Court of Vipers

The Lady of Innislee
Book One

Jacqueline Pawl

Also by Jacqueline Pawl

Defying Vesuvius

A BORN ASSASSIN SERIES

Helpless (prequel novella)

Nameless (prequel novella)

Merciless

Heartless

Ruthless

Fearless

Limitless

THE LADY OF INNISLEE SERIES

Court of Vipers

Copyright © 2022 by Jacqueline Pawl

All rights reserved.

No part of this book may be reproduced in any form or by any electronic or mechanical means, including information storage and retrieval systems, without written permission from the author, except for the use of brief quotations in a book review.

Cover Design by Hannah Sternjakob of www.hannah-sternjakob-design.com

To Mom and Faux Pas
For listening to countless rants about plot holes, reading countless drafts of this book, and shaping Court of Vipers into something readable.

A Note from the Author

Court of Vipers is the first book in a spin-off series set in the same world as the Born Assassin books. While it can be read on its own, I highly recommend reading the Born Assassin series first to see where Riona's story begins, and to avoid any spoilers for that series.

~ Jacqueline

Glossary

RIVOSA

KING DOMHNALL NEVIS: (*Don-ALL NEV-is*) Current king of Rivosa and uncle of Riona Nevis

QUEEN BLAIR NEVIS: Bride to King Domhnall and mother of his children, hails from the Selannic Isles. Sister of Riona's mother, Lady Rhea

PRINCE KILLIAN NEVIS: *Deceased*. Former Crown Prince of Rivosa, killed in a naval battle with the Erdurian Empire

PRINCE DOMHNALL NEVIS: Current Crown Prince of Rivosa, cousin of Riona Nevis

LORD LACHLAN NEVIS: (*LOCK-lan NEV-is*) Lord of Innislee. Younger brother of King Domhnall and father of Riona Nevis

LADY RHEA: (*REE-ah*) *Deceased*. Mother of Riona Nevis and

sister of Queen Blair, of Selannic descent. Killed in a naval battle with the Erdurian Empire

RIONA NEVIS: (*Ree-OH-na NEV-is*) Niece of King Domhnall and Queen Blair. Former bride of Lord Percival Comyn of Beltharos, and one-time queen of Beltharos. (*Stunningly beautiful.*)

AMARIS: (*Ah-MAR-is*) Ward of Lord Lachlan and best friend of Riona Nevis, betrothed to Prince Domhnall. Member of the nobility of the Selannic Isles

CATHAL: (*Ka-HALL*) Current Royal Treasurer of Rivosa and the king's closest advisor. (*Enjoys eating.*)

LORD FARQUAR: (*FAR-kwar*) Former naval captain and current member of the king's council. (*Mysterious and a little cold, but has pretty eyes.*)

LORD WINSLOW, LADY ANNABEL, LORD TRISTAN: Members of the king's council alongside Lord Lachlan and Treasurer Cathal

INNISLEE: (*IN-iss-lee*) Capital of Rivosa. (*Edinburgh, but make it fantasy.*)

ERDURIA

EMPEROR HYPERION: (*Hi-PEER-ion*) Emperor of Erduria and sworn enemy of King Domhnall Nevis of Rivosa

PRINCE DRYSTAN: (*DRIS-tan*) Crown Prince of the Erdurian Empire

PRINCE AUBERON: (*OH-ber-on*) Younger son of Emperor Hyperion. (*Dreamy dimples. A bit of a smart-ass.*)

WALTHER: Spy for Emperor Hyperion

TORCH: Capital of the Erdurian Empire

KOSTOS

KING JERICHO: (*JEH-ruh-kow*) King of Kostos. (*Most definitely an asshole.*)

PRINCE EAMON: (*EE-mon*) Crown Prince of Kostos. (*Also an asshole.*)

KENTER

GRAND DUKE AMBROSE: Grand Duke of the Duchy of Kenter, vassal to Kostos

DUKE VALERIAN: Son of the Grand Duke and heir to the Kentari throne. (*Doing his best.*)

THE FINNEGANI FAMILY: (*FINN-ah-gah-nee*) *Deceased.* Former ruling family of Kenter, overthrown by the nobility after a year-long siege by the King of Kostos.

GLENKELD: Capital of Kenter

BELTHAROS

KING TAMRIEL MYRELLIS: (*Tam-REE-el Mur-ELL-is*) Current King of Beltharos

QUEEN MERCY: Current Queen of Beltharos, former member of the Assassins' Guild

LORD NICHOLAS COMYN: (*COM-in*) *Deceased*. Former military general and high-ranking member of the Beltharan nobility. Briefly overthrew King Tamriel and placed his nephew and Riona Nevis on the throne. (*Good riddance.*)

LORD PERCIVAL COMYN: Nephew of Nicholas Comyn. Former King of Beltharos and husband of Riona Nevis. Loyal to King Tamriel

SANDORI: (*San-DOOR-ee*) Capital of Beltharos

GLENKELD

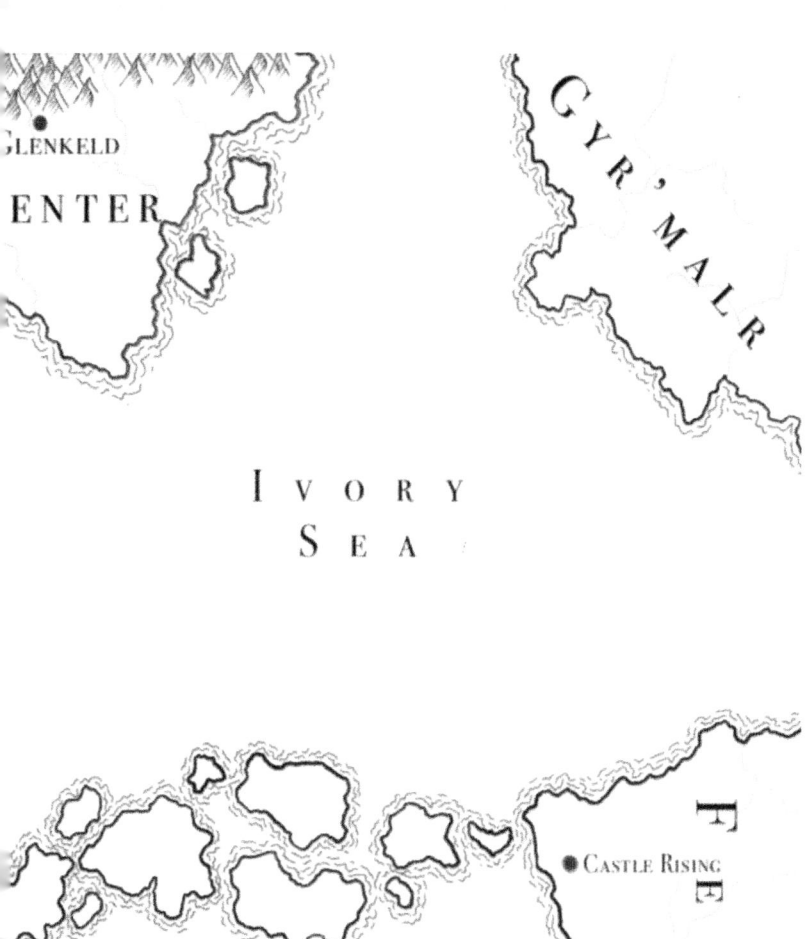

ENTER

GYR'MALR

IVORY SEA

CIRISIAN ISLANDS

CASTLE RISING

FEYNDARA

RHYS

ABRAXAS SEA

Part One
A Gilded Cage

Chapter One
The Lady

I*t appears I've become something of a monster.*

Chapter Two
The Lady

Riona set down her quill and stared at the parchment before her, the elegant cursive in stark contrast to the harsh truth of the words. She knew what the people outside this palace whispered about her. She knew the stories of ruined villages and forbidden magic, of blood and bodies and broken thrones. Perhaps they were right to fear her.

She sat at a long rectangular table in a vast, empty room. The doors behind her were open, and a sweet, floral breeze swept through them, sending the silk of Riona's skirt fluttering against her legs. Everything here was bright and clean: the floor white marble, the walls pale blue, the chandelier a glittering mass of silver and opals. It was so different from the castle in Rivosa, with its iron-latticed windows and drab gray stone.

It appears I've become something of a monster.

She picked up the quill and dipped it in the ink once again.

They stole everything from me. I suppose it was only fair that I repay them for their kindness.

The doors across from her parted, and a boy—no, a man—with unruly curls and a tall, lean build stepped into the room. The quill slipped from Riona's fingers and clattered on the table, leaving a smear of ink on the parchment. It had been a few years since she'd last seen him, and although his hair was longer, his posture more confident, his muscles more sculpted, she would have recognized Percival Comyn anywhere.

He closed the door and leaned against it, crossing his arms. A grin tugged at his lips. "I hear you've been quite busy since you left Beltharos."

"Yes, and look where it has gotten me," Riona responded, her heart aching at the sight of his smile. She'd missed him more than she could put into words. "A prisoner in a gilded cage, once again."

"It also won you the crown on your head."

She reached up and ran her fingers lightly over the emeralds set into the gold band. "A crown I will have little use for if my enemies get their way."

"What enemies? You've killed them all."

No. Not all of them.

Riona folded the parchment and pushed it aside. There would be time for writing—for *explaining*—later. "How have you been?"

"Trying to change the subject?"

"Catching up with an old friend."

Percival's smile faded at that, a mixture of sorrow and nostalgia on his face. He pushed off the door and claimed the seat across from her. "Things have been difficult since Tamriel and Mercy freed the slaves. Many lives were lost to the war with the Cirisians, and those wounds are still healing. The humans like to take their anger out on the elves, and the elves are no longer afraid to strike back. Celeste says that change takes time, but I don't know how much longer we can endure this tension. I'd thought having an elven queen would change things, and it has, but not as much as any of us would have liked." He ran a hand through his hair. "Thank the Creator we're no longer the ones wearing the Beltharan crowns."

"Are Mercy and Tamriel faring well, all things considered?"

"They have each other, which is all they've ever needed. They're still as in love as they were the day they were married."

"I wish I'd been there. I should never have gone back to Rivosa."

Percival smiled sadly. "...No, you shouldn't have."

"I should have done many things differently," she murmured, glancing away. The movement sent flecks of colored light across the room, the sunlight from the palace gardens reflecting off the jewels in her crown. She wore it, even here, even now. The Emperor may have stripped her of her freedom, but he could not strip her of her royal blood. "Well, nothing to be done about it except face what's to come. Have they set a date for my execution yet?"

His brows furrowed. "You haven't been sentenced to execution, Riona. The Emperor wishes to hear your story."

She sat up straighter, surprised. After all this time, he had finally agreed to hear her out? Even if it didn't save her life, at least it would set the record straight, which was all she'd wanted since coming to the palace. People spoke of her all across the northern and southern continents—the girl who had not only stolen a crown, but razed a kingdom. The girl whose blood was something to be feared. They were already telling stories about her; she might as well make sure those stories were true.

"What changed his mind? It took me weeks of asking just to receive those." Riona nodded to the stack of parchment beside her. "Did you convince them to listen to me? Is that why you're here?"

"No, I can't take credit for this, as much as I'd like to. His Imperial Majesty has allowed me to escort you to the throne room, however." He rose and rounded the table, offering his arm. "Are you ready?"

"I've been ready since the moment I arrived."

She slipped a hand into the crook of his elbow, and they left the room together, their footsteps clicking on the tile and echoing down the vast hall that stretched before them. The half-dozen guards assigned to her chambers fell into step behind them. Riona stared straight ahead and pretended not to notice the way their hands hovered over the grips of their swords. Here, as in the rest of the palace, the corridor was tall and airy, made to appear larger by the white pillars and polished mirrors lining the walls. It would have been beautiful, had it not been tainted by the memory of being dragged through these same halls in chains.

Riona watched their reflections as they walked, Percival in the fine tunic and trousers of a Beltharan lord, she in the light, silky gowns she'd always loved. So much had changed, and yet so much felt the same. How many times had they walked arm-in-arm like this through the halls of Myrellis Castle? If she closed her eyes, she could almost pretend they were back there, masquerading as king and queen, as a loving couple.

"So, why *are* you here, then?" Riona asked. "Why aren't you back in Westwater with Celeste and the little ones?"

"You know we have little ones?"

"I may be fighting a war, but I haven't been so busy I stopped keeping tabs on old friends. A daughter and a son, is it?"

"Yes, and I love them more than I ever thought possible." A beaming grin spread across Percival's lips. Life with Celeste was doing him good; Riona could count on one hand the number of times she'd seen him genuinely smile in Beltharos. Now, he couldn't seem to stop.

Percival paused in the middle of the hall and took her hands. It struck her then that he still wore the same crooked, wire-rimmed spectacles he had in Beltharos. "All I want is for you to find the same happiness. As for *why* I've come, did you honestly think I wouldn't sail here immediately after finding out the Emperor had taken you into custody? You stood by me against my uncle. I will stand by you through this."

"Even after everything I've done?"

"Some of your actions have been...questionable, true," he conceded. "But that doesn't change what I said."

Love for him rushed over her, and she threw her arms around him. "Thank you, Percival," she breathed.

He hugged her back just as fiercely. "There is no need to thank me."

She took a deep breath to steady her nerves, then pulled back and slipped her hand into the crook of his arm once again. "Alright. Take me to the Emperor."

Riona held her chin high as the throne room doors parted, revealing a sea of courtiers in the bright, vibrant colors favored in the Erdurian Empire. It seemed every member of the nobility had come to see what the Emperor would do to his prisoner. She kept her expression neutral, as she'd learned to do long ago in the presence of a royal court, but her white-knuckled grip on Percival's arm betrayed her nerves. He said nothing as he escorted her into the room, even though she was squeezing his arm tightly enough to bruise. The nobles sat on benches on either side of the aisle, their gazes weighing heavily on Riona. The Emperor stared at her, stone-faced, from his throne. When Riona laid eyes upon the man who stood before the dais, she stopped in her tracks.

A dagger in her palm.

"Riona!" Percival cried, grabbing her arm as she sent the weapon flying through the air.

Shouts of alarm filled the room. The Emperor shot to his feet as the traitor turned and stumbled backward in surprise, the dagger nicking his shoulder and clattering against the dais steps.

Damn you, Percival, Riona thought as royal guards shoved them apart, wrenching her arms behind her back hard enough to send her to her knees. Her crown clattered to the ground and rolled away, gemstones glittering. *I would have struck his heart if you hadn't stopped me.*

The traitor lifted a hand to the slit in his linen tunic, and his fingers came away red. He clicked his tongue in disapproval. "Now, now, is that any way to say hello?"

She glared at him, loose braids tumbling down around her face. "It's the only greeting you deserve."

"How did she find a dagger?" the Emperor demanded, scowling at the guards. "Did you search Lord Percival for weapons before he went to see her?"

"I didn't give it to her!" Percival objected. Two guards had seized him and were holding him immobile while another patted him down, searching for the dagger's sheath. "What the *hell* were you thinking, Riona?"

"Oh, let him go," the bastard said with a lazy wave of his hand. "She's clever enough to procure a weapon without help. I'd be dead if he hadn't knocked her arm aside. We owe him a debt of gratitude."

The Emperor nodded, and the guards released Percival. He straightened his tunic and shot Riona a look that said, *I told you I would stand by you, but I might have reconsidered if I'd known you were going to do that.*

I'm sorry, she mouthed.

"You're on thin ice, Riona," Emperor Hyperion said, his voice carrying through the vast room. "This is your one chance to tell your side of the events that led to the destruction of Kostos. An entire kingdom was brought to its knees because of you. Buildings leveled. Fields razed. People slaughtered. Do not squander this opportunity."

"Your Majesty."

"Your *Imperial* Majesty," one of the guards corrected, but Riona silenced him with a glare.

"No. 'You're on thin ice, Your Majesty.' I am still a queen, and you will address me as such." She looked up at the Emperor. "Condemn me for my actions if you must, but I have fought, bled, and killed for my crown. As long as I wear it, I expect you to show me the respect I've earned."

"As long as you wear it?" the traitor echoed, glancing at the crown lying near Percival's feet. A viper's smile skated across his lips. "Poor choice of words."

"Why are you here, rather than rotting in some Creator-forsaken corner of the world?"

"You want to tell your side of the story. I'm here to keep you honest."

She scoffed. "That word doesn't exist in your vocabulary."

The bastard merely grinned in response.

Riona had to bite her tongue to keep from retorting. Growing up, she'd always been praised for her mild manners and soft, quiet disposition, but she wasn't that girl any longer. Percival was gaping from where he stood by the rest of the courtiers, staring at her as if he hardly recognized the creature before him.

Good. I may be monstrous, but at least I am no longer weak.

The traitor stood between her and the dais, looking achingly similar to the last time she'd seen him. He was a little older, a little harder, but he still had that mischievous glimmer to his eyes. The same shock of brown hair hung over his brow, woven with strands of a deep auburn. Their gazes locked, and the tension between them pulled taut as a bowstring. So much history lay between them. So many nights in a dark theater, blades flashing in the candlelight, music dancing in the air. So many fights, so many deaths, so much blood spilled. And yet, something kept bringing them back together.

Some might have called it fate, and Riona would have called them fools.

"Prince Auberon," she said, her voice icy.

He gave a single nod. "Your Majesty."

One night in particular haunted her, and she could tell by way he was staring at her that he was thinking of it, too. They had never spoken of it. They'd never had the chance, because he had left long before she had even realized what was happening. What he'd done. Whose life he'd claimed.

Now, everyone would know. Everyone would understand why she had done what she had.

"You want to hear my side of the story?" Riona asked, shifting so she could look Emperor Hyperion in the eyes. "Very well. It begins with a cup of wine."

Part Two
Blood of my Blood

Chapter Three
The Lady

Two dozen heads were staked over Sandori's southern gate, and they were screaming.

Terror sank its claws into Riona's heart as her carriage rolled toward the capital city's exterior wall. The heads had been there for a while. Their flesh was black and sunken, sagging over the skulls, and bits of white bone peeked through where scavengers and insects had eaten away at the skin. Keening, haunting cries tore from thin, bloodless lips. Riona clapped her hands over her ears, but it didn't help. She could still hear them.

As her carriage neared the gate, the bloodcurdling screams gradually began to take shape:

"RUN! RUN! RUN!"

She grabbed the handle and pushed, but the door didn't budge. Riona slammed her palms against it, panic rising within her, then whirled around in search of another escape. The windows were too narrow to climb through, and there was no other door. She was trapped.

The carriage rolled to a stop, and a man approached one of the windows. He wore the livery of a royal guard, but the fabric over his heart was bare. He'd torn off the patch bearing the seal of the Myrellis family.

"Let me out," Riona pleaded, the gut-wrenching wails nearly drowning out her words. "Please, just let me out."

"Why? Are you afraid the same thing will happen to you? You don't have to be, as long as you do as you're told. They were traitors." He nodded toward the head in the middle of the line. Its eyes were empty sockets, and its nose had rotted away, leaving behind a gaping hole. Beside it was a bare skull, the only one of the lot. "The mad king, who was content to chase ghosts around his castle while the rest of us watched the plague claim everyone we loved. And next to him, the filthy knife-ear who stole his heart."

Riona's stomach turned. She started to back away from the window, but the guard's arm shot out and grabbed her, his fingers tangling in her long braids.

"Look at them," he snarled, twisting her head toward the gruesome display. "They were traitors, one and all. Soon, King Tamriel's head will join them—his, and that of the knife-eared bitch who warms his bed. You think this is terrible? This is justice."

"This is savagery."

"If that is what you would brand those who wish to protect their country, let us all be savages, then."

He released her, and Riona scrambled backward until she hit the opposite wall of the carriage. The guard nodded to someone outside her line of sight, and she heard the clanking of the gate opening. Through it all, the heads wailed. The sound made the hair on the back of her neck stand on end. Nicholas Comyn was sending a message. He could have let her enter from the western gate—where most visitors from Rivosa would enter the city—but he had wanted her to see those heads, to know what he'd done.

To know what he could do to her.

The driver snapped his reins, and the carriage jolted into motion, carrying her into the city that would be her prison. The gate clanked shut behind it. The heads continued to scream, their voices growing distant as the carriage advanced into the heart of the city.

"TRAITOR!"

"Liar!"

"murderer..."

"...monster..."

The gravel of the castle's carriageway crunched under the wooden wheels, and the carriage rolled to a stop before the grand entrance. A royal guard opened the door and gestured for her to climb out. Every instinct within her rebelled, but she had no other choice. If she disobeyed, the guard would simply drag her out. If she tried to run, he would kill her. She lifted her chin and climbed out. A man stood on the carriageway beside the guard, and Riona's heart stuttered at the sight of his smug smirk, his blind eye, his grizzled, scarred face.

Nicholas Comyn smiled at her, malice glittering in his good eye. "Welcome to Sandori, Lady Riona."

"Riona? *Riona!*"

She jolted awake, her breath catching when she realized she lay in the dim interior of a carriage. This time, though, she wasn't alone. Lord Winslow, her father's oldest friend, was leaning forward from the opposite bench, reaching out a hand as if to comfort her. Concern shone in his pale blue eyes.

"You were having another nightmare. I should have woken you sooner, but you've had such little rest since we left Sandori."

"Not that I rested much *in* Sandori," she replied, pushing herself upright. Her waist-length braids hung loose around her face, devoid of her usual gold beads, and she wore a simple linen traveling dress.

"Do you want to talk about it?"

She shook her head, her fingers rising to the eudorite pendant at her throat. It was shaped like a crudely-carved arrowhead, its facets smooth as glass, its edges sharp as a blade. The metal was warm from her skin. *Nicholas Comyn is dead,* she reminded herself, *and we will soon be home.* The words brought her some comfort, but not nearly enough. The memory of those horrible rotting heads was too fresh in her mind.

"It'll be better when we're back in Innislee," she said. "I've missed Father terribly."

Winslow smiled and reached out to part the curtains over her window. "Take a look outside, my lady."

She winced as bright sunlight flooded the carriage. Once her eyes adjusted, her heart leapt. Beyond the fields of long, swaying grass, Innislee rose tall and regal in the distance, framed by low, rolling hills. They were close enough to the capital that she could make out the ancient walls surrounding the city and the dark, pitched roofs of the houses within. The sun was high, and its rays sparkled on the Royal Theater's gilded spires. Above it all, Innislee Castle sat proudly atop its rocky crag, overlooking the sprawling city.

"We weren't gone for even two months, but it feels like a lifetime," Riona murmured, more to herself than Winslow, as the carriage rolled up the cobblestone road toward the eastern gate. "I thought I was going to die in that wretched city."

"In truth, I feared the same," he confessed, shuddering. "After what Percival did at your wedding celebration—killing all those nobles—Nicholas Comyn would have happily executed you both if King Tamriel's army hadn't arrived. Another day, and your heads might have joined the ones outside the city gate."

The carriage passed through the gate and joined the bustle of traffic on the King's Road, its wooden wheels bouncing over the pitted, ancient cobbles. Riona gazed out at the tall row-houses that lined the road, their façades covered in lattices of ivy that danced in the languid breeze. Even in the city, greenery bloomed everywhere she looked: ivy crawling up the sides of the houses; window boxes bursting with flowers; trees rising high from each side of the road, lanterns dangling from their boughs to light the city at night. As they continued along the King's Road, the buildings grew larger and grander, wood becoming stone.

They continued up the gently sloping road and came to a

stop in the castle's forecourt. Her father was already waiting for them before the heavy portcullis gate, accompanied by a handful of royal guards. Although he was quite a few years younger, Lord Lachlan was a near double of the king—tall and broad-shouldered, with large hazel eyes and rich ebony skin. He beamed when Riona stepped out of the carriage and ran to him. He met her halfway and crushed her in a vice-like hug.

"You're home, my darling girl. Really, truly home," he sighed. "I can hardly believe it."

A lump formed in her throat. In Sandori, she had been a stranger in a foreign court, alone and at the mercy of a power-hungry tyrant. It had been hard not to resent her father for remaining in Innislee. He'd had court duties to attend, of course, but there had been so many nights she'd wanted nothing more than a hug from her father and a promise that everything would be alright.

"I should have ridden to Sandori the moment we received your letter asking for aid." He held her at arm's length and scanned her from head to toe, searching for injuries. "If something had happened to you, I never could have forgiven myself for sending you to that Creator-forsaken kingdom."

Yet you were content to marry me off to a man I'd met once, years ago, Riona thought, but she held her tongue. There would be time for that conversation later, when they didn't have an audience. She nodded toward Lord Winslow, who had climbed out after her, and the guards riding on horseback behind the carriage. "I'm fine, thanks to them."

"I'll see to it that you're well rewarded for your service to my daughter," Lachlan said to the guards, then turned and clasped his old friend's hand. "Winslow, you have my unending gratitude for accompanying her. As much as I dread what shall come of saying it, I owe you."

Mirth sparkled in the lord's eyes. "After all these decades, you've owed me for many things, and I you. For both our sakes, let's call it even, shall we?"

"You certainly won't hear any protests from me. Now come, there's much to be done."

Her father led them through the portcullis and onto the castle grounds, dismissing the guards with a wave of his hand. Unlike the royal residence in Beltharos, Innislee Castle consisted of several buildings arranged in a spiral shape, linked by a wide cobblestone path. The servants and guards bustling from building to building paused to bow as the Lord of Innislee passed. As she walked, Riona surreptitiously smoothed the wrinkles from her dress, conscious of the image she presented. She would never be a warrior like Tamriel or Mercy, and her court finery was her armor. Without it, she felt strangely vulnerable.

"Relax, Riona." Her father gave her hand a gentle squeeze. "You've returned to us after facing execution and a bloody civil war. Do you think anyone cares what you're wearing?"

"I know the importance of keeping up appearances."

"Then it's fortunate you won't be in the presence of the court today. Queen Blair and Amaris are waiting for you in the queen's chambers. Winslow, the advisors have already gathered in the council chambers. I'll meet you there."

Winslow nodded and excused himself, and they continued up the winding path to the royal apartments. It was the largest and grandest of the castle's buildings, with tall stained-glass windows and ornate scenes from the Book of the Creator carved into the stone façade. Lachlan led her through the foyer and up a twisting flight of stairs to the queen's bedchamber.

She only made it two steps into the room before Amaris leapt to her feet, tripped over the cushion on which she'd been sitting, and nearly bowled Riona over in a bone-crushing hug. Before she could say a word, Amaris stepped back and frowned at her outfit. "Did you dress that way *voluntarily?* I've never seen you leave the house without enough gemstones to finance a small kingdom. Come, we'll fix that."

Riona shot her father an amused look as Amaris dragged her over to the bed, where a gown of emerald silk was spread out beside a tray of jewelry. He shook his head, chuckling. "I'll leave you to it. I've already kept the king and council waiting too long. There's much to discuss in the aftermath of the battle of Sandori."

"I'll meet you there once I've dressed. Please pass along my apologies for my tardiness."

He crossed the room and pressed a soft kiss to her temple. "Worry not, my love. Spend time with Amaris and your aunt. I'll see you both at home for supper."

"But—"

"Your opportunity to speak with the council will come soon enough, I promise. At the moment, there are important matters to be settled now that we have no marriage alliance with Beltharos. For now, enjoy your return."

He turned on his heel and walked out of the room before she could formulate a response. Dejected and a little stung by the dismissal, Riona sank onto the foot of the bed and muttered, "Welcome home, indeed."

"It never changes, does it?" Amaris murmured, her tone laced with bitterness. "We're raised to marry well and secure a political alliance, and then we're cast aside once we've outlasted our usefulness. Even your father, good and honorable as he is, knows no better. That will end when I become queen."

"I hope so. If anyone can change it, you can," Riona said. Amaris was the daughter of a Selannic nobleman, and she'd lived in Innislee as a ward of Riona's father since her betrothal to the Crown Prince. In the following eight years, she and Riona had grown as close as sisters. "Speaking of queens, where is my aunt?"

"She stepped out to speak with one of her ladies, but she'll be back soon enough. In the meantime, let's make you look like yourself again." Amaris gestured for her to stand, and Riona obeyed, pulling her dress over her head and tossing it over the nearest armchair. *Good riddance*, she thought as Amaris helped her into the emerald gown.

"Let's discuss your marriage to Nicholas Comyn's nephew.

Tell me about Percival. Was he a monster like his uncle? Worse, did you consummate the marriage before it was annulled?" She poked Riona's stomach teasingly. "Will we have a little Comyn running around the castle come summer?"

"By the Creator, no!" Riona swatted Amaris's hand away. "We were friends, nothing more. And he is everything his uncle was not: kind, selfless, brave... I was lucky to meet him."

A stab of longing struck her. Percival had been the only honorable man in that violent, deceitful court, and she had fallen head over heels for him during her time in Beltharos. He had fallen in love as well...just not with her. She couldn't blame him, no matter how much the knowledge hurt. His monster of an uncle had controlled every aspect of his life since the day his parents died, and he deserved something that was his alone. He deserved to forge his own future with the woman he loved at his side. Even if that woman wasn't *her*.

So, Riona had convinced the High Priestess to annul their marriage, and then she set off for Rivosa. It had been the best decision for them both, even if leaving had felt like carving her heart out of her chest.

Amaris heard the slight hitch in her voice. Her expression softened, and she pulled Riona into her arms. "Oh, Riona, I'm sorry."

"There is no reason to be sorry. I was the fool who fell in love."

"There is nothing foolish about love. Now let me finish my work, and we'll turn the conversation to happier topics."

As Amaris worked, humming softly under her breath, Riona studied her reflection in the windowpane before her. The vibrant silk was striking against her ebony skin, made even more stunning by the collar of raw emeralds that Amaris clasped around her throat, just above her eudorite pendant. The sight reminded her of sitting on her parents' bed as a child, watching her mother dress for an important state function.

Men like to mock the court ladies for their silks and their jewels, her mother had told her once, gripping Riona's chin in her slender fingers. *But there is power in being beautiful, and even more so in being beautiful and clever. Do not ever forget that, blood of my blood.*

"There," Amaris breathed once she'd finished. She moved to Riona's side and clasped her hand, gazing at the glass's reflection alongside her. "Now you look the part."

Chapter Four
The Lady

"When will Domhnall return from Sandori?" Riona asked as she and Amaris settled on the lavish cushions in the queen's sitting room. Her eldest cousin, the Crown Prince, had led his father's army to Beltharos to help King Tamriel reclaim his stolen throne. After the battle, he had chosen to stay behind with his men while healers tended their injuries.

"Within a week," Amaris said, grinning. "It's a miracle you both survived the battle. I tried to convince him to stay here and let another commander lead the army, but he refused. He would do anything for you."

"He would do anything for either of us. Have you set a date for the wedding yet?"

"No, but we're in no rush. He won't ascend the throne anytime soon." She toyed with the ruby ring on her finger. Prince Domhnall had given it to her for her fourteenth birthday, and Riona had never once seen her without it in all the years since. "A wedding won't change anything. I love him, and he loves me."

"Oh, I know. I still remember the look on his face when you stepped off the boat from the Isles. I've never seen my cousin speechless before."

Amaris winked. "We Selannic women tend to have that effect on men."

"That we do," a feminine voice said from the doorway, the words steeped in a heavy, melodic accent. Riona rose and curtsied as the queen strode into the room, and her aunt scoffed. "Don't be ridiculous, my love. Is that how we greet family now?"

The queen pressed a light kiss to each of her closed eyelids in the traditional Selannic family greeting, then took Riona's hand and guided her down onto the cushions. "I'd bet my crown your Percival was struck senseless the first time he saw you."

Riona's chest tightened, but she forced a smile. "I hope so."

She had met him once as a child, when his uncle brought him to Rivosa to negotiate the betrothal, but they'd barely spoken a word to each other. Percival had been portly and round-faced, a shy, nervous boy who was more at home in a library than playing with the other court children in the castle's gardens. In the years since, he had thinned and grown taller, the youthful roundness giving way to a charming, bookish exterior. He'd become *handsome.*

The day she arrived in Sandori, he'd been standing with his uncle outside the castle's main doors, and his eyes had widened to saucers the moment she stepped out of her carriage. When they exchanged greetings, Percival had barely managed to get one word out without stumbling over his tongue. The exchange had endeared him to her immediately.

"We were just discussing Prince Domhnall's return," Amaris cut in, tactfully changing the subject.

The humor on the queen's face faded. "That boy. As proud as I am of his courage, I hate that he insists on fighting alongside the soldiers. He could train with them, command them, but to fight on the battlefield? And after his brother's death..." She shook her head. "Sometimes I wish he were an only child. That way, he couldn't go off and do half the reckless things he does."

"If your pleading and mine can't change his mind, I'm sure

that wouldn't stop him. Stubbornness is in his blood." Amaris shot a look at Riona. "In the blood of your whole family."

Riona grinned. "I can't help it if I live up to the Nevis name."

"By the Creator, you're all going to send me to an early grave."

Queen Blair laughed and clasped Amaris's hand. "Just wait until you and Domhnall have children, my dear. You'll never live a day in peace again."

That evening, Riona and Amaris strolled together along the path toward the castle's gatehouse, where a carriage was waiting to take them home for supper. It struck her as they walked that there were more servants and guards about than usual. Many carried crates of fruit and vegetables, others casks of wine, some bolts of luxurious fabrics.

"The king is preparing a banquet in honor of you and Domhnall," Amaris said, catching Riona's curious look. "Within a few weeks, details of the battle of Sandori will spread across the kingdom—our fearless, noble prince charging alongside the army, fighting on the front lines, and our beautiful lady standing against a tyrant."

The words sent a shiver down Riona's spine, the memory of those staked skulls still fresh in her mind. "Domhnall can have all the glory. I just want to return to my life here."

As they approached the gatehouse, the sentinels standing watch pulled the doors open for them. Amaris's voice dropped to a whisper as they entered the building. "Riona, I'm sorry to tell you this, but I don't think you should expect life here to return to the way it was. Your uncle sent you to Beltharos to marry Percival, and you've returned without a husband. You may be blood, but he is still your king, and you disobeyed his orders."

"I know." Her stomach knotted with unease. Whether they were in love or not, she and Percival should have remained married until death parted them. "And I will accept whatever punishment he sees fit."

Amaris opened her mouth to say more, but a distant voice cut her off. "What did she think would happen when she returned? She'd be given a position as an advisor to her uncle? If he valued her opinion on state matters, he wouldn't have sent her away in the first place."

Riona slowed, conscious of the click of her heels against the tile, and gestured for Amaris to be silent. The courtiers were discussing *her*, their voices drifting through the open doors that led to the forecourt. She slipped off her heels and crept closer to listen.

The other courtier chuckled. "My thoughts exactly. She's ninth in line for the throne and will never wear the crown. Her only value lies in the price she'll fetch as a bride."

"Then it's a good thing she's beautiful."

"Yes, but a pity she's not stupid. Stupid girls are content to sit around in their pretty dresses and do as they're told. She'll always fight for more."

"Fortunately, that's a problem for her future husband. Not for us."

Amaris glanced at Riona and whispered, "Don't take what they say to heart."

"Do you think me so thin-skinned that I would be wounded by court gossip?" She'd spent most of her life in the castle, listening to nobles and advisors vie for the king's attention; she knew those voices as well as she knew her own. "If Lord Tristan is so interested in the affairs of others, perhaps someone should tell him that his wife has been sleeping with his cook for the last year and a half."

Amaris's brows shot up. "Truly? How do you know?"

"I have my methods. I'm told his infant son has his true father's nose." Riona shot her a wicked grin. "I doubt Lord Tristan would care much, though. He's sleeping with the captain of the city watch."

Before Amaris could sputter a surprised reply, Riona pulled on her heels and strode out of the gatehouse, offering only a passing glance to the two council members who stood nearby. Amaris hurried after her. Lord Tristan, a barrel-chested man with a thick, dark beard, dipped his head in respect as they approached the royal carriage awaiting them. Riona heard Amaris stifle a laugh as she nodded in response.

"You never breathed a word of that to me!" she accused once they were both settled in the carriage. "Why did you never tell me? And why didn't you say anything to him just then? He must have realized we overheard his conversation."

"If he cared about that, he wouldn't have discussed me in the castle. Everyone knows the walls of this place have ears." She cast a sidelong glance at Amaris. "You must not repeat what I told you. Secrets are a commodity in a city like this."

Amaris made a small huff of assent, still looking slightly annoyed that Riona had kept such intriguing information to herself.

Riona studied the lord as the carriage lurched into motion. If the revelation that he was a cuckold, father to a bastard, and an Unnatural spread around the court, Lord Tristan's family would be disgraced. He wouldn't be stripped of his place on the council, but he'd lose all respect in the court, and it wouldn't be long before he resigned his position. Riona didn't want to be the cause of his downfall. Unlikable or not, he was a good leader and advisor, and the people of his sector had flourished since he'd inherited his father's position. Still, it didn't hurt to have one piece of scandalous information at her disposal, should she need it.

Her gaze slid to the advisor at Tristan's side. Lord Farquar was the newest member of the king's council, a former captain of the Rivosi navy. He was tall and well-muscled, with the fair skin of the southern lords. He had retired from the navy earlier that year to assume his father's position on the council when the older man's health began to fail. Riona had heard the stories of his victories in the war with Erduria, but she didn't know the man personally, and that made her uneasy. There was something about the steady, appraising look in his cool emerald eyes that reminded her of Nicholas Comyn.

She shook off the thought and closed the curtains over the window. Farquar was not Nicholas. Both had been respected military leaders, but that was where their similarities ended. Nicholas had been a monster. Farquar was only a man.

Chapter Five
The Lady

The second the council chamber doors opened, a flood of overlapping voices spilled into the hall. Riona held her head high and shoulders back as she walked into the room, the conversation fading to a hush as she dropped into a low curtsy before the long table that dominated the space. Her skin prickled under the weight of the advisors' stares.

"Your Majesties," she intoned, her gaze trained on the floor. "My lords and ladies."

"Rise, my dear," King Domhnall said. He stood on the opposite side of the table, dressed in a gold-trimmed black doublet. Her uncle shared his brother's broad-shouldered build and regal features, but his dark curly hair and short beard were woven through with strands of silver. "Welcome home. It's nothing short of a miracle that you have returned to us, and I thank the Creator every day that you're safe."

Some of the tension in her chest eased at the warmth in his voice, the dread from the previous night's conversation fading as she claimed the empty seat beside her father. As soon as she sat, the queen reached across the table and clasped her hand. "After you left last night, Domhnall filled me in on what Lord Winslow shared at yesterday's meeting. I scarcely believed it when he told me that you joined the battle of Sandori. That was incredibly brave of you."

"Brave, but foolhardy," Lord Farquar said. "His Majesty sent her to Beltharos to be a bride, not a martyr."

Her father opened his mouth, but Riona cut in before he could speak, shooting the lord a scathing look. "Nicholas Comyn betrayed his king, stole the throne, slaughtered countless innocents, and sentenced his nephew and me to execution. It is true that I am not a warrior, but I would not leave my husband to face a bloodthirsty tyrant alone—especially one who had tormented and manipulated him all his life."

"A decision few would've had the courage to make, my lady," Treasurer Cathal interjected, dipping his head in respect. He was a short, portly man with an easy smile and eyes perpetually hidden behind thick-framed spectacles. He grinned at her before turning to the former naval captain. "Honestly, Farquar, is that not the loyalty one would desire of his wife?"

"I am speaking of pragmatism, not loyalty. We needed that marriage with Percival Comyn to settle the border disputes."

"And what value would there be in a marriage if both Lady Riona and Percival had been executed?"

The lord did not falter. "The marriage was dissolved *after* the tyrant was defeated, not before. The fact remains that *Percival* is alive, and *Lady Riona* is here."

The king held up a hand, and the advisors abruptly stopped bickering. "Treasurer Cathal, write to Lord Percival Comyn in Westwater and inquire about the state of his family's troops. Perhaps he will be willing to dispatch some to help quell the unrest between our peoples. While you're waiting for a response, arrange for shipments of food and money to the border villages, and see if our outposts have the numbers to increase patrols."

"Yes, Your Majesty."

"As for you, Riona..." King Domhnall looked pointedly at her hand, and she stiffened, fighting the urge to tuck it under the table to hide the fact that she no longer wore a ring. "Lord

Farquar is right. You and Percival survived the battle, and he has inherited the Comyn fortune and lands. Lord Winslow told me yesterday that it was you who convinced the High Priestess to annul your marriage. Why?"

Because he fell in love with another woman. Because I could never bear the pain of loving someone who did not love me back, and I would not condemn him to a life without Celeste. But she could not admit that—not to anyone save Amaris.

So instead, she held her king's gaze and lied.

"The Comyn fortune is a fraction of what it once was. The allies Nicholas could not sway with promises or threats, he swayed with coin. I assure you, Percival is the only one who would have benefitted from our marriage," she said, the words falling easily from her lips. "Since our vows were made under duress, the High Priestess agreed that they were not binding. I'm sorry I did not consult you before I made the decision, Your Majesty, but I thought only of the future of our kingdom."

He regarded her with disappointment. "The decision was not yours to make. Duress or not, you have a duty to your country. My niece, it gives me no pleasure to tell you this so soon after your return, but you've left me no other option. I have written to the heirs of several powerful and influential thrones, and three royal suitors have expressed interest in pursuing a marriage alliance."

The news struck Riona like a blow. She turned to her father and found guilt scrawled across his face. He had known. Of course he had; he was the Lord of Innislee. He had probably penned the letters on his brother's behalf. Betrayal ignited within her. When she spoke, her voice came out low and cold. "I have been in this city for all of one day, and already, you are prepared to cast me out again."

"Riona—"

"I married Percival. I watched Nicholas beat him, manipulate the court, and slaughter those who dared to oppose him. I faced *execution*." She turned back to the king, her blood boiling. "I risked my life to restore the rightful king to his throne. Have I not earned my own future? My freedom? Am I nothing more to my kingdom than a prize to be sold to the highest bidder?"

"Mind your tongue," her father commanded. "Remember to whom you speak."

King Domhnall's gaze never strayed from her. "Let her speak her mind, Lachlan. Better she does it now than when the suitors are here." All the warmth vanished from her uncle's eyes, leaving them as cold and hard as eudorite. "The blood of kings flows through your veins, Riona. That blood comes with a cost."

"The cost of my dowry, apparently."

Heavy silence settled over the room, each person waiting with bated breath to see how the king would respond. Riona had never spoken to her uncle so brazenly before, and the fact that she had spoken to him in that manner in front of the council added another level of insult to the breach of etiquette. She didn't care. She wouldn't allow her anger to get the better of her, but neither would she blindly submit to another marriage with a stranger.

The king glanced at the advisors. "Leave us."

With no sound but the scrape of chair legs and the scuff of shoes against stone, the council members filed out of the room. Her father squeezed her shoulder in a silent warning before following them. When the doors swung shut, only Riona, King Domhnall, and Queen Blair remained.

Her uncle sank into his chair, his expression softening. "I understand what you must be thinking, my dear niece, and believe me when I say that if I could, I would not be asking this of you."

"Why can't I serve my kingdom as a member of your council? I've spent half my life at court. I know it better than Lord Farquar."

"You would limit yourself to the role of an advisor, when you could be a queen?" he asked, his brows furrowing in genuine puzzlement. "Why?"

Why? "This is my home. I nearly lost it once, and I will not do it again."

"Do go into this with an open mind, my love," her aunt said with an encouraging smile. "I know how terrifying it is to marry a stranger. Your mother and I both did it, and look how well it turned out for us. Wherever you go, you will thrive. I am certain of it."

"I am affording you what little allowance I can," the king added. His voice was kind, but there was no mistaking the command underscoring his words. She had disobeyed his orders in having the marriage annulled, and her behavior in front of the council hadn't won her any sympathy. "I could have sent delegates to each suitor to discuss the terms of a potential marriage alliance, but instead, I invited them here so you may get to know them during the negotiations. Do not squander this opportunity."

"But—"

"This is not a debate. The suitors will arrive by the week's end, and you will smile, charm them, and mind your tongue. Once they are settled, your father and I will meet with them to negotiate the terms of an alliance. Creator willing, we will have a marriage arranged by the new year."

The floor seemed to drop out from under her. "The new year? That's less than two months away!"

Riona looked to her aunt for support, but Blair offered her nothing more than a sympathetic look. She shouldn't have expected anything more. Blair was a queen in name only, content to spend her days wandering the royal gardens with her court ladies and doting on the four heirs she'd given the king.

Riona could see that future stretching out before her, closing around her throat like a noose. A husband she did not love, a country she did not know, a title that was no more than a formality. No purpose beyond warming her husband's bed and bearing him sons.

Desperation began to bleed through her anger. "There must

be some other way. There is nothing a political marriage could solve that cannot be resolved with gold, gifts, and goodwill."

The king fixed her with a look that cut straight through her heart. "And what makes you think you're worth that price?"

"*Domhnall,*" Blair snapped, aghast. "You don't mean that."

He leaned forward, ignoring his wife's objection. "We have been warring with the Erdurian Empire for control of the Tranquil Sea for the last three decades, and contrary to what you may believe, our coffers are not bottomless. You were supposed to be wed to Percival Comyn, but you had your marriage annulled and returned here. Now I am left to clean up the mess you've made. You will marry one of the suitors, and you will be grateful that I have given you a chance to meet them at all." Domhnall stood and turned his back on her, clasping his hands behind him. "You may leave."

Rage rolled over her in a black wave, but Riona forced herself to stand and curtsy. Arguing would get her nowhere. "Farewell, Your Majesties."

Her aunt nodded in response, a wordless apology in her soft smile, while the king said nothing. Riona straightened and walked out of the room, ignoring the intrigued looks from the council members waiting in the hallway just outside. Her father opened his mouth to speak to her, but she strode right past him without a word.

"Riona, have you lost all sense of propriety?" her father demanded, catching her arm and pulling her around to face him. She had managed to make it out of the castle's main building before he caught up to her on the cobblestone path, halfway to the gate. This high above the city, the wind whipped around them, tugging at the skirt of Riona's gown.

"Propriety?" she hissed, conscious of the servants walking along the path, bustling from chore to chore—preparing the castle for the suitors' arrival, she now knew. "Before I even returned, you were planning to send me off to marry yet another stranger. And you speak to *me* of propriety?"

"The king is doing you a kindness by inviting the suitors here. Have you stopped to consider how much this endeavor will cost? Banquets, feasts, entertainment... Think of what it will mean for the future of Rivosa if you marry into one of the most powerful royal families in the northern continent."

Riona went still.

"The northern continent?" she echoed, her anger faltering. She shouldn't have been surprised; Beltharos didn't have an heir to marry, and neither did Feyndara—at least, not one close enough to the throne for her uncle's liking. Still, marrying a lord from Beltharos was very different from marrying a northern royal. "Who have you invited here?"

"Duke Valerian of Kenter, Prince Eamon of Kostos, and..." Her father hesitated for just a moment before finishing, "Prince Drystan of the Erdurian Empire."

"I will never marry an Erdurian," she snarled. "I will never serve the Empire. Do you expect me to smile and charm Prince Drystan, knowing what Emperor Hyperion did to Mother? Knowing that his orders sent her ship to the bottom of the Tranquil Sea?"

At once, the anger bled from his face, giving way to heartbreaking sorrow. "I understand, my love," he breathed, gently tucking a stray braid behind Riona's ear. "Do you think it has been easy for me to face the likelihood of your marriage to the prince? The Emperor took the love of my life from me, and now his son is poised to take my only daughter. It will kill me to watch you leave again, but this is what must be done—"

"For the good of Rivosa," Riona finished with a sigh. "I've heard this story before."

"I want what is best for you, my love. *Never* doubt that. Do not assume that because I did not speak up today, heated words have not been exchanged behind closed doors. Your uncle and I have fought long and hard about this, but in truth, I see no other route to ending the war without further bloodshed. If this is the sacrifice our kingdom demands of us, we must pay it." Her father tried for an encouraging smile, but didn't quite manage it. "Whoever you marry, someday you and your husband will sit on the thrones of the land you will soon call home. And if you are fortunate, you will grow to love him and his people, just as your mother did. That is better than sitting on some council, is it not?"

Better than losing everything and everyone I love, so I can join the court of the man who ordered the attack on my mother's ship? Who would just as easily bury a dagger in my back?

No. I almost lost everything once before, and I would sooner die than let it happen again.

She lifted her chin, holding her father's gaze. "I will find another way."

"It's not going to work, my love. The suitors will arrive within the week, so consider this matter closed." He shook his head sadly. "By the year's end, you will be married."

Chapter Six
The Liar

A blade arced toward Auberon's face.

He knocked it aside and swung his sword low, aiming for Walther's stomach. Steel flashed in the sunlight as Walther parried, his sword cleaving the air with a shrill whistle. The edge caught the side of Auberon's bicep, and a thin line of blood welled under the slit in his tunic.

"You'll have to be faster than that," Walther taunted, grinning. Sweat shone across his brow, plastering his dark curls to his forehead. "Next time, it won't be your arm that I hit."

"Do it again."

Auberon sank into a defensive position. His muscles ached from sparring, and the cloudless sky offered no reprieve from the sun, blazing even at the end of autumn. His tunic was already soaked through with perspiration—a fact which served only to excite the young noblewomen watching from the pavilion to his left, giggling and whispering to one another behind their lacy fans.

Walther's sword sailed toward Auberon's chest. He met the blow with one of his own, locking the blades between them. Auberon's arms shook with the effort of holding his friend at bay.

Walther was twenty-one, only a year older than Auberon, but he was huge—muscle from head to toe.

Without warning, Auberon twisted and dropped into a crouch, pulling a small dagger from the leg of his boot in one fluid movement. He sprang to his feet just as Walther regained his balance and turned, stopping short when Auberon leveled the blade at his throat.

"Not faster," he said, panting. "Just smarter."

Walther stepped back, wiping sweat from his face with the back of his arm. "What if my blade were poisoned?"

He smiled and returned his sword to the sheath at his hip, then the dagger to the one in his boot. "Then you'd better hope it was quick enough to kill me before I repaid the favor."

A steward clad in the crisp white livery of the royal staff started toward them from the far side of the gardens, his hands clasped behind his back. Beyond him, the palace seemed to glow under the sunlight, all pristine white stone and gleaming golden domes. It was a vast, sweeping estate with elegant curves, gilded spires, and intricately carved pillars—the beating heart of the Erdurian Empire.

"Looks like the Emperor has need of you," Walther said, nodding toward the steward who was swiftly approaching.

"Yes, he no doubt wants to make sure I haven't forgotten my orders—as if it were remotely possible to forget something of this magnitude. I'll find you later."

Walther bade him farewell, and Auberon followed the steward across the gardens, winking at the court ladies who blushed as he passed. They walked through a series of stone archways covered in ivy and climbing roses, then into the southern wing of the palace, their footsteps echoing down the bright, airy corridor. When they arrived at the outer chamber, Auberon sprawled across the settee while the steward poured tea from a set on the low central table. He idly ran his fingers over the scratch Walther's blade had left in his bicep. It was the first time his friend had landed a blow on him in a week and a half.

"That's not very princely posture," Emperor Hyperion said as he strode into the room. He was not a tall man, nor especially well-muscled, but his movements were laced with a regal authority Auberon had always envied. He dismissed the steward with a wave of his hand, his slate gray eyes following the man as he bowed and left the room.

Auberon folded his arms behind his head and grinned. "Oh, but I'm so very good at posturing."

Hyperion shot him a look that was half weary, half amused, and gestured for Auberon to join him at one of the floor-to-ceiling windows. Through the glass, they could see beyond the gleaming white manors of the upper district to the southern port. Large sails emblazoned with the royal crest stretched high into the sky, their gentle flapping giving the double-headed eagle the appearance of flight.

"Everything has been prepared for your voyage to Rivosa. You and Drystan will cast off tomorrow at dawn, and you'll be traveling with a complement of two dozen guards. Keep them close while dealing with the Rivosans. With the bad blood between our countries, they are certain to see you as a threat." Hyperion glanced at him sidelong. "Brigham and Osric have apprised you of the task I've given you?"

He nodded. "In short, verify that the eudorite mines exist and secure as much of the ore as possible for the Empire."

"Exactly. The Howling Mountains span the northern coasts of Beltharos and Rivosa. It's not surprising that the Beltharans have not tried to mine the eudorite ore; they've been led by a weak, unstable king for decades, and their country has been plagued by war these past several months. Rivosa, however, has had no such troubles."

As he spoke, Hyperion crossed the room and sat in the large armchair by the hearth, a thoughtful expression coming over his face. Auberon sank onto the settee and handed him one of the teas the steward had poured. The Emperor accepted it with a grateful nod, but made no move to drink it. His fingers curled around the cup, whorls of steam dancing in front of his face as he stared into the crackling fire.

Finally, he said, "Based upon the limited information we have, we believe eudorite ore forms only in the Howling Mountains. When forged into a blade, it is supposedly sharper than steel and harder than a diamond. If King Domhnall is mining it, he will be able to supply his soldiers with weapons and armor impervious to common weapons. His troops may become unstoppable, and we would be their first target."

Unease filled Auberon. Rivosa and Erduria had a long history of bloody battles for control of the Tranquil Sea, and the enmity between the lands had only grown since the king of the Selannic Isles closed the ports to Erdurians and gave Rivosa sole access to the master shipwrights of the islands eight years ago. If King Domhnall had them outfit his ships with eudorite hulls and weapons, his navy would become all but invincible.

"As far as we know, he isn't doing anything," Auberon said. "So, assuming there is an ample supply of ore, he either isn't mining the Mountains, or he's doing it in secret."

"Precisely. I want you to find out what you can while you and Drystan are in Innislee. King Domhnall is too clever to leave such a valuable resource just sitting in those mountains." A shadow passed across his face, and his fingers tightened around the mug. "Creator have mercy on us all if he really is mining eudorite, for his troops will have none when they land on our shores."

A shiver of dread crept down Auberon's spine. "I won't let you down."

The ghost of a smile passed across the Emperor's lips. "I know you won't, my son."

A thick blanket of clouds had swept over the city by the time Auberon arrived at the lower district that night. After leaving the outer chamber, he had cleaned the cut in his arm, bathed, and changed into a fresh—albeit worn—tunic and trousers. The simple garb was a far cry from the finery he wore at the palace, but it enabled him to move unnoticed through the poorer sections of Torch. Unlike the upper district, with its wide avenues and well-maintained lamps, the road he followed was lit only by the occasional lantern. Despite the late hour, people flowed in and out of the taverns, chatter and music spilling through the open doorways.

When he reached a narrow, slouching building in the middle of the next block, he turned down the alley and climbed the twisting metal staircase affixed to the side of the building. On the street behind him, the sound of shattering glass cut through the music, followed by a burst of drunken, boisterous laughter.

He jogged up the stairs and climbed onto the building's flat roof. It was the middle of the night, but everything within him felt alive, charged with energy. Too much of his time was spent shackled to the court, listening to the bickering, preening nobles and their petty disputes. Tomorrow, he would set sail for Rivosa. And despite the countless warnings he'd been given about entering the court of his enemies, the prospect of traveling invigorated him.

Auberon sat cross-legged at the edge of the roof. A musician sat strumming a lute on the street corner, an overturned cap at his feet to collect coins. An elven woman danced in the road before him, the plunging neckline of her dress exposing a swath of pale, flawless skin. The tips of her pointed ears stuck out from her dark locks, but that wasn't all that made her stand out. It was the sultry, self-assured way she held herself as her hips swayed with the melody. She hailed from the upper district, without a doubt, and had come to the lower town for a night of revelry and perhaps a bit of sin. She would dance and drink to her heart's content, then stumble back to her manor in the early hours of the morning, bursting with stories to delight and amuse her highborn friends. Auberon knew the experience well; he had done it plenty of times himself when he needed a break from the monotony of the palace.

Sometimes, he would sit in this exact spot, seeking a moment alone with his thoughts. Other days, he charmed his way into a group of strangers, making friends for the night and treating them to drinks until his coin purse ran empty. He savored the way their faces would light up when he volunteered to treat them to another round of drinks, or to buy a song from whichever traveling minstrel had set up shop in the tavern that day. The people he met that night would forget him by morning, he knew. He would be nothing more than a kind stranger who had entertained them for an evening. That was enough to appease the restlessness within him for a short while, but it always returned with a vengeance.

Even now, a pang of something akin to longing lurked underneath his good mood. It was a constant companion, a strange sort of tether that pulled him to the lower district on nights like this. Something always drew him to this spot, a place where he could both be an observer and participant in the night's revelry. Seen and unseen. A half-forgotten memory clouded with the haze of drink. He stood with a foot in each world—one in the opulent, dazzling halls of the palace, and the other here in the dirty, rundown taverns, the smell of alcohol and the blue-gray haze of *aljar* smoke hanging in the air.

"I thought I'd find you up here."

Auberon glanced over his shoulder to find Walther standing at the top of the stairs. He was dressed in all black and would have been nearly invisible in the nighttime darkness had it not been for the oil lantern dangling from his hand. Despite his towering height and considerable muscle, he knew how to blend in, how to move silently—perks of being one of the crown's highest-ranking spies.

"You know me too well."

"Unfortunately, aye." Walther sat next to Auberon and set the lantern on his other side, its warm light limning the sharp planes of the man's face. "I've known you since you were fourteen years old, and you always come here to sulk."

"I'm not sulking. I just needed out of the palace."

"So you chose to spend your last night in Torch sitting on some rooftop feeling sorry for yourself? Or are you just practicing that whole *dark, mysterious prince* nonsense for all the beautiful women you'll meet in Rivosa?" He set a hand over his heart and affected a rather atrocious impersonation of a lilting Rivosi accent. "Oh, but he's just so distant and emotionally tormented! I should go talk to him, because nothing could possibly go wrong with trying to romance a clearly dangerous man I know absolutely nothing about."

For once, Auberon didn't rise to his friend's joking tone. "It's not that simple."

Walther sighed. "With you, it never is."

He fixed his attention on the street once more. Down below, the elven woman tossed a handful of coins into the lute player's cap, then approached a circle of people chatting outside a tavern. She said something that made them laugh and was swept into the group as they filtered back inside. Part of Auberon yearned to follow, an inexplicable wave of something like homesickness rushing over him.

"When I was younger, I spent a lot of time traveling, as you know," Auberon began. He lay back, his hands linked behind his head, and watched the clouds churn high above the city. "I'd traveled half the northern continent by the time I was fourteen. These past few years, I've just felt…restless. Unmoored. Like I'm searching for something, only I don't know what it is. This is my home—I should be happy here. But all I feel is lost."

A few beats of silence stretched out between them. "I wish I knew how to respond to that," Walther finally said. "I'm not good with this kind of thing. Stabbing people? I'm your man. Heart-to-hearts? Not so much. You just need direction, I think. Your entire life has been shaped by the decisions of the people around you. Sometimes you have to stop and think about what you really want."

The words came to Auberon immediately. "I want to serve the Empire."

Walther studied him through eyes that had watched courts crumble and kingdoms fracture. He suddenly felt as if he'd been laid out for the spy to dissect. "Do you?"

"Of course I do," he snarled, annoyance flaring. He pushed himself upright and flung a hand out toward the city. "What else do I have? *Nothing*."

When Walther spoke again, his voice was careful. "You have a lot more than that, and you know it."

Auberon's anger faltered, and his shoulders slumped. Walther was right, of course. He had no idea why he always felt so...adrift. He loved Torch, and he loved serving his people, but part of him wanted more. The problem was, he didn't know what that *more* was.

"You're doing it again," Walther said, drawing Auberon out of his thoughts.

"Doing what?"

"Sulking."

He lifted a finger. "I'm brooding. That's what distant, devastatingly handsome, emotionally tormented princes do."

"I don't remember saying the handsome part."

"It was implied."

Walther chuckled. "Your ego knows no bounds."

"Another thing common among princes. Right, then. If you think you know me so well, cheer me up."

His friend grinned and nodded at one of the taverns below. "A game of Seven Deadly Kings? Fifty gold regents to the winner?"

"Make it a hundred and the people will hail you a hero when they take it from you. That'll set them up for life."

"Aye, 'cause they'll drink themselves to death before dawn," Walther said, a mirthful lilt to his words. He stood, picked up the lantern, and hauled Auberon to his feet. Perhaps he was right; he just needed something to take his mind off his troubled thoughts. A drink or two—or ten—wouldn't hurt, either.

"Seven Deadly Kings," Auberon agreed, starting toward the twisting metal staircase. "I'll use the money to buy all manner of delights in Rivosa. Perhaps even a few of those beautiful women you were talking about."

"Ha. We both know your skill with the game. The only way you'll win is if you cheat."

He grinned at his friend over his shoulder. "The only way you'll know I cheated is if you catch me. And we both know how likely that is."

Chapter Seven
The Lady

You would limit yourself to the role of an advisor, when you could be a queen? Why?

The question burned within Riona as she silently swept into one of the private boxes in the Royal Theater, the familiar scents of varnished wood and old velvet wrapping her in their embrace. In the near-empty theater below, clusters of candles and lanterns were scattered across the stage, casting dancing lights across the twisted, skeletal metal trees that made up a ghostly, ethereal forest. Young girls—the eldest no more than thirteen or fourteen—spun and leapt among them, moving gracefully to the melody pouring from the piano at the corner of the stage. A voluptuous brunette sat on its bench, watching the girls with a sharp eye as her fingers danced across the keys.

If this is the sacrifice our kingdom demands of us, we must pay it.

Riona's hands curled into fists. Again, she was to be a political prize, a bride cast from her homeland and married to a stranger the moment it suited her king's whims. Nothing she had done in Beltharos mattered. Nothing she did ever mattered; it wouldn't change the fact that she was ninth in line for the throne and would never wear the crown.

She thought of the queen, content to enjoy the extravagant lifestyle her position afforded her without devoting a moment's thought to the state of her kingdom. She loved her aunt, but she could not admire or respect the woman. Blair had had no choice in sailing to Rivosa to be Domhnall's bride—yet another in a long line of marriages between Rivosa and the Isles, demanded by their ages-old treaty—but she had gladly left the running of the kingdom to her husband.

That would never be Riona. As her uncle had said, the blood of kings ran through her veins. Rivosa, Innislee, everything that she loved about her wild and untamed land—it *was* all in her blood, and no suitor would ever tear her from her home again.

In the theater below, one final note lingered in the air, fading to a soft whisper before giving way to silence. The dancers slowed and stilled, falling into a fantastical scene frozen in time. A forest of phantoms.

Then the mistress of the theater closed the lid over the piano keys, the wood striking with a low *thunk*, and the illusion shattered. The girls fell out of their poses and rushed over to her, clamoring for praise and chattering about one aspect or another of the dance. The woman indulged them for a few minutes, then waved a hand in dismissal. The girls curtsied and filed out of the theater in clusters of twos and threes, their pealing laughter echoing through the vast room as they made their way into the foyer and out of the building.

As soon as they had left, the mistress of the theater set her hands on her hips and looked directly into Riona's box. "I was wondering how long it would take you to show your face around here. I should feel insulted you waited so long. A whole *day?*"

Riona left the box and descended to the main floor of the theater. She smiled as the woman walked down the aisle and pulled her into a hug so tight it stole the breath from her lungs. "I came as soon as I could, Mistress Rosalie. The girls have improved a lot since I left."

"They've been practicing more since we learned that you

would be returning to the city. They want to dazzle you with a private performance." Rosalie released her and returned to the piano, gathering the sheets of music in two heavily bejeweled hands. Her full skirt swished against the stage as she began extinguishing the candles. "You should come watch their practice one day. It would mean the world to them, seeing as you fund the lessons of half the girls here."

"I'll try, but I can make no promises. My uncle intends to keep me quite busy over the coming weeks." Riona climbed the steps and sat on the piano bench. "He plans to marry me off again."

Rosalie whirled, her expression thunderous. "Again? *Already?*"

She nodded. "The suitors will be here within a week. If the king has his way, my new husband and I will set off for the northern continent by the year's end," she said bitterly.

"If I had *my* way, you'd be the lead among my dancers, and that king would have no more say over your life than he does any of his subjects," the mistress of the theater huffed. "Which suitors?"

"Kenter, Kostos, and Erduria."

Her face blanched, but she forced a smile. "Well, come now. Surely there are worse ways to spend one's time than in the company of a bunch of handsome royals. You may not want to marry any of them, but enjoy the north's finest stock while you have the chance. Perhaps I'll even steal one for myself." She shook her head. "If only you'd been born a man. Even with royal blood, you'd have the choice of marrying, joining the council, or serving in the military. Although I can't say I'd rather see you follow Prince Killian into the Tranquil Sea than marry an Erdurian."

"Some fates are worse than death."

"Yes, but I know you better than you think, my dear. Even in Erduria, you would find a way to carve out a place for yourself. You'd have them wrapped around your finger before they even realized what had happened." A tender expression swept across the woman's face, and she crossed the stage to clasp Riona's hands. "I only had the pleasure of meeting your mother a few times, but even in those short encounters, she struck me as a remarkable woman. I see her strength in you. Even if the worst comes to pass, Erduria will not break you."

"No, they will not," Riona said, resolve hardening her voice. "Nor will I give them the opportunity to try."

Chapter Eight
The Liar

Walther was waiting at the southern port when Hyperion, Drystan, and Auberon arrived, the dawn tingeing the eastern sky a rosy pink. After exchanging warm greetings with the Emperor and Crown Prince, he led their small party toward the huge carrack that would carry them to Rivosa. Sailors and fisherman paused to gawk at the royals as they passed—and then they caught sight of the huge man at their fore, the *not-quite-rightness* of the spy sending them skittering on their way with a whispered prayer.

When they reached the gangplank, Hyperion turned to Auberon. "Now, remember, should anyone ask why you are accompanying Drystan to Innislee, you simply wish to attend the negotiations and make contacts in the Rivosi court. If you can, convince the king to promise his niece to Drystan. It will go a long way in securing peace and ending the war."

"I know. I won't disappoint you."

"I have no doubt of that. Be safe, my son." Hyperion clasped his shoulder with a warm smile, and then gestured for Drystan to follow him onto the ship to speak with the captain.

As soon as they were out of earshot, Walther turned to

Auberon, a knowing grin on his lips. "Are you ready for the voyage? Think you can handle a week at sea?"

"Of course. I have the memory of last night's victories to cheer me up when I'm feeling ill." He smirked and patted the coin purse in his pocket. They'd challenged some strangers to a game of Seven Deadly Kings and played for hours, quickly drawing a crowd. They had played hand after hand, the purse of a hundred gold regents—a small fortune—passing back and forth among the players. Auberon had eventually won the pot, but by then, he'd already spent twice as much buying drinks for the tavern patrons.

"Cheater."

"Sore loser."

Walther rolled his eyes, then clapped a hand on Auberon's back. "Good luck, my friend. I'll see you in a few weeks with Prince Drystan and his blushing new bride in tow. Who knows, maybe while you're gone, you'll find whatever it is you've been searching for all this time."

A flush of embarrassment crept up his neck. He had always been careful not to speak of his discontent to anyone—even Walther—but last night, the thought of spending weeks in the court of his empire's enemies had loosened his tongue more than was wise. "Maybe," he replied, doubtful.

He climbed the gangplank, trying to focus on anything but the way the ship rocked beneath his feet. A bird diving into the waves to snatch a fish. A fisherman swearing loudly as he attempted to untangle a caught net. The double-headed eagle crest proudly emblazoned on the sails, one head wearing the Imperial Crown, the other holding a bundle of arrows in its beak. Even so, his stomach lurched as he crossed the deck. There was nothing he loathed more than sailing. Except perhaps mushrooms.

Hyperion bade farewell to the captain and returned to the dock, joining Walther by the water's edge. Pride shone on his face as the crew finished loading the ship and preparing to set sail, masking whatever fear he felt at sending them into the heart of Rivosa. Once the last crate of supplies had been stowed and secured, the ship hands pulled the gangplank, spread the sails, and cast off.

Auberon stood at the railing, watching the coast of Erduria steadily grow smaller. The capital city sat nestled against the bay, the sparkling sands giving way to twisting cobblestone roads. The buildings were all made of the same pale stone, but every single one was decorated with bright splashes of paint, murals that sometimes spanned multiple buildings. Only the palace was a pristine, regal white. Auberon surveyed the scene, admiring the way the reds and oranges of dawn played across the palace's gilded domes. The last time he saw this beautiful sight, he'd been fourteen years old, exhausted from his long journey from Kenter. Seasick and shaking, he had vowed that day that he would never set foot on a ship again. And yet, there he stood, not a decade later.

The things I do for my country...

Footsteps sounded behind him, and he turned to find Drystan approaching from across the ship. The Crown Prince was a year and a half older than Auberon, with the same dark hair and lean build as the Emperor. They even shared the same quiet, powerful grace of a born ruler. Auberon, on the other hand... Well, his personality was the complete opposite of Drystan's, but the differences in their appearances were subtle enough to be negligible: Auberon's hair was more auburn than brown, and his eyes more blue than Drystan's slate gray.

"Brooding again?" Drystan asked as he leaned against the railing. "Walther's right. You seem to have developed a habit."

"Just preparing for the Rivosi court," Auberon responded with a roguish grin, unabashedly stealing Walther's joke from the night before. "*You* may be competing for Lady Riona's hand, but fortunately, I am not. So, while you're off charming the king and council, I'll be spending my time in the arms and beds of the loveliest ladies the kingdom has to offer."

"You wish. Father would have your hide for abandoning the assignment he gave you."

"I know, but a man can dream, can't he?" He let out a mock long-suffering sigh. "I am far too dedicated to our country, which is why I will deny my roguish instincts and keep my hands to myself."

"What a sacrifice you're making."

"I expect to receive a hero's welcome upon our return to Torch. The minstrels will recite ballads in my honor." Auberon straightened, fingers tapping idly on the railing, as the city faded in the distance. Far below, waves lapped against the ship, sparkling under the sun's rays. The sight would have been beautiful if he weren't already feeling ill. He sought a distraction and seized the first topic of conversation that came to his head. "We're sailing all this way so you can marry a woman you've never met, which strikes me as a truly terrible way to begin a relationship. Tell me, what do you *actually* know about the Lady of Innislee?"

"Not much," Drystan admitted, looking slightly uncomfortable. "We've all heard the rumors of her beauty. I know some of the details of what happened in Beltharos during the civil war, but not much about her role in it. News travels too slowly across the Tranquil Sea. Apparently, she was made queen, but she gave up the crown to fight for the rightful king."

"I meant in terms of her personality."

Drystan went quiet.

"Are you truly interested in marrying her, Drystan? Or are you just doing this because you're the Crown Prince and you want an end to the war?"

He shifted, tugging at the sleeve of his doublet. "Regardless of my opinion on the matter, marrying her and ending the fighting is the right thing to do. We shall see if she and I warm to each other when we finally meet, but I have a very clear idea of how the Lady of Innislee will greet the men responsible for her mother's murder."

They fell silent at that, each consumed by their thoughts. Auberon wasn't sure which of them had the more difficult task: Drystan, having to navigate court politics in the heart of a kingdom that would rejoice to see his blood spilled, or Auberon, who would spend every day and night trying to uncover a secret that could prevent the slaughter of his people.

Eventually, Drystan spoke, staring toward the horizon as if he could see all the way to Rivosa's distant shore. "One day, I'll be the ruler of the greatest empire in history. It is an incredible privilege, and I need a wife who will rule by my side and care for our subjects as if they were her own. I don't know if Lady Riona and I will ever fall in love—you and I have witnessed too many unhappy political marriages to believe that is a certainty—but if she serves our people well and rules them justly, that will be enough."

"A noble response. Well, for now, we have a week of doing nothing ahead of us, and I'd like to have some fun before seasickness entirely incapacitates me." Auberon slung an arm around Drystan's shoulders and led him toward a group of sailors sitting around a makeshift table. "Come, play Seven Deadly Kings with us."

"I don't know that game."

Auberon drew back. "*Everyone* knows that game."

"Need I remind you that I'm the Crown Prince? I have better things to do with my time than sit around seedy taverns and gamble all my money away, unlike *some*."

He grinned conspiratorially. "It's only a gamble if you lose."

Drystan shook his head, chuckling, as Auberon dragged him over to where the sailors were sitting. Four piles of worn cards were spread out across the table's surface, the faces of the royals faded from age and use. Auberon gestured for Drystan to sit on one of the crates, then turned to the crew and pulled the bag of gold regents from his pocket. The coins clinked against one another as he tossed it onto the center of the table.

"Gentlemen, let's teach our Crown Prince how to have fun."

Unfortunately, years of traveling had failed to instill in Auberon a tolerance for long voyages. Day and night, his stomach churned with no hope of relief. Most days, he could barely keep his meals down—a fact which amused Drystan to no end. He reveled in the crumbling of Auberon's usual haughty, sarcastic façade. Even so, there was an undercurrent of pity in the Crown Prince's laughter.

When the coast of Rivosa finally appeared on the horizon, a cheer rose from the ship's crew. Auberon would have wagered every gold regent he owned that no one had ever been as happy to see that slender strip of sand as he was in that moment.

He gripped the railing tightly as the ship approached the harbor of a town called Crafford. What little he could make out of the land was beautiful, the coast dusted with sand that gleamed a pale pink under the late morning sun. In the distance, barely visible, rose the range of limestone karsts that spanned the northern coasts of Beltharos and Rivosa—the Howling Mountains, purportedly home to the fearsome stone creatures known as the Rennox. According to rumors, the king and queen of Beltharos had been attacked by the Rennox earlier that summer, but Auberon doubted there was any truth to the story. He prided himself on a rather grand imagination, but the thought that there were creatures of living stone lurking within the dark caves was a stretch, even for him.

Two other royal vessels already sat in the harbor. Auberon shielded his eyes with a hand to better make out the sigils emblazoned on their sails: the soaring griffon of Kostos, and Kenter's rearing stag, wreathed in flame. The sight of the latter sent a pang through Auberon, memories of a country of rolling hills and luscious verdure flooding his mind.

He turned away and returned to his cabin, donning an embroidered doublet and leather boots. They still had a four-hour ride to the capital city, but he was much too vain to be seen in sailor's roughspun by any save for the ship's crew.

By the time he returned to the deck, the ship had docked, and the crew was already unloading their belongings. Auberon followed Drystan down the gangplank and let out a sharp breath of relief when his feet hit the dock. It felt good to be back on land, even if the ground swayed beneath him and the reek of fish made his stomach turn. He paused, waiting for the world to right itself before joining Drystan and their retinue of royal guards at the carriage awaiting them on the street. Its doors bore the crest of the Rivosi royal family: a dragon with wings outstretched, a column of flames pouring from its mouth.

Auberon climbed in behind Drystan and claimed the seat opposite him. Their guards mounted the horses they had brought from Torch, then fell in behind the carriage as it pulled onto the road, joining the rush of traffic around the harbor.

"Kostos is half the size of Erduria," Drystan scoffed, gazing at the Kostori ship through the open curtains. "Prince Eamon is going to have quite the time trying to convince the king to accept a marriage alliance."

"Yes, but his father's health has been failing these last few years, remember? Many speculate it will not be long before Prince Eamon ascends the throne. By marrying him, Lady Riona would also have jurisdiction over the Duchy of Kenter. It's a vassal to Kostos."

"And yet poor Duke Valerian has come to try his luck at winning the lady's hand." He shook his head in feigned pity, then paused, his expression turning thoughtful. "Do you think he hopes that by marrying Lady Riona, he would be able to use Rivosi forces to reestablish Kenter's independence?"

Auberon shrugged. "Could be. Kenter has only been a vassal

to Kostos for, what, fifteen years? Many in the court remember what it was like to be independent, and there's bound to be some tension between Valerian and Eamon. Use that to your advantage."

Drystan sat back against the wall of the carriage, grinning as he appraised Auberon. "Remind me never to attend court without you. You're much better at remembering all the intricacies of court politics than I am."

"What can I say? It's a gift."

"Oh, that it is."

Comfortable silence descended once more as the carriage continued through Crafford. Auberon watched the townspeople they passed, considering what likely awaited them in Innislee. Over the next several weeks, he would live in Rivosa's capital and dine with some of the most important people in the country. While Drystan charmed Lady Riona and won over the court, Auberon would be free to speak with the king's advisors. He would dine with them, ply them with drinks, and gain their trust, as he had so many times with strangers in Torch's taverns. Before they knew it, they would tell him everything he needed to know about the mines.

Chapter Nine
The Lady

"You look as if you're headed to the gallows, rather than a banquet in your honor," Amaris murmured as they followed Riona's father through one of the castle's corridors. At the end, the doors to the banquet hall stood open, and elegant music drifted from within.

"Really? And here I thought I was hiding it so well."

Amaris shot her a look and moved closer, whispering, "I know you have your doubts about the suitors, but please, try not to make any enemies tonight. I'll be the queen of Rivosa one day, and I'd rather not be left to clean up any messes that sharp tongue of yours makes of our politics."

The teasing words brought a smile to Riona's lips. "No promises."

"Well, at least you won't be the only one drawing blood tonight. How long do you think it'll take the suitors to begin tearing one another apart?"

"About three minutes."

"You think so? I'd have said five."

Riona's father shot them a warning look, and they fell silent. Riona ran her hands over her gown, steeling herself for the banquet. The dress was made of ivory silk, with a fitted bodice, thin straps that bared her arms, and intricate whorls of gold embroidery that climbed its full skirt. She had commissioned it from the royal tailors years ago, modeling it after a traditional Selannic robe her mother had brought from her homeland. She could still picture her mother sitting at their grand breakfast table, the pale fabric ethereal against her dark features, her eudorite pendant hanging at the hollow of her throat.

You see this necklace, my love? her mother had asked the day she'd left for her ill-fated voyage. She had let the chain dangle from one slender finger, and Riona had stared at it, mesmerized, as it slowly spun. In her eleven years, she had never seen her mother without it. *I want you to keep it safe for me while I'm in the Isles. Do you know what they say about eudorite? Do you know why it's so prized?*

When Riona shook her head, her mother had continued, *Once eudorite blades are forged, they will retain their form until the end of time. The sharpest blade cannot scratch it. The hardest stone cannot blunt it. Remember that, blood of my blood. That is what you must become if you are to survive in the court.* As her mother spoke, she had gently turned Riona around, swept aside her braids, and clasped the necklace. Even now, eight years later, Riona could feel the ghost of her mother's touch against her skin. *Unbending. Unyielding. Remember that, and the vipers in the court will never have power over you.*

They passed through the doors to the banquet hall, and the sight before her took her breath away. Her uncle had pulled out all the stops for the arrival of the suitors. The entire hall was steeped in the rich browns, reds, and golds of late autumn. Crimson tablecloths covered the two tables that ran the length of the room, set with gold tableware and adorned with centerpieces of fallen leaves and gold-painted gourds.

Most stunning, however, were the thirty-foot columns that supported the room's vaulted ceiling. Stone dragons coiled around the columns and blasted plumes of flame at the ceiling, the candlelight reflecting off their onyx eyes and claws. Their scales were painted a shimmering blue-black, their flames rendered with red, orange, and the slightest hint of gold. They looked so realistic, they might have taken off and soared around the hall.

And perhaps cooked a few members of the court while they were at it, Riona thought with a wry smile.

King Domhnall and the rest of the royal family were standing atop the dais at the far end of the room, overseeing the final touches on the night's preparations. The three younger heirs—Gearald, William, and Namira—were already seated, wriggling with excitement. Standing just behind them, Prince Domhnall II looked resplendent in a crimson doublet and a diadem of gold and rubies. Riona heard Amaris's breath catch when she saw her betrothed. She ran across the room and bounded up the steps of the dais, laughing as he swept her in a tight embrace. Riona's smile grew as Amaris pulled back and kissed him.

The king met Riona and her father in the center of the hall, grinning as he spread his arms wide. The return of his eldest son seemed to have vanquished whatever anger he'd held for Riona's outburst at the council meeting earlier that week. "Well? What do you think of the decorations? They're lovely, are they not?"

"They're wonderful," Riona said, dipping into a curtsy. She hoped he couldn't hear the hint of acid in her tone. They hadn't exchanged more than pleasantries since her outburst in the council chamber. For the sake of the court and suitors, she would remain civil tonight. "I'm sure the suitors will be impressed."

Her father clasped Domhnall's arm and leaned in close, lowering his voice. "This extravagance is too much, Domhnall. The expense—"

"You are welcome to concern yourself with finances any other day, Lachlan, but not tonight. Save your objections and enjoy the evening. Your daughter is the guest of honor, after all."

"I... Very well."

"Good. Now, if you don't mind, I'd like to have a word with my niece."

"Of course." Lachlan dipped his head in respect, shot Riona a look that warned her to hold her tongue, and started toward the head table. She watched him greet the Crown Prince with a clap on the shoulder, wishing she could join them.

She braced herself for reproach, but when the king turned back to her, he looked amused. "Don't pay any heed to your father's worries. He's been serving this kingdom for so long, he has forgotten what it means to relax." His expression softened as he took in her ivory gown. "You look beautiful, my dear. The spitting image of your mother, Creator watch over her. She would have been so proud to see you here today."

Her chest tightened. "Thank you, Your Majesty."

He took her hands in his own. "I know you are wary of entering into another arranged marriage, but rest assured that I will do everything in my power to secure you a good, honest husband."

And I will do everything in my power to keep you from auctioning me off like a prize mare. "Thank you, Uncle."

The music swelled as courtiers began filing into the banquet hall. Riona schooled her features into a polite, neutral mask and followed her uncle to the head table, where the seat of honor had been left for her beside the queen. She sank into her chair, and her aunt leaned over to kiss her cheek and croon over her beautiful gown.

When the last courtier was seated, King Domhnall stood and offered a few words of welcome. As he spoke, Riona lifted her chin and squared her shoulders, her stare boring into the banquet hall's double doors. Any second now, the suitors would make their grand entrance.

"Now, Master Kaiden," the king finally said, his deep voice filling the room, "please present Lady Riona's suitors to the court."

Murmurs of excitement spread through the banquet hall as the Master of the Guard disappeared into the hallway. A few moments later, Kaiden returned with four young men in tow.

Four? Riona thought, her polite smile faltering. Her uncle had said three suitors would be vying for her hand.

"May I present to Your Majesties the Crown Prince Eamon of Kostos, Duke Valerian of Kenter, and Crown Prince Drystan and Prince Auberon of Erduria."

Each suitor dropped into a bow as his name was spoken. Riona studied them in turn: Prince Eamon, with his ink-black hair, muscular build, and strong, regal features. Duke Valerian, with his golden curls, easy smile, and toned, lean physique. Prince Drystan and Prince Auberon with their dark hair and tanned skin. Surveying the gathered nobles, Riona spied at least a dozen court ladies fawning over them...and a few young lords eyeing them with interest, as well. Riona wondered idly how the Erdurian princes would respond to the slight of being introduced after the other suitors.

They climbed the steps of the platform to join the royals at the head table. As soon as the suitors had claimed their seats, a fleet of servants poured in from the kitchen. A divine aroma wafted through the air as they set plates before Riona and the others. Conversation and music gradually filled the hall.

"I've not had the pleasure of visiting Rivosa before," Prince Eamon said to Riona in the common tongue of the south, his words tinged with the refined accent of northern nobility. "What I've seen of your country so far has been beautiful—almost as lovely as you."

Creator, spare me. "Thank you, Your Highness. Your position does not allow much time for travel, I take it?"

"Not to the southern continent, unfortunately. The unrest in Kenter often demands my attention."

"Unrest?" She glanced at Duke Valerian, who was glaring at the prince. The negotiations would not begin for a few days, but every interaction provided an opportunity for one of the suitors to tip the scales in his favor, especially when the king was within earshot. She locked eyes with Amaris, who was hiding her grin behind the lip of her goblet. Three minutes, just as she'd said.

Further down the table, Prince Auberon smirked and shot his brother a look that seemed to say, *I told you this would happen.*

"The dissidents are nothing but a vocal minority," Valerian said curtly. "Our politics certainly do not require the attention of a foreign king."

"Of course they do, if you can't maintain control yourself. My father's troops have been keeping the peace on the Grand Duke's behalf for years," Eamon explained to Riona. "He's the one who *gave* the duchy to Valerian's father. Whenever there is trouble in the court, we step in to ensure it reaches a peaceful resolution."

Valerian scowled. "The *trouble* is little more than the grumbling of a few distinguished families. Grand Duke Finnegani may have lost his life along with his throne fifteen years ago, but his friends in the nobility are still alive. Every few years, they gather and demand justice for him, along with a change in leadership." The duke turned to Riona. "My father swiftly shuts them down every time, right before the Kostori king or his son shows up to claim credit for 'keeping the peace'. They are *not* a threat. The lies Prince Eamon spreads to exaggerate his father's influence, however, are a different story."

Valerian and Eamon locked glares. The tension grew for several charged moments, until Prince Auberon chuckled. "Oh, of course they're not a threat. The Finnegani family was soundly defeated in the Kostori siege. There's no sense in demanding justice for dead men."

The duke sat back, visibly relaxing. "No, certainly not." He offered Auberon a grateful look before changing the subject, clearly relieved to return to neutral topics of discussion.

Riona half-listened to their conversation, focusing her attention on the younger of the Erdurian princes. It was odd that the Emperor has sent two of his sons to bid for her hand in marriage. Drystan was the Crown Prince; surely Emperor Hyperion knew that her uncle would favor the heir to the throne. So why had Auberon really come?

Just as she thought it, the prince turned and caught her staring. He raised a brow and shot her a crooked grin, mistakenly assuming she had been ogling him. The gesture revealed dimples that would make most noblewomen swoon.

Riona smiled coyly in response. *Let him think me vain. Let him think I can be taken in by a pretty face.* While it was true that he was hardly lacking in looks, she was far more interested in the threat he and his brother posed to her country and her future. Between Kenter, Kostos, and Erduria, the Empire was by far the wealthiest—a fact which would undoubtedly benefit them in the negotiations.

Fortunately, Erduria also had the bloodiest history with Rivosa.

Prince Auberon held her gaze and lifted his goblet in a silent toast. In the flickering candlelight from the chandelier, the planes of his face were cast in sharp contrast, emphasizing the height of his cheekbones and the angle of his jaw. He drank deeply from his cup, then nodded to her own as if in challenge. A shock of hair fell into his eyes as he watched her. *Trust me,* his grin seemed to say.

Riona lifted her goblet and took a drink. The flavors of the spiced wine danced on her tongue, and she savored it for a moment before setting her goblet back on the table.

Give me one reason to, her sly smile responded.

Chapter Ten
The Liar

Auberon trailed his fingers along the rim of his goblet as the servants cleared the last of the dinner plates. A sour taste filled his mouth as he watched Prince Eamon take Lady Riona's hand and sweep her onto the dance floor, joining the rest of the noble couples gathering before the dais. He disliked everything about Eamon, and it wasn't just because he was competing against Drystan for the lady's hand. Auberon had plenty of reasons to detest the Kostori, but chief among them were; one, they refused to put an end to the barbaric practice of keeping slaves, and two, they were bastards.

He nudged Drystan's arm and nodded toward the king and queen. "Now's your chance. Don't sulk because Eamon asked the lady to dance before you could. Go over there and woo the king. He hasn't bothered trying to hide the fact that you're his least favorite suitor."

"The king? Lady Riona—"

"Undoubtedly has little say in whom she will marry. Eamon was clever with those quips at Valerian's expense, but he made the mistake of trying to charm Lady Riona. It's not *her* you have to convince, it's her uncle."

"Good point," Drystan said, rising from his seat.

"That's what I'm here for." Auberon downed the last of his wine. "To give invaluable counsel, and look incredibly handsome doing it."

Drystan merely shook his head and walked away.

Turning back to the court, Auberon studied the way the nobles moved from conversation to conversation, tracking which lords and ladies attracted the most attention. It seemed to be concentrated around a group of men and women seated at the closer end of one of the tables. The advisors, presumably. As the song drew to a close, Duke Valerian practically leapt from his seat for the chance to dance with Lady Riona. Auberon fought the urge to roll his eyes. *Amateurs.*

He rose and descended from the dais. On his way, he snagged a pitcher of wine from a passing servant's tray and refilled his cup. He took a sip as he leaned against one of the pillars lining the hall to watch Riona and Valerian dance. Noble couples spun around them in a sea of lace, silk, damask, and brocade, but every woman paled in comparison to the Lady of Innislee.

Since King Domhnall's invitation arrived at the royal palace in Torch, hardly a day had passed in which Auberon wasn't regaled with tales of her beauty: her striking blue eyes, flawless ebony skin, and full lips. The rumors hadn't been exaggerated. Lady Riona was so beautiful it took his breath away. She was tall and willowy, with waist-length braids woven through with strands of gold ribbon. Even if there hadn't been whispers of potential eudorite mines, it wouldn't have been a mystery why the heirs to three thrones sought her hand in marriage.

As she spun, Riona's unusual necklace caught his attention. The pendant was made of a metal that resembled obsidian, jaggedly cut into a shape like an arrowhead. Eudorite. He had never seen the strange metal before, but there was no doubt in his mind. The pendant looked like nothing else he had ever seen. Auberon took another drink as he surveyed the other ladies of the court. Every wrist, neck, and ear dripped with priceless jewelry, but no one wore anything remotely close to

Riona's eudorite pendant. Even the queen's jewels were mere rubies.

At the head table, Drystan bowed to the king and queen, then approached the Lady of Innislee to finally claim his dance. Auberon noted the way the king's attention lingered on the prince, his lips pursing in thought. *See, Drystan? Invaluable counsel.*

He set his goblet aside and turned his back to the royal family. Eventually, he would have to dance with Lady Riona for propriety's sake, but he had much more important matters to attend to at the moment.

Most of the council members were still lounging at one of the tables, chatting. As he started toward them, he reached into his pocket and pulled out the glass vial tucked inside, breaking the wax stopper with his thumb. It contained a diluted form of the poison known as gloriosa tansy. In its pure form, it mimicked extreme inebriation before ushering its victim to a swift death. Diluted, it served to dull one's inhibitions. He dumped the contents into the wine pitcher. A little alcohol, dosed with the drug, would simply loosen the tongues of the council members. If any of the advisors had knowledge of the mining operation, he would find out before the night was over.

"Oh, you think I'm exaggerating, my friends? The hounds tracked his scent to the larder, where they found him without a stitch of clothing. He had a pie in one hand and was using it to cover his... Well, I'm sure you can imagine." Auberon grinned as the advisors roared with laughter. He stood, pitcher in hand, and refilled each of their goblets with the drugged wine. "I swear it on my life! That was the last time I saw that *particular* stableboy, although stories about him ran rampant through the palace for weeks afterward."

"What a rogue!" Lady Annabel exclaimed, fanning herself

with a hand. To her right, her husband gasped for breath, laughing so hard he nearly fell off his seat.

"Truly, truly!" Auberon turned to the Royal Treasurer—a short, round-faced man named Cathal—and lowered his voice to a conspiratorial whisper. "Some say he has a dozen half-noble bastards throughout Torch, and he's barely a year older than I! Can you believe it?"

"By the Creator, no!"

He raised a brow. "You haven't any wild tales like that from your youth?"

"Oh, I didn't say that. If I admitted to half the idiotic things I did when I was young and foolish, I'd have to resign." The portly, red-faced man hiccuped, then took a long swig of his wine. Auberon's smile took on a sharp edge. The diluted gloriosa tansy had most certainly taken effect. "One doesn't become Royal Treasurer by—*hic!*—gallivanting around with the ladies of the court. I'm married to my—*hic!*—my work."

"And she is a cruel mistress, isn't she, Cathal?" Lord Farquar asked, good-naturedly shoving the man's shoulder. "I don't envy you, my friend."

"That she is, but I love her so."

Out of the corner of Auberon's eye, he saw Prince Domhnall cross the room and grasp his cousin's elbow. He and Riona exchanged a few quick words before slipping through a door tucked into the side of the banquet hall, half-hidden from sight by the wing of a stone dragon. Making a quick escape between songs, it seemed. He turned back to the advisors and kept his voice carefully nonchalant. "That necklace Lady Riona is wearing. It's eudorite, is it not?"

"Quite unusual, no?" Cathal said between hiccups. "It was her mother's, given to her just before her death. A tragedy, that. Her ship sank a few years back."

"It was struck down by Erdurian ships eight years ago," Farquar corrected, directing his response to Auberon. The mirth in his voice had faded, replaced with the pure loathing of a man who had watched too many friends die in battle. "On her annual visit to the Selannic Isles, which was protected by a Rivosi fleet and flying flags of neutrality. She should have been safe."

His words hung in the air. The knowledge that the fighting had claimed Riona's mother settled heavily on Auberon's chest, but he would not apologize for it. They were at war. Innocents died, and pretty words wouldn't bring them back. He knew that better than most. Around them, the council members turned to their drinks, the humor on their faces dying. Farquar stared straight at him, his fingers tightening on the stem of his goblet as if he were imagining wringing Auberon's neck.

"We paid our price for the attack," Auberon said carefully. "Because of Lady Rhea's death, no man or woman with a single drop of Erdurian blood is allowed to set foot on the Isles."

"You lost some trade," the lord responded, his voice like steel. The words were slightly slurred from the drugged wine, but not nearly as much as Auberon would have liked. "The queen lost her sister. Lord Lachlan lost the love of his life. The price you and your people paid is nothing in comparison."

One of the council members cleared his throat loudly, and Auberon inclined his head, eager to steer the conversation in a direction that was *slightly* less confrontational. "My apologies for bringing it up. I shall give Lady Riona my condolences."

The tension on some of the council members' faces faded, but Farquar did not look appeased, his cold stare fixed on Auberon. Yet he did not object as Lady Annabel reached over and patted Auberon's hand. "I'm sure she would appreciate that, Your Highness. It would mean a lot coming from one of the Emperor's sons." She turned toward the head table, where the king and queen were watching over the celebration. "Her Majesty took the loss of her sister hard. They sailed here from the Isles together, did you know? Two royal sisters for two royal brothers."

"Does Queen Blair have a necklace like that, then? Could the eudorite have come from the Isles?"

"I don't think so," she responded, and the others nodded in

agreement. "According to the stories, eudorite is only found in the Howling Mountains. Not that our *brave* king would risk angering the Rennox by mining it." Annoyance flashed across her face, and she reached across the table to refill her goblet once again, sloshing a bit of wine over the rim in the process. "Everyone knows they disappeared over twenty years ago."

"The king and queen of Beltharos were attacked by Rennox just this past summer," Farquar said. "This topic has come up in meetings before, Annabel, and we're all in agreement. Between the Rennox, the caves, and the sinkholes, it's much too dangerous to even *attempt* to mine the Mountains."

"Maybe for mortal men. Send a ship to Gyr'malr and hire some of those reptilian Qadar to mine the ore. Their scales are said to be nearly indestructible."

He scoffed. "We've all heard of the battle that took place between the Beltharan army and the Assassins' Guild. The Guildmother was Qadari, and her cruelty was unparalleled. There's no place for her ilk in Rivosa. I say, leave the Qadari in Gyr'malr, and let those Creator-forsaken Rennox have all the eudorite they like."

As they spoke, Auberon studied the Royal Treasurer, noting how quiet Cathal had become at the mention of the Mountains. If anyone outside the royal family knew of the eudorite mining, it would be him. The king would need someone experienced in finance to address wages, supplies, and the like—and who better than the man who had served as Treasurer for decades?

Lord Farquar abruptly stood and extended a hand to Annabel. "I'm tired of this political talk. This is supposed to be a celebration, after all. Seeing as your husband is too drunk to tell his right foot from his left, will you dance with me?"

"I don't think you're far off, yourself," she said, laughing, "but it would be my honor."

Auberon objected, wishing to continue his questioning, but they paid him no heed as the lord took Annabel's hand and swept her off to the dance floor. Beside him, Lady Annabel's husband lifted his goblet to his lips and muttered something crude under his breath. Cathal burst out laughing, rocking back so far he tumbled off the bench, dragging the tablecloth along with him. Auberon leapt up as goblets overturned, spilling wine across the table and over Cathal's doublet. The Treasurer only roared louder.

"By the Creator, man!" one of the nearby nobles exclaimed, carefully skirting the drugged Treasurer. "How much have you had to drink?"

Auberon swore under his breath and reached down to pull Cathal to his feet. He *may* have given the Treasurer a *bit* too much of the drugged wine. The toxin was too diluted to kill him, but he would wake with a pounding headache in the morning. "Come, let's get you some fresh air."

Cathal beamed at him and slapped a meaty hand on Auberon's back so hard he grimaced. "What a gentleman. Our Lady Riona would be lucky to marry one so well-mannered!"

He refrained from reminding the Treasurer that he was not, in fact, a suitor. He slung Cathal's arm around his shoulders and led the man out to the balcony, into the sobering embrace of the cool night air. Thankfully, there were only a few other people outside. Auberon guided the Treasurer to the railing, relieved to see that it was high enough that Cathal wouldn't somehow fall over the side. That would be the *last* thing he needed.

He glanced over his shoulder to check that none of the other people had wandered into earshot, then murmured, "What can you tell me about the mines, Cathal?"

The Treasurer slowly dragged his gaze from the sprawling city. "Mmmmines? What mines?"

"The eudorite mines in the Howling Mountains. I know they exist."

"There're no mines, boy. The Rennox will never allow it. Did you know they have hearts of stone and eyes of onyx? That's what the stories say, anyway." The Treasurer paused, frowning thoughtfully. "But they also say that anyone who enters the

Mountains is never seen again. So how're there stories, hm? Tell me that."

"Cathal, focus," Auberon hissed. "If King Domhnall mined the eudorite, he would be able to outfit his troops with the strongest weapons and armor in the world. His army would be unstoppable. Isn't that what he's planning?"

Cathal let out a choked sound that was somewhere between a laugh and a sob. "It's not as simple as you make it sound, son."

Auberon opened his mouth to respond, but held his tongue as a pretty elven servant emerged from the banquet hall with a tray of goblets balanced on one hand. She smiled as she handed them each a goblet, then moved on to the other nobles milling about on the far side of the balcony. As soon as she was gone, he said, "What do—"

The Treasurer suddenly thrust his goblet into Auberon's hand and lurched backward, his face turning a sickly shade of green. "I think I'm going to be sick."

He hurriedly set both drinks down and steadied Cathal with a hand as the man doubled over and retched over the railing. Frustration and impatience swept through him, along with a rush of defeat. Cathal couldn't stay at the banquet in this state, and it was clear Auberon wasn't going to get any useful answers out of him tonight. "Alright, my friend," he sighed. "I think it's time you went home."

The Treasurer slapped his hand away. "No, no—my office. I have a cot. I'll sleep off the drink in there."

Auberon caught the eye of a guard inside the banquet hall and waved him over. "It seems our friend here has indulged in a bit too much wine," he said when the man reached them. "Would you please take him to his office, and see to it that he drinks plenty of water. And please—be discreet when leaving. I doubt the Treasurer would want anyone to see him in this state."

"Yes, Your Highness."

The guard slung Cathal's arm over his shoulders and led the Treasurer away. Auberon watched them leave, then turned back and gazed out at Rivosa's capital city, seeking a few moments of peace before he had to return and play the courtier once again. *So this is where my empire's greatest enemy lives,* he thought as he took in the sight before him. The city spread out in every direction, warm golden light glowing from the large bay windows of the manors that surrounded the castle. Unlike Torch, the manors here were a dark gray stone, greenery climbing the old bricks. As they approached the tall walls that surrounded the city, the buildings grew smaller and narrower, cramped row-houses lining the twisting cobblestone roads. It was striking how different the two capitals were: Torch was pristine and uniform, vivid colors and sterile whites; Innislee was ancient and scarred from countless battles, all labyrinthine alleyways and sharply pitched roofs, new buildings built upon the bones of the old. It was a city that *survived.*

The start of another song drifted through the open banquet hall doors, and Auberon sighed. It was growing late, and soon someone would question his absence. He grabbed the goblets of wine and returned to the hall, pausing for a moment to scan the room. The music was still playing, nobles still dancing, chatter still filling the air. Some servants had cleaned up the mess Cathal had made; the table where the advisors had sat was empty, the stained tablecloth replaced with a fresh one.

Auberon was considering wading through the crowd in search of another council member when his gaze landed on Lady Riona, who was quickly making her way toward the musicians' platform at the far end of the room. She had her head bowed, clearly trying to stay out of sight. Perfect. It would give him a chance to speak with her before the suitors could claim her attention once again. He set one of the goblets on the nearest table and started toward her. He may have learned nothing from Cathal, but she was wearing a necklace of eudorite, and her father was Lord of Innislee. Riona or her father had to know something about the mines.

He drained the wine as he neared her, savoring the spices that danced on his tongue. It was so much more flavorful than the cheap, watered-down ale he always drank in the taverns in Torch. He set his empty goblet on a passing servant's tray as he neared the Lady of Innislee. She turned just as he smiled and dropped into a low bow.

"Lady Riona, would you honor me with a dance?"

Chapter Eleven
The Lady

Riona followed Prince Domhnall into the courtyard at the center of the building and shivered as a chill crept across her skin. The balcony had been prepared for the guests, but she was glad Domhnall had taken her somewhere private. She needed a break from the court. Unfortunately, they had about five minutes before the king or queen would notice their absence and summon them back to the banquet.

"I thought you'd want to slip away," her cousin said as she sank onto one of the stone benches and tugged off her heels, breathing a sigh of relief. "Clearly, I was right. As I so often am."

"Humble, too."

Domhnall sat beside her and bumped her shoulder. "That's a strange way to say thank you. Pick up those manners in Beltharos, did you?"

She pressed a hand to her heart and fluttered her lashes at him. "Why, thank you, my dashing savior. My brave prince. How could I ever repay you?"

"That's much better."

"Happy to oblige. How are the troops faring after the battle of Sandori?"

"Quite a few were injured, but we didn't lose as many as I had feared, so I thank the Creator for that small mercy."

"Your father still disapproves of your commanding the army, I take it."

Domhnall sighed. "Have you ever known him to change his mind? He takes no issue with my *commanding* the army. It's the fighting he abhors, ever since Killian died. He's terrified of losing another son, but I refuse to sit in this castle and drink spiced wine while our people give their lives for us. Until the crown passes to me, I will stand with them."

Riona smiled, even though she dreaded losing another cousin to an enemy's blade. Prince Domhnall had chosen to fight, and nothing would change his mind. *Nevis stubbornness,* Amaris would have said. "Your subjects don't know how lucky they are to have you. You'll make a wonderful king someday."

"And I have no doubt you will be a wonderful queen...or duchess...or empress. Now, I've waited long enough. Which suitor do you favor?"

She drew back. "None of them. I've known them for all of a few hours, Domhnall."

"Really? The way Amaris was swooning over Prince Eamon, you would have thought *she* was the one marrying him."

"She very well could. She *is* Selannic nobility, after all."

The prince fixed her with a flat look. "Very funny. She's betrothed to me, in case you've forgotten. And you're avoiding the question."

"Precisely. Who does your father prefer?"

He leaned back and gazed up at the stars. "The obvious choice is Prince Drystan. Erduria is rich, has an—"

"I will not marry a prince of Erduria," Riona snarled. "We can find a resolution for the battles over the Tranquil Sea another way. Marriage is hardly the only method for securing peace."

"I know, and the blood that has been spilled between our lands won't be forgotten anytime soon," he said, setting a hand atop hers. "Moreover, rumors about the Emperor's spy network are concerning. My father fears that if we agree to a marriage alliance, he will have essentially handed his crown to Emperor Hyperion. He doesn't want to risk our kingdom's independence."

"If Hyperion wanted to send spies into our court, he would do it regardless of a marriage alliance."

"Yes, but a treaty would make it easier for him to maneuver us into becoming part of his empire. He is the ruler of the largest empire in our people's history, Riona," he said, a sliver of fear sliding into his voice. "Men don't become as powerful as he is without mastering the art of manipulation. Give him an inch, and he will take from us everything we have fought to protect these last thirty years. We'll be no better off than Kenter."

The certainty in his tone—the fact that there was no doubt in his mind that Emperor Hyperion was capable of such deception—sent a chill down Riona's spine. Along with a rush of relief that her uncle, too, had reservations about her marrying Drystan. "What about the others?"

"Prince Eamon would not be a bad choice. Kostos is smaller, but it has control over the Duchy of Kenter. For less reward, there's also less risk." He shrugged his broad shoulders. "We shall see which way my father leans once the negotiations begin."

Riona nodded, mulling over what he'd said. All of it made sense...except that he'd overlooked someone. "What of the other Erdurian prince? He certainly wasted no time in befriending the council."

"He must be trying to sway them to his brother's side. My father said Prince Auberon isn't here to bid for your hand. He only came to attend the negotiations."

She laughed softly. "Then Auberon has just become my favorite of the lot."

An elven servant appeared in the doorway across the courtyard. "Your Highness, my lady, His Majesty requires your presence."

It has been more than five minutes, Riona thought as she

tugged on her heels, her sore feet protesting. *He's feeling generous today.*

"Thank you," Domhnall responded, rising and offering her a hand up from the bench.

She waved it away. "Go in without me—I just need a few more moments of peace before I resume being the night's entertainment. *Go*," she insisted when he wavered. "I'm sure Amaris is waiting to dance with you, and you can distract the nobles until I return."

"Don't take too long. The suitors will be missing you."

Then they can have a lesson in disappointment. "I'll be in soon."

He nodded and left, the elven servant dipping her head in respect as he passed. The second Riona heard the distant door to the banquet hall latch shut, she turned on the elf. "Why wasn't I told the suitors would be arriving, Ophelia? You and the others didn't think I should know that my uncle was planning to marry me off again?"

"I wanted to tell you, my lady," she responded, fidgeting with the small obsidian pendant hanging at her throat, usually tucked beneath the collar of her castle livery. It was a cheap imitation of the eudorite necklace Riona wore, a way of marking the *helpers* she had among the staff. "But Aeron... He insisted we let the king inform you of his plan."

"Why?" Riona asked, bewildered.

The elf's expression softened. She took a step closer and said in a soft voice, "Because he couldn't bear to break your heart, my lady. None of us could. You've endured so much these past few months, and we knew how happy you would be to return to your city. We couldn't take that from you."

Whatever reproach Riona had been about to give died on her tongue. Ophelia and the few others she paid to be her eyes and ears in the castle were more than her employees; many of them had become her friends. They were the one thing Riona had in this kingdom that was truly her own.

She rose and crossed the courtyard. "Thank you for trying to spare my feelings, but I cannot be blindsided the next time something of this magnitude arises."

Ophelia dipped her head in respect. "Yes, my lady. I'm sorry."

"Please call me Riona," she said as she started down the corridor. Ophelia fell into step beside her. "You needn't cling to court titles, my friend. I held your baby brother in my arms and sang to him when he was sick. We are more than noble and servant to each other."

She smiled. "If you insist, Riona."

"I do."

Ophelia nodded and left, slipping into the banquet hall and melting into the crowd like a phantom. Riona paused on the threshold, dreading the hours ahead. The nobles' faces were flushed with alcohol and merriment, and a bright, lively melody filled the hall. In her absence, the suitors had taken to dancing with ladies of the court. Luckily, no one seemed to have noticed her return yet. Riona stuck close to the wall as she made her way toward the far end of the room, glad to be spared the court's attention, if only temporarily.

Just as she reached the platform where the musicians were playing, movement in her periphery caught her eye. She turned as Prince Auberon dropped into a low bow before her. "Lady Riona, would you honor me with a dance?" he asked, looking up at her with a charming grin.

I would rather follow my mother into the depths of the Tranquil Sea.

Riona bit back the words. As much as she detested the thought of spending even one second in the prince's company, a single word from him could launch a hundred Erdurian ships and slaughter a thousand of her uncle's soldiers. She took his hand. "The honor would be all mine."

Prince Auberon led her to the center of the dance floor, and excited whispers rose from the courtiers as the musicians began to play a soft, slow song. He slipped an arm around her waist and held her close, his free hand clasping hers. With her heels, she was only a couple inches shorter than he, and they stood almost nose-to-nose. He grinned at her as they began to move in time with the music.

"Why do you smile so much?" she asked, keeping her voice low to preserve what little privacy they had among the other dancing couples.

"Why do I smile? My lady, you have spent far too much time with the unhappy creatures of the court if you find my good mood unusual. I am a guest in a foreign kingdom, eating the finest food and dancing with a beautiful woman. What is there to complain about?"

She leaned back, trying to maintain what little distance there was between them. "Beautiful? Careful, Prince Auberon. Your brother might think you're trying to steal me away."

"He might think so, but he would be wrong. It would be unseemly for me to seduce the woman my brother might one day marry. Fortunately, I happen to find you exceedingly repulsive."

Riona couldn't help the surprised laugh that escaped her. "*Repulsive?*"

"Oh, incredibly so. I prefer my women with bald patches and eleven fingers. Maybe a vestigial tail or two. You just don't reach my lofty standards."

"I'll try not to cry myself to sleep tonight."

Auberon nodded solemnly. "Do your best."

Curse him, he *was* charming, and that made him more dangerous than any other man in this room. Auberon had come here to help his brother win her hand in marriage. Every honeyed word out of his mouth was intended to break down her defenses. "My cousin told me you're here to attend the negotiations. Is that true?"

"It is. I'll serve Drystan once he ascends the throne, and he will expect me to travel and act on his behalf. Negotiations like these will become routine, and I intend to gain as much experience as I can. I doubt there are any more challenging negotiations than those between countries with as bloody a history as ours."

"It helps when you sway the council to your side," she responded, looking pointedly at where Lady Annabel and her husband were dancing. Both were giggling and stumbling, clearly drunk. She doubted they would remember much of the banquet come morning, save for the impression Auberon had made. He seemed the type that wasn't easily forgotten.

"Please. That's hardly an uncommon tactic. The only noteworthy thing about it is that Eamon and Valerian didn't think of it." He spun her under his arm. When they came together again, her breath caught as he pulled her flush against him. "I'm not going to lie—I will win over the court for my brother. He wishes to marry you, and I will serve him in any way I can. I will do anything for Erduria."

Before she could respond, he leaned in and whispered in her ear, "But I also get the added benefit of making Eamon jealous. Watch."

He turned them in a slow circle, his cheek pressed to hers. Sure enough, the Kostori prince shot a murderous look at Auberon's back as he waltzed past with Lady Annabel's daughter. Riona laughed softly, and Prince Auberon drew back, wearing a knowing expression. "One would think you two were already married by the way he's glaring at me. Has he burned a hole in the back of my doublet yet?"

"Not yet, but I suspect you won't want to dance with me again, just to be safe."

Prince Auberon dipped her low, his arms strong and steady around her. "I'll take my chances," he said softly, a crooked grin on his lips.

He pulled her up, and Riona looked everywhere but at him as they danced. *Do not be taken in by his charm.* She'd been watching him from the corner of her eye all evening, and she hadn't missed the ease with which he had slipped into the advisors' conversation. The smiles and jests were nothing but a pretty façade. She could never forget who he was. The Emperor wasn't a man who feared the cutthroat machinations of the court; he was a man who turned them to his advantage, and his sons were no different. She could see it in the gleam in Auberon's eyes, as dark and unforgiving as the Tranquil Sea's tides.

"You don't...care much for politics, do you, Lady Riona?" Auberon said, slightly out of breath. Over the course of the evening, the temperature of the room had risen considerably, and perspiration shone across his brow.

"What makes you say that?"

He raised a brow. "That laugh with which you graced me earlier was the first time I heard you laugh all night. You've smiled through every dance, yet—yet it has never once reached your eyes. You hate it here."

Alarm bells rang through her head. *He sees too much.* "Do not presume to know a single thing about me," Riona hissed.

"I'm not blind, my lady. You may be a good enough actress to...trick every—"

The word ended in a gurgle as he doubled over and coughed, blood splattering across the ivory silk of Riona's bodice. She froze in shock as the prince staggered back a few steps and wiped his mouth with the back of a hand. It came away crimson. The couples around them recoiled. Several noblewomen let out shrieks of horror and fear when they saw the prince gasping, a smear of blood across his lips.

Drystan leapt from the dais and shoved through the crowd. "Auberon! Oh, by the Creator—"

"My bag," Auberon interrupted. He gripped his brother's arm. "There's a small...wooden box inside. Bring it to me...*now.*"

Drystan didn't waste a second. He helped Auberon into one of the seats at the head table, then rushed out of the room, pushing gawking nobles out of his path. Chaos erupted. Guards and servants rushed in, herding the nobles toward the rear of the room and the suitors to the dais. The king commanded Master

Kaiden to fetch a healer as Auberon doubled over and coughed again, bright red droplets pooling on the marble at his feet.

Riona stared at the blood, frozen in place. Auberon's doublet strained as he sucked in several wet, shallow breaths, his knuckles white around the arms of his chair. He lifted his head, a shock of chestnut hair falling over his brow, and his wide eyes met hers. The pure terror she saw in their depths hit her like a physical blow. Without a word, she climbed the steps and sank to her knees beside him, heedless of the blood staining her ivory skirt.

"You're going to be okay," she murmured, setting a hand atop his. He said nothing, blood dripping from his lips, but he released his vice grip on the chair's arm and instead clasped her hand. "The healer is on his way. He'll be here before you know it. You're going to be okay."

Auberon could only nod.

Riona looked him over, belatedly realizing that the perspiration beading on his forehead had not been a result of the warmth of the room, but of fever. His eyes were shiny, unfocused, and his hands had grown clammy. Riona cursed herself for not seeing it sooner. The realization of what had happened settled over her just as he lifted his head and mumbled *Osha's Kiss* through bloody lips.

Someone had poisoned Prince Auberon.

Chapter Twelve
The Liar

Auberon was dying.

He fought for breath through failing lungs as the celebration devolved into chaos around him. He was doubled over, staring down at the flecks of blood dotting his shiny leather boots, and he could hear the jumble of voices echoing throughout the hall. The king snapping orders. The queen comforting her children. Guards herding people away from him. Somewhere in the hall, metal rang against stone when someone knocked a tray of goblets to the floor.

Yet through it all, he could hear Riona.

"You'll be okay," she kept saying, over and over and over again. He clutched one of her hands, and the other was on his back, rubbing gently, keeping him focused on her voice. Auberon coughed, the taste of copper filling his mouth. Blood dripped from his lips and splattered on the floor, soaking into the skirt of her gown. "You're going to be okay. Healer Barra will help you. He'll— Oh, thank the Creator! Your brother's here."

Auberon pushed himself upright as Drystan dropped to his knees beside the chair, a small wooden box in his hands. Without hesitation, Auberon snatched it and scanned the labels of the bottles within, recalling the hours and hours of lessons he'd taken in the palace library. *Osha's Kiss. Osha's Kiss. Counteracted by...maryglove!*

His hands shook as he pulled the bottle out and broke the wax seal, then poured the contents into his mouth. The dried blossoms were bitter and earthy, but at the very least, the taste cut through the horrible tang of blood. He prayed he hadn't taken the antidote too late. Already, his heart was racing, his chest rising and falling rapidly, his lungs filling with fluid. He doubled over and coughed again, wincing at the spray of blood that splattered across the floor. His vision was growing hazy.

The banquet hall doors flew open, cracking against the walls, just as everything went black.

Chapter Thirteen
The Lady

"No one is to leave the banquet hall until they've been questioned by a member of the royal guard," King Domhnall said to Master Kaiden as he stormed into the throne room, his face contorted in fury. "Not a servant, not a cook, not a courtier. Someone tried to kill the son of the Erdurian Emperor in *my* castle, and I will not allow him to walk free. I don't care how long it takes. I will not be forced into another damned battle."

"Yes, Your Majesty."

Kaiden bowed and hurried out of the room, dipping his head in respect as he passed Riona, her father, and Prince Domhnall. The king let out a string of oaths as he paced before the throne, running an agitated hand over his short hair. "Of all the things to befall us tonight, a poisoning!" he snarled. "You had all better begin praying that Prince Auberon survives the night, because if he dies, it'll be all our heads. The Emperor will rip the whole *kingdom* from us if his son dies tonight."

"Barra is the best healer in the kingdom," Lachlan said, holding his hands up to calm his brother. "He will save the prince's life, and we will find and punish the person responsible for this attack. If we have to promise Riona to Drystan in order to avoid another battle..." He hesitated, pain flashing across his face. "We will do it."

"We will not," Riona snapped.

"If it comes to it, we'll fight," Prince Domhnall said, setting a comforting hand on her shoulder. He turned to his father. "Do you truly believe the Emperor and his sons didn't plan this? They knew that if something like this happened while Drystan and Auberon were your guests, it would give him every right to demand a betrothal. I didn't think he would risk his own son's life to further his political goals, but one can never overestimate the cruelty of an Erdurian."

Could it be true? Riona's tutors had taught her about the Emperor's ruthlessness, but she had seen the genuine terror on Auberon's face. Her hand still ached from how tightly he'd been clutching it. Nicholas Comyn had been a master of deception, but even he wouldn't have been able to fake the fear she had seen on Auberon's face.

Do not be taken in by his act. He is the enemy. Everything he does is in service to the Empire—he said as much earlier.

"Prince Auberon had the poison's antidote in his bag," Riona said, and the king stopped pacing mid-step. All three of them turned to stare at her. They'd been too distracted by the chaos to notice that Drystan had retrieved that small wooden box for his brother. "It seems too fortunate to be mere coincidence, but I saw the terror on Prince Auberon's face, and I don't believe he knew of the poisoning beforehand. Still, they cannot be trusted. The wisest course of action would be to send them back to Erduria as soon as the prince is well enough to travel."

King Domhnall sank onto his throne. "If I had the evidence to support that claim, I would have both princes thrown onto their ship tonight, peace treaty be damned. Whoever organized the attempt on Prince Auberon's life chose a perfect time to strike. There were so many people in attendance tonight, it would have been easy to slip poison into a goblet or onto a plate without anyone noticing. Unless we find undeniable proof that this was a plot by the Emperor himself, we must act as if the poisoning were genuine."

They continued discussing the events of the night, but Riona hung back, frowning. Something about what the king had said troubled her. The Empire had always been more powerful than Rivosa; it was the most powerful country in the northern continent, and they were already at war. If Emperor Hyperion wanted to invade, he wouldn't have risked his son's life in the process. He would have simply attacked.

Doubts filled her mind, but she held her tongue. Whether the Emperor had been behind Auberon's poisoning or not, she wouldn't protest if the king decided to send the princes back to the northern continent. Once they were gone, she would only have to rid herself of the other two suitors.

"Whatever comes of tonight's interrogations," King Domhnall said, "speak of your suspicions to no one. For all intents and purposes, we—"

Shouts rose from beyond the closed doors, and the king rose as a Rivosi guard rushed into the room. "Your Majesty, it's Prince Drystan. He says—"

"Let him in."

The man bowed and pulled one of the doors open wide. Prince Drystan stormed in, flanked by more than a dozen Erdurian guards. Rage rippled off him with every step. A contingent of Rivosi royal guards rushed in after them and made to form a line between the prince and their king, but King Domhnall held up a hand to stay them. Riona edged closer to her father and cousin, fearing that the night would end in further bloodshed.

"Not one day in the city, and my brother is lying in the infirmary, fighting for his life," Drystan spat. "Is this how you welcome all your guests into your home, Your Majesty, or just the Erdurian ones?"

"Prince Drystan, what happened to your brother was terrible, and we're praying for his swift recovery," the king said, gazing down at the prince with a calm, level expression. "We will find the person responsible for this attack and he will be punished accordingly."

"I expect so. I also expect, Your Majesty, that certain *concessions* will be given during the negotiations to make up for this breach of trust."

"We will discuss that when the time comes," King Domhnall replied coolly. "For now, let us focus our efforts on finding the attacker and praying for your brother's survival."

Drystan's gaze slid to Riona, and she stiffened, bracing herself for his demand for their marriage. Hatred for him, for his brother, for the Emperor, burned within her. *I will never become your wife,* she silently vowed.

Instead, he turned to the king. "According to your healer, Osha's Kiss is only effective when administered orally, and it kills its victims within fifteen minutes of ingestion. Have your guards question the people who were pouring and serving the wine. You'll find the would-be killer among their ranks."

Domhnall nodded to one of the Rivosi guards, who bowed and left to pass on the orders. With that, Prince Drystan turned on his heel and walked out of the room, his guards falling into step behind him. As soon as they disappeared into the hall, the king waved away the remaining men and turned his back on the room, shaking his head. The tension in Riona's chest gradually eased, and she sucked in what felt like her first full breath since the prince had barged into the room. He hadn't demanded her hand in marriage. Thank the Creator for small miracles.

"Lachlan, speak to the commander of the city watch and have them increase patrols," the king said. "Domhnall, help Master Kaiden organize the royal guard, and see if you can calm the nobles while you're at it."

"Yes, Father."

"And Riona, get close to the princes and see what you can learn about them. They're eager to impress you, and that will loosen their tongues. Just...be cautious."

She curtsied and followed her father and the Crown Prince out of the throne room. Once the doors swung shut behind them, her father turned back and kissed her temple. "Go back to the house and get some rest, my dear. Domhnall and I will oversee the interrogations."

"I want to help," Riona said. She needed to find Ophelia and her other helpers, see if they had witnessed anything that would aid in the search for the would-be assassin.

"As much as I would appreciate that, we'll have a hard enough time calming the courtiers without the sight of the blood covering your dress," he said, nodding to the red-brown splotches marring the once pristine silk. "It's late—go home and rest so you can help tomorrow. I'll send Amaris home soon, as well. She stayed behind to help Blair with the little ones."

"...Fine."

She bade them farewell and started down the corridor, trying to ignore the cold brush of the bloody gown against her skin as she walked. Her already low mood plummeted. It seemed silly to mourn for something as trivial as a gown, but the dress was one of the few things she owned that tied her to her mother.

She turned the corner into the great hall and paused when she saw Prince Drystan sitting with his head in his hands on one of the benches that lined the room. His guards lingered near the entrance, giving him a moment of privacy to compose himself.

"It's the middle of the night, Your Highness," Riona said as she approached, and he looked up at the sound of her voice. "You should go to your guest house and try to sleep."

Drystan shook his head. His face was bloodless, his hair unkempt. "Healer Barra said that Auberon should pull through, but...there's still a chance he could die. I don't want to sleep in case something happens. I just needed a moment away from that cold, sterile infirmary."

"I understand. And I know this will put a strain on the negotiations. No one will blame you if you and Prince Auberon decide to return to Erduria while he regains his strength. My uncle will be more than happy to send delegates to discuss the terms of a potential betrothal."

"Thank you for your concern, but we've sailed all this way. I'm not leaving until after the negotiations are finished." A weary smile tugged at his lips. "Plus, I'm fairly certain *I* would be the next one in the infirmary if I told Auberon he had to endure another week of sailing. He can't stand being on a ship."

Her own smile faded. "Then he's welcome to stay in the infirmary as long as he needs."

"Thank you, my lady."

Riona curtsied and started to walk away, then turned back. "Why didn't you demand my hand in marriage when you spoke with my uncle, Your Highness? I saw you contemplating it. Why risk losing me to Prince Eamon or Duke Valerian when you could have won your prize tonight?"

The corners of his mouth turned downward at the word *prize*. "Why did you comfort Auberon earlier? Our countries are enemies, yet you sat with him and held his hand while everyone else panicked. Not many people would do that."

"I think that says more about other people than it does about me."

His eyes bored into hers. "No, it doesn't."

Riona opened her mouth to respond, then closed it. Why *had* she helped Auberon? After three decades of fighting, no one would have condemned her if she had left the prince to await the healer alone. Yet she couldn't stop seeing the terror on Auberon's face as he choked on his own blood. She couldn't stop hearing the prince's wet, ragged gasps for breath.

"You and Prince Auberon are strangers in a foreign kingdom, hundreds of miles from your home," she finally said. "After my time in Beltharos, I know how it feels to be alone and surrounded by enemies. To fear that each day would be your last. I did what I would have wanted someone else to do if I had been in Prince Auberon's place. It is as simple as that."

Drystan was silent for several moments, warring emotions on

his face. When he eventually spoke, all he said was, "Thank you for your kindness, my lady. I am more grateful for it than you can imagine. Auberon is, as well, but he'll be too proud to admit it."

A faint smile touched her lips. "Somehow, that doesn't surprise me."

He chuckled as she started toward the exit, the Erdurian guards parting before her. One had just opened the door for her when Drystan called, "Because it was the right thing to do."

Riona turned back. "I'm sorry?"

"Why I didn't demand your hand in marriage tonight. What happened to my brother was terrible, and the person behind the attempt on his life will pay dearly for what he has done. But if we are to be wed, I don't want it to be through political manipulations. Forcing you to become my wife is not the way I plan to heal the rift between our countries. I will not make you my prisoner."

She sank into a curtsy, the tension in her chest unspooling. "Goodnight, Prince Drystan. I hope for your brother's swift recovery."

Chapter Fourteen
The Liar

Auberon was miserable. His lungs burned with every breath. His mouth tasted like copper, his throat was dry, and his stomach churned.

But he was awake, and that meant he was alive.

He peeled his heavy eyelids open and winced at the sunlight streaming in through the open window. He lay on a cot in a sparsely furnished, unfamiliar room. The infirmary. He vaguely recalled someone mentioning the healer before all had gone black. A bedside table with an unlit lantern and a cup of water sat to his right. A lightweight blanket covered him from the waist down, and his chest was bare. His doublet and tunic had been neatly folded and left on a chair tucked into the corner of the room.

He turned his head. A table stood against the wall to his left, laden with bottles, vials, bandages, and countless medical implements. A man was hard at work grinding something with a mortar and pestle. He jumped when Auberon coughed, blood flecking his lips.

"Your Highness! You're awake!" the stranger exclaimed. He handed Auberon a handkerchief to wipe his face, then opened the door and said to someone in the hall, "Send for Healer Barra and the prince. He's awake."

The prince? Auberon straightened. *Drystan is here?*

The man grabbed a vial from the table and lifted it to Auberon's mouth. "Drink this, and drink all of it. It'll ease your pain."

He obeyed, wincing at the bitter burn of the tincture against his throat. Just as he swallowed the last drop, Drystan and two guards hurried into the room, an elderly man with frizzy gray hair close on their heels. The stranger—presumably Healer Barra—moved to the table and began speaking with the other man in a quiet voice.

"I can hardly believe you're alive," Drystan said as he dragged the chair over to Auberon's bedside. He looked awful: his hair was loose and unkempt, his skin pale, his eyes underscored with dark shadows. If Auberon hadn't felt as if he'd been trampled by about a dozen horses, he would have thought *Drystan* was the one who had nearly died the night before—which didn't bode well for his own appearance. "How do you feel?"

"Oh, I've certainly felt better," he rasped. "I suspect I've looked better, too."

Drystan shook his head, chuckling softly. "Even after being poisoned, you're as vain as ever."

"I strive for nothing if not consistency."

Healer Barra moved to the other side of the cot, his assistant hovering over his shoulder as he checked Auberon over, listening carefully to his breathing. The expression on his weathered face did not change throughout his ministrations. For several minutes, the only sounds were Auberon's shallow, wheezing breaths.

Finally, the healer straightened. "You're doing well, Your Highness—as well as one could hope after a poisoning of that nature. As long as you take it easy, you'll make a full recovery. I'd like you to stay here for at least two weeks so we can keep an eye on you. Talcott here will oversee your recovery."

Auberon's gaze snapped to Drystan. *Two weeks?* "But—"

"I'd prefer it if he stayed with me, where our guards can watch over him," Drystan said.

"I understand, Your Highness, but it's not wise to move him right now. The poison weakened him considerably, and there is still blood in his lungs. Moving him to the guest house will do more harm than good. You're welcome to leave guards here, however."

Drystan glanced at Auberon for confirmation, then nodded reluctantly. "I trust in your judgment, Healer Barra. Thank you for helping him."

"You're very welcome, Your Highness. We'll give you two some privacy. One of my assistants will prepare some tea for you."

A shadow passed across the prince's face. "No, thank you."

The healer opened his mouth, closed it, then said, "If you are concerned about poison, I must assure you that you can trust every member of my staff, Your Highness."

"That's what I thought about the banquet staff. No tea."

"I... Very well. Call if you need anything." With that, the healer and his assistant bowed and left the room, shooting wary glances at the Erdurian guards as they filed into the hall and closed the door.

Drystan slumped in his seat and ran a hand down his face. "Father warned us of the danger of entering an enemy's court, but I didn't expect one of us to be targeted our first night in the kingdom. Thank the Creator you came prepared."

"The first rule of being a spy: always prepare for the worst. And Osha's Kiss is about as bad as it gets."

"So I saw. I thought I was going to watch you die right in front of me."

"Unfortunately, you're not quite that lucky."

Drystan shot him a weary grin, but it quickly slipped. "One of the Rivosi guards came by earlier with an update. They've questioned all the servants who worked in the kitchen and banquet hall last night, and they haven't yet found the person responsible for your poisoning."

"That's not what's most important right now. It *isn't*," he pressed when Drystan opened his mouth to argue. "We'll find the poisoner eventually. In the meantime, think of the advantage this will give you in the negotiations! I almost *died*. If King Domhnall wants to avoid retribution, he'll fall at your feet to give you anything you ask. He'll hand you Riona *and* the eudorite mines."

"I already spoke to the king. I didn't demand her hand in marriage."

Auberon jerked back, his brows furrowing. "What? Why not?"

"I want a wife, not a prisoner. I will not make her my captive."

"No, you fool. You'll watch her become someone else's."

Drystan scowled. "I made my decision, and it is not your place to question it, Auberon."

"Yes, I'm well aware." He shook his head, muttering a curse. "If only I'd been born the Crown Prince. You are too kind for this. I'll do what I can, but if you lose her to Eamon or Valerian, it's your own fault."

"Back to the task at hand. When did you start feeling the poison's effects?"

"Halfway through my dance with Lady Riona. I couldn't catch my breath, but by the time I realized what was happ—"

He broke off with a bout of painful, wet coughs. The taste of blood filled his mouth, and he wiped his lips with the handkerchief Talcott had given him. It came away crimson. Guilt flashed across Drystan's face as he handed over the cup of water from the bedside table.

"It should have been me," he murmured as Auberon drank. "I'm the Crown Prince—I'm the one competing for Lady Riona's hand. Why didn't the poisoner target me?"

"Perhaps he saw my breathtakingly good looks and grew jealous."

"Please, I am begging you, be serious for once in your life. You first felt the effects of the poison during your dance with

Lady Riona, so you must have ingested it only minutes before. Can you recall who had access to your drink in that time period? Who might have had a chance to slip something into your wine?"

Auberon frowned, attempting to recall the details of the night before. His memories were hazy from the pain and poison. He had been sitting with the council members for most of the evening, trying to learn about the kingdom's politics and the eudorite mines. He had drugged their wine. And then he had dragged Cathal out to the balcony so they could speak in private. The only thing he'd consumed within that time period was the wine that servant had served them.

Realization struck him like a crossbow bolt. *Oh, Creator...*

Drystan was right: if someone had intended to poison one of them, the obvious choice would have been the Crown Prince. Auberon's assassination—while *undeniably* tragic—would only have favored Erduria in the negotiations.

He hadn't been the intended target of the poison.

Auberon pushed himself forward, wincing at the agony that tore through his battered lungs, and gripped Drystan's arm with white knuckles. "Has anyone checked on the Royal Treasurer?"

"Not that I've heard. Is he the one who poisoned you?"

"No—it was meant for him, I'm sure of it. Send a guard to his office. He spent the night there." Cathal had shoved his drink into Auberon's hands when he'd started to feel sick. He must have mixed them up when he returned to the banquet hall.

Drystan nodded to one of the guards, and the man swiftly left the room. As the door swung shut behind him, the prince frowned and said, "Why kill the Treasurer?"

"Right now, the *why* isn't important. As soon as I made my grand show of nearly dying, the killer would have realized that they'd poisoned the wrong person. They've had hours to come up with a new plan." Dread rose within Auberon. "Treasurer Cathal might already be dead."

Chapter Fifteen
The Lady

He had been murdered in a brothel.

Cathal's body lay sprawled atop the mattress, his torso shredded to ribbons. His face was pale, still twisted in pain and surprise. As Riona stared at the body, she could hear the grunts and moans of pleasure from the rooms on either side. Business continued, even as the Treasurer's body lay cooling in one of the rooms. Master Kaiden's voice drifted in from the hall, where he was speaking with the mistress of the brothel, but it was too low to make out their conversation.

"It doesn't make sense," Prince Domhnall said, stalking across the room. "Not just the murder, but the brothel. I didn't think he was one to…indulge."

Riona skirted the pool of blood that had spilled over the edge of the mattress and leaned in to examine the Treasurer's body. The sight of his torn flesh made her sick to her stomach, but she fought the bile rising in the back of her throat and forced herself to focus on the corpse. His arms were splayed to either side of his body, and his hands bore countless cuts. Some were bone-deep. Riona pictured him fighting desperately, trying in vain to ward off the attacks, as the prostitute straddled his hips and drove the dagger into his chest over and over and over again. She'd stripped the money and valuables from his body—even down to the gold buttons on his shredded doublet—and then fled. According to the guards' questioning, none of the other girls had seen her leave. Most had been otherwise occupied at the time, likely committing deeds that would have made their fathers fall to their knees and weep. Some reported hearing shouting, but hadn't bothered to call for the guards. Apparently, in a place like this, shouting and crying out in pain weren't cause for alarm. The thought sent a shiver down Riona's spine.

Someone cried out—in pleasure this time—in the room to Riona's left, and her cousin's gaze shot to her. "You should go back to the castle. This isn't a fitting place for a lady."

She crossed her arms. "Are you afraid I'll catch a fatal case of depravity? It's not a place for Crown Princes, either."

"Just don't pin the blame on me when your father asks why you were in the seediest, gaudiest brothel in the city."

"Well, I certainly didn't come for the company."

He rolled his eyes and muttered something about stubbornness and glib responses. Riona turned her back on the corpse and crept closer to the doorway, trying to listen in on Master Kaiden's conversation. The Master of the Guard hadn't been happy to discover her here, among the lowest of Innislee's citizens, but she couldn't have cared less. Anything to keep her away from the suitors.

The second she passed through the castle's portcullis gate that morning, she had known that something was wrong. Guards and servants had been rushing up and down the cobblestone path between the buildings, frantically snapping orders to one another. Prince Auberon was alive and awake, a guard had informed her, and he feared that the poison had been intended for the Treasurer. Riona had found Prince Domhnall organizing search parties in the garden and insisted on accompanying him.

Cathal's body had been discovered half an hour later, but they were still no closer to finding answers. Whether the prostitute had committed the murder or was merely framed for it, no one was certain. All they knew was that Cathal was dead, and the last person to see him alive had vanished.

King Domhnall walked into the room, Master Kaiden and the mistress of the brothel—clad in her cheap silks and fake gemstones—on his heels. Riona expected some reproach for avoiding the suitors, but the king didn't even seem to notice her. His attention was solely focused on the body of his Treasurer. "By the Creator and all the Old Gods..." he breathed, the blood draining from his face. "What happened? What have you learned so far?"

"According to the Treasury guards, he spent the night in his office and left early this morning, claiming that he had a meeting somewhere outside the castle," Master Kaiden supplied. "He didn't say where, or with whom, just ordered the guards to await his return. Half an hour ago, his body was discovered here. I have men searching for the woman who was with him as we speak. She would have been covered in blood, so it shouldn't be hard to track her down. She'll have left a trail."

Riona frowned as he spoke. The Treasurer was notorious for only taking meetings in his office; he didn't like the thought of sensitive documents leaving the security of the castle's walls. The prince glanced at her, and she knew he was thinking the same thing. It had been a lie to cover the fact that he was coming here, but as Domhnall had said, Cathal hadn't seemed the type to solicit whores—especially not in a place where the mattresses were hay-filled and suspended with ropes, the sheets stained and worn. One could catch a half-dozen diseases just from setting foot beyond the door.

The king turned to the owner of the brothel. "How often did he come here?"

"Every week or so, he'd visit one of my elven girls, Faylen," she responded, her voice thick with the rolling rural accent of the south. "But that stopped quite a while ago, Your Majesty."

"Why?"

"She's pregnant. That's usually the reason they stop showin' up."

They all turned to her, surprise rippling through the air. "... Pregnant?" the king echoed, looking as if he hoped he'd misheard her. "With his child?"

"I don't know, and I didn't ask. All I know is that he was coming here about once a week, and then he just stopped. Not sure why he came back today, but he just rushed in and said he needed to speak with 'er. I assumed it was about the child." Her gaze drifted to Cathal. "She must have been angry that he had stopped visiting."

The king stepped forward to examine the Treasurer's body. Just as he clasped his hands behind his back, Riona noticed that they were trembling badly. He was fighting to keep his expression neutral, but the loss had to be hitting him hard. Treasurer Cathal had been his closest advisor. "It just... It just doesn't seem like him..." he murmured. "None of it does."

Riona stepped into the hall and started toward the exit, seeking a moment away to absorb all that had happened over the last several hours. Most of the rooms she passed were only sectioned off with archways draped in thin, gauzy curtains, and she caught the silhouettes of writhing bodies in her peripheral vision. A few had wider archways where a handful of beady-eyed men lingered, hooting and hollering as they watched the people within.

One caught Riona's arm and yanked her close to him, a hand rising to squeeze her breast. "Beautiful girl," he slurred, his breath sour with the scent of cheap ale. "How much you charge to open those nice legs of yo—"

He froze when the tip of Riona's eudorite pendant cut into the soft flesh of his neck, drawing a slender rivulet of blood. She'd taken it off and wrapped the chain around her hand the second she'd arrived at the brothel. It wasn't much of a weapon, but it was better than nothing. The man's eyes widened in fear. Even in his inebriated state, he understood that one wrong move would mean his death.

Riona smiled. "You should take more care when speaking to ladies. We're not all as helpless as we seem."

His throat bobbed, causing a second trail of blood to join the first. Behind him, the others didn't so much as glance in their direction, still focused on the entertainment inside the room. "Apologies, milady," he mumbled. "Didn't mean nothin' by it."

Riona pushed the man away, disgusted. He stumbled into the person behind him, who cursed and shoved him back. She ignored their bickering, continuing down the hall and out the building's main doors. A fresh breeze swept over her, chasing away the stench of blood and cheap perfume. She pulled a handkerchief from the pocket of her gown, wiped the blood from the edge of her pendant, and clasped the chain around her neck.

The links in the brothel's hanging sign—which bore the face of a bear, cheekily stylized to resemble a man and woman locked in passion—squeaked as the wind sent it swaying. *The Bear and the Maiden.* Riona approached the carriage she and Domhnall had taken and idly patted one of the horse's necks as she surveyed her surroundings. The wooden buildings were low, narrow, and looked as if they were seconds from crumbling to a pile of kindling. The cobbles in the street were cracked and uneven, and sewage pooled in the depressions.

What brought you here, Cathal? she wondered, running her fingers through the horse's thick mane. If he'd wanted someone to warm his bed, there were several more reputable pleasure houses he could have chosen. And if he'd wanted more than that, he could have had his pick of the noblewomen in court. Any one of them would have leapt at the chance to marry the king's right-hand man. *Of all places, why this?*

Grief swelled within her. She'd always liked Cathal. Whenever she'd accompanied her father to court events as a child, he had found a way to sneak her a treat from the kitchen. He had always been kind

—eager to tell her a new joke or story or challenge her with a riddle. She tried to hold that image of him in her mind, rather than that of his bloody, battered body lying on the mattress inside that seedy brothel.

Everything about the situation was odd. If Cathal and that Faylen girl had indeed fought, who had tried to poison him at the banquet? Poisoning was a cold, calculated method of murder; the grisly scene inside the brothel was anything but that. Riona would bet every jewel she owned that the poisoner had followed Cathal to the brothel and ambushed him there. Then he'd made Faylen disappear.

The king and his son emerged from the brothel then, wearing identical troubled expressions. King Domhnall merely glanced at her and gestured for her to climb into the carriage, too grief-stricken to care about the impropriety of her presence at a pleasure house. "I must discuss what has happened with the council," he murmured as he and the prince climbed in after her. "The funeral must be planned, and someone will have to fill Cathal's position until I choose a permanent replacement."

"I'll do it," Riona blurted. Tragic as it was, this could be her chance at freedom. If she did her job well and secured favorable alliances with the northern countries, her uncle would have to grant her the position permanently. "I want to help. I can do the work around my obligations with the suitors. I'll start by corresponding with Percival about settling the border disputes."

"No, no, Lord Winslow or your father can manage Cathal's responsibilities. You'll be busy enough with the suitors."

"But—"

"Please, my dear, not today," King Domhnall said softly, his voice so thick with grief that it halted the objection on Riona's tongue. "Let us make it through the funeral without arguing."

The driver snapped his reins, and they rode in silence for a while, watching the buildings grow larger and grander, the streets wider and cleaner. Eventually, Riona said, "I don't believe that Faylen killed him."

"Nor do I," her uncle sighed, "but I believe she witnessed the attack. Master Kaiden has already sent orders to the guards at the city gates to check everyone trying to leave the city, and to the city patrolmen to search the area around the brothel. Alive or dead, we will find her."

"What do you mean, he *burned* all his records?"

"They're—They're all gone, Your Majesty," a young guard named Art stammered as he led them through the halls toward the Treasury. The sleeves of his uniform were rolled back, his hands and forearms streaked with soot. "Everything has been destroyed save for the documents he left with this morning. Niall and I assumed they were materials for his meeting."

Prince Domhnall shot Riona a confused look before turning to his father. "Did Master Kaiden or his men find any documents with the body?"

"No, nothing." King Domhnall flagged down a passing guard and instructed him to send word to Kaiden about the missing documents, then turned his attention back to Art. "Was Cathal acting oddly this morning? Did he give you any reason to believe anything was wrong?"

"No, Your Majesty. He seemed shaken when Niall and I told him of the prince's poisoning, but anyone would have reacted the same way. Although... He did refuse breakfast this morning. He wouldn't even open the door to let the servant in, just shouted that he didn't need food and left about half an hour later. He couldn't seem to get out fast enough. I assumed he was running late for his meeting."

He wasn't running late, Riona thought, a terrible sense of certainty coming over her. *He was fleeing.*

But why to the brothel?

When they arrived at the office, Art pulled out a heavy iron key and unlocked the door. The king entered and stopped just beyond the threshold, taking in the sight before him with a mixture of confusion and disbelief. Riona glanced at her cousin, who looked every bit as perturbed by the sight as his father. She had never set foot in Cathal's office before, but she had caught glimpses of its interior in passing. The desk was usually laden with stacks of papers, scrolls, and books. Now, it was not merely pristine; it was *barren.* Not even a scrap of parchment rested on its worn, ink-stained surface.

While her uncle stepped further into the office, circling the desk as if willing some explanation to appear from thin air, Riona followed Prince Domhnall to the other side of the room. A cot was crammed into the corner, tucked between two bookshelves.

"I still can't believe Cathal slept here," Riona said, picking at the rumpled sheets. "He lived ten minutes away."

"That's what he said when he requested the cot, although he managed to make it sound like a far distance."

Riona opened the door to the adjoining chamber—the sitting room where Cathal took his meetings—and the acrid stench of smoke washed over her. She wrinkled her nose and stepped inside, Prince Domhnall and Art trailing behind her.

"Treasurer Cathal pushed fabric under the doors so we wouldn't smell the smoke," the guard said, pointing to a tightly-rolled wad of fabric wedged in the gap under the door to the hall. Several of the windows had been left open to air out the room. "He did the same under the door to his office. He didn't want anyone to discover what he'd done until it was too late."

"You're certain it wasn't his killer who destroyed the documents?" Riona asked. "Perhaps they were trying to hide something."

Art shook his head. "No one entered these rooms after he left, and the windows are a straight shot down the cliff. It's a hundred-foot drop, too treacherous for anyone to climb. He burned them."

As he said it, Riona walked over to the open window, where a metal chamber pot sat on the sill. Prince Domhnall followed her, and together they stared down at the remains of the Treasurer's documents. Riona picked it up, tilting it from side to side to see if anything had survived the flames, but only ashes remained.

"Why? What was he trying to hide?"

The prince shook his head sadly. "I'm not sure. It seems we did not know our Treasurer as well as we thought we did."

Chapter Sixteen
The Liar

Auberon was sitting upright in his cot, anxiously awaiting news of the Royal Treasurer's fate, when a knock sounded on the door. At a nod from him, one of the guards opened it, and his brows shot up when he saw who stood just beyond the threshold.

"I hope I did not wake you, Your Highness," Duke Valerian said with a small bow. He spoke the common tongue of the southern continent fluently, but his words were lilted with a soft Kentari accent.

"No... No, not at all," Auberon replied, trying to mask his surprise. He smoothed the wrinkles in his tunic, infinitely grateful that Drystan had thought to send him a fresh change of clothes. It was rumpled from lying in the cot, but it was better than nothing. "Come in."

Auberon gestured to the chair beside his bed and, as the duke sat, exchanged confused looks with the guards standing watch at his door. He had barely spoken to the man. Why had Valerian come to visit his infirmary room? "Are there any updates on the situation with the Treasurer?"

"They found his body in a brothel, stabbed to death. I believe they're still searching for his murderer, but the guards are trying to keep it quiet for now."

Auberon sagged against the cot's headboard, his shoulders slumping. Cathal was dead, and whatever knowledge he held about the supposed eudorite mines had gone to the Beyond with him. Worse than that, he'd liked the man. Useless as he'd been the night of the banquet, Cathal had struck him as kind and good-natured, with an easy smile and a loud, warm laugh.

He shook his head. "Word of the murder will spread across the city by nightfall, if it hasn't already. Seems life in the court will get much more interesting before the negotiations are over."

"That's...part of the reason why I came here today, Your Highness. I wanted to say thank you for speaking up last night in the dining hall—when Eamon brought up the tensions in my father's court. Anything I said would have come off as defensive. You helped diffuse the tension, turn the focus away from me. So...thank you."

Auberon raised a brow. *That* was why the duke had come? "You don't need to thank me. I'll take any opportunity to knock Eamon's ego down a few levels. The man is an ass."

Duke Valerian grinned. "In that, you and I are in total agreement, Your Highness. Believe it or not, this is him on good behavior. I pray the king does not promise his niece to Eamon; she will see the true face of that snake when they sail to Kostos."

"You know each other well, then?"

A shadow passed behind Valerian's pale green eyes. "It's my great misfortune to say that we are better acquainted than I would have ever liked. Every time there is so much as a hint of unrest in the duchy, Eamon's father sends him to put an end to it. He marches into Glenkeld with hundreds of soldiers at his back, makes a grand speech and some thinly veiled threats, and then demands that we throw a feast in his honor. The man is nothing more than a thief."

"Thieves have principles."

"He's a parasite."

With that, Auberon wholeheartedly agreed. "He and all his people."

The duke tilted his head. "Why do *you* dislike him, Your Highness? If you don't mind my asking."

"Dislike is too kind a word." It made his blood boil to know that Eamon was out there, charming the king and council, while Auberon was stuck in the infirmary. "If I recounted all the reasons why I detest Eamon and his father, you'd be here all day."

Valerian nodded, although he looked disappointed. "Another time, then. As much as I would like to bond over our mutual loathing for that blight on the world, I should leave you to rest. Healer Barra threatened to have the guards throw me out if I disturbed you for too long, and I'm only half-convinced he was joking."

The duke started to rise, until Auberon asked, "Did Eamon's father really give your father the duchy?"

Valerian's grip on the chair's arms tightened, his fine features twisting in anger. "King Jericho did not *give* my father anything. My parents were steadfast supporters of Grand Duke Finnegani for decades, but after King Jericho declared war on us, they watched the Grand Duke flounder, losing city after city to the Kostori. The year-long siege on Glenkeld was the final straw. The people of the city were starving, and our dead were piling up in the streets. After my sister died, my father led several other noblemen to the Kostori camp under a flag of truce and negotiated the city's surrender."

The duke's gaze had gone distant and haunted as he spoke, lost in the memories of those terrible days. Images filled Auberon's mind: bodies slumped in alleys, poisoned wells boarded up, columns of smoke rising in the air. A sea of army tents beyond Glenkeld's mighty stone walls. The people, gaunt-faced and hopeless, waiting for the reprieve of death.

"They let King Jericho's troops into the city and helped them root out the Grand Duke and his family," Auberon finished quietly. "They had planned to publicly execute them for failing their subjects, but the building caught fire, and the Grand Duke and his family were trapped inside. They burned to death."

"Afterward, when the nobles were fighting over who would take the throne, King Jericho supported my father. The others quickly fell in line, and my father has been the Grand Duke ever since." Valerian studied him, clearly impressed. "I thought you didn't know much about our history, Your Highness."

"My tutors taught me the basics, but it's quite different to hear it from someone who actually witnessed the war."

"I was only five when it happened. Most of what I know is from my father's stories. Some call him traitor, but he did what was best for our people. He refused to watch more innocent civilians die." Valerian glanced at the window. The sun was just beginning to set, painting the sky with streaks of pink and orange. "I should leave you to rest. Before I do, there is just one thing I would like to share—something that often brings me comfort. It's an ancient saying from Old Kentari: *Rijat du'omo, Iei sao.* 'Until the end, I fight.'"

"I've never heard it before."

"One of our old heroes, a knight who spent his life in service to the Grand Duchess during the Year of One Night, wrote those words in his journal the evening before he fell in battle. His sacrifice allowed the duchess to escape and give birth to their son, who rebuilt the country from its ashes. It has become a motto for our men in the army," he said. "A few years ago, during my first trip to Kostos, my driver lost control of the horses and our carriage crashed, shattering one of the bones in my leg. I was bedridden for weeks in a dirty tavern in the middle of nowhere, stranded, agonized, and alone save for my guards. Whenever the agony became too much to bear, I repeated the words to myself until the pain subsided. *Rijat du'omo, Iei sao.* Something to think on while you're stuck in this room."

The duke stood and clasped Auberon's shoulder in what he assumed was intended as a friendly gesture. Coming from a near perfect stranger, it felt more than a little awkward. Something else caught his attention, however. Even through the fabric of his tunic, he could tell that Valerian's hand was hot—much more so than it should have been. He jerked away from the duke's touch as if he'd been scalded.

"What did you just do to me?"

The guards stiffened, their hands going to the swords at their hips, but Valerian merely smiled and started toward the door. "I hope your recovery goes well, Your Highness."

"No, wait—" Auberon pushed off his blankets and leapt out of the cot, swaying with the rush of vertigo that followed the sudden movement. He braced a hand on the wall to steady himself. "Stop—"

He doubled over and coughed, pain shooting through his battered lungs. The copper tang of blood filled his mouth as the guards rushed forward to help. Behind them, Valerian silently slipped into the hall. Auberon tried to order the guards to stop him, but he couldn't stop coughing, couldn't catch his breath. All the while, his shoulder throbbed as if it had been branded by a hot iron.

"Stop—" he finally managed to gasp. "Stop him."

"Call for Healer Barra," one of the guards snapped to the other. The man ran into the hall, shouting for the healer and his assistants.

"Stop the duke," Auberon insisted, pointing to the door. "Don't let...him leave."

"The duke?" The guard's brows furrowed. "The only person who has come to see you is your brother, Your Highness."

Auberon barely had time to comprehend the absurdity of the statement before Healer Barra rushed into the room, his weathered face pinched in concern. "What's the problem? What caused this?"

"I don't know. He just jumped out of bed and started coughing up blood. Could the poison have affected his wits?"

"No, no. Hold him steady now—I'll need to give him a sedative." Barra hurried over to the desk and shuffled through several drawers before turning back, holding a syringe. Auberon struggled to free himself from the guard's grip on his arms, but it wasn't much of a fight. He could barely breathe.

"The duke..." he protested as the guard forced him onto the cot. The heat in his shoulder throbbed, pulsing in time with his frantic heart. What was happening to him? Why were they acting as if Valerian had never come?

"You've undergone a lot of stress, Your Highness, and your body is still weak," Barra said as he jabbed the syringe into Auberon's arm and pressed the plunger. "Some rest will do you good."

"No..." Auberon shook his head as the sedative flooded through him. "The duke..."

Within moments, spots of darkness bloomed in his vision, and his body gave in to unconsciousness.

Chapter Seventeen
The Lady

Riona stood in the hall outside the treasury, watching through the open doorway as several royal guards searched for any documents that may have survived the burning. As far as they could tell, Cathal had destroyed everything: there wasn't so much as a scrap of paper left on or inside the desk, and all the bookshelves contained were dry texts on economic theory and treasury records that were too old to be of any use.

Nothing made sense. Cathal had served the crown faithfully since before King Domhnall ascended the throne. Clearly, he'd been trying to hide something, but what? What had been so secret, so terrible, to warrant burning all the treasury documents? To warrant his *murder*?

Had he discovered something unsavory in the records? That was easier to accept than the theory Prince Domhnall had suggested before leaving for an emergency council meeting: that perhaps Cathal had been helping another member of the court steal money from the crown. With forty-odd years of experience in the treasury, it wouldn't have been difficult for him to manipulate the numbers. Perhaps his partner had decided to kill him to cover their tracks. Even so, Riona didn't believe him capable of betraying the crown's trust. Cathal had earned a reputation in the capital as a good, honest man, and she didn't want to consider the fact that it might have been a lie.

Nicholas Comyn was one of the most respected generals in the history of Beltharos, a doubting voice whispered. *No one ever expected him to turn on his king, and yet he didn't hesitate to do it. Is it really so hard to imagine that a man like him existed in your uncle's court?*

She turned away from Cathal's office. Men would do terrible things if they grew desperate enough, but Cathal had lived comfortably in the wealthiest part of the city, and he'd had no family to support after his wife passed before she could give him an heir.

Corruption festered within the heart of her uncle's court; Riona knew it instinctively. She refused to believe that the man who had teased her and joked with her, who had snuck her treats from the kitchen, who had stood up for her against Lord Farquar's cold judgment, would betray his king.

She would do whatever it took to find the man responsible for Cathal's murder. Perhaps then her uncle would see her true worth and grant her a council position, leaving her free to remain in Innislee.

Even if she failed to secure her independence, at least Cathal's murderer would face justice.

Riona quickly left the building, the wind tugging at her dress as she wandered along the cobblestone path, her thoughts tumultuous. The sun was low in the west, and the fat gray clouds on the horizon promised an impending storm.

She paused at a flowerbed and ran her fingers over the velvet-soft petal of a Selannic lily, trailing her thumb along the strip of pink from its center. They were too fragile to withstand Rivosa's winters, and every spring, Queen Blair brought some back to be planted fresh after her annual journey to the Selannic Isles. Riona's mother had loved them. She bent down and breathed in the flower's familiar scent, letting it wash away the day's events. She would find Cathal's killer. She would earn her freedom.

"I owe you an apology, my lady."

She straightened to find a young man standing at the entrance to one of the royal gardens, half-hidden by the mass of climbing roses twisting its way up the stone arch. He was tall for an elf, his servant's livery fitting snugly across his broad shoulders and lean, muscular build. His wavy brown hair fell to his shoulders, the sides tucked behind the points of his ears. He lifted a hand to his heart and bowed low.

"Aeron," she breathed, ducking into the garden to speak with him. "You needn't apologize for trying to spare my feelings. Just, in the future, keep me apprised of anything important you learn —*especially* if it concerns the future of my kingdom. What did the guards discover in their interrogations last night? I haven't had a chance to find Ophelia or any of the others."

"Precious little. By the time Prince Auberon was poisoned, most of the courtiers were too drunk or too distracted by the presence of the suitors to have noticed anything suspicious. No one from the kitchen or serving staff has provided any useful information, either," he said with a frown. "Little wonder why the would-be assassin chose that night to strike."

"What of the servant who served them the poisoned wine? Has she been identified?"

Anger flashed across Aeron's face. "A few people recalled seeing her on the balcony, but their descriptions of her are vague at best and conflicting at worst. They're nobles. They saw the pointed ears and elven features, and looked no further."

"Meaning?" Riona asked carefully. Slavery had been outlawed in Rivosa for generations, but she knew the class divisions between the human nobles and elven workers were as stark as ever after years of escaped Beltharan slaves crossing the border to seek freedom. Their economy was shaky enough after decades of war with Erduria, and many of the cities had more poor elves seeking work than businesses that could afford to hire them.

"Meaning we know she is an elf, female, and has dark hair," Aeron said, a bitter edge to his voice. "Do you know how many women in the kitchen and serving staff fit that description? The guards questioned them multiple times, but none admitted to going out on the balcony last night."

Riona sighed. "Make some inquiries if you can, and tell me if you discover anything. Prince Domhnall seems to believe that one of the courtiers was behind the poisoning and murder."

He dipped his head in respect and stalked off, crossing the garden to gather the practice swords some members of the royal guard had left behind after their drills. Riona stepped through the archway and stopped when her gaze landed on the double doors to the castle's infirmary. *Prince Auberon.*

Her uncle's orders to get close to the Erdurian princes rang in her ears as she crossed the cobblestone path and pulled one of the doors open, striding through the empty sitting room until she came to a short hallway. An Erdurian guard stood watch outside the door at the opposite end.

"May I speak to the prince?"

"He's resting now, my lady."

"It's important—it's about his poisoning," she insisted. "Please, if Prince Auberon is awake, ask him if he will see me."

The guard bowed and retreated into the room. A few moments later, he returned and opened the door wide for her. "Make it quick, my lady. He's had an...eventful day, and he's only just awoken from a sedative."

She thanked him and entered the room, the door swinging shut behind her. Another guard stood stiffly near the healer's worktable, watching over his prince, and Riona nodded a greeting to him before focusing on the man sitting in the cot before her. Prince Auberon looked awful—his hair tousled, his eyes heavy-lidded and groggy—but he visibly perked up when he saw her.

"Lady Riona, I—" He stopped and looked to the guard. "You see her too, don't you?"

"Yes, Your Highness."

"Good." Before Riona could ask what he'd meant by the odd question, Auberon turned his attention back to her. "Have you spoken to Duke Valerian today, by any chance?"

She faltered, confused by how quickly the conversation had gone off track. "No, I haven't."

"Well, that makes two of us, then. Interesting." He frowned, then shook his head as if to clear it. "Can I help you, my lady? Or have you simply come to finish our dance? I'm sorry to inform you that I'm not quite as steady on my feet as I was yesterday. Something's come up, you see."

By the Creator, how does anyone hold a conversation with this man? Riona had hoped that he'd be too exhausted to act like the cocky, irreverent prince he'd been at the banquet, but no. Nearly dying had had no effect on his personality. "You were poisoned yesterday—"

"Hm? Oh, yes, I had noticed that."

Her eyes narrowed. His grin widened.

She tried again, exasperated. "You were poisoned yesterday, and I want to know what you remember from the banquet—anything that might help with the investigation into the attempt on your life."

His expression turned somber. "And the murder of the Treasurer, I presume. I was sorry to hear about his death. He seemed like a good man."

"...I always thought he was. I hope I'm right about that."

"I do, too. I don't remember much from last night, just the broad details: speaking with the council members, going out onto the balcony with Cathal, dancing with you. I assume Drystan relayed everything I told him to the king and his men. Why has His Majesty sent you?"

"You don't remember anything else?" she pressed, perching on the edge of the chair beside his cot. "Who served you the poisoned wine?"

"Answer my question, and I'll tell you."

Riona fought to keep her rising frustration in check. She couldn't admit that she wanted to find Cathal's killer on her own; she was supposed to be devoting her time to entertaining the suitors. If anyone in her family discovered her plan to earn her freedom, the king would assign guards to shadow her every step and make certain she was attending to her court duties. "I should think you'd prefer to aid in the search for your would-be killer, rather than waste time playing petty games, Your Highness," she said, a slight edge to her voice.

His expression hardened at that. "I would *prefer* for Drystan to march up to your uncle and demand your hand in marriage, but unfortunately, he is too kindhearted to take what he is owed. He hopes to court you." Riona scowled, opening her mouth to tell him just what she thought of that, but he pressed on. "I will not go against his wishes outright, but I believe you and I can help each other. I assume you came here because you think to find the Treasurer's killer yourself. Frankly, I don't care about your reasons for doing so. I *do* care that you'll likely endanger your life in the process, and my brother can't marry a corpse. So, I will help you find the killer if you convince your uncle to agree to the alliance between our countries."

Riona tried not to let her surprise show. She couldn't tell her family or anyone in the court about her plans, and he was offering her a lifeline. Even in an enemy kingdom, Auberon was powerful. It would be wiser to have him as an ally than an adversary.

"It will take time to convince my uncle," Riona hedged, hoping that she wouldn't come to regret this decision. If she could delay upholding her half of the deal long enough for them to find Cathal's killer, there would be no need for her to marry Drystan. She had no intention of ever binding herself to the Emperor's court.

"That's fine. I'll need time to heal, and I'd rather my brother didn't know we made this arrangement. Better he believes he convinced King Domhnall through the negotiations than I through my meddling."

She raised a brow. "You already admitted that you were trying to sway the council last night."

"Yes, but *influencing* people and arranging my brother's marriage are two entirely different things. His efforts to persuade your uncle to accept the peace treaty will only aid your own." His gaze dropped to the eudorite pendant hanging at her throat, then flicked back up. "Do we have a deal?"

Riona lifted her chin, ignoring the warning bells clanging in her mind. "We do."

"Excellent. Then we'll need somewhere to train. If we're going to hunt down a murderer, you should be able to defend yourself." He scanned her from head to toe, looking utterly unimpressed by what he saw. "I'm guessing you haven't held anything sharper than a butter knife in your life."

"I'm guessing it wouldn't be terribly difficult to slip another dose of poison into your next meal."

He huffed a soft, tired laugh. "Clever. It's a wonder no one in your court sees it."

Riona frowned, uncertain whether he was complimenting or mocking her. She stood and smoothed the wrinkles in her gown. "If you're finished scheming, Your Highness, would you please tell me what you remember about the servant who gave you the poisoned wine?"

"I didn't get her name, but she was short and fair-skinned, with long, dark brown hair. Pretty. Maybe twenty-five or twenty-six years old," he said, his brows furrowed as he sifted through his memories of the night before. "She's the only person I saw handle the goblets."

"Was she pregnant?"

"Is your uncle in the habit of keeping pregnant servants in his service?"

That's a no, then. She brushed off his comment and said, "It's funny how much one can recall after making an underhanded political deal."

Auberon smiled. "It does wonders for the memory."

Riona shook her head and left the room, glad to leave that infuriating man behind. The Erdurian guard waiting outside dipped his head in respect as she passed, quickly making her way down the hall and out of the infirmary. As soon as the doors latched shut behind her, Riona leaned against them and clutched her mother's eudorite pendant, the metal smooth and warm under her fingers. She closed her eyes and let out a soft breath.

Creator, tell me I've not just made a terrible mistake.

Part Three
Court of Vipers

Chapter Eighteen
The Lady

Four days later, Riona sat stiffly in one of the Church's pews, listening to the High Priestess's melodic voice fill the grand prayer room. Cathal's body lay in its casket near the bowl-shaped altar, his bloody, ruined chest patched together and hidden beneath a sapphire doublet. Riona stared at him, unable to tear her eyes from the royal crest sewn just over Cathal's heart.

Rumors had already taken root in the court. Some speculated that the Treasurer had been stealing money from the coffers and lavishing it upon his secret lover. Others believed the murder was merely the unfortunate result of a heated argument. A few questioned whether Cathal's death had been connected to Auberon's poisoning, even going so far as to allege that Prince Drystan had arranged the Treasurer's assassination as repayment for the attempt on his brother's life. *That* rumor was the most absurd; anyone who had seen Drystan after the banquet would have known that the prince had not spared a thought for anything save his brother's survival.

The High Priestess dipped a slender finger into the vial of holy oil hanging from the cord around her neck, then traced the sign of the Creator over Cathal's forehead as she led a prayer.

Riona's gaze slid to the council members as the gathered nobles joined in, suspicion swelling within her. In the days since Cathal's murder, she had researched Osha's Kiss. The plant from which the poison was extracted was native to Rivosa, but vast quantities were needed to produce a dose suitable to kill a full-grown man. It wasn't common or affordable—especially for an elf in the cheapest brothel in Innislee. Someone of means had bought it, and then framed Faylen for the murder when the poison failed.

A handful of royal guards stepped forward to carry Cathal's casket out of the church. Once they had left, the nobles rose from the pews and began filing toward the exit, many sniffling and drying their eyes on handkerchiefs. As her father crossed the aisle to speak with his brother, Riona followed Amaris toward the wall nearest them, where a display of lit candles burned beneath a massive stained-glass window. In it, the Creator extended a hand to the body of a slain woman, his palm glowing with ethereal golden light. Riona knew the story from the Book of the Creator; it was the moment he had cleaved the realms of their world apart, crafting the In-Between and the Beyond. The same window existed in every church across the country. Rivosi custom dictated that for each person who died, one candle would burn for seven days to guide the spirit into the Beyond.

As she and Amaris moved through the room, Riona caught snatches of conversation, spoken in hushed voices:

"—*stole from the treasury—*"

"*It was all a misunderstanding. A fight that ended badly. A damn shame...*"

"*—put a babe in that whore of his, I heard. A bastard, and an elf-blooded one, at that. It would've ruined him.*"

Amaris stopped beside the display of candles and shot a dirty look at the nobles. "What despicable people. I've heard what they're saying about Cathal, and while I can't claim to know the truth behind his murder, I knew the man. He wouldn't have done half the things they're accusing him of. How long do you think it'll take someone to leap for the chance at his position?"

"It only took me about thirty minutes after learning of his death," Riona responded, and Amaris shot her a sharp, surprised look. "What, did you think I would pass up the opportunity for a place on the king's council?"

Her face softened with understanding. "I would give anything for you to stay, Riona, but the king is not going to let you out of an arranged marriage. The suitors are already here, and his Majesty has gone to great expense to host them during the negotiations. If you hope to find a way out of this, you will be disappointed."

"What happened to all your talk about being powerless? About changing the court? We are more than brides."

"That's right. We will be *queens*. You cannot change anything if you are chained to a treasury position here in cold, rainy Innislee. What will you do, count coins and collect taxes? Is that the legacy you wish to leave?"

"I will be *free*."

"Yes, but you will also be a fool. Do you think I don't dream of returning to my home in the Isles? Of seeing my family again?" Amaris asked, the words laced with pain. "I have given up all of that to put an end to *this*—the trading of sisters and daughters like cattle. When I am queen, your little cousin, Princess Namira, will be free to marry whom she chooses. My daughters will marry whom they choose, or they will marry no one at all. Do you see nothing noble in sacrificing so other girls will have that freedom?"

"I don't have to be a queen to change things. If I served my kingdom well as its treasurer, wouldn't that prove that all royal-blooded women can be more than just pawns?" She shook her head. "I will not sit like a meek little mouse and let men dictate my future."

As soon as the words left Riona's lips, all the warmth vanished from Amaris's face. "Is that what you truly think of me, then? A meek little mouse? A foolish girl who will do as she's told because some boy has promised to put a crown on her head?"

"No, I—"

She scoffed and walked away. "I wish you all the luck in the world, Riona. You may not believe that, but it's true," she said, tossing the words over her shoulder. "Try not to set your heart on staying in Innislee. It's been broken once before."

Riona turned away from her, her hands curling into fists. Amaris was no fool; when she became queen, she *would* change things for the girls of the court, but she was also in love with the prince. She had no reason to object to the marriage. Even to those who loved her, Riona had never been anything but a puppet.

Well. If they would not fight for her, *she* would fight for *them*.

Riona left the church, ignoring the nobles who stepped into her path, trying to draw her into a conversation about the suitors. She walked alone along the twisting cobblestone roads until she arrived at the grand entrance of the Royal Theater. Its tall mahogany doors were decorated with swirls of iron, crafted into images of flying dragons and swirling plumes of flame in honor of the royal family's patronage. They looked heavy, but they swung open at a single soft push, the only sound a whisper of well-oiled hinges. The polished metal mirrors in the walls of the theater's foyer reflected slivers of Riona's burgundy mourning gown as she slipped into the theater proper, blinking against the sudden darkness. As before, the stage was lit with candles, their flames bobbing in a draft.

Mistress Rosalie was sitting at the piano, playing a melody from one of the theater's most popular ballets. She paused when she saw Riona, her smile faltering at the sight of her mourning gown. "I heard the Treasurer's funeral was today. May the Creator watch over his poor soul."

"And guide him to peace eternal," Riona said, finishing the prayer. "Mistress Rosalie, I came to beg a favor. I was hoping you would allow me to use the theater late at night, once everyone has left."

Rosalie raised a brow. "Oh? Planning some illicit meetings with the handsome young suitors who have just arrived at court, are we?" She waved a hand in dismissal. "I'd never be one to stand in the way of a bad decision, my dear. The theater is yours. But if anyone asks, I never knew you were here."

Riona smiled. While Rosalie was a glutton for petty gossip, she wouldn't dare speak of this for fear of the king's wrath. She led Riona out of the theater and into her office, where she plucked a ring of keys from a drawer and dropped them into Riona's hand. "They're the extras. Keep them as long as you need. I'll leave the candles burning for you, so just make sure to extinguish them on your way out."

Riona thanked her and left the theater, slipping the keyring into the pocket of her gown as she walked up the gently sloping King's Road. The tension in her chest eased with every step. Auberon was no different from the rest of the court. He may have acknowledged her clever mind, but he still saw her as a prize to be won for his beloved empire. He thought he could use her to further his own goals, and that mistake was her key to buying her freedom.

A few minutes later, the Church came into view before her, the royal family standing in a small circle just beyond the doors. The queen's somber face brightened when she saw Riona. "I was wondering where you had wandered off to, my dear," she said as she cupped Riona's cheeks and gently pressed a kiss to each eyelid. "I hope today wasn't too difficult. Cathal always had a soft spot for you."

"I just needed some fresh air. Seeing him in the casket reminded me of the day we...found him," she said, the words not entirely a lie.

"I know, love. You just need to take your mind off of it. Thankfully, Prince Drystan and Prince Eamon are waiting for you at the castle. I had Lady Annabel arrange a day in the public gardens for you all."

Riona forced a thin smile. "That sounds lovely, Your Majesty."

Queen Blair patted her cheek before leading her husband into one of the carriages. Once the Crown Prince and the younger heirs had followed them inside, Lord Lachlan led Riona and Amaris to another waiting carriage. Amaris settled on the bench beside her, but did not look in Riona's direction. If her father noticed the tension between them, he didn't say a word, perhaps mistaking their anger for grief.

"Did the search of Cathal's estate reveal anything?" Riona eventually asked, breaking the silence. "The missing treasury documents?"

Her father shook his head, looking troubled. "The guards searched it from top to bottom, but found nothing out of order."

"So what does that mean? You believe the killer has them?"

"It's possible, but it's too soon to be certain. We're not yet ruling out the possibility that Cathal hid them before his killer caught up to him. Something in those papers was worth saving, else he would have burned them along with all the other documents. He was clever. If he had realized that someone was coming to kill him, he would have stashed them somewhere the assassin wouldn't find them. Now it's a matter of *us* finding them."

"And the elven prostitute?"

A spark of frustration lit his eyes. "No news yet."

Riona let the conversation drop, frowning. What had been different about those documents? Why had Cathal thought them worth saving, when he destroyed all the other treasury records? Too many questions. Hopefully, with Prince Auberon's help, she would discover the answers soon enough.

After several minutes, the carriage rolled into the forecourt, and the three of them climbed out. Amaris made to follow the royal family into the castle, but Riona caught her wrist, stilling her. "I'm sorry for what I said earlier," she whispered. "You know I didn't mean it that way. Please forgive me."

Amaris looked down at the hand on her wrist, then up at Riona. "You needn't ask forgiveness. More than anything, I want you to be happy, Riona. Just...don't overlook the possibility of finding happiness with one of the suitors."

Chapter Nineteen
The Liar

"I must say, Your Highness, you are recovering extraordinarily quickly," Healer Barra said, incredulous. His assistant hovered behind him, scrawling notes on a piece of parchment while wearing an equally bewildered expression. "I admit, I'm shocked by how well you are faring."

"All due to your skill and knowledge, I'm sure. Still, I'd be lying if I said I wasn't eager to return to court," Auberon responded, trying to ignore the unsettling warmth emanating from his shoulder. It pulsed like a heartbeat, even days after the duke's visit. "Am I free to go?"

Barra's gaze swept over him, and Auberon fixed him with an imploring look. The king would choose Riona's husband by the end of the year. Already, a week had slipped through his fingers. His only solace was that Treasurer Cathal's death had delayed the start of the negotiations.

The healer nodded. "Try to take it easy for a while, Your Highness. Your lungs may not be bleeding anymore, but they're still healing."

Auberon let out a relieved breath and swung his feet over the side of the cot. It felt good to finally be released from the infirmary. He'd nearly gone mad after being forced to sit still for so long, trapped within the same four walls. "Thank you for everything you two have done for me. I owe you my life."

"You owe us nothing, Your Highness," Barra replied as he and his assistant bowed. "We merely did our duty."

Auberon gathered his belongings—a couple of books and some changes of clothes, courtesy of Drystan—and followed the men out of the room, his guards trailing behind him. Drystan was waiting in the sitting room, and he jumped to his feet when he saw Auberon.

"You're okay, then? You're cleared to leave?"

He nodded, and the tension on Drystan's face melted away. After thanking the healers one more time, they left the infirmary and started up the path to the guest house they'd been given. Auberon sucked in a breath and instantly winced at the burn of cold air against his battered lungs. He stopped, doubling over, as a painful coughing fit overtook him. Drystan grabbed his elbow, steadying him, as he wiped his mouth with a handkerchief. To his immense relief, it came away without any trace of blood.

"Are you sure you're ready to leave the infirmary? You won't be able to complete the assignment Father gave you if you have one foot in the Beyond."

"I'm fine."

Drystan shot him a doubtful look but didn't argue. When they arrived at the house, he dismissed the guards with a wave of his hand as he followed Auberon up the stairs to his bedchamber. He leaned against the doorframe, arms crossed over his chest, and watched in silence as Auberon returned his belongings to the chest in the corner of the room, still packed with the things he'd brought from Erduria.

"There's...something we should discuss," Drystan began after the silence had stretched out a few beats too long. His tone was casual, but Auberon could hear the undercurrent of concern—and worse, *doubt*—in his voice. "A few days ago, the guards told me you believed that Duke Valerian had visited you in the infirmary. They said it worked you up so much that you had to be sedated. What happened?"

His fingers tightened on the lid of the chest. *I'm not mad. I know what I saw.* "They still claim that he was never there?"

The guards had *let* Valerian into his room. How could they have no memory of the encounter? As his frustration mounted, the heat in his shoulder stuttered and picked up in pace, thumping like a second heart.

"...You were alone with the guards."

He slammed the lid shut and turned on Drystan. "Our ship is waiting for us in the harbor at Crafford. If you think I'm mad, send me back to Torch."

"That's not what I was saying, and you know it."

The prince's mild response only fueled his ire. "Who has spent countless hours studying the deadliest poisons in the northern and southern continents? Who prepared tonics and tinctures to counteract those poisons? Who will be risking his life so you can spend your days drinking wine and dancing with beautiful noblewomen?" Auberon spat, the searing heat in his shoulder sending waves of agony through him. "So, I will leave you to your politicking, Crown Prince, if you will leave me to do my job."

Drystan sighed and pushed off the door frame. "Get some rest. We'll be meeting with the king tomorrow morning to begin the negotiations." He paused, then added, "For what it's worth, I'm glad you're back."

With that, he left, closing the door behind him.

Auberon whirled on the polished metal mirror in the corner of his room and pulled his tunic over his head. There was no mark on his right shoulder where Valerian had touched him, his hand burning like a hot iron. If not for the heat pulsing just below his flesh, Auberon would have thought he really *had* lost his wits. But it was there—relentless, foreign, maddening. He hadn't spoken of it to the healers. How could one explain a wound that left no mark, from a person no one but he had seen?

One went straight to the source.

He found Duke Valerian and Prince Domhnall chatting outside the throne room doors.

"Good afternoon, Your Highness. Your Grace," he called, not particularly caring that he'd interrupted them mid-conversation. They turned, surprise flashing across their faces when they saw him. Auberon smiled, masking the dark wave of fury that rose within him at the sight of the duke. "It's been a while."

"You're looking well, Prince Auberon," Domhnall said. "I was under the impression you'd be in the infirmary for at least another week."

"So was I, but it seems I'm a fast healer." His gaze slid to Valerian. "Or perhaps I simply met with a miracle."

The Crown Prince chuckled, oblivious to his anger. "Whatever the reason, we're all glad that you'll be able to join the negotiations. Please, allow me to apologize on behalf of my family for the accident that befell you. My father's men are working around the clock to track down the person responsible for the poisoning. He will be brought to justice, I swear it."

"Creator willing," he said dryly. Not one member of the royal family had bothered to speak with him since that first banquet, save for Lady Riona. For all their talk of peace and welcome, it was clear just how far their hospitality extended to those of Erdurian blood. He turned to the duke. "I'd like a word with you in private, Your Grace."

Valerian hesitated. "I will be meeting with the king and his brother shortly—"

"It'll take but a moment, I promise," he said in a voice that made it clear he would brook no argument. "Come."

When the duke nodded reluctantly, Auberon led him around the corner and into the first empty room he found, closing the door behind them. In a heartbeat, he had Valerian pinned against the wall, one arm braced against his chest, the other leveling the edge of his sword to the duke's throat. Valerian made a small noise of protest.

"Be quiet, or I'll slit your throat," Auberon snarled. "What did you do to me? And why don't my guards remember you?"

"I have no idea what you're talking about."

"Don't deny it. You touched my shoulder before you left, and ever since, the throbbing has been driving me mad. I can feel this—this pounding, this *heat*, in my shoulder. And my guards don't remember you coming into my room. It sounds insane, I know, so you can rest assured that I would not be asking about it if I were not *certain* you had done something. No one heals this quickly after being poisoned with Osha's Kiss."

Valerian said nothing, just kept that infuriatingly calm expression firmly in place.

"What. Did. You. *Do?*"

The duke lifted his chin, exposing more of his neck to Auberon's blade. "I'd advise you to put away your weapon, Your Highness, lest you get blood on my doublet. I doubt my death at your hands would benefit you and your brother in the negotiations."

"In about two seconds, the negotiations will be the least of your concerns," Auberon spat, but through his anger, the rational part of his mind insisted that the duke was right. He couldn't kill Valerian—not *here*, at least. Not now.

"Sheathe the sword, and we'll speak like civilized men. Eamon would struggle with the concept, but it shouldn't be too difficult for you and me."

Begrudgingly, Auberon released him and slid his sword into its sheath. He expected Valerian to shout for the guards, but the duke merely smoothed the wrinkles in his doublet and ran his fingers through his golden curls. When he caught Auberon's wary look, he said, "I'm not going to call for the guards, nor am I going to tell the king what you just did. You and I are aligned in our hatred of the Kostori, which means that we can help each other."

Auberon narrowed his eyes. "How so?"

"Without your brother as a potential suitor, the king would undoubtedly promise Lady Riona to Eamon. My country is too small and too insignificant to be of much value to him. I want to marry her, but if I end up losing her to your brother, so be it. I'll gladly watch her marry Drystan if it spares her from a lifetime as Eamon's wife. Now, if you'll excuse me—"

He turned to leave, but Auberon stepped in front of him. "Tell me what you did to me. That pounding, that heat... It's driving me mad."

Unease flashed across the duke's face. "I did you a favor, Your Highness," Valerian said, a warning in his voice, "and that is all. It would be best if we did not discuss this further. Trust me."

"You *did* heal me. How?"

"I cannot say more, Your Highness. You owe me a debt—if not for healing you, then at least for not telling the king and his men that you threatened to kill me—and you may repay it by keeping what you have learned to yourself." Valerian dipped his head and stepped around Auberon, heading to the door. "Thank you in advance for your discretion."

As soon as Valerian's footsteps faded, Auberon pinched the bridge of his nose, muttering a curse under his breath. He couldn't afford to lose his temper again. Making a mistake like that could cost his life, and it would certainly cost Drystan his chance to win Lady Riona's hand in marriage—to say nothing of his own mission to learn more about the eudorite mines.

He pushed thoughts of the duke away as he started toward the great hall. He didn't trust Valerian, but he supposed he didn't have to; he only had to trust in Valerian's hatred of the prince of Kostos. In that, at least, they were aligned.

And after the welcome Auberon had been given by the Rivosi court, he would take any ally luck sent his way.

He was halfway to the guest house when an elven servant

approached him and dropped into a low bow, proffering a folded piece of parchment. Auberon accepted it and broke the wax seal, unfolding it to find a short note inside. It was unsigned, but the distinctly feminine cursive and overly formal (yet still somewhat condescending) tone left no doubt of its author.

I've secured a place for us to meet, Riona had written. *When you are well, we may discuss what to do next at the Royal Theater. Let's see just how adept you are at slipping through the cracks in the castle's security.*

Auberon studied the elven servant. Bowed as he was, the neckline of his servants' livery dipped just enough to reveal a glimpse of a small obsidian pendant—one that looked remarkably like the eudorite necklace Riona wore. "What is your name?"

The elf did not rise. "Aeron, Your Highness."

"I take it you're a friend of Lady Riona's, then?"

He stiffened. "I wouldn't say that, Your Highness. I serve all the members of King Domhnall's family."

"Oh, no?" Auberon leaned in and smiled. "Then you may wish to hide the mark of her favor a little better," he said, nodding to the pendant. As Aeron rose and tucked it back under his tunic, he continued, "Can you fetch me a quill and a pot of ink?"

Aeron nodded and disappeared, returning a few minutes later with the items he'd requested. Auberon took the quill, dipped it in the ink, and scrawled, *How about tonight?*

He sent the elf off with the note, and Riona's response returned in minutes.

I'll see you at midnight.

Chapter Twenty
The Lady

"I've been thinking about what you said at the banquet the other night. About the unrest in Kenter," Riona said as she and Prince Eamon walked arm-in-arm through the public gardens. The sun was shining brightly—a rare event for Innislee—and several noble couples were out enjoying the weather, walking the gravel paths or sitting by the edge of the pond at the park's center. "I was in Beltharos during the civil war, and after nearly losing my life because of it, I have no desire to bear witness to any more fighting. I wanted to ask if you believe that the rebels in Kenter will revolt against the Grand Duke. Or if they will tire of Kostori occupation and attempt to cast you off entirely. Do you fear that they will turn on you?"

Prince Eamon didn't respond immediately, seeming to consider his words carefully. As they walked, a handful of Rivosi guards trailing just out of earshot, Riona gazed toward the pond. Shortly after arriving at the public gardens, they had stumbled upon Lord Winslow, who had offered them warm greetings before taking Prince Domhnall aside to discuss some matter pertaining to the negotiations. They were sitting at one of the white marble benches by the water's edge, their heads bent in conversation.

"The Grand Duke's court can be...volatile at times," Eamon finally said. "As you have seen, our involvement in Kentari politics is a sore spot for Duke Valerian. He is loath to admit it, but his people have enjoyed fifteen years of peace precisely *because* of our occupation."

They are enjoying that peace because you *decided to stop invading their land. Now, when you terrorize them, you claim it is because they are your vassal, not because they are your enemy,* Riona thought, but she kept the response to herself. She knew few details about the siege fifteen years ago, but she saw a glimmer of Nicholas Comyn's arrogance in Prince Eamon, and it left no doubt in her mind who was the villain in that particular tale. Still, she chose her words wisely. She didn't have to like the Kostori prince, but she had to forge an alliance between their lands.

"There must be some cause for concern if your father sends you to Kenter every time the nobles demand justice for the former Grand Duke and his family," she said lightly. "Certainly if it were only grumbling, as Duke Valerian claimed, he and his father could handle it. That was the point of them becoming a vassal, was it not? Your father didn't annex the duchy into his kingdom."

The prince faltered, and Riona fought to keep the smirk from her lips at the trap she'd laid. At the banquet, he had tried to harm Duke Valerian's position in the negotiations by making the Grand Duke seem a weak and ineffective leader, unable to quell even the slightest hint of unrest without Kostori aid. Yet if he exaggerated his claims too much, he risked scaring the king into rejecting a marriage alliance with both Kenter and Kostos. Her uncle would not send her to a country bound to be mired in a years-long war, one for which he would be honor-bound to provide military aid. He had enough troubles with the war against Erduria.

"Valerian's father does his best, but the duchy is large, and the war left his country in shambles," Eamon finally replied. "Without my father's troops, the Grand Duke would not be sitting on his throne today, and Valerian often chooses to forget that little fact." Prince Eamon sniffed in disdain, dismissing the idea with a flick of his hand. "He thinks it is long past time his country reclaimed its freedom, but he fails to realize that his comfortable, luxurious life will come to a swift and violent end if it does. He is as likely to be stabbed in the back by one of his own people as he is by one of mine—*if* he and his father step out of line."

"Hm," Riona murmured mildly, not deigning to respond. She'd spent about as much time as she could stomach with the Kostori prince. "If you will excuse me, Your Highness, I should see how Lord Winslow is faring after Treasurer Cathal's death. They were quite close."

He frowned, but nodded, reluctantly releasing the hand she had slipped into the crook of his arm. "Of course, my lady. It was a pleasure speaking with you, and I hope we may do it again soon —preferably *without* the company of His Imperial Highness," he said with a sharp look at Drystan's back.

"I'm sure that can be arranged."

She curtsied and quickly joined Drystan and Winslow where they sat on the marble bench. "I'm sorry to interrupt your conversation," she breathed when she reached them, "but I was hoping, Lord Winslow, that you wouldn't mind entertaining the Kostori prince for a few minutes."

"You mean you want me to spare you his charming company?" Winslow quipped knowingly. "Prince Drystan here told me His Highness practically attached himself to your side the moment you stepped out of the carriage."

"To my great misfortune."

"Then of course I will come to your rescue, my lady." The lord rose and bowed. "I shall take my leave of you, Your Highness. Lady Riona."

He started toward Prince Eamon, and Drystan gestured for Riona to take the spot on the bench that Winslow had vacated. "Finally managed to extricate yourself from Eamon's grasp, I see," he said as Riona sat, the marble cool through the silk of her skirt. A crooked grin, so like his brother's, tugged at one corner of his mouth. "I should have warned you that he would attempt to steal you away at the first opportunity."

"He's very...determined."

Drystan laughed, a warm, rich sound. "Not exactly the word I would have chosen for him, and most definitely not the one Auberon would have chosen."

"You know each other well, then?"

"I know his reputation, and that of his father, and I am content to leave it at that. Auberon, however..." The prince paused, seeming to search for the proper words to describe his brother's relationship with Eamon. In the end, he simply shook his head. "That is a story too long to recount. Auberon is skilled at reading people, and he is quick to decide whether someone is deserving of his time or his mockery. Once his mind is made up, there is little chance of changing it."

"I see why he accompanied you here, then."

He nodded. "He's very protective. Sometimes to an infuriating degree." Drystan turned to face her fully. They sat so close, Riona could see that his eyes were a deep steel gray, without a hint of Auberon's blue. "But after the way you comforted him at the banquet, there is no doubt in our minds that you are worth every second we spend here."

He wishes to court you, Auberon's voice whispered in her mind. She could see it, too. The prince was careful to keep a polished mask over his face, but he couldn't quite hide the glimmer of hope in his eyes as he regarded her, a slight smile on his lips. The sincerity in his words reminded her of the night after the poisoning, when she had found him sitting on that bench in the great hall, his head in his hands as he attempted to compose himself.

The night Auberon shouldn't have survived.

"Why *did* Prince Auberon have the poison's antidote in his bag?" she asked, finally voicing the question that had been nagging at her for days. "And how did he know which poison he'd ingested?"

Drystan rolled his eyes. "Part of it is just Auberon being Auberon. He has always been fascinated with things of that nature—the Assassins' Guild, poisons, swordplay, archery. As you can imagine, there are many people who would like to see themselves on the Empire's throne, and because of that, our father insisted our tutors include lessons in poisons, healing, and self-defense. Auberon simply took to it better than I did. He doesn't travel anywhere without that box of antidotes."

Riona found herself smiling at the affection in the prince's voice. "You're lucky to have a brother like him."

"Yes, I must remind myself of that every time he makes one of his smart-mouthed comments," Drystan said, chuckling. "Anyhow, that's enough about him."

He gazed out at the gardens, a field of lush foliage spreading out before them. Even though it was late in the year, many of the blossoms still clung to their bushes, dotting the landscape beyond with vibrant splashes of color. He drew in an awed breath. "This place truly is beautiful," he said, watching a young boy and girl chase each other along the edge of the pond, giggling. "Do you spend much time here?"

"Not anymore," Riona responded, a familiar ache tugging at her heart. "My mother used to bring me here when I was little for my lessons in the Selannic tongue. She said it reminded her of the gardens at the royal palace. She always claimed it would help me connect with my roots."

At the note of grief in her voice, Drystan's expression softened. "Have you ever been to the Isles?"

"Never. It's a long voyage, and my mother always wanted to wait until I was older to take me on her annual visit. And after..." She stopped. *After her ship was destroyed, my father became terrified of losing his only daughter to the war, as well.* "I haven't had the chance."

The prince seemed to hear her unspoken words. "I'm sorry

for what the war has cost you. Nothing I can do or say will bring your mother back, but I hope you and I can create a future in which no other girls must lose their mothers to a needless war," he said. "If you return to Erduria with me, we will stop in the Isles so you can meet your mother's family. We will stay as long as you like."

Riona opened her mouth, then closed it, unsure how to respond to the kind offer. Part of her was touched by the sentiment. She didn't know much about her grandfather's court, and she'd always wanted to meet the family her mother had left behind.

Thankfully, she was spared having to answer by the arrival of Eamon and the Rivosi guards, who informed her that it was time to return to the castle. She followed them to the carriage waiting outside the garden, and the three of them fell into easy, light conversation as the wheels clattered over the cobblestones. As they passed the Royal Theater, Riona reached into her pocket and ran her fingers over the piece of parchment tucked inside, Auberon's response to her promise to meet him there at midnight. It held three words, scrawled in the prince's cramped, hurried hand:

I can't wait.

The king was on his knees in the royal chapel, sobbing.

Riona had accompanied the princes to their houses and bade them farewell, then wandered up toward the royal apartments, savoring the peace and quiet. Her uncle would be hosting a court dinner in Cathal's honor, but she had a little while before she had to return to her father's estate to change. She'd been seeking out a moment alone with her thoughts when she'd spotted the small royal chapel. Its doors were ajar, a handful of royal guards bracketing the entryway, and through the gap she had spotted her uncle's broad shoulders, shaking with silent sobs.

She approached the doors, and one of the king's guards stepped in front of her. "It'd be best not to disturb His Majesty, my lady."

At the sound of the man's voice, Domhnall turned and spotted her through the opening. "It's alright, Donnic. Let her in."

The guard stepped aside, and Riona slipped into the chapel. The building was small, meant only for the royal family and close friends, and only a few pews sat on either side of the narrow aisle. The lanterns and torches scattered throughout the prayer room were unlit, leaving it illuminated with only the colored light filtering through the stained glass windows. In the center, before the bowl-shaped altar, knelt the king.

"We will find the man responsible for Cathal's murder," Riona breathed as she sank to her knees beside her uncle, "and we will bring him to justice."

"Will we?" He turned toward her, tears shining against his dark skin. Riona wondered if this was the first opportunity he'd had to grieve his friend since the day they learned about his murder. For as long as she could remember, her uncle had always been a king first, and a man second. He had even managed to hold himself together long enough to meet with Duke Valerian about the negotiations for her hand. "If the world were just, the man who committed this crime would suffer for it a thousand times over. But you and I both know the world is rarely that fair."

Riona clasped her fingers around the eudorite pendant, feeling the ghost of her mother's touch on the back of her neck. "No, it isn't, but that doesn't mean we stop trying to make it better."

"I admire your optimism, my dear niece. I wish I shared it." King Domhnall slipped an arm around her shoulders and kissed her temple. She leaned against him, her head resting against his chest. Although she was still angry with him for inviting the suitors, she could not bear to see him in such pain. "I will carry this grief with me every day of my life. Grief and guilt."

"Guilt?"

"He was my closest friend and confidant. What use is being king if I cannot protect the people I love?"

"This is not your fault. No one could have foreseen what happened."

"I should have known," he insisted, his voice thick with emotion. "How much more loss can we bear? First your mother, then the Selannic royals. Then Killian—my *firstborn son*. And now Cathal. I know you're angry with me for inviting the suitors here, my dear, but you must understand why I insist on sending you away with such haste. I misjudged Nicholas Comyn, but I had hoped that sending you to Beltharos would spare you from the curse on this kingdom. I can live with selecting a husband who will protect you and give you a proper position. I could not endure the death of another person I love."

"But surely you see that there is danger anywhere I might go. I could have died in Beltharos. We are at war with Erduria. Kenter may go to war with Kostos. I am in no more danger here than I am anywhere else. Allow me to stay."

He shook his head. "I do not wish to argue with you, Riona. Not today. If that were the only reason, I might reconsider. Please, trust that I am trying to do what is best for you and for our kingdom. There are no easy answers when it comes to ruling a kingdom, especially in times of war." King Domhnall's arm fell from her shoulders, and he bowed his head once more. "Shall we pray for Treasurer Cathal?"

Riona nodded and clasped her hands, fixing her gaze on the stone beneath her knees.

"Creator, watch over our dear friend, Cathal, and guide him to everlasting peace at your side. He was taken from us too soon, and we shall cherish his friendship and faithful service every day," he breathed. "Damn the man who committed this terrible crime, and forgive us who allowed it to come to pass."

Once he had finished, Riona murmured the words of a prayer commonly spoken at funerals, but the words rang false as they left her tongue. She attended church with her family and said all the proper words, but she had lost all faith in the Creator the day they had learned of her mother's death. She would not worship a god who stole a little girl's mother from her.

When she fell silent, the king rose and offered her a hand up. His tears had dried, but his face still bore the evidence of his grief. "Forgive me. It is improper for a king to display such weakness, and I beg your discretion on the matter," he said softly.

Riona pulled him into a tight embrace. "Right now, you are not a king. You are merely a man in mourning. Do not be ashamed."

"Thank you, my darling niece." He hugged her for a few heartbeats, then stepped back. "I've kept you too long. You should go and prepare for the banquet."

"Would you care to walk with me?"

"No, I'll remain here with my thoughts for a little while longer. Go ahead. I'll see you at dinner."

"Very well." She curtsied and started toward the exit, but his voice halted her halfway down the aisle.

"You are wiser and stronger than you know, Riona. Wherever you go when the negotiations are finished, your new people will be lucky to have you. You will lead them well."

Chapter Twenty-One
The Liar

Auberon arrived at the Royal Theater at midnight, his heavy wool cloak dripping from the downpour that had begun minutes after he'd left the castle. The main doors were unlocked, and as he walked into the foyer, he admired the soaring ceiling and the sculpted golden ivy climbing the walls. Stone dragons with onyx eyes and claws glared at him from the corners of the room as he trudged toward one of the many curtained archways on the far wall, the hem of his sodden cloak dragging across the ornate rug. The distant strain of a piano drifted through the opening.

He slipped through the curtains and continued into the theater, the dark room sprawling before him. The only light came from the stage, which was decorated with tall trees crafted of twisted bits of metal, their branches skeletal and unnatural. Bits of white fabric hung from them like spectral leaves. The scene was ghostly and ethereal, like something out of a storybook.

Riona was seated at the piano on the edge of the stage, her profile gilded by the light of the scattered candles—high cheekbones, full lips, straight nose. Her hands danced over the keys, filling the air with a haunting, beautiful melody. Auberon stopped mid-step when he recognized the song, feeling as if the

Creator had just reached out and stolen the breath from his lungs. He watched, transfixed, as Riona played.

Her eyes were closed, her fingers gliding faultlessly over the keys. The melody slowed, notes straining with a sense of melancholy and longing that Auberon felt in the pit of his stomach. It was a song that made the world stop for a few precious seconds.

Finally, the last note faded, and silence settled over the theater. Riona's lids remained shut, her fingers lingering on the keys. Auberon took what felt like his first full breath in ages. He didn't want to move, to break the beauty of the moment.

Riona's hands fell into her lap, and she opened her eyes. "Your Highness."

"I—I didn't know you could play like that. Where did you learn that song?"

"My parents took me to the ballet when I was young. After we returned home, I sat at our piano and played it from memory." A wistful smile tugged at her lips. "It's called—"

"The Fall of the Faeries," he breathed, lost in the memories the song had unearthed. "It's my mother's favorite song. She used to play it for me when I was younger. Even tried to teach me once, but I was terrible. I couldn't have played worse if I'd been using my feet."

Riona's smile grew, then she abruptly stood and closed the lid over the keys, a cold mask slipping over her features. Auberon cursed himself as he saw her defenses rise. Could she even look at him without being reminded of the last time she'd seen her mother's face?

"So tell me: how did you manage to slip out of the castle?"

He shot her a crooked grin. "I spent the day making no secret of my love of drinking and gambling, which is why the guards at the gate found it not at all surprising when I told them I planned to spend the night enjoying all the delights Innislee's taverns had to offer."

"The day before you meet with the king for negotiations?" Riona asked, raising a skeptical brow.

"I spent the last five days in a cot in the infirmary, my lady. Creator forbid I wanted to celebrate my newfound freedom with a drink or two."

He wasn't certain whether she believed what he'd said, but it was the truth; with the suitors and courtiers otherwise occupied, he had been free to search for a hidden servants' entrance. All castles had them—unmarked exits, discreet passages, escape tunnels—but he'd only been able to dedicate an hour to his search before his lungs had begun to burn. For now, lying to the guards would have to suffice. To maintain appearances, he'd brought a handful of Erdurian guards with him and left them standing watch on the streets surrounding the Royal Theater.

He shucked off his sodden cloak and slung it over the back of the nearest seat, noting the way Riona's wary gaze dropped to the emerald-hilted dagger sheathed at his hip. He turned and scanned the room, taking in the worn seats and skeletal trees. "This isn't *quite* what I had in mind when I told you we'd need somewhere to train, but I suppose it will work."

"So pleased to have your approval, Your Highness," Riona responded, crossing her arms. Her braids hung in one long, thick plait over her shoulder, and she wore a long-sleeved tunic and fitted black pants tucked into knee-high leather boots. The simple ensemble clung to her figure, leaving no curve to the imagination. She was stunning, even as she glared at him with absolute loathing. Here, away from the court, she had no reason to hide the depth of her hatred for him. "But we're not training tonight. We're going to a brothel."

He set a hand on his heart in mock horror. "What about my pristine reputation? My chastity?"

She laughed, but there was no humor in the sound. "Your country rests on the graves of those your father, and all the emperors before him, slaughtered. Your rivers run with their blood, and their remains fertilize your fields." Riona stalked down the steps of the stage. "What about that makes a reputation worth preserving?"

"You do not know of what you speak," Auberon said, his voice deathly soft. "So I would advise you to hold your tongue."

Riona stopped before him, mere inches between them. "Is that a command, Your Highness? From the son of a tyrant?"

"A *tyrant?*" Anger flared within him. "I am no tyrant, and neither is my father. You mistake us for the Kostori. Eamon is the one of whom you should be wary."

"The Kostori did not send a neutral ship to the bottom of the Tranquil Sea."

"No, they only laid a year-long siege on the capital of Kenter after devastating the countryside. Duke Valerian can tell you all about it. They killed farmers and fishermen, burned fields and razed towns. Stole livestock. Poisoned water sources. Flung disease-ridden corpses over Glenkeld's walls," he retorted. "That's war. No one survives without the blood of innocents staining their hands."

"Do not use their crimes to justify those of your people."

"No ruler alive is a saint. Far from it. They do what they must to win wars, or more people die. More people like your moth—"

Before he could finish the word, Riona pulled the dagger from the sheath at his hip and leveled it at his chest. "Do not," she warned, "speak of my mother."

Auberon forced himself to take a deep breath, tempering his anger. "I am sorry for her death, truly. I am sorry for the pain and grief you have endured because of it. But I am not to blame for the attack on her ship," he said as placatingly as he could. "I am here to help you."

Riona held his gaze for several heartbeats, her cold expression betraying no hint of the thoughts racing behind that calm veneer.

When she started to lower the dagger, he caught her hand and wrapped his fingers around hers, repositioning the angle of the blade. "The way you were holding it, you would have struck one of my ribs. If someone were attacking you, the dagger would have gotten stuck between the bones and been wrenched out of your hand before you could land a killing blow." He moved it back to the way she'd been holding it, then showed her the correct position again. "Like this. Straight through the ribs."

A shadow passed through her eyes. "Like Cathal..."

She saw the body, he suddenly remembered. It hadn't taken long for word of the Treasurer's bloody, brutal death to spread through the castle. Auberon gently tugged the dagger from her grip and sheathed it, then shot Riona a cocky, roguish smile. "Are you sure you don't want to train tonight? Seems like you could use a bit of practice."

Riona turned away and grabbed a wool cloak that she'd left draped over the back of one of the seats. She slipped it over her shoulders and tied the strings at her throat, then drew up the hood. "Your lungs still need time to recover from the poison," she responded as she returned to the stage to extinguish the candles. "We're going to the brothel. One of the elves who worked there may have witnessed Cathal's murder, and I want to learn everything I can about her."

He shook his head, feigning resignation. "Very well. I suppose I can accompany you to a house of lust and debauchery." She started down the aisle, toward the light bleeding in from the foyer, and he trailed after her. "Never been in one of those before."

"Prince Auberon?"

"Yes, my lady?"

"Do you ever stop talking?"

He grinned as he fell into step beside her. "When one finds himself graced with natural charm and blade-sharp wit, one must not deprive the people of charming witticisms."

"If only I knew someone like that. Perhaps he would drown out your incessant noise."

Auberon's grin grew, and he lapsed into silence as they left the theater and stepped out into the pouring rain. Riona led him away from the heart of the city, and the streets grew narrower and more twisting as they neared the poorer section of Innislee. The same streetlamps lined the roads here, but unlike the main avenues, many of the lanterns were cracked and unlit, leaving large patches of darkness. They didn't pass a single carriage for hire, so they ran from building to building, ducking under awnings or into the covered alleyways that were common in the city. It wasn't long until they were soaked through and shivering.

When they passed under the light of a streetlamp, Auberon saw the flicker of disgust and shame that crossed Riona's face. She didn't want a foreign prince to see this side of her beloved city—the streets uneven and missing stones, the houses with broken shutters, the sewage rotting in the alleys. It was nothing to which he was unaccustomed, considering how much time he spent in Torch's lower district. He opened his mouth to tell her that, but the drumming of the rain and the roar of the wind were so loud they would certainly drown out his voice.

Still, he couldn't help but curse her as they continued along the streets, holding their cloaks closed with one hand and their hoods up with another. "You couldn't have chosen a more perfect night for a tour of the city, my lady!" he yelled, his eyes slitted against the stinging rain.

"WHAT?"

"I said—"

"*WHAT?*"

By all the gods, the Creator must be looking down at us right now and laughing.

He thought it just as Riona stopped before a low, wide stone building, its hanging sign swaying too violently in the wind to make out its name. The brothel. Warm light filtered out around the edges of the shutters, and Auberon let out a sigh of relief. He held the door open for Riona, who nodded in gratitude as she slipped into the building, then followed her into the pleasure house.

Chapter Twenty-Two
The Lady

The night was black as pitch outside, and the brothel wasn't much brighter. The small main room was furnished with tables and chairs, and a wooden counter by the far wall functioned as a makeshift bar. A few men sat at the various tables, drinking or dragging from pipes whose smoke left a blue haze throughout the room. Working girls flitted between them, clad in scraps of silk that left little to the imagination. A couple of young girls sat on stools beside the bar and played a tune on some old instruments.

Behind Riona, Auberon coughed, a dry and ragged sound. "Not that I'm complaining about the sights in this fine establishment, but what exactly are we doing here?"

"Observing."

Ignoring the suggestive grin that danced across the prince's lips, Riona hung her cloak on a peg on the wall, then took a seat at one of the tables in the corner of the room. Goosebumps crawled across her flesh. Despite her efforts to hold her cloak closed as they'd crossed the city, her clothes were soaked, and they clung to her skin. Without a word, Auberon went to the bar and returned a minute later with two cups of whiskey. Riona accepted hers with a murmured thanks and took a drink. The whiskey was cheap and watered down, but the burn of the alcohol helped to chase away the chill which had seeped into her bones.

They drank in silence. Across the room, a woman perched on the edge of a table and leaned over the man sitting there, offering him an ample look down her top as she purred soft words into his ear. Auberon watched as the woman drew the man to his feet and led him into the hallway.

He leaned forward. "Please tell me again what we're doing here. This isn't exactly where one would expect the Lady of Innislee to spend her free time. Especially not in the company of an Erdurian prince."

"Precisely. Look around us," she said, gesturing to the women—their cheap silks, their fake gemstones, their painted faces. "Does this seem like a place one of the most powerful men in Rivosa would spend his time? There are plenty of pleasure houses in the city, most far nicer than this one. Cathal apparently favored one of the prostitutes here and kept it so secret, not one person outside this brothel knew about it. The question is: Why?"

"And if he figured out that the poison was meant for him, why would he come here instead of fleeing the city?" A sly grin spread across Auberon's lips. "Perhaps he just wanted to die doing what he loved...or *who* he loved."

Riona scowled. "That's crass."

"But a logical conclusion. If you loved someone and knew that you might die in a matter of hours, wouldn't you want to spend your last moments with that person?"

The image of Percival's smile, his eyes shining behind his crooked spectacles, flashed through Riona's mind. Her chest tightened. Rather than responding, she picked up her cup and drained the last of her watered-down whiskey. "The point is, I need to learn as much about Faylen as possible. She's the only lead I have."

"I didn't hear a *we* in that answer, and I'm almost positive you didn't invite me here for my charming personality. What do you need me to do?"

"Provide a distraction." While they were sitting there, she'd watched the mistress of the brothel collect the money from the bar and slip through the doorway behind the bartender. Riona nodded toward it. "I need to get into the owner's office."

Auberon grinned. "Say no more."

He rose, and Riona grabbed his arm. "Don't let them hear your Erdurian accent."

"Don't ye worry, milady," he said in a perfect imitation of the rural Rivosi accent, which he must have picked up from some of the castle staff. "I've spent half my life travelin' the northern continent. Tongues and accents come easily to me." He winked. "Just one of my many talents."

Auberon rose and grabbed the two cups of whiskey, then stumbled into the hall where the prostitute and her customer had disappeared. After a few heartbeats, he cried with a drunken slur, "There ye are, ye Creator-damned harlot! I knew I couldn't trust ye! Oh, I listen to the men at the warehouse and treat mysel' to a night in a woman's arms, and this is how ye repay me? By leavin' a pox on my manhood?" He let out a sound that was half-hiccup, half-sob. Riona turned her face toward the wall and coughed to hide her surprised laugh. "Get out, friend! Do ye hear me? Get out, save yer coin, and seek comfort in the company of yer hand! At least ye know where that's been!"

As he continued to shout, the men in the main room glanced at one another, their faces paling in horror. As one, they rose and tripped over themselves and the barstools in their haste to leave. The prostitutes rushed after them, clutching their sleeves and begging them to stay. Someone ripped the door open, and a gust of wind sent it cracking against the wall, extinguishing the candles on many of the tables.

Taking advantage of the chaos, Riona rose and skirted the edge of the room as the bartender ran down the hall to quiet Auberon's drunken rambling. The mistress of the brothel hurried after him, snapping commands to her women to get their clients back. While they were distracted, Riona slipped into the office, locked the door behind her, and began searching through the drawers of the desk. They didn't contain much: jars of cosmetics, pouches of coin, pieces of jewelry, and bottles of what looked like some sort of contraceptive tonic.

Finally, she found a sheaf of records detailing each woman's information, including her age, full name, date of employment, and client history. Riona brought the papers closer to one of the candelabras and skimmed them until she found Faylen. The record listed her simply as *Faylen of Sandori, elf, twenty-nine years of age.* Sandori? Considering she'd been an elf in the Beltharan capital, it was likely that she had been a noble's slave. The date listed for her acquisition was only a few months prior, shortly after the end of the Beltharan war against the Cirisian elves. She must have fled the city in the fighting and come to Innislee in search of freedom.

Some freedom she found, Riona thought, *if she had to work in a brothel.*

Most interesting was the record of payments from Faylen's clients. For the first month or so, she'd been visited by many different men. After Cathal's name appeared the first time, all other clients ceased. Riona trailed a finger along the orderly boxes on the paper, totaling the numbers. Cathal's visits had been sporadic, but he had paid hundreds of aurums to ensure that Faylen would not see any man save for him.

Perhaps he truly did love her, and he was trying to spare her the pain of working in this dreadful place.

Through the door, Riona heard Auberon return to the main room, pretending to be somewhat mollified. She returned the papers to the drawer in which she'd found them and then stepped out of the office, silently closing the door behind her. Many of the men from before had left; only a few remained, arguing with the prostitutes about payment for their services. The mistress of the brothel was speaking with Auberon near the front door, her hands out in supplication. The bartender hovered nearby with his arms crossed over his chest, watching with disapproval as Auberon drank straight out of a decanter of whiskey.

"Fine, fine. I'll keep my mouth shut about this," he slurred, "but don't think I'll be comin' back anytime soon. Well, not 'til my...uh, *problem* has resolved itself. I 'spect that ye'll keep a closer watch on yer girls, else the next time I come back, it'll be with the city guards."

"Of course, my friend," the woman said, her smile sharp as a blade. She grabbed Auberon's cloak from the peg and swept it around his shoulders, all but strangling him as she tied the laces at the neck. "Nothin' like this will ever happen again, I swear it. I would not tarnish my name by housin' unclean girls."

"I should hope not. Word of this gets out, men'll be cursin' ye from here to the Abraxas Sea." Auberon laughed at the outraged look on her face and took another long swig of whiskey. "Don't ye worry. I'll speak none of this to the men at the warehouse. What they do with their coin don't matter to me."

Riona crept along the edge of the room as the mistress of the brothel ushered Auberon out, and she quickly donned her cloak and slipped out behind them. The storm had eased to a soft rain, and she walked at a leisurely pace along the street as Auberon reassured the mistress of the brothel of his silence one final time. A few moments later, he jogged up to Riona's side with a bright, smug grin on his lips.

"That was fun," he said, dropping the Rivosi accent. "Did you find what you were looking for?"

"Enough for tonight, at least. I think you were right about Cathal loving Faylen. He'd been visiting her for months and paying extra so she would see no one but him. He wouldn't do that if he had just wanted someone to warm his bed."

"Well, I do know a lot about the subject."

Riona shot him a sidelong glance. "Love?"

"Brothels."

She rolled her eyes, then nodded to the decanter of whiskey he was holding. "Where did you get that?"

"From the owner. A gift to mollify me, or a bribe to keep my silence. Take your pick."

"And how much have you had to drink?"

He lifted the decanter and squinted at the amber liquid inside. "Enough to ease the sting of the cruel words you said to me earlier this evening. Not enough to dull the pain from that damned poison. Perhaps I should have listened to the healer and rested." They passed a streetlamp, and in its soft glow, Riona saw Auberon grimace as he rubbed his chest. "Too late to do anything about it now. Come, I'll walk you home."

"That's not necessary. We'll part ways when we reach the King's Road, and you can spend the remainder of the night resting."

He scoffed. "Nonsense. Haven't you heard the news, my lady? There are murderers about."

As they neared the King's Road, the streets grew brighter, lit with lanterns that made the wet cobblestones glisten. In the distance, the Royal Theater's gilded dome reflected the nighttime sky, distorting the moon and stars along the curve of the metal. The scents of rain and earth hung heavily in the air—the scents of Innislee. The scents of *home*.

When they finally arrived at her father's estate, she was relieved to find that all the windows were dark. Thank the Creator, neither her father nor Amaris had awoken and discovered her missing. Before leaving, she had dosed their tea with Oil of Ienna, a sleeping aid. The last thing she needed was one of them sounding the alarm that she'd vanished.

Before she could open the gate, Prince Auberon caught her hand. She turned back, and her breath caught at how close he stood, only a few inches separating them. She could smell the scent of the storm on his clothes. "I want you to know that I understand why you hate us for what happened to your mother," he murmured, a hint of whiskey on his breath. "She should have been protected. She should have been *safe*."

Riona reached up with her free hand and grasped her mother's eudorite pendant. Grief buried its claws into her heart as she said, "Thank you. And...I am grateful for your help tonight, Prince Auberon."

Auberon squeezed her hand once before letting go and starting back the way they'd come. "We are both children of war, my lady," he said over his shoulder. "We must help each other when we can."

Chapter Twenty-Three
The Liar

Auberon kept his gaze fixed straight ahead until he reached the street corner, and then his resolve failed him. He turned back just as one of the second-floor windows in Lord Lachlan's manor grew bright, the room beyond filled with soft candlelight. As he watched, a silhouette moved to the window and started to close the curtains, then paused. From the distance, he couldn't make out her face, and she certainly wouldn't be able to see his. Even so, he knew Riona was staring at him.

His hand flexed at his side, remembering the feel of her palm against his. He hadn't intended to reach for her hand; he had acted on impulse. Auberon took a long swig from the whiskey decanter and told himself it was a combination of the alcohol and the desire to gain her trust that had driven him to do it.

He gazed at her until she snapped the curtains shut, breaking the spell, then returned to the Royal Theater to collect his guards. As he walked, he considered all that Riona had told him. Most of the courtiers had accepted the story that the prostitute was responsible for Cathal's death, but a murder born of passion or rage did not explain the poisoning and missing documents. Somehow, the mines were tied to the Treasurer's death.

The morning of his murder, Cathal had realized that the poison was meant for him, burned most of the records in his office, and smuggled the missing documents out of the castle. If they held information about the mines, what had the Treasurer achieved by destroying the rest of his records? He would have known that the guards would search his office following his abrupt flight, so perhaps he had sought to protect the king from scrutiny. With four foreign royals in the castle, he wouldn't have wanted the guards to be gossiping about the state of the kingdom's finances. But still, *burning?*

Questions nagged at him as he and his guards continued toward the castle, walking along the rain-soaked streets. Puddles had collected in the depressions in the road, and they reflected the imposing façades of the manors surrounding him. He was careful to stick close to the buildings and keep his head low. No one who happened to look out at the street would recognize him, of course, but it was a force of habit. Cities like Innislee and Torch never slept. The fewer people who knew an Erdurian prince was wandering about late at night, the better.

When the castle's portcullis came into view before him, he let his grip on the decanter slacken and stumbled toward the gate. A half-dozen guards stood outside. He felt their eyes follow him across the forecourt, assessing whether he would be a threat or a mere nuisance.

"Play along," he told his guards.

"Identify yourself," one of the men at the gate called.

"The greatest player of Seven Deadly Kings in the world," he responded with an elaborate bow, the whiskey sloshing against the glass.

When the torchlight struck his face, he saw recognition spark on their faces. A couple of the guards cracked grins at his disheveled appearance, and one gestured for the gate to be opened. "Did you enjoy your night, Your Highness?"

"With a strong drink and good company, how could I not?" Auberon took another swig of whiskey, savoring the way the world had begun to grow fuzzy around the edges. He leaned in and lowered his voice to a conspiratorial whisper. "Perhaps tomorrow, I'll find my way into the arms of a beautiful noblewoman."

"Perhaps you will, Your Highness."

Auberon bade them farewell, then sauntered up the cobblestone path with his guards in tow, humming an old Kentari drinking song. He maintained the charade until the guest house appeared before them.

"There's an elven prostitute missing from one of the cheap brothels in the southern sector of the city. *The Bear and the Maiden,*" he said to one of his men as he approached the house. The storm had been too violent to make out the sign, but he'd gathered the name of the brothel from the rather graphic artwork he'd passed in the hall. "Her name is Faylen. Send some men to search for her, but be quiet about it. If you find her, set her up with a room in a tavern and send for me."

The guard nodded, and Auberon slipped into the house and crept up the stairs to his room, trying not to awaken Drystan or the slumbering guards. Once he had shut the door, he set the whiskey on the table, shucked off his wet clothes, and climbed into bed.

Minutes passed. He lay there wide awake, staring up at the ceiling. The heat in his shoulder pulsed like a brand under his chilled flesh, reminding him of his conversation with the duke. By the Creator, Auberon had no idea what to make of Valerian. They weren't enemies. The Duchy of Kenter was a vassal to Kostos, and—personal grievances aside—Kostos and Erduria were neutral toward each other. Thanks to the Kostori control over the duchy, Valerian and his father were little more than figureheads. The duke was nothing to him.

And yet, Valerian had healed him and asked only for discretion in exchange.

After Auberon threatened to kill him.

He could continue to pressure the duke into revealing what he had done, but it would be wiser not to risk his and Drystan's places in Innislee. If King Domhnall discovered that Auberon had threatened one of the suitors within his walls, he and Drystan would immediately be cast out of Rivosa. Prince Eamon would win Riona's hand.

Although the alliance was shaky, he believed that Valerian was sincere about wanting to prevent Eamon from marrying Riona. He could trust that the duke wouldn't say a word about Auberon's threat. He could overlook Valerian's strange ability for now. Frankly, he had so much on his mind that uncovering what the duke had done to him was the *least* of his concerns.

He closed his eyes, trying to sleep, but his thoughts kept drifting to Riona. He hadn't gone to the theater intending to antagonize her, but as soon as he walked through the archway and heard the song she was playing, he hadn't been able to stop the flood of memories that had overcome him. He had spent so many nights in his mother's music room back home, lulled gently to sleep by the very same melody Riona had been playing. He could still picture her dark, wavy hair falling over her shoulder as she swayed in time with the music. Those nights felt like a lifetime ago. The boy he had been then would not recognize the man he had become. He wasn't sure whether he should feel pride or shame about that.

He had been harsher than he should have been with Riona, but he hadn't been able to bear the grief in her eyes, nor the pang of sorrow and longing that had lodged in his heart. Nothing would bring Riona's mother back. Nothing would return him to those nights of falling asleep in his mother's music room. It was time they each accepted that.

Auberon closed his eyes and splayed a hand over his heart, exactly where Riona had placed the tip of his dagger. Although she had never been trained to fight, there was something fierce and unforgiving about her. It was entrancing.

That night, he fell asleep with the scent of Riona's perfume in his nose and the sound of her laughter filling his ears. Just as the darkness swept over him, he sent a silent entreaty to Drystan:

Please, forgive me.

Chapter Twenty-Four
The Lady

The sound of ringing steel greeted Riona when she arrived at the castle's main garden the next morning. In the center of the grass, Prince Domhnall and Prince Eamon were slashing at each other with blunted practice swords, to the delight of the courtiers and council members gathered around them. Eamon twisted a second too late, and her cousin landed a blow to the prince's upper arm, earning a smattering of applause from the onlookers.

Riona scanned the garden. A few yards away, Duke Valerian stood watching the match and sipping from a goblet of wine, an unreadable expression on his face. Despite the early winter chill in the air, he wore only a simple tunic, the loose neckline revealing a swath of suntanned skin shiny with perspiration. His stare never strayed from the Kostori prince. When Eamon disarmed Prince Domhnall and leveled the edge of his practice blade at the Crown Prince's throat, Valerian's lips turned downward in distaste.

"Good morning, Your Grace," Riona said as she approached him. She gestured toward her cousin and Prince Eamon. "From the look on your face, one might think you were wishing the blades were real. Hoping to repay Prince Eamon for his comments about your country's political turmoil, are you?"

"That, and everything else he and his father have done to Kenter," he muttered. "I would not be surprised if he spent the entirety of your outing yesterday regaling you with stories of my father's failings."

"Oh, not the entirety, but a good portion," Riona responded lightly. "Not to worry—I take everything he says with a grain of salt. As I do with all of you suitors."

Duke Valerian laughed. "Good. If you took him at his word, I would seriously question your judgment. And my own in trying to win your hand."

She smiled. "I'm sorry we've not had much time to speak since your arrival. I trust that your meeting with His Majesty went well yesterday?"

"There's no need to apologize, my lady. Considering everything that has happened, I was amazed the king still insisted on speaking with me at all. Your uncle is a strong man."

"Yes, he is," Riona responded, recalling the sight of him kneeling before the altar in the private chapel, tears streaming down his cheeks. She had arrived at the court dinner not one hour later, and if she hadn't seen him in mourning, she might have thought him perfectly unruffled by the events of the last week. "What are you asking for in addition to my hand? Trade? Resources?"

"An army."

Riona's brows rose. She was surprised that the duke would state it so plainly, when Prince Eamon had danced so carefully around the topic of war. "Truly?"

"Yes. I will not deny it." His expression hardened with resolve as he glanced back at Eamon and Domhnall, their blades slicing through the air with undeniable skill. "The Kostori have controlled my country for almost as long as I've been alive. I will not watch them bleed us dry any longer."

"Have the Kostori done nothing worthy of praise in Kenter? Eamon's father gave your father his position."

"That's what King Jericho would have you believe. My father

sits on our country's throne and takes the blame for our problems while the Kostori grow fat on our food and conscript our men for their army. I assured you at the banquet that Eamon was exaggerating our political unrest, and that was true," he said, his pale green eyes cutting back to her. "The noble families who demand justice for the former Grand Duke are nothing but a vocal minority, powerless. But they desire to see our country freed, just as my father and I do. If we were able to gather a force large enough to reestablish our independence, Kenter would flourish once again."

She tilted her head, considering what he'd said. "But do you not fear that in allying with us, you will be trading one foe for another?" Riona asked, as casually as if they were discussing the weather. "Once you win your freedom, who is to say that my uncle will not demand your aid in the war against Erduria?"

A flicker of uncertainty passed across the duke's face, but he quickly blinked it away. "If you were to help us regain our independence, we would owe it to you to fight at your side. You and I would stand against the Empire together."

If Riona knew one thing for certain, it was that Duke Valerian was not a coward. Admittedly, she hadn't expected much from him when he was presented before the court on his first night in Innislee. He was tall, corded with lean muscle, and his pale eyes and golden hair gave him a deceptive air of softness. In fact, he had reminded her a little of Percival, with his quiet, bookish manner.

The thought chipped away at her innate dislike of the suitors. She could tell by the conviction in Valerian's voice that he meant every word he said. She suspected that if it came to war, he would fight on the battlefield alongside his men, just as King Tamriel and Queen Mercy had. Somehow, she would find him the army he needed, and not just because she wanted her own future. She truly hoped to see him succeed in freeing his country.

Still, she had to think first and foremost about her freedom. Duke Valerian was courageous, but he was no fool. If she planted the doubts in his mind, he would soon realize that he couldn't stand against Kostos and Erduria in the negotiations for her hand. He couldn't afford the cost of a marriage alliance with Rivosa.

"It would be an honor to stand by your side," Riona said, surprised to find that she meant it. "How many men are in your army right now?"

"By law, my father is allowed to have only eight thousand at his command. We could call on another twelve thousand to join us, but they're troops that are held and commanded by the Kentari nobility. He would require their support to lead them in battle, which is problematic because the nobility is divided in its loyalty to Kostos and to my father. That is why I need your uncle's aid."

"So, twenty thousand total—*if* you and your father manage to convince the nobles to support your war for independence," Riona mused. "Kostos has been benefiting from your country's resources for the last fifteen years, so they'll have the supplies to endure the fighting. My uncle will help where he can, I'm sure, but it'll be difficult to send aid if we're still fighting the Empire for control of the Tranquil Sea. It'll be easy for them to set up blockades around Kenter's ports. Still, I'm certain we will find a way. My uncle has managed to hold the Erdurian navy at bay for thirty years. He can do it a little while longer."

"I'm...sure he can." Duke Valerian smiled, but Riona didn't miss his unease as he looked away.

Across the garden, Prince Domhnall's sword flipped out of his hand and landed in the grass at his feet. He lifted his hands in surrender as Eamon leveled the point of his blade at the Crown Prince's heart. "Yield," Domhnall gasped, sweat dripping down his face.

The courtiers applauded as Domhnall offered the Kostori prince a good-natured slap on the back, then bent to pick up his sword. He didn't even have time to straighten completely before Amaris ambushed him, wrapping her arms around his neck and pulling him into a kiss. Eamon chuckled at them as he returned his practice sword to the weapon stand on the far side of the garden. He scanned the crowd, his expression brightening when he spotted Valerian.

"Ready for our match, Your Grace?" he asked as a servant rushed forward with a goblet of wine for him. He took a sip and raised a brow at the duke. "I do hope you've been practicing since the last time we sparred."

Valerian's fingers tightened around the stem of his own goblet, but his smile was as easy and polished as ever. "Of course. I don't intend to lose to you twice. I don't think your ego could handle it."

Eamon ignored the jab, draining his wine and gesturing for the duke to follow him to the sparring ring. Valerian offered Riona an apologetic smile as he set aside his goblet and followed the prince. As soon as they picked up the practice swords, the nobles circled around them, excited to see what would come of this volatile match.

A soft touch brushed Riona's arm.

She turned to find a young girl—no more than fourteen years old—standing in the shadow of the wall that surrounded the garden, nervously eyeing the gathered courtiers. The knees of her servant's uniform were streaked with dirt, marking her as one of the gardeners. "Aeron sent me, my lady," she whispered. "He has found the servant who gave the poisoned wine to Prince Auberon."

Her grave tone sent a chill down Riona's spine. "And?"

"She's dead."

Dead. A stone sank to the pit of Riona's stomach. How many more bodies would stack up before the Treasurer's killer was found? "Do the city watch or royal guard know?"

"They know that she hasn't reported to work since the banquet, but nothing more. One of Aeron's men found her body dumped in an alley. She was badly beaten, but...he managed to identify her," the girl said, tripping over the words. "Aeron sent me to find out what you want us to do next."

Riona glanced at the courtiers, all distracted by the sparring match. She wanted to go and examine the servant's body herself, to glean what information she could about the woman's murder, but she couldn't leave just yet. "Have him meet me at the Royal Theater tonight, at midnight. I want to examine the body."

The girl curtsied and started to turn away, but Riona pulled a small piece of paper from her pocket and handed it to the servant. "Please deliver this to Prince Auberon."

She nodded and left, and Riona turned her attention to the suitors. Valerian's and Eamon's blades were locked, sweat pouring down their faces as they glared at each other, each trying to gain the upper hand. The nobles were wholly focused on them, engrossed in the match. She couldn't leave the castle, but she could slip away for a short while without her absence raising too many questions.

Without a glance back, Riona stepped through the archway and left the garden behind.

Chapter Twenty-Five
The Liar

"Did you hear a word I said?" Drystan asked, his sharp tone drawing Auberon out of his thoughts. They were standing in the hall outside the throne room, awaiting the king's summons. "Have you been listening *at all?*"

"I'm listening, I'm listening." Auberon rubbed his tired eyes with the heels of his palms. When he finally fell asleep the night before, it had been a fitful, uneasy rest. "In summary, you want me to stand back and say nothing while you make a bid for the lady's hand. Oh, and keep any smart comments to myself. Does that about cover it?"

"I think I put it in somewhat kinder terms." Drystan's expression softened as he studied Auberon. "Are you sure you don't want to go back and rest? You're still recovering from the poison."

"That was nearly a week ago. I'm fine. Besides, you've proven that I can't leave you to negotiate alone. You already passed up one opportunity to make Riona your bride, and I will not allow you to do it again."

An elven servant opened one of the throne room doors. Drystan shot Auberon a look that was part amusement, part warning before following the woman inside. As in the banquet hall, stone dragons coiled around the pillars that supported the second-story gallery, where minor nobles would be allowed to watch the proceedings during court events. Their onyx eyes glimmered in the light from the stained-glass windows, making them seem eerily alive.

At the far end of the room, King Domhnall sat tall and proud on his throne, flanked by Lord Lachlan and Prince Domhnall. Not a flicker of emotion passed across his face as Drystan and Auberon stopped before the dais steps and bowed low.

"Prince Drystan and Prince Auberon of Erduria, Your Majesty," the servant announced, curtsying.

"Thank you, Ophelia. That will be all."

She rose and turned to leave, brushing shoulders with Auberon as she passed. Her hand found his, and she pressed a small, folded piece of paper into his palm. He closed his fingers around it as she walked away.

As soon as she left, King Domhnall said, "I won't waste time mincing words. Prince Drystan, considering the history between our countries, I am sure you understand why I am resistant to sending my niece into your father's court."

Drystan offered the king a practiced smile. "My father treats his friends well, and I have come here to see that my brother and I depart as your friends, not your enemies. We can unite our countries and end this war. A marriage would show our people that we are willing to forgive past conflicts and heal together."

"Would you call the deaths of my eldest son and sister-in-law mere *conflicts?*" he asked, his voice low and even. "What about the assassinations of half the Selannic royal family? Was that a conflict?"

Auberon stiffened at the fury in the king's voice, his grip tightening on the little paper in his hand.

Drystan's smile faded. "Their deaths were tragedies, Your Majesty. With all due respect, I will remind you that my father denounced the attack on the Selannic royals and ordered the arrest and execution of every man involved as soon as word reached us in Torch. The assassins were not working under my father's orders."

"I find it hard to believe that Emperor Hyperion had no prior knowledge of an attack that resulted in the deaths of half my wife's family."

"And I find it fortunate for you that only lesser members of the royal family were killed in the assassination. The king, queen, and heir all emerged completely unscathed, but not without a renewed hatred of the Erdurian Empire."

The king's eyes narrowed. "I know, Prince Drystan, that you are not implying that I somehow had a hand in this tragedy. That I sought to benefit from their murders."

"No, of course not. I was merely making a point—rather indelicately, I will admit—about the efficacy of throwing around baseless accusations," Drystan said smoothly, looking not in the least bit regretful.

King Domhnall bristled. Behind him, Lord Lachlan and the Crown Prince remained stone-faced, watching over the proceedings in silence. Auberon stood taller at Drystan's side, his chest filling with pride. He knew how to sway people with sly words and clever turns of phrase. Drystan did it with all the regal authority of a man who had been born to lead the greatest empire in the world.

"The Erdurian navy broke the laws of neutrality and sank a ship bound for the Selannic Isles," the king finally said, "resulting in the death of Lady Riona's mother. In breaching those laws, Emperor Hyperion has proved himself to be a man without honor. Why should I send my niece into the court of such a man? If we ally, what will prevent him from one day turning my own kingdom into a vassal?"

"If he wished to expand his empire, he would have invaded long ago. We seek only an end to the fighting, which would benefit both countries greatly. Trade would flourish. You would have access to our resources and the support of our military, should you ever require it."

King Domhnall shook his head. "A chance at peace is not worth risking my country's independence."

Because you know that you only have to wait until you have enough eudorite weapons to launch an attack on Erduria, Auberon thought with mounting frustration. *With eudorite blades and eudorite-hulled ships, our navy wouldn't stand a chance. You're planning a slaughter.*

Unable to remain silent any longer, Auberon slipped the folded note into his pocket, then stepped past Drystan and held up his hands in placation. "Come now, Your Majesty. It looks to me like Rivosa would benefit much more from an alliance with Erduria than we would with you. What precisely can *you* offer *us*? Beyond your beautiful niece, of course."

Admit you're mining eudorite, he silently challenged. *Prove to us that your kingdom is worth something.*

Heavy silence descended over the room. Lord Lachlan did not move, but the Crown Prince shifted uneasily, glancing from Auberon to his father and back. They could all feel the ghosts of those the war had claimed crowding the room, waiting for an answer.

Today, the decades-long war between Rivosa and Erduria could finally end.

At last, the king laughed—a soft, humorless sound. "You are almost as skilled with your words as the man who sired you, Prince Auberon. Let us speak plainly. As valuable as your troops and trade may be, I do not trust your father, and I have yet to hear a reason why I should entrust him with my niece's safety.

"A sea may divide our lands, but tales of your father's bloody, brutal ways spread well beyond the borders of your precious empire. His spies were responsible for the crumbling of the court in Camrone. His army leveled the city of Orbury because its leader dared to demand independence. And yet you ask me to betray my subjects and entrust the future of my kingdom to him? Unless you can allay my concerns, my answer is no."

Drystan's hands curled into fists, the only outward sign of his growing anger. "I hope you will reconsider in the coming weeks, Your Majesty. It would be a great honor to marry Lady Riona and peacefully end the war."

King Domhnall nodded. "You are dismissed, Your Highnesses."

They bowed stiffly, then left the room. If Auberon had had any doubts, they were gone now. King Domhnall had no intention of agreeing to a betrothal. If he allowed everyone else to believe that Drystan would win Riona's hand, Eamon and Valerian would be forced to offer better terms. He was playing them against one another, knowing that the Erdurian Crown Prince would be too proud and stubborn to give up.

Cunning bastard.

"I'm sorry for interjecting," Auberon said as he followed Drystan through the halls. "I couldn't stand there and listen to that any longer. If I had been in your place, I don't know that I would have been able to hold my tongue."

"You *didn't* hold your tongue," Drystan replied. "But thank you for trying to put him in his place."

He nodded, and they walked in silence. Politics had always intrigued him, but this was not politics—this was patronizing. If they had only come for the betrothal, Auberon would have suggested sailing back to Erduria and ruining the king's game. Unfortunately, they were stuck: Auberon had to learn about the mines, and Drystan desperately wanted the betrothal and peace treaty. It would not be easy to overcome the king's open hostility, but they would find a way.

King Domhnall's paranoia had cost them a chance at peace, and every death that occurred on the Tranquil Sea from this day forward would be on his hands.

Auberon would not rest until every person in this kingdom knew it.

When they reached the guest house, he and Drystan went their separate ways. Auberon stepped into his bedroom and closed the door, leaning against it as he unfolded the note the servant had given him. It was crumpled from how tightly he'd been gripping it, but the elegant cursive was still perfectly legible.

Meet me again tonight. Same time and place.

Chapter Twenty-Six
The Lady

Riona crouched behind one of the throne room's wide stone pillars, peering through the gaps in the railing that surrounded the second-floor gallery. As soon as the Erdurian princes left, Prince Domhnall slumped onto the top step of the dais and rubbed the back of his neck, letting out a long sigh.

"Are you certain this is the best course of action, Father?" he asked. "We cannot afford to antagonize Erduria, especially after Prince Auberon's poisoning. You did promise Prince Drystan that there would be some concessions during the negotiations."

"My *concession* is that I have not tossed him and his insolent brother on a ship bound for their precious empire!" The king's voice rang through the room, making Riona flinch. "They threaten *every* aspect of our kingdom's future. Unless I hear some undeniable reason to trust them—and to entrust Riona's safety to them—I will not bend."

"But the war—"

"We will end it another way." King Domhnall glanced over at his brother. Riona shifted closer to the railing, peering down to try and catch a glimpse of her father's expression as her uncle continued, "We have lost too much. I swear it on my son's grave:

this war will not end until the Tranquil Sea runs red with Erdurian blood."

The icy promise in his voice sent a shiver down Riona's spine. Her uncle had been fighting to limit the Emperor's influence since he took the throne, so hearing her king's resolute words should have filled her with pride. Yet the mental image they evoked—ships burning on the water, bodies bobbing on the waves—was unsettling. Rivosa and Erduria had been trading blows for so long. How many bodies had stacked up between them? How many children like her had lost parents to the fighting?

How many more deaths would occur because of the king's refusal?

Riona padded silently across the cold stone in bare feet, her heels dangling from one hand as she descended the twisting spiral staircase and stepped into the hall, where she paused and pulled on her shoes. If only she had been able to eavesdrop on the negotiations with Valerian. Auberon's poisoning gave weight to Drystan's claim for her hand, but her uncle had made it clear he would rather die than entrust the future of his kingdom to Erduria, even at the cost of continued fighting. The marriage alliance would fall to Eamon or Valerian, and Riona knew her uncle favored the Kostori prince.

If she could help Valerian level the scales, it might delay the king's decision long enough for her to find Cathal's killer.

She found the duke and a few of his guards in the garden, speaking with Lord Farquar. The matches now finished, the nobles had left, and the weapons rack had been removed so that the only remaining evidence of the sparring matches was the patch of flattened grass in the center of the garden.

"Please pardon the interruption," Riona said as she joined them, setting a hand on Valerian's arm, "but I was hoping I could steal the duke for the afternoon. We haven't had much time to get to know each other, and I'd like to make it up to him."

"Of course, my lady," Farquar said with a dip of his head. He turned to Valerian. "I will share what you have told me with the other lords and ladies of the council. Creator willing, we may be able to aid you."

"Thank you, my friend. My father will see that you are rewarded handsomely for it."

"What were you discussing?" Riona asked once the lord had bowed and excused himself.

"The Kostori king's mistreatment of my people. If we are married, I'll need the support of your uncle and his council to go to war for my country's independence. Lord Farquar is sympathetic to my cause, and I was hoping he would speak to the rest of the council on my behalf. Plus, the promise of gold and land always manages to sway even the most reluctant."

"True, but you need support from more than the nobles. You must earn the hearts of the people." Riona offered Valerian a sly grin. "Fortunately, I can help. Send for all the guards at your disposal, and have them bring as much money as you're willing to invest in your bid for our marriage. We're going to need a few extra sets of hands."

A few hours later, Riona and Valerian walked side-by-side through the heart of the city's poorest district, leading a procession of Kentari guards through the narrow, winding streets. Tall, cramped buildings lined the road, and several children peered out at them with curiosity, their round faces just visible through the cracked and grimy windows. Riona smiled and waved at them. Duke Valerian stood tall at her side, striking in black trousers and shining leather boots, his doublet of violet and gold brocade shining under the sunlight.

Every Kentari guard held a crate in his arms, laden with bread, fruit, vegetables, containers of stew, and more. They had spent most of the afternoon in Innislee's largest market, strolling in plain view of the townspeople as Valerian purchased crate after crate. He had spoken to the merchants, charmed the young women, and treated the children they'd met to toys from the market stalls. Watching him interact with her people, Riona had been struck with admiration. Genuine delight had shone in his eyes as she led him through the market, introducing him to vendors and artisans she knew.

The cramped buildings gave way to a small square, a dry fountain at its center. A crowd had gathered behind them as they made their procession through the sector, and the people watched with curiosity as Valerian nodded to the guards, who immediately set the crates down around the fountain and began unpacking the contents. He led Riona to the center of the square and surveyed the humans and elves around them.

"My name is Duke Valerian, and I have come from Kenter to bid for Lady Riona's hand in marriage," he said, his voice clear and confident. "I hope these gifts will ease the burden the war with Erduria has placed on your shoulders, and remind you that the Kentari people stand with you. Please, take what you need."

As Riona watched, the wariness on the people's faces eased, and they began to line up in front of the Kentari guards. Many were haggard-looking women in long, worn dresses, young children clinging to their skirts. Valerian's expression softened as he watched a little girl hesitantly accept a loaf of bread from a guard and rush back to her mother's side.

"I remember standing beside my father after the Kostori siege ended," he murmured, "and watching a line of merchants file into the city. The gates had been closed for more than a year. People lined the streets, shouting and cheering. Someone in the square below brought out an old lute and began to play, and I realized then that it was the first time I had heard music since the siege began. I was only five years old, but I remember that moment as if it were yesterday. We finally had hope again. I am glad to give hope to these people, even if it is only for a short while."

Riona nodded, surveying the gaunt faces around them. "The

war has been difficult for us all, but it hits this part of the city the worst. The factory owners can't afford to pay their workers after the Erdurians sink their trading ships, and many of the men are forced to join the navy to support their families. Few come back alive."

Valerian turned to her. "If we marry, my father and I will help. Our navy is small compared to your uncle's, but if he will provide ships, we can send food and goods to be distributed to those most affected by the war."

"You have enough to spare?"

He nodded. "Kostos demands most of our resources, but I've been building stockpiles in Glenkeld and some of the other major cities. Once we reestablish our independence, I'll be able to divert some of those supplies to Rivosa."

Riona smiled, touched by his generosity. She watched the people move from guard to guard, collecting everything from bowls of soup to swaths of fabric to leather shoe soles. Every single one of them bowed or curtsied to her and Valerian once they'd finished, tears in their eyes as they stumbled over words of gratitude. Riona smiled and bade them farewell, but inside, her stomach knotted. If her uncle sent Prince Drystan away without a treaty, how long would the war with Erduria continue? How long could these people endure the fighting?

"If my uncle chooses one of the other suitors," Riona began when they had a moment alone, "would you still provide aid to my people? If you and I were to secure the army you need another way, would you help us?"

"What do you have in mind?"

"I can't promise that King Tamriel and Mercy would pledge you troops, but I do have some good will in Beltharos from my time there. I could write to them." She had fought to restore the rightful king's throne, and she knew that Tamriel was grateful to her and Percival for their aid. If she wrote to him, he would at least *consider* providing Valerian the men he needed.

"Do you have such little faith in my negotiating abilities, my lady?" the duke asked, a wry smile tugging at one corner of his mouth. "I know Eamon and Drystan have more to offer your uncle, but I don't think I should give up hope *this* early."

"No, no, of course not. I wouldn't have suggested this if I didn't want you to have a better standing in the court." She nodded to the crates of goods at the guards' feet, trying not to betray how much she wanted Valerian to secure troops from Beltharos. That would leave her with only Kostos and Erduria to contend with as the negotiations progressed. "Still, I thought you should be aware that Beltharan aid is an option. Even if we are not married at the end of the negotiations, I hope that you will be able to reclaim your country's independence."

"Thank you, my lady. I appreciate your help, but there is no need to write to King Tamriel just yet, with the negotiations only just beginning."

They turned as a young, weary-looking mother approached them to give her thanks, a pair of round-faced little boys clinging to her skirt. While Riona spoke with their mother, Valerian knelt and dazzled them with the flash of a gold Kentari coin, whispering something about them bringing good luck as he passed one to each child. Their mother curtsied and thanked him profusely before herding her boys down the street, a basket of food swinging from one arm.

They remained there into the evening, handing out food and goods and speaking with the people of the sector. By the time Riona returned to her father's estate, her cheeks ached from smiling. Still, she couldn't seem to stop. After a while, she had even forgotten that she had organized the display to aid Duke Valerian. It had simply been nice to leave the confines of the castle and spend time amongst her people.

She climbed the stairs and started toward her room. As she passed one of the open doorways, Amaris poked her head out and called, "I heard about your little outing. Did you enjoy your time with the duke?"

"Yes," Riona answered. "I truly did."

Without waiting for a response, she slipped into her bedroom and closed the door, then sat at her desk and pulled out a piece of parchment, a quill, and a pot of ink. After lighting the candelabra, she picked up the quill, dipped it in the ink, and began her letter to King Tamriel Myrellis.

Chapter Twenty-Seven
The Liar

Auberon was still fuming about the negotiations when he arrived at the Royal Theater that night. Riona was already there, dressed in the same dark, fitted clothing she had worn the night before. Her long braids were twisted into a knot atop her head, and every strand sparkled with gold beads. She stood among the skeletal trees atop the stage, hacking at a wooden costume mannequin with a prop sword she must have found among the theater's stores. She was clearly untrained, but her movements held a dancer's natural grace—that much was undeniable. As was the spark of desire that flared within Auberon as he watched her fight her inanimate opponent.

"I think you've killed him," he said as he bounded up the steps. "Despite doing just about everything wrong."

Riona frowned at him over her shoulder. "I wasn't doing *everything* wrong. I know which side of the sword to hold." She lifted the weapon in emphasis, then sent it sweeping toward the mannequin. "And I know where to hit."

"Oh, aye. A stunning maneuver. Mannequins everywhere are quaking."

She spun and lunged toward him, the sword slicing through the air. Auberon stepped to the side and, with a raised brow, grabbed the blade with his bare hand. It was metal, but dulled to a blunt edge. "First lesson: use a proper weapon."

He yanked it sharply, pitching her off balance. Riona stumbled forward, and he caught her, an arm slipping around her waist. Auberon heard her breath hitch when she realized that they stood chest-to-chest, her soft curves pressed against the hard planes of his torso. His gaze roved from the thick lashes framing her blue eyes to her high cheekbones, then down to her full, perfect lips. For a moment, the world seemed to stop.

"You see?" he breathed, his heart pounding. "Now I've disarmed you."

"Only because I let you get so close," she huffed, looking down at where his fingers were still wrapped around the dull blade. "I'm doing my best. Some of us didn't grow up with the luxury of a private swordplay tutor."

His smile faded. "I should think the greater luxury is not having to grow up with one at all."

Riona faltered, guilt filling her expression. He saw her gaze drop to his mouth, where a faint, pale scar cut into the edge of his lower lip. "...Perhaps you're right."

Just then, the curtains at the far end of the theater parted. Riona released the sword and jerked away from Auberon, self-consciously running her hands down the front of her tunic, as a man stepped through the archway. She didn't look at Auberon as she started down the steps from the stage. "Aeron," she said, picking up a cloak she'd left on one of the theater seats and sweeping it around her shoulders. "I'm glad you came. Will you take us to the servant's body?"

Whatever desire he'd been feeling abruptly left him at those words. "What body?"

"We found the woman who served you the poisoned wine dead in an alley. At least, the woman we believe served you the wine. I suppose you'll be able to confirm her identity, Your Highness," the stranger said as he walked down the aisle. The candlelight revealed the pointed ears sticking out from his wavy hair, along with the mistrust with which he regarded Auberon. "I wasn't aware we would have company, my lady."

"Prince Auberon is helping me find the person who attempted to kill him. You will tell no one of this, and you will keep any opinions of his Erdurian blood to yourself."

Aeron continued staring at Auberon, but he nodded. "I won't say a word, my lady."

Auberon bristled at the contempt in the elf's voice, but said nothing as he set aside the prop sword and descended the stage steps. Aeron turned and started back toward the archway, Riona walking close at his side. Auberon trailed behind them as the elf led them out of the theater, along the King's Road, then down several narrow, twisting streets. The night was clear, a blanket of brilliant stars sparkling high above the city. Yet their beauty dimmed when Aeron started down a close—one of the narrow, covered alleyways that were characteristic of Innislee—and the stench of decay and rotting meat washed over them.

"By the Creator," Auberon hissed, lifting a hand to his nose. "How is it possible that no guards or city patrolmen have discovered the body when it smells like this?"

Aeron shot him a withering look over his shoulder. "We're in the slums, which is occupied almost entirely by starving, out-of-work elves. Finding a body in one of the closes is hardly noteworthy to the city watch."

He led them a bit further and stopped before a doorway that only came up to his shoulder, the door hanging on broken hinges. "This is where we found her. Lady Riona... You may want to wait outside."

"No," she said, although her voice came out strained. "No, I don't."

The elf nodded and picked up a lantern someone had left beside the doorway. He struck a match and lit the wick, turning the flame as high as it would go before leading them inside. The floor immediately dropped, having been dug out so whoever was inside could stand fully upright. It was a...flat, Auberon realized as he surveyed the room in the light from Aeron's lantern, although he pitied anyone who had to live in such cramped quarters. It consisted of a single room with a dirt floor, a rickety table and chairs pushed into one corner alongside a wood-burning stove. On the opposite wall stood a simple wooden cot, where a figure was curled beneath layers of thick, ratty blankets. The putrid odor that emanated from it was nearly unbearable.

Riona reached for the blankets and wavered, looking as if she was about to be sick. Auberon stepped around her and pulled the covers back.

A cloud of flies burst from the corpse. Auberon bit back a startled cry as they shot past him and out the door. His heart hammered against his ribs as he examined the body, fighting to hold down his dinner. Aeron moved to the foot of the cot and held the lantern high, his face pale and grim under the flickering light. The woman lay on her side, facing away from them, her long brown hair spilling across the mattress. Her face was bloated and swollen with dark bruises, most of the delicate bones badly broken. Her head was bent backward at an awkward angle, and when Auberon leaned forward, he saw why.

The elven girl's throat had been slashed from ear to ear, straight through the jugular. Auberon swallowed, feeling the blood drain from his face. "Creator preserve us..."

"It's her, isn't it?" Riona asked softly. "The servant?"

He nodded. Although her face was mutilated and mottled with bruises, he could still see a glimmer of the girl who had served him the wine that night.

"The castle had no record of where she lived," Aeron said. "It was only through sheer luck that my man stumbled upon her body. Whoever was behind the attempt on your life used her to deliver the poison, then murdered her to ensure her silence."

"We... We should search the room," Riona added. "There may be something here that can lead us to the murderer."

They began to rifle through the flat's meager furnishings. Riona searched the few cupboards that made up the kitchen, climbing onto one of the chairs to see if anything was hidden on top of the shelves, while Aeron and Auberon quickly peeled back the rest of the blankets to further examine the body. The elf was clad in two layers of tunics and pants, an attempt to guard against the dank chill of the flat, and the rest of her body was untouched. She had first been killed, and then her murderer had mutilated her face in an attempt to keep her from being identified.

He was weary and heartsick by the time they emerged from the close, frustrated by the fact that they'd found nothing of note. A small chest at the foot of the bed had held her servants' livery and a few other changes of clothes, along with a small bag of coins, but that was it. There were no notes, no vials of poison or weapons, no evidence of any payment from the murderer for her aid in the poisoning. They'd even gone so far as to examine the walls for loose stones where the elf might have hidden any evidence of her involvement in the attempt on his life.

Nothing.

No one spoke as they made their way back to the Royal Theater. When they stepped through the curtained archway into the theater proper, Riona slung off her cloak and flung it over the back of a chair, then slumped into one of the seats in the first row. "Send anonymous notes to the royal guard and city watch that the body has been discovered," she said to Aeron in a quiet voice, "and then get some rest. I'm sorry for dragging you out in the middle of the night."

He pressed a hand to his chest, just over his heart. "You do not have to apologize. I am yours to command, my lady."

Aeron bowed and left, not even bothering to shoot Auberon a hateful look as he passed. Once he was gone, Auberon sank into the seat beside Riona's, wishing he could scrub the night from his mind. "I think that elf's in love with you," he teased, trying for a lighthearted tone.

"He's not," Riona responded, the words flat. "His wife died of a wasting sickness three years ago, and he hasn't been the same since. He still loves her. It's part of the reason why he has such hatred for the nobility. She..." She stopped and shook her head. "He wouldn't want me to speak of his affairs. Just know that he can be trusted."

"I can see that. I think he'd fall on his own blade if you commanded it."

Riona met his gaze, something haunted and defeated in her eyes. "I think serving me is the only thing that keeps him from falling on his blade most days."

Auberon fell silent, having no response to that. The quiet of the theater was a heavy, somber thing, filled with the horror of what they'd seen that night. Another body. Another brutal murder. Riona was so careful to play the polished court lady at the banquets, but he could see now the toll that the senseless deaths were taking on her. She had faced execution and survived a tyrant's reign in Beltharos only to find her own court festering with corruption. When he could stand her sorrow no longer, he stood and offered her a hand.

"We will find the person responsible for this, Riona," he said, and she looked up in surprise at his use of her name—no title, no teasing quips. "But as we've seen tonight, we live in a world rife with weapons and bastards who know how to use them, so you should learn how to protect yourself. Which is why you're incredibly lucky to have my expertise at your disposal. I'm an excellent teacher."

A spark of life returned to her eyes, and she fixed him with a skeptical look. "Among other things, I'm sure."

He winked as she took his hand and rose. "I'm more than just a pretty face, my lady."

Chapter Twenty-Eight
The Liar

"All teasing aside, you show promise," Auberon said as he moved the mannequin to the edge of the stage, out of the way. When he returned to Riona, he gestured for her to lift the prop sword and corrected her grip. "You're a skilled dancer—you have control over your body and you're aware of the space around you. Use that to your advantage." He stepped to her side and nudged her foot with his until she shifted, moving her weight to the balls of her feet. "You're tall, but most of your opponents will be larger and stronger than you. So use your grace and speed against them. Let them tire themselves out with brute force, then strike."

Riona laughed softly. "You make it sound so simple."

Auberon reached over to correct her grip on the sword again. "Eventually, your body takes over, and you don't have to think. Same with a dance. You adapt and learn."

"Or you die."

"Which is what I'm trying to help you avoid. If you end up in Erduria with Drystan—or in Kenter with your darling, selfless Valerian—you will face many enemies simply because of the man you marry."

She raised a brow at him over her shoulder. "*You're* my enemy, Your Highness."

"Yes, but I've had the very unfortunate experience of having been charmed by you," Auberon responded, his voice sickly sweet. "As much as it pains me to admit it, I would very much hate to see you dead."

"I believe that's the kindest thing you've ever said to me."

"Don't get used to it. Your stance is absolutely dreadful." He pushed her foot back to where he had placed it before, then stepped back and crossed his arms. "Forget what I said about your dancer's instincts. I'll need a miracle to turn you into a proper warrior."

That familiar flash of annoyance returned to her face. "I may surprise you yet."

He grinned. "My lady, I don't doubt it."

Auberon walked her through the proper stance one more time, then demonstrated a few simple drills—blocking, slashing, stabbing, disarming an opponent. A little furrow of concentration formed between her brows as she followed him through the movements. Without music, without anyone else around, the theater was as silent as a tomb. The only sounds came from the soft scuff of Riona's boots and the whistle of her blade through the air.

After an hour, Auberon caught her arm, stilling her. "Now try to strike me."

"Already? I hardly know what I'm doing!"

"Better than fighting a wooden dummy." He nodded to the mannequin as he retrieved a prop sword from backstage. His lungs still ached from the poison, but the pain was easing every day. "You should practice fighting an opponent who can react to your attacks. Your enemies aren't going to stand still and wait for you to kill them."

"Will *you* stand still and let me try?"

He chuckled at her irritated tone. "I think, *aramati*, that you have forgotten I am doing you a favor by teaching you. Would you rather I take you to the Erdurian court and throw you to the wolves?"

"If they're anything like you, they're all bark and no bite. Give me a couple days, and I'd have them eating out of my hand."

Auberon shot her a knowing look. "Tell me, how did that confidence help you while you were awaiting execution in Beltharos just a few short weeks ago? For all your courtly manners and lovely smiles, you still ended up a prisoner. Your head would have been staked to the city gate alongside all the others if not for the arrival of King Tamriel's army. Men with swords. That's what saved your life. Not the court maneuvering you so love."

Riona glared at him. "I do not love it."

"Lie to yourself, but not to me. That little display of charity with Duke Valerian earlier today? Oh, yes, I heard about it, and I have no doubt the rest of the city did, as well. Just as you intended," Auberon said, stalking forward. She lifted her chin and held his gaze, her grip tightening on the sword. "You don't care about the people. You care about the way your little act makes you look, and the way it's going to affect Valerian's standing in the negotiations."

"Say what you will about me," Riona responded, her voice quiet and cold, "but don't believe for one second that I would not give anything for my people."

"Yet you will dance and drink and charm the court while our people fight for their lives on the Tranquil Sea. You will pull your little strings and pit Eamon and Valerian against each other, all while knowing that your inaction sends more innocent people to their graves. So who are you really doing this for: your people, or yourself?"

That was enough. Riona lunged, slashing low. Auberon lifted his sword and knocked the blow aside with ease. She huffed and tried again, fury twisting her features. He blocked. The third time, she feinted right, then twisted past him and aimed at the back of his thigh. He turned and caught her blade with his own before it could make contact.

"I detest you," she snarled, retreating and falling into the stance he had shown her.

"Apparently, as you haven't yet convinced your uncle to accept my brother's offer and end the bloodshed between our countries. How many more people will you allow to die, just so you don't have to marry Drystan?"

Fury twisting her features, Riona rushed at him again, driving the point of her sword toward his chest. Auberon met her blade with his own and twisted, sending it skittering across the stage. He smacked her arm with the flat of the blade, and she yelped, glaring at him.

"Second lesson: don't let your emotions get the better of you. It's a perfect way to make a mistake and—"

Riona ran across the stage and scooped her sword off the ground. Auberon lifted his own as she charged at him, slashing at his arms, his face, his chest, all with renewed vigor. He knocked her blade aside every time, a grin spreading across his face. Her movements were clumsy, but she was no longer thinking about anything except for the fight. No doubt. No hesitation.

"You're laughing at me," she spat as she swung at him.

"No, I'm not."

"You're toying with me."

"A little bit, yes."

Riona slashed at his side. Auberon knocked the sword from her hand, but she kept moving, ducking low and darting behind him. When he turned, he came face-to-face with the point of his dagger. She had pulled it from the sheath at his hip. Riona had sacrificed her own blade, letting him believe her anger had made her clumsy, and outmaneuvered him. Auberon lifted his hands in surrender.

On the other side of the dagger, Riona's eyes were wide. She was as surprised as he was that it had worked. "I'm a quick learner," she said, trying to seem unaffected by her victory. She lowered the dagger and sat on the piano bench to catch her breath.

"You did well. Even if I *was* going easy on you." Auberon

crossed the stage and sat with his legs hanging over the edge, grimacing as he rubbed his chest. His lungs burned from the latent effects of the poison. The heat still pulsed in his shoulder, but it was finally beginning to fade. *Thank the Creator.*

"Are you in pain?"

"A bit. It's not too bad, but the exertion made it worse."

"Good. You deserve it."

He lay back, chuckling. "You're not overly sensitive to my plight, *aramati*. After all the hard work I put in teaching you."

Riona was quiet for a few moments, and when Auberon glanced back, he found her studying the dagger in her hands. He rose and sat beside her on the bench. "I've been carrying that dagger for as long as I can remember. It was a gift from my father—a family heirloom. Keep it with you at all times, and pray that you never have to use it."

Riona looked at him sharply. "I can't take this."

She tried to give it back to him, but he caught her hand and closed her fingers around its grip. "Trust me. Better to be armed and not need it than to be caught unprepared. As I said earlier, I have a vested interest in keeping you alive. Not just for my brother, but for both our countries. I don't want to see any more people killed in the fighting over the Tranquil Sea."

"Nor do I."

"Then speak to your uncle. Convince him to choose Drystan," Auberon implored her, leaning forward so she was forced to meet his eyes. Every day she delayed cost them more lives. "I understand why you want to help Valerian in the negotiations. I understand why you want to stay in your home for as long as possible, but trust me when I tell you that it is not worth the price."

Riona looked away, lowering the dagger to her lap.

"You believe that my brother and I are heartless. You believe that my father is a monster. Riona, who came here asking for peace?" Auberon pressed. "I have reason to believe that your uncle is mining the Howling Mountains and crafting weapons of eudorite ore to wield against my father's navy. If I'm right, he will not stop fighting until one of our countries is decimated. Hate me all you like, but do not condemn your people and mine to death. Do not make them pay for a war they didn't choose."

"You say that as if I have a choice in the matter. My uncle doesn't value my political opinions. If he did, do you think he would be selling me off to a complete stranger?" she asked, a note of bitterness slipping into her voice.

"You must try," he insisted. "If not for the people, then do it for Treasurer Cathal. I believe the eudorite mines are somehow tied to his murder, and I fear that the king or a powerful member of the court may have had a hand in the assassination."

Riona stilled, anger flaring. "Explain."

So he did.

Chapter Twenty-Nine
The Lady

Once he'd finished, Riona sat in silence for several long minutes, considering all he had said. "It doesn't make sense," she finally responded. "If Treasurer Cathal knew about the mines and kept them secret for years, what reason would one of the courtiers have for ordering his assassination? Cathal was one of the king's closest friends and advisors. What could have caused someone to question his loyalty?"

"I'm not sure, but there's a reason Cathal didn't just burn those missing documents along with the rest of the treasury records. Think about it—if you realized that someone was coming to kill you, why would you risk your life to smuggle some papers out of the castle?" Auberon asked, leaning close. "I've heard the rumors around the court. If he were stealing from the treasury, he would've simply destroyed the evidence and fled the city. Those documents are important. I believe that they hold information that could affect the future of your kingdom, and that someone powerful—maybe even your uncle—ordered Cathal's assassination to keep him silent."

"You're wrong."

Sympathy shone in his blue-gray eyes. "I don't think I am, *aramati*."

Riona turned away, shaking her head. He was only suspicious of the king because of the direction the negotiations had taken. Her uncle was cold and unyielding when it came to the war with Erduria, but he would never be so heartless as to order the death of the man who had served him for decades. She had seen him mourning in the private chapel, tears of pure grief running down his face.

"If my uncle were behind the murder, he would already have the missing documents in his possession. The assassin would have taken them from Cathal's body and delivered them to the king, but that didn't happen. The guards are still searching."

"Which must mean that Faylen has them. Don't you see? *That's* why Cathal went to the brothel that morning. He must have known he would be followed if he tried to leave the city, so he gave her the papers and told her to disappear. The king knows that if he finds her, he'll find the documents, too."

As far as anyone knew, Faylen had simply vanished. It would have made sense for Cathal to give her the documents and tell her to meet him somewhere safe outside the city. The Royal Treasurer drew attention wherever he went, but an elven woman would have been able to join the bustle of traffic through one of the city gates without anyone noticing.

Riona stood and crossed the stage, wrapping her arms around herself as doubts began to creep in. "Cathal slept in the castle all night after you were poisoned," she said, turning back to face Auberon. "The murder didn't occur until the next morning. If my uncle had been behind it, he would have sent someone to kill Cathal the moment he realized the poison had gone to the wrong person."

Auberon shook his head. "The assassin knew to wait until the right opportunity presented itself—first, during the chaos of the banquet when any jealous courtier could have slipped poison into the Treasurer's goblet, and then in a brothel, where the murder could be explained as the result of a fight between lovers. If not for the burned and missing documents, it would have been dismissed as a mere coincidence that it happened after the attempt on my life. Find those papers, and you may find your killer's motive."

Then I must find Faylen, Riona thought, *and I must do it alone.* If the documents were truly as important and confidential as Auberon believed, she could not allow them to fall into his hands.

Mistaking her silence for uncertainty, Auberon picked up the dagger and approached her. "I know this is hard to hear, but if we hope to find the man responsible for Cathal's murder, we must examine every possibility. For your sake, I pray that I am wrong. But I cannot overlook my duty to my country and my people. All of this—the war, the assassination, the mines—is tied together somehow."

This war will not end until the Tranquil Sea runs red with Erdurian blood.

Auberon took her hand and set the dagger in her palm. "You don't have to trust me," he breathed, "but trust that I love my people as deeply as you love yours. I will do anything to protect them. If I'm right, you and I can prevent a slaughter that would claim thousands of Rivosi and Erdurian lives."

There was nothing but sincerity on his face. Nothing but desperation in the way his hand gripped hers.

"Do you trust in that?" Auberon asked, his eyes searching hers.

"Yes," she responded softly. "I do."

Chapter Thirty
The Lady

Two weeks passed with infuriatingly little change. Almost every day, Auberon was occupied with negotiations or meetings with the council members, attempting to convince the advisors to endorse Drystan for the betrothal. With a few well-chosen words to the right people, he had ensured that news of the king's refusal of a peace treaty spread like wildfire. People gathered in the streets every time Riona accompanied the suitors on a public outing, and as the days passed, their looks toward the Erdurian princes shifted from hostile to wary, and from wary to hopeful. The tide was turning in their favor.

As soon as Riona had noticed the shift, she redoubled her efforts with Valerian. At every opportunity, they took food and supplies to the poorest sections of the city or chatted with townspeople in the public gardens. She had even taken him to meet the dancers at the theater, all of whom had blushed and stuttered at receiving the slightest bit of attention from him. Rumors of the duke's kindness and generosity spread as quickly as Auberon's planted barbs, and it wasn't long before crowds began forming in the gardens and market for a glimpse of the golden-haired duke. Valerian still had the least to offer the king in terms of an alliance, but he had earned the hearts of the people, and that held its own weight.

Every day provided another chance to tip the scales. Auberon's criticisms about the ongoing war put pressure on King Domhnall to choose Drystan, while Valerian's popularity among the people bolstered his favor in the court, much to Eamon's chagrin.

Every night, Riona and Auberon upheld their shaky alliance. The prince wasn't happy about her helping Valerian gain favor, but even he admitted that it was a good strategy. The longer the negotiations continued, the more time they would have to hunt down Cathal's killer and learn about the eudorite mines. Still, it didn't stop him from making sarcastic, mocking quips at every possible opportunity. Riona snapped a response every time. She resented that he was sowing doubt among the courtiers, manipulating them to turn against their king. After a while, they came to the unspoken agreement to only discuss matters concerning their partnership, and nothing more.

As far as either of them could tell, the royal guards and city watchmen had come no closer to finding Cathal's murderer. Neither they nor Riona's helpers had been able to find any trace of Faylen in the city or surrounding towns. Doubts festered within Riona, only growing stronger with every day that passed. Where had Faylen gone? What was she planning to do with the documents Cathal had given her?

Late one night, she stood on the side of the stage with her prop sword, watching Auberon demonstrate a drill. Earlier that evening, he had tossed his doublet over the piano bench, leaving him in his fitted trousers and loose linen undershirt. The open collar revealed a swath of his suntanned skin and toned chest, the muscles sculpted from years of swordplay. The sight sent a warm —and horrifying—rush of desire through Riona. Curse her, she couldn't deny that he was handsome. Something about the little furrow of concentration between his brows, the sleeves he'd rolled up to his elbows, the shock of rich auburn hair hanging over his forehead, had her studying him in a different light.

He glanced over at her, and she quickly tore her gaze away, a flush rising to her cheeks. "Try again, *aramati*," he said, oblivious to her traitorous thoughts. "This time, see if you can land even one blow. A hundred aurums says I strike you first."

"You've been training all your life. Of course you're going to hit me first."

"You know, one of the things I admire most about you is your infallible optimism. Now quit talking and attack me. If you strike me first, I'll double the bet."

"I'd settle for five minutes without a sarcastic quip at my expense."

Auberon's smile grew. "Deal."

Riona charged forward, slashing at his face, his arms, and his chest in quick succession. Auberon knocked her blade aside every time. His sword swung low, and she brought hers up to meet it before it could strike her side. He murmured praise as she lunged and parried, trying to break through his defense. When he swung to meet her next blow, she twisted, bringing her blade down in a whistling arc. Before the blow could connect, he snaked his ankle around hers and slammed into her shoulder, throwing her off balance. She landed hard on the stage, a bright flare of pain shooting through her hip. Auberon smirked as he leveled the point of his sword at her face.

"Alas, you remain the subject of my mockery. What was your mistake?"

"Got too close." She grimaced and sat up, rubbing her sore hip. "I didn't leave myself enough room to swing."

"Well, at least you know what you did wrong. You're not completely hopeless."

He lowered the sword and offered her a hand up, which she accepted, wincing when she put her full weight on her leg. "If someone asks me why I'm walking funny tomorrow, I'll leave you to explain it," she said as she crossed the stage and poured a cup of water from a pitcher she had stolen from the theater's stores.

Auberon's grin turned wicked. "Are you certain that's a wise idea?"

Her flush came back with a vengeance. "By the Creator, forget I said anything."

He slipped the toe of his boot under Riona's sword and flipped it into the air, catching it with his free hand. He chuckled when Riona muttered, "Show-off."

"Sore loser." Auberon walked over and handed her the prop sword. The emerald-hilted dagger was strapped to her thigh in a sheath he had given her earlier that week, but neither of them trusted her with a real blade yet. "Try again."

Riona set the cup down and followed him to the center of the stage, pushing the braids that had fallen from her topknot over her shoulder. She lifted her sword and let Auberon attack first. He moved like a phantom, like the wind through the narrow city streets, swift and precise. No mirth in his eyes. No smug, mischievous smile. This was the real Auberon. Not a prince. Not a courtier.

A warrior.

She did her best to block his attacks, her arms shaking with the effort of holding him at bay. Her muscles ached. Not a day passed that she didn't wake up sore and in pain, her bruises throbbing. But she *was* improving, or so Auberon claimed. Sometimes, she wasn't certain whether he was telling the truth or trying to spare her feelings—if he were even capable of such a thing.

Riona lunged, driving her sword toward Auberon's chest at the same time as he swung low. The point of her blade came to rest just over his heart as his sword struck her side.

"A draw," he said. "We're both dead. Want to try again?"

She sat on the piano bench and shook her head. "No more. Not tonight."

"Fine by me." He tossed his doublet aside and sat next to her.

Riona was exhausted, but he was energetic, alive. His cheeks were flushed, and his gray-blue eyes were alight in a way she had never before seen them. Sparring always seemed to help him work off the frustration from the negotiations. "Don't be so hard on yourself. It's only been a couple of weeks since you started training. Like I said before, you have a dancer's instincts. That already aids you more than you realize."

Riona shifted, grimacing at the bruise forming on her hip. "Doesn't feel like it."

Auberon grinned—not one of his practiced court smiles, but a bright, genuine one. "We've all felt the pain of swordplay training. Now it's your turn, *aramati*."

"You keep calling me that. What does it mean?"

"*Beloved one*," he said with exaggerated sweetness, pressing a hand to his heart. "I told you, your charm and poise have utterly entranced me, my lady. It's no wonder the heirs to three powerful thrones have come to claim your hand. Minstrels will sing of your unmatched beauty until the end of days."

What a flirt. "Well, they certainly won't be singing about my battle prowess."

"Yes, but I wasn't going to point that out. At least not while you have a dagger within arm's reach."

Auberon rose and pulled on his doublet. As he started to work on the line of buttons along its front, Riona lifted the cover over the piano keys and played the first few notes of the song she had been playing their first night in the theater. Auberon's back was to her, but she saw the almost imperceptible tightening of his broad shoulders as the melody drifted through the air. He turned toward her as she continued to play, the doublet's buttons forgotten.

"Sit down," she said, nodding to the bench beside her.

"Why?"

The word came out little more than a breath, and the expression on his face was almost...*startled*.

"I know I'll never be skilled with a sword, but I was helpless as a hostage in Nicholas Comyn's court, and I will never be that weak again," she said. "This is my thank you for helping me. You can delight your mother by playing for her when you return to Torch."

"When *we* go to Torch," Auberon corrected, but he didn't move. His eyes were fixed on her hands, her long fingers dancing over the keys. A flicker of emotion passed across his face, there and gone too quickly for her to identify it.

Riona nodded to the bench. "Sit. Please."

Auberon rounded the piano and sat beside her. She began the song again, playing the first few notes and watching him attempt to replicate her movements. He hesitated between striking the keys, but Riona nodded, repeating the section whenever he faltered. Bit by bit, line by line, the song filled the empty theater. As its haunting, mournful melody wrapped around them, Riona realized why she hadn't been able to place the expression on his face: for the first time, he had looked *vulnerable.*

Auberon turned toward her, and it was only then that she realized the piano had fallen silent; he was waiting for her to continue the song. Instead, she asked, "What happened to your mother? That first night we met here, you spoke about her as if she were dead."

The prince let out a quiet, humorless laugh as he stood and moved to put away the prop swords. "My mother is very much alive, although sometimes it feels as if she has died. I grew up believing that my mother was a goddess among mortals. But eventually, there comes a day when you realize that the person you worshiped as a child is just as fallible as the rest of us. We have had some difficulties in recent years, she and I."

Auberon shoved the swords into a crate full of other props, then turned back to her. The candlelight cast his features in sharp lines, emphasizing the angle of his jaw, his high cheekbones, and straight, regal nose. A shock of chestnut hair hung over his brow. The urge to brush it away, to coax another genuine smile to his lips, ignited within Riona. She focused instead on the piano.

"The Erdurian court changed her, didn't it?" she asked, gripping her eudorite pendant until the edges began to cut into her fingers. *Remember who he is. Remember who you are.*

"One could say that." Auberon crossed the stage and offered her a hand up from where she sat on the piano bench. She accepted it and rose, but he didn't let go.

"Make no mistake—a court as large as my father's is a dangerous place. There are always whispers of revolt among the border cities and vassals," he said, his voice low. "When you marry Drystan, his allies will become your allies. His enemies will become your enemies. But if anyone comes for you, I swear, I will make them wish I had given them the mercy of a swift death."

Chapter Thirty-One
The Liar

The pale light of dawn was just beginning to grace the eastern sky when Auberon stepped out onto the King's Road. His clothes were rumpled and worn, smelling of whiskey and cheap perfume, and the coin purse in his pocket was noticeably lighter than it had been when he'd left the Royal Theater. After walking Riona home, he had wandered into the first tavern he'd found and challenged the patrons to countless rounds of Seven Deadly Kings. He had been doing the same thing almost every night for the last few weeks. In addition to giving him an excuse for leaving the castle late at night, it provided him the opportunity to earn the trust of the commoners. He charmed them with jokes and rounds of drinks, and as their inhibitions eased, they told him what the people of the city were saying. Duke Valerian and Riona had made a half-dozen trips to the markets and poor neighborhoods in the last fortnight. A man had been dismissed from the city watch after speaking out against the king and denouncing the war with Erduria. Prince Eamon had made an attempt to get to know the people in the market, but his words had rung as hollow as his intentions.

No news of Faylen, save for the fact that the royal guards and city watch were still searching for her. No whisper of eudorite mines. Nothing about the Treasurer's death save for the usual rumors.

Nothing. He had been in Innislee for three weeks, and he had nothing to show for it. So, he had decided to drown his disappointment in alcohol—not enough to get terribly drunk, of course, but the world had a pleasant haze to it as he started up the King's Road toward the castle. Drystan would be furious, but frankly, he didn't care. He was allowed one night to lament his lack of progress.

At this hour, the roads were already starting to fill with traffic: carriages carrying nobles to the castle, carts laden with goods heading to the market, and workers bustling to their various jobs. Most of the people he passed paid Auberon no heed, thinking him just another tavern patron stumbling home after a night of gambling. A few recognized him, however, and waved or offered a greeting as he made his way to the castle. He was glad to see that the wariness with which they had regarded him and Drystan on their first few days in the city had vanished. At least one thing was going their way.

After a few blocks, he slowed, his skin prickling. Someone was watching him. Feigning a nauseous spell, he stopped and set a hand on his stomach, taking the opportunity to scan the street. Initially, all looked as it should. Then his gaze snagged on the mouth of one of the closes. Someone was lingering just within the alley. His face was concealed by shadow, but his muscular build made it evident that he was a man. A city watchman or royal guard, perhaps? Auberon wouldn't have been surprised if the king had ordered someone to tail him, but it didn't make sense. If the man had been following him long enough to see Auberon meet Riona in the theater or walk her to her father's estate, he would have reported it to the king immediately. Auberon was certain that King Domhnall would waste no time in forbidding him from speaking to Riona, lest he somehow taint her with his Erdurian blood.

His pursuer had been sent by someone else, then. Auberon

frowned, trying to wade through the haze in his mind. Creator curse him for drinking so much, and curse him again for not sensing his pursuer sooner. He was still in an enemy kingdom, and he could not afford to let his guard down. Auberon turned toward the castle and started walking, pretending he hadn't noticed the man on his heels. Even so, he did not allow his hand to stray far from the dagger sheathed at his hip, a simple blade to replace the one he'd given Riona.

He abruptly turned and started down one of the side streets, shoving his hands into his pockets and whistling a Kentari drinking song as he wandered in the direction of the brothel where Cathal had been killed. He did not look behind him, but he could feel the weight of the stranger's gaze on his back. It never wavered. He continued down two more streets, then ducked into one of the closes and pressed flat against one of the doorways halfway down the alley, hiding himself from view. The close was cluttered with sewage and refuse, rotting food and the contents of emptied chamber pots leaking along the edges of the narrow footpath. Auberon had to hold his breath to keep from upending the meager contents of his stomach.

Soon enough, he heard his pursuer turn into the alley, and Auberon pulled the dagger from the sheath at his hip. He waited until the man had almost passed him, then lunged, shoving him up against the wall. The edge of his blade dug into the man's throat.

"Who sent you?" Auberon snarled. It was dark, but he could make out the fact that the man had an unremarkable face, with fair skin, thick brows, and a clean-shaven jaw. He wore plain black clothing, without a single mark that might betray his identity. "Who ordered you to follow me?"

The man brought his knee up into Auberon's groin, then rammed his fist into Auberon's stomach as he doubled over. Searing pain ignited within him. He had enough presence of mind through the alcohol and the pain to lash out with his dagger, catching the man's upper arm with the edge of his blade.

His pursuer hissed an expletive and grabbed Auberon's wrist, wrenching it until the dagger slipped from his grasp and landed somewhere amidst the puddles of foul-smelling liquid at their feet. With almost comical ease, the man shoved him into the wall of the alleyway and knotted his fingers in Auberon's hair, pressing his face into the rough stone. Auberon squeezed his eyes shut, grimacing at the scrape of the cold, dank stone against his cheek, and spat a string of oaths. He should have been able to avoid that attack with ease. The whiskey must not have been as watered-down as he'd thought.

Drystan was going to be *furious*.

"Stay away from Lady Riona," the man hissed into his ear. "This is your one warning."

Auberon would have come up with a sharp retort, if he weren't entirely focused on keeping the contents of his stomach *within* his stomach. Apparently satisfied, his pursuer released him, shoving him into the doorway where he'd originally hidden. Auberon caught his balance on the frame and turned just in time to see the man leave the alley. He didn't bother trying to follow him. There was no point.

His pursuer had been wearing plain, simple clothing, and his face had had no distinguishing scars or marks, but he had made the mistake of speaking. The man had softened his vowels and rounded his words, attempting to adopt a neutral Rivosi accent, but it hadn't fooled Auberon. After all his traveling, he had an ear for accents. The man who had pursued him was Kostori.

Prince Eamon had sent one of his guards to spy on him.

Chapter Thirty-Two
The Lady

"How can there be no news yet? The king's men have been searching for Faylen for weeks, and as far as I've been able to discern, they've gotten no closer to finding her," Riona said to Amaris and Prince Domhnall as they crossed the great hall, following the current of courtiers and advisors who were making their way toward the banquet hall.

Amaris shook her head. "I still can hardly believe what's happened. First Prince Auberon, then Cathal, and now that servant? And to think the guards have no leads! I know the circumstances are unusual, but one would expect that they'd have narrowed it down to a few suspects by now. What does Master Kaiden say, Domhnall?"

The prince ran a hand through his hair and let out a long, weary breath. "He's doing his best with what little information we have. The prostitute is missing, Treasurer Cathal's body and office have proved useless, and the search of that servant's body yielded no clues."

"Have they questioned the council members again?" Riona asked, thinking back to the suspicions Auberon had shared so many weeks ago. As unwilling as she was to believe one of the king's most trusted advisors—or, Creator forbid, the king himself

—was behind the murders, they had the most resources at their disposal to do so. "I thought you suspected one of them was working with Cathal to steal from the treasury."

"More accurately, I had a *hunch*, and I cannot go demanding the financial records of every member of the council without cause, as my father and Master Kaiden have both informed me," he huffed. "Until we have evidence of wrongdoing, my hands are tied."

"I just want this all to be over," Amaris said, slipping an arm around Domhall's waist and pulling him close. "I never expected Cathal to frequent a brothel, and that has somehow become one of the *lesser* revelations of the past few weeks. I'm eagerly awaiting the day the assassin is found and brought to justice."

Domhnall draped an arm over her shoulders. "The most important thing is finding Faylen."

"Finding her, or finding her body?"

His grave expression made it clear which answer he considered more likely. "Considering she was *in the room* with Cathal when he was killed, it's unlikely she managed to lose the assassin and flee the city. If she's alive, there's no reason why she wouldn't go to the guards for protection. She has no reason to hide."

Unless she knows something about the king or council that would warrant her death, a voice that sounded suspiciously like Auberon's whispered in Riona's mind.

They arrived at the banquet hall just then, sparing Riona from having to respond. She followed Amaris and Domhnall to the dais, where her father and the king were already standing, speaking with their heads bent and voices low. A flash of movement caught her eye—Duke Valerian leading the suitors into the hall. When their eyes met, his expression brightened. She started to smile, but faltered when she saw Auberon file into the room behind him. The prince was dressed in his usual finery, but his cheek and the side of his forehead were scraped raw, shadowed with faint bruises. Even so, he offered the courtiers a polished smile as he crossed the room to greet some members of the council.

Prince Domhnall pulled out a chair for Riona, but she waved him away with an apologetic look. "Go ahead and take your seat. I'll be back shortly."

Before he could object, she rounded the head table and descended the steps of the dais, brushing aside the courtiers who tried to speak with her as she made her way toward Auberon. He was standing beside one of the wide stone pillars, smirking as he wove some tale that made Lady Annabel and her husband chuckle.

"Don't worry about him, my lady," a voice said from somewhere to her right. Riona turned to find Prince Drystan approaching her, a goblet of wine in each hand. He offered her one, which she accepted with murmured thanks. "The fool had the excellent idea to overindulge in a tavern last night and brawl with someone on his way back to the castle this morning."

"Is he alright?" She knew Auberon frequented the taverns along the King's Road to provide a cover for his comings and goings, but as far as she knew, he had never gotten drunk. "Do you know with whom he fought?"

"Some man on the street. I don't think Auberon even got his name. From what he said, it sounded like nothing more than a drunken scuffle, and he swore that nothing more would come of it." Drystan shook his head in disappointment. "I want to assure you that it is not in his character to behave so poorly. Auberon can be...*impulsive*...but he is neither a drunkard nor a brawler. I hope you can forgive him. He is here as a representative of Erduria, and he has proven himself an embarrassment."

"We've all made mistakes, Your Highness. From the look of it, he's trying to earn your forgiveness by charming the court on your behalf," Riona said, watching him continue to chat with Annabel and her husband. Lord Farquar and Lord Tristan had joined their small group, along with Prince Eamon. Even though Auberon kept the crooked grin on his lips, Riona did not fail to notice the dark look he shot Eamon every time the opportunity presented itself.

Drystan nodded. "Yes, and it's hard to stay angry at him when he is so dedicated to his duty. I suspect he was feeling frustrated with the lack of progress in the negotiations, and he sought a reprieve. I can hardly blame him for that."

Riona took a drink of wine, savoring the taste of the spices on her tongue. "My uncle has been fighting your people since the day he was coronated. The war is all he has ever known. It is near impossible for him to see you as anything but the enemy."

Drystan took a half step closer, a grin on his lips and mischief in his eyes. At that moment, he looked so much like his brother that it made Riona's heart stutter. They didn't look as alike in appearance as she'd initially thought—she'd come to know them well enough to see that Drystan's hair lacked his brother's auburn strands, that his bone structure was softer and more refined, that his eyes had no hint of Auberon's blue—but his manner was entirely his brother's as he said, "And you, Lady Riona? Do you still think of us as your enemies?"

She held herself perfectly still, fighting the urge to glance at Auberon. A traitorous answer sprang to her lips, burning like a brand, but she refused to say it aloud. She certainly didn't trust Auberon, and she would never forgive Erduria for all that the Empire had taken from her and her family, but the past few weeks had changed the way she viewed the princes.

"I...don't know," Riona admitted. She was spared having to say more by the arrival of a fleet of servants from the kitchen, carrying platters of food and drink.

Drystan offered her his arm as the rest of the nobles and royals began taking their seats. "Well, I'm glad to hear that your answer isn't an outright yes. Perhaps there is hope for us yet."

Riona merely nodded, uncertain how to respond. As they walked the length of the room and climbed the steps of the dais, her fingers drifted up to the eudorite pendant at her throat. How could she speak and laugh with the Erdurian princes, knowing that their navy had sent her mother's ship to the depths of the Tranquil Sea? Knowing that their father likely ordered the breach in the laws of neutrality? Guilt sank its claws into her heart as Drystan guided her to the head table and pulled out her seat for her. She sat and forced a small, grateful smile.

"I would be honored if you would grant me the first dance tonight, Lady Riona," Prince Drystan said. "Allow me to give the court something to talk about besides my brother's less than regal appearance."

"Of course, Your Highness. I look forward to it."

Her father leaned over as Prince Drystan rounded the table and sat in his assigned place. "It looks like you're starting to come around to the idea of marrying one of the suitors," he whispered. "I'm glad to see it, my love."

"Do not mistake kindness for acceptance," she responded as servants began setting plates down along the length of the table. "I would sooner die than marry an Erdurian."

Her father flinched. "In all likelihood, you will not be forced into marriage with Prince Drystan. Your uncle doesn't trust them. As desperately as I would like to see the war ended peacefully, I would do anything to avoid sending my only daughter into that den of vipers Emperor Hyperion calls a court. I nearly lost you to Nicholas Comyn's cutthroat court, and I will not lose you to another."

The musicians began to play, and they shifted to lighter topics as servants moved throughout the room, setting down plates and goblets of wine. Riona half-listened to the suitors' conversation as she ate, watching out of the corner of her eye for a glimpse of Aeron. She hadn't seen the elf at all over the past several days, and she wanted to find out if he or any of her other helpers had gotten any closer to discovering Faylen's whereabouts.

It felt like an eternity passed before the meal drew to a close. She ate and chatted with Eamon and the others, forcing a smile, forcing a laugh, all while waiting for a glimpse of Aeron. A few of the servants in the banquet hall wore markers of loyalty to her, but she couldn't risk asking them about the missing prostitute within earshot of the suitors and the royal family.

"You look troubled, my lady," Prince Drystan murmured as they danced, his hand resting on the curve of her waist. "What's wrong?"

"Nothing. Everything's fine."

He raised a brow. "I may not have my brother's knack for reading people, but even I know that was a lie. Is it to do with our conversation earlier? I'm sorry if my mention of the war upset you. You have lost more than most to the fighting, and I should have spoken with more tact."

"No, it's not that. It's...everything."

As the prince turned her under his arm, Riona's eyes met her uncle's. He was still sitting at the center of the head table beside the queen, and the dispassionate way he was studying them sent a chill down her spine. *Is Auberon right?* she wanted to ask him, hating that the prince's suspicions had dug their way under her skin. *Do you know the truth about Cathal's murder?* She didn't want to believe that her uncle was responsible for the murder of the Treasurer and the servant, but how else could one explain the fact that the guards had found *nothing* in the weeks since the first banquet? Who else would have had the power to terrify Cathal into attempting to flee the city? Why wouldn't he have gone to the king for protection?

She turned back to Drystan. "I'm not sure who I can trust anymore."

The prince's gaze drifted to the king. "Then you are wiser than you know, my lady."

Chapter Thirty-Three
The Liar

Auberon stood with a group of council members, idly swirling his wine as he feigned interest in a story Lady Annabel was telling—something about an intimate relationship between one of the minor noblemen and a kitchen scullion. Across the banquet hall, Riona and Drystan were dancing together to the delight of the nobles crowded around them. They both wore smiles, but neither seemed particularly happy. Auberon knew the feeling well. He'd been in a foul mood since Eamon's lackey accosted him that morning. If Walther were here, he would have reprimanded him for his carelessness and stupidity until he was blue in the face. Drystan had done an admirable job of it in the spy's absence. Even now, Auberon could see the anger simmering beneath Drystan's polished smile.

His attention slid to the Kostori prince, who was speaking with Prince Domhnall and Duke Valerian near the head table. He hadn't told Drystan that Eamon had been behind the fight this morning, or that someone had been following him; all he had admitted to was getting into a drunken brawl. If he'd told the truth, Drystan would have insisted on confronting the prince, which Auberon most certainly did *not* want to do. Eamon believed he had the upper hand, which meant that Auberon could have some fun tonight.

Earlier, in the height of his anger, he had wanted to use the same trick he'd done the night of the first banquet, when he'd slipped diluted gloriosa tansy into the council members' wine. It wouldn't be strong enough to affect the prince's health, but it would render him exceptionally obnoxious—even more so than he was on a day-to-day basis. But Auberon had discarded the idea not long after it occurred to him. He wanted Eamon fully in command of his faculties. He wanted the bastard to watch the tide of the court's favor turn against him.

"Do you know why I loathe the Kostori prince?" he suddenly asked, drawing the attention of the council members around him. Lady Annabel, Lord Winslow, and Lord Tristan turned, the mirth fading from their faces at the sight of his dark expression. "I have a great many reasons—more than I could share tonight— but my main problem is that he has no qualms with the Kostori's barbaric practice of keeping slaves."

"Yes, we're well aware of that, Your Highness," Lord Tristan said, looking uncomfortable with the direction the conversation had taken. "It's an appalling thing, slavery. We've raised our concerns with the king on that front, but it is His Majesty's decision whether or not to enter into an alliance with the Kostori. He will do what he believes is best for Rivosa and her people."

"Will he demand the liberation of the slaves as a condition of the alliance?"

"He could certainly try, but it's unlikely that King Jericho or his son would agree to it. As horrible as the practice is, their country has been built on the backs of slaves, and they are set in their ways."

"Set in their ways? If we did not try to change things, my lord, we would never progress." Auberon turned to Lord Winslow. "Have you not considered what it would be like for Lady Riona to marry Prince Eamon and adopt his kingdom as her home? Do you want her to become queen to an enslaved people?"

A shadow passed across Lord Winslow's face. "Of course not. If it were up to me, Prince Eamon would have never received an invitation to come to Innislee."

Good, Auberon thought, hearing the fierce protectiveness in the lord's voice. Lord Winslow and Lord Lachlan were close—he had seen them talking often at the banquets, and he could tell by the way that Lord Winslow spoke that he cared for Riona. That was one council member he didn't have to bother turning against Kostos.

To Lady Annabel and Lord Tristan, he said, "And you, of course, must agree with him. We've all heard how the tensions between the humans and elves progressed in Beltharos over the last twenty years. First, the king's elven mistress is murdered, then Cirisians march to war to free their brethren, and then King Tamriel is deposed for his sympathy for the slaves. Who is to say something similar will not happen to Lady Riona if she is married to Prince Eamon?" Auberon asked, a thread of fear unfurling within him at the thought. "What will she do when she becomes their queen? Either she remains silent and allows her subjects to suffer, or she voices her opposition and paints a target on her back."

Concern flashed across Annabel's face, but Lord Tristan merely waved a hand in dismissal. "What she does is her own business. If they are married, her safety will be the concern of her husband and his royal guards, not ours. She will obey him if she knows what's best for her."

Anger rushed over Auberon at the lord's blatant lack of concern for Riona, but he was careful to keep his expression neutral. As Riona had said, most of the advisors had only ever treated her like a prize to be trotted out at court events and state functions. The thought infuriated him.

"Perhaps she will, and perhaps she will not," Auberon said, "but judging from what I know of her actions during the

Belthran civil war, she doesn't seem like the type to sit quietly and say nothing while her people are being mistreated. She will do what is right, regardless of the risk it may pose to her safety."

Annabel's brows rose, and she glanced sidelong at Lord Winslow. "I wasn't aware you were so well acquainted with our Lady Riona, Your Highness. You speak very highly of her."

"I'm only repeating what my brother has told me," he responded smoothly. "My point was simply that you cannot maintain a marriage alliance with a country if the bride gets herself killed."

"And we cannot demand that Kostos free its slaves without risking war, Your Highness," Lord Tristan cut in. "Anyway, we are debating hypotheticals and discussing politics when we should be enjoying the banquet. If you will excuse me..."

The lord started to leave, but Auberon's response halted him before he could take more than two steps.

"I saw a young girl being whipped in the square before the castle for stealing a roasted chicken from her master's kitchen," he said. "She couldn't have been more than eight years old, and she was so thin that one could see her ribs through her threadbare tunic. Her crime was presented before the court and King Jericho passed his judgment. Do you know what that monster did to her?"

Lord Tristan turned back, opening his mouth to answer, but Auberon cut him off before he could speak.

"Because she ran from the guards, he had her feet lashed until the soles were bloody ribbons of flesh. Because she stole, he had her pinkies cut off so all who saw her would know she was a thief. And because she would not stop crying as her punishment was meted out, he had her gagged and bound to a post in the square for all to watch her humiliation as she was whipped."

Lady Annabel's face turned a ghastly shade of white, and she reached out to Lord Winslow for support. "He did that to a *child?*"

"Don't listen to him, Annabel," Tristan snapped. "He's

Erdurian, and he will say anything to better his brother's position in the negotiations. If this story were true, he would have told it to the entire court his first night here."

"I don't blame sons for their fathers' crimes," Auberon retorted, "no matter how terrible. I had hoped that time away from that monster would do Prince Eamon some good, but he has proved himself to be just as despicable a man as the one who sired him. If you allow Lady Riona to be married to Prince Eamon, you will send her to her death. When she sees the way slaves are treated in Kostos, she will not be able to, as you said, *hold her tongue*."

Lord Tristan scoffed. "As you stated, a son is not responsible for his father's crimes. Even if this were true, Prince Eamon is not at fault."

Auberon shook his head, his already foul mood darkening at the memory of that terrible day. The young girl's cries echoed in his ears, thick with pain and terror. He would never forget the impassive way King Jericho and Prince Eamon had looked on as the girl sobbed and begged for mercy. Auberon had already hated the Kostori by then, but at that moment, he had vowed that he would someday bury a dagger into those monsters' black hearts.

"Perhaps in the girl's punishment, that is true," Auberon said. "But if you doubt the truth, ask Prince Eamon about it. Ask him if he remembers the boy who ran out of the crowd and grabbed the whip from the guard's hand. Ask him if he remembers sentencing that boy to thirty lashes for his compassion."

Lady Annabel lifted a hand to her mouth, tears welling in her eyes. "I... I'm sorry, I cannot listen to more of this. I had heard some of the stories from Kostos, but I didn't know Prince Eamon was as cruel as his father. Tomorrow, I will find out if the king knows anything about this. Lord Winslow, will you help me find my husband? I think it's best I go home now."

Lord Winslow nodded and slipped an arm around her waist, allowing her to lean against him. "Of course, my lady. Goodnight, Your Highness. Lord Tristan. We will continue this discussion at a later time."

They wandered off, and as soon as they were out of earshot, Lord Tristan leaned in close. "Your clever words may be working on some of the weaker members of the council, Your Highness, but I see through this little game you're playing. I may not care for Prince Eamon or his country, but I don't trust Erdurians. Deceit is in your blood."

Auberon smiled. "Ask Eamon about that boy. Then you shall see whether I am lying."

Chapter Thirty-Four
The Lady

Something changed over the course of the banquet. It hadn't been immediate, but by the time the night started to draw to a close, it felt as if all the air had been sucked out of the room. On the surface, everything looked the same—the courtiers milled about in their small groups, the servants cleared away the goblets of wine, and the musicians played a lively melody —but the tension settled around her like a too-tight bodice. Riona finished her dance with Duke Valerian, dipped into a curtsy, and then joined Amaris and Prince Domhnall where they stood at the rear of the room, near the platform where the musicians sat.

"What happened?" she whispered. "Did I miss something? It feels like the moment before a storm breaks out."

Amaris slipped an arm through hers and drew her close. "Apparently, Prince Auberon has leveled a rather weighty accusation against Prince Eamon. He told some of the council members about the horrible mistreatment of a Kostori slave and alleged that Prince Eamon sentenced a boy who tried to protect the child to thirty lashes. He says he witnessed it all, but Prince Eamon denies it outright."

Riona's stomach twisted. She didn't know much about the

Kostori treatment of slaves, but she had been a hostage in Beltharos and seen the depth of their hatred for elven slaves. She had watched Nicholas Comyn beat his own nephew for daring to help a handful of slaves escape their chains. If the two countries were at all similar in their mistreatment of the slaves, she could only imagine the poor elf's punishment. "And is what Prince Auberon says true?"

"I don't know. I won't deny that I don't care much for the Kostori prince, but I also know better than to take the Erdurians at their word. The suitors are here to win your hand. They will say anything to put the others down."

"I think Amaris is right. It's a lie," Domhnall said, scowling. "Prince Eamon is the most likely candidate for your hand, and Prince Auberon feels threatened by that fact. He knew that appealing to our sympathies for slaves would win him and his brother some favor in the court."

"So now the courtiers are taking sides," Riona guessed.

"Precisely."

She shook her head. All this politicking would be useless if she managed to find Cathal's killer and prove her worth to her uncle. As she thought it, her gaze snagged on one of the elven servants, and she realized that she still had yet to see Aeron. She turned back to Amaris and Domhnall. "If you'll excuse me, I need some fresh air. I'll be back in time to bid everyone goodnight."

Before they could respond, Riona slipped her arm out of Amaris's and left the banquet hall. As soon as she passed through the grand double doors, she let out a breath of relief. The tension that had settled on her chest eased with every step she took away from the banquet.

Riona started down the corridor, hoping to find Aeron, Ophelia, or one of the other servants who acted as her eyes and ears in the castle. She was just about to turn the corner when she heard someone in the next hall call out, "Leaving so soon, Your

Highness? Why not stay and enjoy the celebration? You did, after all, turn it into quite the interesting affair."

Riona slowed, recognizing Prince Eamon's voice. When no response came, she pulled off her heels and crept forward on silent feet, peering around the corner. Auberon was stalking down an empty, rarely-used corridor with his back to her, anger evident in the tight line of his broad shoulders. Prince Eamon stood in the center of the hall behind him, watching the prince walk away, his arms crossed loosely over his chest. From his stance, he looked almost *amused*.

"I know you're bitter over the fact that despite your best efforts, your brother will *still* lose Lady Riona's hand in marriage," Prince Eamon continued. "No matter what lies you tell the court, it won't change the fact that I will win the betrothal. Valerian is weak and powerless, and your father has spent his life making Rivosa his enemy. You can try to turn the council against me all you like. It'll make it even more embarrassing for the mighty princes of Erduria when you lose."

"They aren't lies, Eamon," Auberon said, his voice surprisingly calm. He continued to walk away. "Sooner or later, the Rivosi court is going to see you for the snake you are."

Prince Eamon shook his head, clicking his tongue as if he were reprimanding a child. "So much anger. Why do you care so much about your enemy's niece? You see, I think you've failed your brother so you can keep Lady Riona all to yourself."

The prince kept walking, saying nothing.

"What do you do with her all those nights in the Royal Theater, Auberon? Do you kiss her? Do you *fuck* her?"

Auberon went still. Riona's mouth dropped open, and she set a hand on the wall beside her, willing herself to simply stand and watch. She waited to see how the prince would respond. Auberon's fingers curled into fists at his sides, but still, he kept his back to Eamon. She would have given anything to see the look on his face at that moment.

"I've been silent thus far to avoid shaming Lady Riona in

front of the court, but how do you think the king will react when I tell him what you've done? You and your brother will be cast out in disgrace, with no hope of ever achieving peace. Don't worry—Riona's secret will be safe with me. I am gracious enough to marry her, sullied or unsullied." Eamon lowered his voice, his words dripping with arrogance. "Let us just hope that you have not put an Erdurian-blooded bastard into her, hm? Or else the palace in Torch will receive a rather unwelcome delivery in about nine months' time."

Auberon turned, strode to the prince, and punched him in the face.

Eamon reeled back, a hand flying up to his cheek. "Erdurian snake!" he spat, launching himself at Auberon.

"Kostori filth."

Eamon swung a fist, but Auberon caught the prince's wrist and twisted it behind him, slamming Eamon into the wall. "Speak one more word against her," he snarled, his face contorted in fury, "and I will cut out your tongue and feed it to you."

"You wouldn't dare."

"Try me."

Riona smoothed her features into a cool mask and stepped around the corner. Both men froze when they saw her, and she graced them with a smile that promised she had heard every word of their exchange.

"How nice it is to hear that you are concerned about my honor, Prince Eamon," she said as she approached, savoring the fear that flashed through the Kostori prince's eyes. "You'll have to take my word that I am, to use your own phrasing, *unsullied*. Unless you propose that I spread my legs so you can check?"

"No, my lady," Eamon blurted, horrified. "That's not what I meant at all."

"Then I would advise you to keep your concerns about my virtue to yourself. Have I made myself clear?"

"Yes, Lady Riona."

"Good. Prince Auberon, you may release him."

Auberon begrudgingly let go and took several steps back, although his icy glare never left Eamon. A bruise was already discoloring the prince's cheek. In an effort to appear unruffled, Eamon straightened his doublet and ran a hand through his hair, shooting a hateful look at Auberon.

"If the story that Prince Auberon shared with the court wasn't enough to turn their favor against you, Your Highness," Riona continued, "your behavior tonight certainly is. Go to your guest house and tend to that bruise. We shall see in the morning if the king still deems you worthy of a place here in Innislee."

"My lady, I did none of the things of which he has accused me. I am sorry for allowing my anger to get the better of me, but I will not tolerate slander against me and my kingdom."

"And yet you felt it appropriate to accuse Prince Auberon and me of an intimate affair," she snapped, allowing her anger to bleed into her voice. "Watch your step, Prince Eamon. I may be too much of a lady to resort to threats, but the next time you make speculations about my private life, I may not be there to keep Prince Auberon from following through on his."

Another flicker of fear passed across Eamon's face, and he dropped into a low bow. "Of course, you're right. I beg your forgiveness, my lady."

"Then I suggest you demonstrate you are worthy of it. Leave us."

Surprise, anger, and indignation flashed across Eamon's face, but he merely straightened and murmured a farewell before making his escape. As soon as he turned the corner, Auberon leaned against the wall and crossed one leg over the other. He frowned as he examined his knuckles. "Perhaps punching Eamon in the face wasn't the wisest thing I could have done in that situation, but it *was* the most satisfying."

Riona walked toward him and took his hand, frowning as she studied the bruises already forming on the ridges of his knuckles. "Is there any truth to the story you told the court?"

"Have you ever known me to lie, Lady Riona?" he asked, one

corner of his mouth rising into a smirk. "You can stop fussing over my hand. I've suffered much greater wounds than a few bruises, and I have a feeling I'll suffer a few more where you and Prince Eamon are concerned."

She released him and took a step back. "Thank you for defending my honor."

"You're welcome. I'd marry Eamon myself before I ever allowed him to speak one word against you."

Although anger still blazed in Auberon's eyes, there was a flicker of something deeper there, too—something that caused Riona's pulse to stutter. She looked away, telling herself she'd imagined it. "How does Prince Eamon know that we've been meeting in the Royal Theater? Aeron didn't tell him, if that's what you suspect."

"I know he didn't. Eamon had me followed," Auberon said, his tone laced with frustration. He rubbed the back of his neck and muttered a string of oaths under his breath. "I should have realized it sooner. I was...distracted this morning, and his spy caught me by surprise."

"Is that why you told the court about the slave? You wanted to get back at him?" she asked. "Now he'll tell the whole court that you and I have been sleeping together!"

"He won't say a word. He's a coward and a snake, but he won't insult you and your king by tarnishing your reputation. He only hoped to scare me into silence. Since it didn't work, he's going to slink off to his chambers and nurse his wounded pride."

Before she could say a word, Auberon pushed off the wall, stalking forward until they stood almost nose-to-nose. Riona sucked in a breath at his sudden proximity.

"One would think that if he did speak, you would be relieved, if not grateful, *aramati*," the prince said, his voice icy. "You promised me that if I helped you, you would speak to your uncle on Drystan's behalf. Do you think I haven't realized that you're just biding your time and hoping to find a way to avoid an arranged marriage? Well, Eamon has just handed you the way out.

You could have simply wandered into the nearest brothel and had your pick of the whores, but sleeping with an Erdurian prince—and not the one who came for your hand in marriage—would be unforgivable in the eyes of the court. You'd be free."

Riona seethed, insulted that he would think her so shallow. "If I were to find a way out, it would be on the merit of what is between my ears, not what is between my legs."

"Ah, I see. You're a noble with principles."

Her hands curled into fists at his mocking tone. "One of us has to have them."

"Might I remind you that *I'm* not the one whose uncle is trying to sell her off to a stranger?" Auberon stepped closer, forcing her backward until she was pinned against the wall. He braced one hand on either side of her head. His expression hardened, his blue-gray eyes as deep and cold as the Tranquil Sea. "One word from me could launch a thousand warships. One word could send soldiers into this very city to claim you for my brother, since he was too kindhearted to demand the marriage after my poisoning. What could you do to stop it? Tell me, what use are principles when one is powerless?"

Riona glared up at him. "When one has lost everything, principles are all we have left."

"And what do you do when even those have been stripped from you?" Auberon asked. He dipped his head and whispered in her ear, his breath soft against her neck, "What do you do when everything that made you who you are has been destroyed?"

"Are we still talking about me, Your Highness, or you?"

Auberon stilled. His head was bent so she couldn't make out his expression, but Riona saw the way tension corded through his shoulders just before he pushed off the wall and turned his back on her. "You should return to the banquet hall before someone comes looking for you. We wouldn't want to add fuel to any rumors that may arise in the coming weeks."

Riona nodded, seeing that he did not want to continue down the path their conversation had taken. He stood facing away from her, watching the flames from torches along the walls crackle and dance. His hands curled into fists at his sides. Part of her wanted to ask what was bothering him, what he'd almost admitted, but she could tell by the way he held himself that he was waiting for her to leave.

"Goodnight, Your Highness," she said softly as she walked away.

Auberon didn't try to stop her.

Chapter Thirty-Five
The Liar

By the Creator, he'd wanted to stop her.

Every step she took away from him, every sharp click of her heels against the stone, sent another dagger through his heart. When the sound of her footsteps finally faded, Auberon slumped against the wall and buried his face in his hands. A small flare of pain shot through his cheek when his fingers brushed the shallow cuts the alley wall had left in his skin. He shouldn't have come to the banquet. He had managed to do nothing except shatter whatever fragile trust he'd built with Riona. *Why* had he pressed her on the matter of the arranged marriage? Why had he taunted her about her principles, when they were what he admired most about her? Why had he insisted on making such a monumental ass of himself?

Auberon flexed his right hand, the tender bruises across his knuckles aching. He knew why he had pushed her. Watching her paste that practiced smile on her lips and dance with the suitors night after night bothered him almost as much as the advisors' dismissal of her. Riona had been a vision as she strode down the hall, rage pouring off her as she glared at Eamon. He always enjoyed fracturing her careful façade with his mocking quips and pointed comments when they met in the Royal Theater, but she still played the obedient little noblewoman before the courtiers. It infuriated him. If she wanted to, she could bring the whole court to its knees.

Eventually, she would have to accept the fact that her scheming would not save her from an arranged marriage. They had already spent over two weeks searching for Faylen, and they had come up empty-handed. In truth, Auberon only cared about finding Cathal's killer because he'd thought it would lead him to information about the mines. It was time to take another route. He had to convince Riona to persuade her uncle to accept the alliance with the Empire. Her resistance cost both their countries more lives every single day. It would be easier for them all if she stopped delaying the inevitable and accepted the future that lay before her.

If he had to play the villain in order to make that happen, so be it.

Auberon composed himself and returned to the banquet hall, where the night's festivities had just ended. Most of the nobles had left already, and servants bustled around the room, clearing goblets of wine and decorations from the long tables. Riona stood before the dais steps with the king and the rest of her family, speaking with Lord Winslow and Duke Valerian. Drystan was making his way toward them, but he stopped and changed course when he spotted Auberon. They met just inside the banquet hall's double doors.

"Where have you been?"

"Oh, I just stepped outside to have a little discussion with Eamon. He's not too happy with me at the moment, I'm sorry to say, but who can blame him?"

Drystan nodded, smirking. "You dealt him a heavy blow tonight. Good work. He can deny the story all he likes, but even those here in Rivosa have heard tales of the slaves' mistreatment in Kostos. It makes Beltharos look like a paradise in comparison."

"Exactly," Auberon responded, too weary to savor the praise. "Keep reminding the council members of the Kostori brutality—

and Lady Riona's sympathy for the slaves—and hopefully they'll convince the king to reject an alliance. King Domhnall can't risk turning his niece into a martyr."

"You don't fear retribution from Eamon?" Drystan asked, his brows furrowing with concern. "The prince is a proud man, and he won't take kindly to what you've done. And for future reference, I'd like to be warned the next time you turn an evening with the court into a battle."

"We're in Rivosa. Every evening with the court is a battle."

He let out a soft, humorless laugh. "I suppose you're right about that."

"As for Eamon, we don't have any reason to worry right now. He may be proud, but he is also a coward. He'll find some way to repay me, I'm sure of it, but right now he's more concerned about the blow to his ego."

"To his *ego?* Not to his standing in the negotiations?" Drystan examined him with a wary look. "What precisely happened between you during your little chat?"

Auberon set a hand on Drystan's shoulder and propelled him toward the dais. "Nothing that concerns you. Just worry about the negotiations with the king, and leave the other suitors to me."

Across the room, the royal family was bidding goodnight and farewell to the few remaining courtiers. Riona stood at the end of the line, smiling as she spoke with Duke Valerian. He said something that made her laugh, and she tapped on Amaris's arm to draw her into their conversation, leaning in close to whisper the duke's joke into the girl's ear. Amaris chuckled, shooting Valerian a wicked grin.

The second Riona noticed Auberon and Drystan making their way toward her, the humor on her face faded. She kept the smile on her lips as they exchanged farewells with her, Amaris, and Valerian. Yet Auberon could still feel the anger pouring from her in waves. Once the others had moved on to speak with Lord Lachlan and the royal family, Auberon stepped close and murmured, "Think on what I said earlier. You can allow the court to continue to treat you like a pawn and marry you off to the man your uncle chooses, or you can take charge of your future and convince him to pick Drystan. End this war and save countless lives."

"I will counsel him toward peace for the sake of my people, but I will *never* marry an Erdurian."

Auberon shook his head. If she wanted to cling to her deluded belief that finding Cathal's killer would spare her from a political marriage, so be it. They had been working together for weeks and had nothing to show for it. He would find proof of the eudorite mines himself. "Then consider our partnership over, my lady."

He dropped into a low bow and moved down the line to say farewell to the royal family. The entire time, he felt the weight of Riona's glare on his back. She hated him. So be it. They were enemies, and over the past few weeks, they had made the mistake of allowing themselves to believe they could ever be anything more than that. Auberon would not relent until the king accepted the marriage alliance—not only because he had been ordered to do it, but because Drystan was enchanted by Riona. They were perfectly suited to each other: intelligent, regal, poised, and they each knew how to walk the line between diplomacy and cutting, brutal truth.

Whether she would admit it or not, Riona could never be happy spending her life chained to her uncle's court. Even if she somehow managed to convince the king to give her a place on his council, he and the advisors would only ever see her as the powerless little girl she'd once been. Rivosa was too small, too inconsequential, for her. She belonged in Erduria. She belonged on the Empire's throne.

Chapter Thirty-Six
The Lady

The second the banquet hall doors swung shut, Riona turned to the king and queen. "Inviting the suitors here for the negotiations seemed like a good idea at the time," she said, "but this cannot possibly end well. Duke Valerian and Prince Eamon already hated each other, and now Eamon and Auberon are one smart comment away from slitting the other's throat."

"I agree with my daughter on this, Domhnall," her father said, moving to her side. "Is gaining better terms worth destroying the relations of all these countries? We cannot survive without allies, and we certainly cannot demand the respect of our court if we turn every banquet into a damned spectacle."

"*We* did not do anything," King Domhnall replied. "The fault lies with Auberon and Eamon. They are allowing their emotions to get the better of them. Still, I agree with you. It would be wise to give them some time away from the court to relieve the tension. We'll cancel the banquet tomorrow and dine in private."

The queen shook her head. "They're each trying to one-up the others and win your favor. They'll do it regardless of whether the rest of the nobility is there because your opinion is the only one that matters. As long as there is an opportunity to score points, they will be at each other's throats."

"We'd be better off sending them home with our apologies and arranging alliances via emissary," Riona said.

"No. They're here now, and we have invested too much time and money into this to send them home without some sort of resolution. Besides, negotiations like these are better done in person. Communication takes much too long between the northern and southern continents."

"Then at least send the Erdurian princes back," Riona insisted. "They're more trouble than they're worth, and anyone can see that you only keep them around to pressure Prince Eamon and Duke Valerian into offering better terms."

With Auberon and Drystan gone and Valerian potentially able to garner support from Beltharos, that would only leave her Eamon to contend with. She considered revealing the vile things Eamon had said in the hall earlier, but decided to hold her tongue. She still didn't know what her uncle hoped to gain from an alliance with Kostos, and she doubted a few crass remarks would do much to harm Eamon's chances at an alliance.

"We can't send them home," Prince Domhnall interjected, his fingers laced through Amaris's. "Father, I know you don't trust them after everything that has happened, but the Empire has lost much to the war, as well. Prince Auberon and Prince Drystan came asking for a peace treaty, and I must insist again that you accept. Amaris and I will one day rule this kingdom, and we have no intention of dragging out this war any longer than necessary. Think about our future."

"That is *all* I think about," the king responded. "At my coronation, I swore a vow to protect my subjects. I will not bow to Erduria. I cannot risk Rivosa's security. You saw how Prince Auberon turned half of the court against the other with a few clever words. Do you truly believe that Emperor Hyperion would not use tricks like that to expand his influence into our kingdom?"

"So what will we do?" Riona's father asked, shooting a warning look at a group of servants who had paused to listen in on their conversation. Their cheeks flushed crimson as they bowed and rushed off to attend to their duties. "If we cannot narrow the pool and cannot arrange a betrothal via emissary, what happens now?"

"The suitors need some time to cool down," the queen said. "The cooks can deliver their dinners to the guest houses tomorrow night, and we'll simply have to apologize for the change of plans. I'm sure they will understand."

"We should have a public outing," Riona cut in, an idea striking her. "A performance at the Royal Theater. That way, they will be forced to behave themselves, and they won't be caught up in trying to top the others. It'll be nice for them to get out of the confines of the castle."

Queen Blair smiled. "Excellent idea, my love. Domhnall?"

The king nodded. "I agree. In the morning, I'll send word to the owner of the Theater letting her know that we will be using our private box."

"There's no need. I'll do it," Riona said. She was still furious with Auberon for what he'd said earlier, but she owed him for helping her these past two weeks, and this was how she would repay him.

"Thank you, my dear."

She curtsied and bade them goodnight. Together, she, her father, and Amaris made their way to the gatehouse, where her father called for a carriage to take them home. None of them spoke as the wooden wheels clattered and bounced over the uneven cobbles, each mulling over the events of the night. It was Amaris who finally broke the silence.

"I hope you marry Duke Valerian," she said quietly, the light of the streetlamps playing across her face as she stared out the window. "He seems like a good man."

"He does," Riona agreed. "And he deserves a wife who will love him."

Her father studied her for several long moments, his expression unreadable. "Are you so certain you cannot be that wife?"

"I do not intend to find out. With any of the suitors."

He fixed her with an exasperated look. "My love, I wish you could stay here and serve on the council, but that is not the fate the Creator has given you. You will marry one of the suitors, and it is time you accepted that. I don't want to hear another word to the contrary. Have I made myself clear?"

"But—"

"You are a grown woman, Riona," he said, his patience beginning to fray. "You know the cost of the royal blood in your veins. You know the sacrifices our kingdom demands of us. I am sorry to have to speak so harshly, but you must give up this foolish notion of staying in Innislee. It is over. Your uncle plans to select a suitor in one week's time."

Chapter Thirty-Seven
The Liar

The next day, Auberon followed Drystan toward the Royal Theater's open doors, struck by how strange it felt to see the building in use. Instead of the lone few candles to which he'd grown accustomed, every chandelier in the foyer was lit, filling the room with warm golden light. Nobles milled about, each clad in a form-fitting gown or a fine doublet and coat. At a command from a royal guard, they parted to clear a wide path to the base of the theater's grand staircase, dropping into bows and curtsies.

The king and his wife led the procession through the foyer, trailed by Prince Domhnall and his young siblings. Next came Amaris, Riona, and her father, then the suitors. The respect with which the court regarded Duke Valerian didn't escape Auberon's notice. Riona's charitable little excursions had won him the hearts of the people, poor and rich alike. Still, it wasn't terribly concerning. Popularity couldn't make up for the fact that the Duchy of Kenter had little to offer King Domhnall. Plus, he rather enjoyed seeing how the duke's favor grated on Eamon—the latter of whom had managed to secure some sort of cosmetic to cover the dark bruise blossoming across his cheek.

Of their own accord, Auberon's eyes drifted to Riona, and

his chest tightened as he watched her climb the stairs beside her father. She looked resplendent in a floor-length gown of midnight blue silk. The cut of the bodice left her entire back bare, revealing lithe muscle and perfect ebony skin. Her braids were twisted and piled atop her head, and sapphires dripped from her earlobes. Auberon hadn't thought she could look more beautiful than she had at that first banquet, but he'd been wrong. Every time he looked at her, she took his breath away.

The royal guards led them to the largest of the private balconies, where Valerian and Eamon claimed the seats on either side of Riona. Auberon sat beside Drystan and watched over the railing as eager patrons filed into the theater, chattering excitedly. Once they were all seated, theater attendants ran throughout the room, extinguishing the lanterns until the audience sat in a blanket of darkness. Gradually, a low, rolling melody filled the room. The curtains swept open, revealing a stage full of twisting, skeletal trees partially hidden behind a sheer wall of fabric.

Several elven women in silken gowns melted from the shadows. Their fair skin was painted an ethereal silver, and gossamer wings protruded from their backs. They spun and twisted through the fantastical forest like wraiths, their movements laced with the elves' fabled grace. Auberon's heart stuttered as realization swept over him. He hadn't recognized it at first, but he knew the song dancing on the air. It was the opening of his mother's favorite ballet. He should have realized it the second he saw the trees all those weeks ago, but he had never attended a performance before; he had only ever heard his mother play the music.

Something moved in his periphery. He looked over to find Riona watching him, studying his reaction. Had she arranged this? The outing to the theater had been a last-minute plan; he and Drystan had only received the invitation that morning. He thought back to all those nights he had slipped into the theater in secret. There had been no signs on the exterior announcing that they would be performing the ballet, which meant they must have been rehearsing for a future performance. Had Riona convinced the owner of the theater to put on a special show for the court?

A pang shot through his heart at the thought. She didn't owe him anything for all the nights they had spent in the theater. In truth, he had come to enjoy sneaking out and sparring with her more than he would ever dare to admit. The meaning of her gesture was clear enough: it was a goodbye, of a sort. He had ended their shaky alliance. Tonight would be their last night in the Royal Theater, and tomorrow, they would go their separate ways.

The end of the ballet was spectacular. The music swelled as the faerie queen cut down the last human soldier standing in her path. He crumpled, and she knelt beside him, removing the heavy golden amulet from around the man's neck. As she did, the music softened and stretched out to a low, mournful note that gradually faded into silence. Auberon held his breath as the drums began to pound a steady *thump, thump, thump*, like the pulse of a heart. The dancer held the amulet before her as if praying, her lips forming soundless words. Faeries slunk out of the shadows to gather around their queen, watching with astonishment as the sheer fabric hanging over the stage rippled, then fluttered to the ground. The magical barrier keeping them trapped in the forest had been broken.

Thump.

Thump.

Thump.

The faeries let out a jubilant shout and leapt from the stage, twisting and spinning down the aisles. Some even pulled nobles from their seats and drew them into their otherworldly dance, to the delight of the audience. Standing behind them, alone in the small clearing, the queen pressed a hand to her heart and swayed on her feet. The grip of her sword slipped through her fingers, and she collapsed beside the soldier she had killed.

The drums
thump...
thump...
thumped...
and fell silent.

As the curtains swung shut, Drystan and the others rose and applauded. Auberon barely registered it. The slow, steady beat of the drums rang in his ears as his hand wandered to his shoulder, where the warmth from Valerian's touch had once throbbed.

Oh, Creator...

He knew how the duke had healed him.

Theater attendants ran around the floor below, lighting the lanterns, and chatter filled the room as the nobles slowly filtered into the foyer. As someone turned up the lantern's flame in their private box, Auberon rose and walked over to where Valerian stood, speaking with Drystan and Lord Lachlan. He gripped the duke's arm and murmured, "Speak with me in private, right now."

Valerian barely spared him a glance. "Can't it wait until we return to the castle, Your Highness?"

"No."

At the blunt response, the duke turned, his polite smile fading when he saw the rage simmering in Auberon's eyes. "... Very well."

"Should I come?" Drystan asked. "You look a little pale, Auberon."

He heard the words Drystan didn't dare voice in front of Riona's father: *Do you need help?*

"No, I'm sure we won't be long."

Send a guard looking for me if I'm not back soon.

Drystan nodded, and Auberon pulled Valerian into the hall none too gently. He ignored the duke's objections—and the grumbling of the people he jostled—as he pushed through the crowded foyer and out the theater's doors. Several couples lingered just outside, chatting while they waited for their carriages, so Auberon dragged Valerian around the side of the theater, well out of earshot.

"That's enough," Valerian snapped, yanking his arm out of Auberon's grasp. "What in the Creator's name—"

"I know how you healed my lungs," Auberon spat, a black wave of fury swelling within him. "Blood magic."

Part Four
The Darkest Night

Chapter Thirty-Eight
The Liar

"Blood magic."

Valerian froze, and the words hung in the air for several heartbeats. In the darkness, Auberon couldn't make out his expression, but he would bet every gold regent he owned that it was *terrified*.

"That's how you did it, isn't it?"

"Don't be ridiculous."

Valerian started toward the front of the theater, but Auberon stepped into his path and pulled the dagger at his hip. "Oh, no. I'm not letting you go until you tell me *exactly* what I want to know. It's true, isn't it?" he demanded, his skin crawling with revulsion. "Those words you said in the infirmary—they were some sort of...spell or...incantation, weren't they?"

The accelerated healing. The guttural tongue. The pulsing heat. He should have put it together sooner, but he'd thought only elves could use blood magic. That was what the old folk tales claimed, at least. The truth must have been twisted over the generations, but he was certain of one thing: if King Domhnall learned that Valerian wielded blood magic, he would be banished to Kenter before the night was over.

"...Don't tell anyone," the duke breathed. The words came out soft, pleading—not at all how Auberon had expected. "I will answer all of your questions, but you must swear that you will not tell a soul what I've done. I helped you, and this is all I ask in return."

"Make your case."

"I healed you when I could have just as easily let you wallow in that cot for weeks," Valerian whispered. He cast a nervous glance toward the front of the theater to make sure none of the departing nobles would overhear their conversation. "It was a gamble, I know, but what I told you the day you were released from the infirmary was true. It's not likely that I'll win Lady Riona's hand, and I would rather see her married to your brother than Eamon. She deserves a better man than that snake. Please, Auberon, you must believe me."

"I must trust a man who dabbles in forbidden magic?" he scoffed. "Who else have you used your powers on? My guards had no recollection of you visiting me in the infirmary. How did you manage that?"

"An incantation that muddles memories."

"So why didn't you use it on me?"

"Your body was weak from the poison, and the healers' medicine had dulled your mind. I feared the side effects of tampering with your memory, and hoped I could rely on our mutual hatred of Eamon to keep you quiet," he said, his voice tight with desperation. "I know what you must be thinking, but even if I wanted to, I can't change people's thoughts or affect the outcome of the negotiations. What I did to you only increased the rate at which your body healed itself. I've never used the power on anyone else—I didn't know you'd feel that...pulsing, as you called it."

"So I was to be your *experiment?*"

Valerian began to pace, dragging a hand through his curls as his expression grew thoughtful. "It appears to be a mark of the magic, connecting us. Blood magic relies on the user's life force for power. It follows that if I were to die while you were healing, you'd stop receiving the benefits of the magic. I think that's what happened in Beltharos after that Cirisian elf died. The plague vanished, and the corpses she'd raised..." He tilted his head, considering. "Do you still feel it?"

"Is that really your concern right now?" Auberon snapped. "Blood magic is incredibly dangerous."

"So is the dagger in your hand, but it depends on the wielder whether it will be used for good or ill." The duke closed the distance between them and said, "Now, I will answer every question you have, but I don't like discussing this in the open. Auberon, I swear on my life, I have never and will never use my powers against anyone here. You have my word. Do I have yours that you will keep this between us?"

Auberon considered all that the duke had said, wary. There was nothing in Valerian's tone or demeanor that hinted that he was lying. More than anything, he seemed *scared.* The bookish young man standing before him was a far cry from the merciless, power-hungry blood mages from the folk stories. If Valerian had wanted Auberon dead, he could have killed him a dozen times over by now.

"You do," he responded, and the duke let out a relieved breath. "But your secret remains safe only as long as Riona and the rest of her family do, too. If I hear so much as a whisper of blood magic—"

"You won't. I wouldn't think of it," Valerian replied without hesitation, sounding horrified at the mere suggestion. "Come to my house later tonight, and I will explain everything in greater detail."

Auberon agreed, and they returned to the theater. The royal party and their contingent of guards were already waiting for them at the bottom of the grand staircase. As they crossed the foyer, Valerian glanced back, tensing almost imperceptibly—as if fearing that Auberon was going to open his mouth and reveal his secret to everyone. Auberon met his gaze and shook his head once. He had made a vow, and he would keep it until Valerian gave him reason not to.

A row of carriages emblazoned with the royal crest rolled up to the front of the theater, and they filed outside. King Domhnall and his family took one, Amaris, Riona, and her father took another, and the suitors claimed the third. Drystan lingered on the street beside Auberon while Eamon and Valerian climbed inside and took their seats.

"What were you two discussing?" he whispered.

"How best to keep Eamon from winning Lady Riona's hand in marriage."

Drystan raised a brow, skeptical. "Is that all? After the performance, you looked as if you'd seen a ghost."

"I was just struck with horror at the thought of anyone having to spend a lifetime with Eamon. It's not a fate I'd wish on my worst enemy." Auberon nodded to the carriage. "Don't worry about what we were discussing. Focus on wearing down King Domhnall and the council, and leave me to do what I do best."

"And have you made any progress with the mines?"

"Some," he responded. He had spent three weeks in this wretched kingdom, and he had nothing to show for it. Nothing save for a near-death experience and a few secret meetings in a dark theater. "Mostly speculation. I just hope I have enough time to find proof that they exist, otherwise this will all be for nothing."

Drystan clasped his shoulder comfortingly, then climbed inside, Auberon following close behind. The driver snapped his reins, and they started back toward the castle. A heavy silence settled over them. Valerian and Eamon were sharing the opposite bench, and each seemed to be doing everything in his power to pretend the other didn't exist.

When they arrived at the castle, Valerian climbed out of the carriage first and excused himself to retire to his rooms. Auberon made to follow Drystan through the portcullis, but Eamon stepped in front of him, stopping him in his tracks. In the moonlight, the prince's eyes were twin pools of darkness, cold and empty. "Your Highness, I was hoping we could finish last night's conversation on somewhat more *civilized* terms."

"That's an interesting suggestion. I didn't think you were even capable of such a thing."

A barbed smile cut across the prince's face. "You see, I realized that I don't have to say a word about your improper desires to the king and court if I wish to hurt you. I suspect it will be torturous enough for you to stand silent and watch Lady Riona be promised to one of us." He leaned in, lowering his voice. "Tell me the truth: have you fallen for the girl your brother wishes to marry? Do you lie awake at night, wishing you could steal her away for yourself?"

Auberon laughed. Over Eamon's shoulder, he saw Drystan turn around and start toward them, and he held up a hand to stop him. "No, I would never do that to Drystan. He is the sort of man Lady Riona deserves, not I." His voice turned icy as he drawled, "You have no reason to feel threatened by me, Eamon. You will lose Riona, and it will be no one's fault but your own."

He brushed past the prince and walked through the portcullis. Drystan fell into step beside him. "Need we be concerned about him?"

"Not at all."

Drystan didn't look convinced, but he nodded, and they continued through the castle buildings in silence. When they neared Valerian's guest house, Auberon said, "I must have a word with the duke. When you get back to the house, send some guards over here, but tell them they are not to come inside unless I give the command. Just have them stay within earshot."

"Is this something I should be concerned about?"

"Just a precaution."

"Then I will. Be careful."

Auberon grinned. "I always am."

He bade Drystan goodnight and approached the house in which Valerian was staying. The duke's guards were already waiting outside, which meant that they would be able to speak in total privacy. He knocked on the door, the sound jarring in the nighttime quiet. After a few seconds, the duke opened the door, a grim expression on his face. "Come inside, and I'll explain everything."

Chapter Thirty-Nine
The Lady

She had six days left to secure her freedom. Riona could think of nothing else as she walked into her bedroom and lit the candelabra on the vanity table, counting down yet another day that had yielded no answers in the search for Cathal's killer. There, propped against the polished metal mirror, sat an envelope with her name written in elegant cursive. Riona picked it up and flipped it over, her heart skipping a beat when she saw the Beltharan royal sigil imprinted in the wax seal. She broke it open and pulled out the heavy parchment, leaning close to the candelabra to read the lines of script across the paper. When she reached the end, she folded the letter, tucked it back into the envelope, and closed her eyes.

Tamriel and Mercy were glad to hear from her and sympathetic to Valerian's desire to win his country's independence, but their military was in no shape to provide aid. The wars that had plagued their kingdom over the past year had devastated the countryside and their people, and their focus was on rebuilding.

Riona dropped the envelope and rubbed her temples, fighting the wave of hopelessness swelling within her. In the last two months, she had been held hostage and sentenced to execution. She had defied a tyrant and given up the man she loved. She had vowed to find Cathal's killer and proved herself to be as useless as the council members had always believed.

She was a fool.

Something *plinked* against the window. Riona crossed the room and parted the curtains, her heart stuttering at the sight of the cloaked figure standing in the front garden. *Auberon?*

The figure pulled down his hood, and the moonlight struck his pointed ears. Aeron. As worried as she'd been for him, she couldn't deny the unwelcome stab of disappointment that struck her as she shut the curtains and moved to her wardrobe. Quickly, she changed from her gown to a black tunic and trousers, leather boots, and a cloak. Then she grabbed Auberon's dagger from under her pillow and strapped the sheath to her thigh.

She crept down the hall, hoping her father and Amaris were asleep. The house was still, blanketed in a heavy, fragile silence that would shatter with the slightest scuff of a shoe.

Her fingers had just closed around the front door's handle when a light swelled behind her, illuminating the foyer in its weak glow. She whirled around. Amaris stood halfway up the staircase, a low-burning lantern dangling from one hand. "I suspected you'd been sneaking out for a while," she whispered, closing the distance between them. "So I stopped drinking the tea you made us. Every day for the last week, you've left in the middle of the night and returned just shy of dawn."

Riona gripped Amaris's free hand. "You haven't said anything to my father?"

"Of course not. You don't have much time left here, and I won't take what little freedom you still have. Whatever you've been doing all these nights is your business." Amaris paused, searching Riona's face. "I just hope that you've thought this through. In less than a week, you'll board a ship bound for your new home. Make sure you do not leave your heart in Innislee."

"My heart?"

Understanding struck her a heartbeat later. Amaris had assumed that she'd been sneaking out to meet a secret lover. That her desperation to stay in her kingdom and earn a place on the council was born of love for a man, rather than love for Rivosa. It was a misunderstanding Riona would not correct, no matter how much she hated lying to Amaris. It was better to let her believe that than to admit to hunting down a murderer with an Erdurian prince.

Riona stepped closer. "Please, tell no one about this. I will stop seeing him when I am betrothed, but until then...I can't. I can't bear it."

At the tremble in her voice, Amaris set down the lantern and pulled her into a tight embrace. "Savor the freedom you have left," she whispered, her breath tickling Riona's ear, "but don't make your leaving any harder than it must be."

She nodded and backed out of the hug. "I have to go. Thank you, Amaris."

"Anything for you, sister."

Riona waited until Amaris had disappeared up the stairs before stepping through the front door. Aeron was leaning against one of the stone pillars that bracketed the entryway, twisting a wilting Selannic lily between his thumb and forefinger. He dropped it when he saw her.

"Where have you been? I've been worried—"

"We found Faylen," he blurted. "She's alive, and she has the missing treasury documents. We must ride to Crafford right now."

She stopped dead. "You *found her?*"

Aeron nodded, his expression tight. "One of my men spotted her at the port, trying to convince any captain who would listen to give her passage to the Isles. He set her up in a tavern not far from the harbor, said you'd pay her fare if she told you what she knows about Cathal's murder, and she agreed. She will speak only with you."

"Why did he not hire a carriage to bring them here?"

"She refuses to return to the city. Claims that the person who murdered Cathal is searching for her, and she won't risk her babe's life. I have horses waiting. We can go now."

Crafford was four hours away, and if they left now, they wouldn't arrive until four or five in the morning. Even if they only spent an hour speaking to Faylen, they wouldn't return to Innislee until almost midday. The Creator only knew what her father and uncle would do if they woke to find her missing.

Still, she did not hesitate. "Let me grab my things."

She slipped into the house and crept up the stairs as quickly and quietly as she could. In her room, she grabbed her coin purse and all the money she had at her disposal. Then she scrawled a note promising that she would be back the next day and slipped it under Amaris's door on her way out.

When she left, Aeron led her down the road to a tavern where he had tied up two horses. "Calanthe," he said as he handed her the reins to a tall black mare. As he swung up onto his slate gray stallion, his cloak parted to reveal the handle of a sword sheathed at his hip, one he must have stolen from the castle's armory. The sight sent a chill down Riona's spine. "I'd recommend you keep your hood up and your head down, my lady. It'd be best to avoid any city watchmen recognizing you."

Riona obeyed, and they set off, their horses' hooves clacking loudly against the cobbles. The city never truly slept—there were still plenty of carriages and riders on the roads, and boisterous crowds lingering just outside the taverns they passed—but Aeron was still careful to keep them to narrow, twisting side roads. Riona sat hunched in her saddle, tensing every time she caught a glimpse of a city watchman's uniform. Thankfully, they were few and far between. Still, it was all she could do to keep from checking over her shoulder every few seconds, expecting to find her father or a royal guard racing after them.

It was only when they reached one of the city gates that she allowed herself to look back. The castle sat high on its perch over the city, its sturdy gray walls and proud turrets stretching into the nighttime sky. Warm golden light bled from its windows. Despite everything, part of her wanted to send Aeron to fetch Auberon. Riona smothered the urge. She had grown too used to his presence, too reliant on his cocky grins and smart-mouthed remarks chasing away her growing sense of hopelessness. She had chosen to end their alliance, and for good reason. He had been a means to an end, and nothing more.

She dug her heels into her mare's sides and followed Aeron out of the city.

The sky was still dark when Crafford appeared before them, smoke rising from the chimneys of its sturdy wooden houses. Beyond the peaked roofs, Riona could see the stormy gray expanse of the Tranquil Sea, reflections of the stars sparkling on its waves. The suitors' ships were docked in the harbor, their sheer size dwarfing the fishing boats to either side of them. Her gaze snagged on Erduria's double-headed eagle crest, and she pushed thoughts of Auberon away for what felt like the hundredth time since they'd left the capital.

She focused her attention on Aeron as he led her through the outskirts of the town. It was better that they had come alone, even if it meant she'd been forced to endure four hours of riding in relative silence. For all his faults, at least Auberon provided plenty of commentary.

It wasn't long before Aeron stopped in front of a simple two-story tavern. After tying up their horses, he led her inside and up to one of the rooms on the second floor, where he knocked on the door in a peculiar way—three short raps, then a pause, and one more. A few heartbeats later, it swung open to reveal a young elven woman in a worn tunic and skirt, her long brown hair falling in tousled waves around her shoulders.

Riona's breath caught at the sight of her.

Faylen's fair skin was mottled with green and yellow bruises. Her nose had been broken, and it sat among a sea of bruises and shallow cuts. A fresh scar cut across the edge of her narrow jaw, hooking up across her cheek. More gashes crisscrossed her bare forearms and hands, but they were not what Riona's gaze focused on as it swept over her body. It was the curve of Faylen's round belly, heavy with child.

"Were you followed?" the elf asked, leaning forward to peer into the hall.

"No," Aeron said. "Faylen, this is Lady Riona Nevis. My lady, Faylen."

She studied Riona for what felt like an eternity, then opened the door wide. "Come in, then. I'll tell you everything."

Chapter Forty
The Liar

"It's not every day I get to speak to a real-life blood mage." Auberon sat back on the settee and crossed his arms, sarcasm dripping from his voice. "Lucky me."

Valerian held his stare, the light from the sitting room's hearth playing across his features. "Would you rather be back in the infirmary?"

"Is that a threat?"

"I'm pointing out that I risked my neck to heal you so you could help your brother win Lady Riona's hand in marriage. I haven't gained anything from helping you, save for the enjoyment of watching the court's favor turn on Eamon last night. I would appreciate it if you would stop looking at me like you want to flay the flesh from my bones."

"Begin, then."

The duke nodded. "You've heard the folk tales about blood magic, but a lot of truth has been distorted over the centuries, a lot of our knowledge lost. I've been studying it for years, and even I know only the basics. I want to understand it, though. I want to understand why some people are able to wield powers the like of which only the Old Gods knew," he said, a spark of excitement in his eyes. It was the same look that came over Walther's face whenever he described a battle he'd studied—a scholar's excitement. "Even if it never comes back into practice, it is an intrinsic part of our history and religion. If not for blood magic, no one would have survived the Year of One Night. There's no telling how much knowledge we've lost in the millennia since."

"So you're playing with forbidden magic you know hardly anything about, and you had the *gall* to use it on me."

"I did what I thought was best. What I told you when I visited you in the infirmary was true—when I was younger, my leg was shattered in a carriage accident on a journey to Kostos. The healer told me I would never walk again. Blood magic healed it."

Auberon sat silently, waiting for him to continue. He couldn't very well scoff; he'd felt the effects of blood magic, and he couldn't deny that it was capable of remarkable things.

"I'd been studying blood magic for a while, an idle hobby. I never expected to use it, but that day, that saying kept repeating over and over in my head. *Rijat du'omo, Iei sao.* I was in more agony than I'd ever felt in my life." Valerian absently rubbed his thigh, a shadow of that old pain passing across his face. "I can't recall much of that week, but I remember saying those words and begging every god I could think of to help me. The next thing I knew, it felt like my leg was boiling from the inside out. I passed out from the pain, and when I woke up three days later, the bone had begun to mend. A week later, I was able to stand and walk normally. My guards called it a miracle.

"Ever since, I've dedicated every spare moment I can find to studying blood magic. Imagine the miracles that healers trained in blood magic could perform. Imagine the sicknesses they could cure, the pain they could ease, the wounds they could heal," the duke pressed, leaning forward. "All the people who died in the war between my country and Kostos. All those you have lost in the war with Rivosa. How many could have been saved? Since the accident, I've been testing that healing incantation on myself. Minor cuts seal themselves almost immediately. Stab wounds take a little longer, due to the damage to muscles and other tissue, but—"

Auberon held up a hand. "Hold on. You *stabbed* yourself?"

"Who else?" Valerian asked, as if the question surprised him. "There's only one person I would gladly stab, and Eamon doesn't seem likely to volunteer his services anytime soon."

Despite himself, Auberon chuckled and gestured for the duke to continue.

"I told you I'd never used blood magic on anyone else until I helped you. I knew the magic would leave a mark—that warmth you felt—but I had assumed it would occur in your lungs, and that you would dismiss it as a side effect of the poison or antidote. It's interesting that you felt it where I touched you. I hadn't expected that, but I suppose it makes sense. When I used the incantation on myself, the power stayed within me, and it manifested where the injury was. When I used it on you, it created a link between us."

Auberon frowned. All his life, he had heard tales about violent and ruthless blood mages. They weren't men like Valerian —quiet, bookish. At least, they never remained that way for long once they'd gotten an idea of how powerful they could become. "How does it work?"

"I'm still trying to figure that out myself. Few sources survived from the Year of One Night, but I've pieced together some details over the years. First, it's not truly blood magic— not the way people imagine it, at least. To the Old Gods, the magic was as much a part of them as their bones and muscle. It's not infinite power, as the stories claim. Every Old God had a reserve. The Creator's was the greatest, which is why the others grew jealous and launched the War of the Old Gods. They—"

"I'm familiar with the story," Auberon cut in. "Spare me the mythology, if you will."

"Think of it like running. If you sprint as fast as you possibly can, you'll run out of stamina quickly, and you'll need to rest to rebuild it. If you go slower, you can use it for longer, but it's not as effective. That's how the magic works, in a way."

He raised a brow. "Until blood mages start murdering others to make themselves more powerful."

Valerian winced. "Yes, well, the metaphor does start to break down there..."

"You're saying that the magic is bound by physical limitations. A blood mage can use his own reserve to fuel the power, or he can take from others to add to it. So you healed me...how, exactly? Did you feel any differently?" Auberon asked, trying to pretend that his mind wasn't reeling. He followed the Church of the Creator and knew the stories of the Old Gods, but he had only ever considered them in the abstract. It was still hard to accept the fact that the man sitting before him held a sliver of divine power.

"For lack of a better word, it...drained me to heal you. The magic took from me to give to you—a transfer of power, because the world must always be at equilibrium."

"By that logic," he mused, "if you were to heal a mortal wound..."

"I would die," Valerian confirmed, his expression grave. "Unless I drew the power from someone else. I think that's how the Cirisian First managed to grow so powerful. We've all heard the stories of Beltharan and Feyndaran soldiers being slaughtered in the Islands. The First must have taken from them, which allowed her to manipulate the plague and raise corpses," he said, his nose wrinkling with disgust. "People like her are the reason why folk tales warn of blood mages. They never gave of themselves because they knew it would leave them vulnerable. I have no doubt that there were many blood mages who studied it and used it as I do, but history doesn't record those people. History only remembers the worst among us."

Auberon's frown deepened. As strange as it all sounded, it made sense. It wasn't surprising that blood mages would be tempted to kill others to overcome the limitations of their power.

That Cirisian First had razed a third of Beltharos to the ground during the war. She and her soldiers shouldn't have lasted one battle; they had been outnumbered, outmatched, and under supplied. So, rather than lead her people into a slaughter, she had raised corpses to fight alongside them. With the aid of her power, they had managed to march all the way to the capital and breach not only the *city's* defenses, but the *castle's*.

Valerian truly seemed to want to understand blood magic, to find ways to help his people. Had Auberon been in his position —a powerless heir to an enslaved country—he might have been tempted to do the same.

"Do you understand now?" Valerian asked softly. "I wish no ill will on anyone here in Innislee. I only hope to help my people and secure them a better future. That is all I have ever wanted."

"I do, but...if you truly want to free yourself and your country from Kostori rule, why not use blood magic to do it? With enough power, you could fell entire armies without ever meeting them on a battlefield."

"I won't lie and say I've never been tempted to try it. I imagine it every time I see the fields the Kostori have burned. Every time I meet a mother whose son was ripped from her arms to serve in King Jericho's army. Every time I try to picture my sister's face and realize I can no longer remember what she looked like," Valerian said, pure grief in his voice. "I imagine doing the most unspeakable things to the Kostori, and that is precisely why I am here, asking the Rivosi king for troops. I will not allow blood magic to turn me into a monster."

"Even if more of your people suffer because of it?"

"Creator forgive me, even then. I would give my life for them, but I will not give my soul." Valerian stood and gazed down at him. "You'll keep your vow of secrecy?"

Auberon stood, as well. If only he *were* an oath breaker. He understood Valerian's reasoning for studying blood magic, but he also knew how the Rivosans would react if they found out that the duke was dabbling in forbidden magic. If Valerian managed to make it out of the city with his life, he would be forced to flee to Kenter. One more obstacle to Drystan's betrothal would be cleared.

But considering the fact that Auberon was hunting a murderer and searching for the eudorite mines, it would probably come in handy to have an ally who could heal almost any wound.

Auberon nodded, and a look of relief came over the duke's face. "I'm not in the habit of breaking my word."

Chapter Forty-One
The Lady

"I'll sit in the main room and keep an eye out for any suspicious characters," Aeron said as Riona stepped inside. "Shout if you need me."

"Thank you, Aeron."

He dipped his head and left, a hand curled around the grip of his sword.

Faylen shut the door as Riona surveyed the room. It was simply furnished, with a bed, a chest of drawers, a table and chairs, and a tall wardrobe. The lone window was shuttered tightly. Even though it was the middle of the night, the room was pristine, the bed untouched. The only sign that someone had been staying there was the canvas bag sitting on the floor by the door, within easy reach should Faylen need to flee. A lantern sat atop the chest of drawers. Its low flame danced, making the shadows throughout the room pulse with life.

"I haven't been able to sleep much since Cathal... Since I left Innislee," Faylen said, following Riona's gaze to the untouched bed. She sat at the table, her arms curling around her belly. "You'll really help me get to the Selannic Isles?"

Riona pulled out her coin purse she had brought and set it on the table. Faylen's eyes widened at the sound of the coins clinking against one another. "I will. This should be enough to pay for your passage and set you up with a nice life there."

"Oh, thank you! If your man hadn't found me, I don't know what I would have done. I told every captain bound for the Isles that I would work to earn my place on the ship, but none would take me in my condition. Never mind that I have a couple of months before the baby arrives."

"They'll do it for the right pay," Riona said, nodding to the money. "You and your child will be safe."

Faylen's face crumpled, and she looked away. "Cathal... I don't know what to do now that he's dead. He promised that he would take care of me—take care of *us*."

Riona leaned forward, her voice soft. "Will you tell me about him?"

"Where do I begin?"

"Wherever you'd like. Perhaps with how you met."

"I was in the market purchasing ingredients for the contraceptive tonic the brothel owner made for us. The merchant's stock was running low, and he wanted to charge me an exorbitant price—more money than Mistress Lilah had given me, but she would have punished me if I hadn't returned with her order. And the punishments..." Faylen faltered. "She would give us to the customers who hurt women for pleasure. I think that's why no one came to our aid when Cathal and I were attacked. They all thought it was just another monster who'd paid the mistress for the *entertainment*.

"I was arguing with the merchant when Cathal interrupted and paid for everything. Just like that. And once he'd finished, he walked me to the brothel and promised he would come back to see me. That was how it started. For a while, he did nothing more than sit and talk to me, but he paid every aurum the mistress demanded without complaint."

"I know he continued to visit you after that. He even paid so you wouldn't have to entertain any other customers," Riona said. She paused, then asked, "Did you love him?"

The small, grief-filled smile that spread across Faylen's lips was confirmation enough. "I did. I loved him desperately. He was only able to visit me once or twice a week if I was lucky, but during those visits, I could almost pretend I hadn't escaped slavery only to end up in another hell." Her smile turned sorrowful. "For the few hours he was there, that was enough."

"What changed? The owner said he stopped coming to see you."

Shame flashed across her face. "I didn't want him to know about the baby. When it started to show, I refused to see him, but Mistress Lilah wouldn't turn away good coin. She locked me in a room with him, and I shouted the most foul, most despicable things I could imagine. I wanted to hurt him so badly that he would stop visiting. When I was finished, he left without a word, but he continued to pay so that I wouldn't have to take any more clients. He saved me, even when I did everything in my power to make him hate me."

"...Because the child isn't his, is it?" Riona whispered, putting the pieces together. Faylen had only joined the brothel a few months ago. Her pregnancy was too far along for Cathal to have fathered the child.

"It would have been his child in every way that mattered, except for one. *That* honor goes to the man I paid to help me escape my chains back in Sandori," she spat. "I thought he would take me to Rivosa and help me find work, but he had other plans. He kept me with him for a few months, until he discovered that I was with child. Then he dumped me in the brothel with no money and nowhere to go."

Faylen shook her head. Despite the rage and pain and grief in her voice, she did not cry. Riona suspected her tears had run dry long ago. "I was terrified of what Cathal would say when he discovered the truth. And I was ashamed."

Riona reached across the table and squeezed the elf's hand, her heart breaking for the things she had endured.

"I didn't see him again until the morning he died."

"What happened?"

She sucked in a deep breath and looked down at her belly. "I woke to Cathal bursting into my room, spouting nonsense about fleeing the city. I got out of bed to try and calm him, and it was then that he saw my condition. He went completely still, completely silent, but I could see him putting everything together. Cathal vowed then and there that he would take me to the Isles and marry me. He gave me some documents he had smuggled out of the treasury and told me to run. We would meet in Crafford, he said, so we could sail over together."

Faylen squeezed her eyes shut. "The next thing I knew, someone ran into the room and shoved me into the wardrobe. When I turned, they were on the bed, fighting. I saw the dagger plunge into— I saw it plunge into Cathal's chest." She paused and sucked in a ragged breath. Her gaze was distant, lost in the memories of that terrible day. "I launched myself at the bastard on top of him. He elbowed me in the face, and when I fell to the floor, he turned on me. He would have killed me, but Cathal grabbed him and told me to run. Every night, when I close my eyes, I see the hopeless look on his face as he said it. He knew that was the end. He knew that I had to leave him to protect my baby. So I did. I grabbed the documents, fled out the brothel's back door as quietly as I could, then stole a horse."

Riona was silent for several long moments, haunted by the memory of Cathal's body, his chest shredded to bloody ribbons. When she finally found her voice, all she could say was, "You rode all the way here in your condition?"

"What other choice did I have? The bastard was going to come after me once he killed Cathal. I had to leave the city, and a carriage was too slow and too expensive. I'd grabbed a cloak on my way out to cover my face and my belly, and I ran. I... I left him to die alone."

"I am so sorry," she breathed when Faylen met her eyes. Through the sorrow and pain in their depths, Riona saw unparalleled strength. "I promise I will do everything in my power to find Cathal's murderer. What did he look like?"

Faylen shook her head. "The hood of his cloak was up, and I never got a good look at the bastard's face. I can tell you that he was tall and fair-skinned, broad-shouldered like a sailor or laborer. His eyes were dark—green, maybe? Blue? I don't know. I wish I'd seen more."

Riona nodded, masking her disappointment. "Do you mind if I look at the documents?"

"Please do. I never learned how to read, so I can't make sense of them. I've been driving myself mad wondering what information they hold."

Riona grabbed the bag, pulled out the sheaf of parchment within, and spread the papers across the table. Faylen fetched the lantern and carried it over, holding it up so Riona could read. Most looked like regular treasury records—figures written in neat little boxes across the parchment—but the last two were maps. One was of a section of Rivosa's northern coast, where a place called Portcross Castle was marked with a little black X. The other map detailed the wide expanse of the Howling Mountains, stretching from Crafford to the border Rivosa shared with Beltharos. In the pitted, jagged peaks, Riona counted a half-dozen Xs. Five were red, crossed out so many times that the nib of the quill had torn through the parchment in some places. The last X was black.

Riona's heart dropped. "He was right..."

"What?" Faylen's brows furrowed. "What do they mean?"

There was only one reason anyone would brave the Howling Mountains. *Eudorite mines. Auberon was right.*

Riona examined the rest of the papers, her stomach twisting. Many of them were records of the kingdom's accounts—expenditures, taxes, debts, and the like—and dread swept over her as she looked over the numbers. Her kingdom was bankrupt. Her uncle owed hundreds of thousands of aurums to the Selannic Isles, and he was well behind on payments. Every banquet, every outing, every bite of food she and the suitors had enjoyed had been bought with the Selannic king's coin.

That must be why Cathal burned the treasury records. He knew that the guards would search his office after his death, and he needed to make sure no one discovered that the kingdom was bankrupt. At least, not until *after* a marriage alliance had been secured. None of the suitors would enter into an alliance with a kingdom in crippling debt.

And that's why my uncle is in such a hurry to marry me off. He needs an alliance before everyone learns that Rivosa is dying.

"Why did Cathal want to take these documents to the Isles?" she asked, looking up at Faylen. "Did he tell you?"

"He said something about showing the king and buying more time for something, but he was in such a panic I couldn't make sense of half of it. Please, what do they say?" Faylen shifted closer, her voice thick with grief and desperation. "Tell me he didn't die for nothing."

"...I don't believe he did," she responded softly. *Buying more time...* Cathal must have been planning to show the Selannic king proof of the mines, perhaps in an attempt to restructure the repayment of the debt. Eudorite ore was priceless, and striking a deal with the Isles would have saved her kingdom from ruination.

She moved on to the next page, which was a log of prisoners at various prisons across the country. At first it seemed out of place, until she noticed that a steady stream of prisoners was recorded as being transferred out each month, and always to a place identified only by a pair of coordinates. Riona didn't need a map to tell her that it was the location of the mine, or that her uncle was the one running the operation. For something this large-scale, he had to know. He had to be aware that he was sending those prisoners to their deaths.

Riona recalled the day she had found her uncle kneeling in the castle's private chapel, silvery lines of tears trailing down his cheeks. The memory struck her like a blow to the gut. The guilt and grief in his eyes. The bitterness in his voice. The responsibility he'd felt—not for failing to prevent his Treasurer's murder, she now saw, but for *ordering* it. Her uncle mourned Cathal, she did not doubt that, but when he'd been faced with the choice between keeping the mines a secret and allowing the truth of their existence to spread, he had elected to silence the man who had served him faithfully for decades.

We will find the man responsible for Cathal's murder, Riona had promised him that day, *and we will bring him to justice.*

Will we? her uncle had asked, bitterness and self-loathing lacing the words. *If the world were just, the man who committed this crime would suffer for it a thousand times over. But you and I both know the world is rarely that fair.*

Chapter Forty-Two
The Liar

One look at the king's face, and Auberon knew something was terribly wrong.

He picked up his pace and gripped Drystan's arm as they approached the throne room's dais. "Something has changed," he whispered. The king, Lord Lachlan, and the Crown Prince were stone-faced, but Auberon could read the tension between them like words on a page. "I don't know what, but it is enough to completely shake them. Use it to your advantage."

Drystan nodded once, and Auberon released him, falling a few steps back as court etiquette dictated. When they reached the space before the dais steps, they dropped into low bows, and the king dismissed the servant who'd summoned them with a flick of his hand.

"Your Highnesses, I believe I have heard everything you have to say on the subject of an alliance, and I have made my decision quite clear," King Domhnall said, leaning forward in his throne. "We have nothing further to discuss."

Drystan inclined his head and offered him a disarming smile. "Your Majesty, my brother and I are your guests, and we will respect whatever decision you make regarding Lady Riona's marriage. But, betrothed or not, I seek a peaceful end to the war."

"You expect me to make peace with your father? The man who has spent the last thirty years sending my subjects to the depths of the Tranquil Sea? Whose orders killed my sister-in-law, her family, and my eldest son?" the king said, his fingers tightening around the arms of his throne. Behind him, the Crown Prince's concerned gaze flicked to his father, but he was wise enough to hold his tongue. "I will not spit on their graves by making peace with my enemy."

"We have all been touched by the war, both by the loss of someone we held dear and by the blood of those our men have killed in the fighting. With a treaty, we can spare more innocents from losing their lives to these ceaseless battles, Your Majesty. Your people are begging for an end to the fighting."

"Because you and your brother have seized every opportunity to turn them against me and against this war," the king responded coldly. "They do not realize that I am doing this for their protection. Give your father an inch, and he will take everything from us."

Drystan shook his head in disappointment. "I see that there is nothing I can say to change your mind, Your Majesty. Let us speak plainly, then. You never had any intention of approving a match between Lady Riona and me. Your only reason for inviting me here was to force Valerian and Eamon to offer you more favorable terms. You were playing us against each other," he said. "I've grown tired of playing your games. I rescind my bid for Lady Riona's hand."

Auberon whirled toward him. They hadn't discussed this. A marriage alliance was their key to securing the ore from the mines. Without it, they were almost certain to drag the war out to a bloody end.

"By your leave," Drystan continued, "I shall remain in Innislee for one more week, Your Majesty. This is your final chance to negotiate for peace. I advise you, do not squander it."

With that, he bowed and started toward the doors. Auberon hurried after him, still wrestling with the shock of what Drystan had said. As soon as they left the throne room, he tensed, expecting Drystan to explode with anger. But the prince merely continued strolling down the hall, the variegated light from the stained-glass windows playing across his features. The servants they encountered paused and bowed, and he acknowledged them with a nod and a smile as he passed.

"Drystan," he hissed. "What have you done?"

Drystan glanced back at him. "I've done all I can to make him see reason. Whatever happens now, my conscience is clean."

Chapter Forty-Three
The Lady

Riona sat at the table, staring at the documents spread across its worn surface, until the pale light of dawn slipped through the cracks in the shutters. Behind her, Faylen lay curled up in the bed, the blankets tangled around her legs. It hadn't taken much to convince her to rest; she had been alone and on the run since Cathal's death, constantly looking over her shoulder. Riona suspected this was the first time she'd allowed herself to enjoy a full night's rest in weeks. Not that it was truly *restful* sleep—every time she drifted off, it didn't take long for her to begin to toss and turn, Cathal's name on her lips.

When Faylen thrashed again, Riona crossed the room and sat on the mattress beside her. The elf's face was pale and contorted in terror, a slick layer of sweat coating her skin. "Faylen," Riona said, setting a hand on her shoulder. "Wake up."

She murmured something incomprehensible, then jerked upright with a gasp. "He— He was—"

"It was a nightmare. You're safe. Aeron and I will protect you, remember?"

Slowly, the elf's breathing calmed, and she leaned back against the headboard. "It's not enough that I think of his death every day—it has to haunt my sleep, as well." Faylen paused, her eyes roving over Riona's face. "Did you sleep at all? I daresay you look worse than I do."

"No. I couldn't stop thinking about... about everything." *My own uncle ordered Cathal's assassination.* Her shoulders slumped as she tried to wrap her head around all that she'd learned. Did the council know about the mines? Prince Domhnall? Her *father?* "Cathal was only doing his duty as Treasurer. Why would he need to be murdered?"

Faylen's expression hardened. "I don't know, but we must set sail for the Isles today. Cathal wanted those documents presented to the Selannic king, and I will find a way to fulfil his wish."

Riona rubbed her eyes with the heels of her palms. Exhaustion wore at her; she hadn't slept in over a day, and her body was sore from riding the four-hour journey from Innislee. And in her heart, she just felt...weary. After all the horror she had witnessed in the Beltharan court and all the heartache she had endured since returning to Innislee, she wanted nothing more than to renounce her royal blood and turn her back on the politics of the court. But she had vowed to bring Cathal's killer to justice, and that was what she would do—even if continuing down this path meant committing treason.

If it saved her kingdom from ruin, it would be worth it.

The question remained where to go next. They could sail to the Isles and reveal the existence of the mines to her grandfather in the hope of reducing Rivosa's enormous debt, but eventually, she would have to return to Innislee. Perhaps her grandfather would provide her protection for her return to the castle, when she would confront her king about Cathal's murder. It was a dangerous path, and one wrong step would mean her death. If she did not play her cards exactly right—if she did not have undeniable proof of what her uncle had done—*she* would be the one meeting the executioner's blade.

Riona wrapped her arms around herself, suddenly wishing Auberon were there. She could picture him lounging on one of the chairs, his legs propped up on the table amidst the spread of parchment. The light would play across the planes of his handsome face as it had so many nights in the Royal Theater, catching on the auburn strands in his hair. *Cheer up, aramati,* he would say, a cocky grin on his lips. *I've been telling you all along that your uncle was a bastard. Are you upset because of what we learned, or because you realized that I was right?*

Her gaze wandered to the table, where the treasury documents betrayed the true state of her kingdom's finances. She thought of Innislee—the pitted cobblestone roads, the worn and weathered buildings, the lampposts with their missing panes. She had always thought them part of the charm of her ancient city, but now she saw them for what they really were: the scars of a dying kingdom.

Riona rose, gathering the papers into a pile and slipping them into the canvas bag. "I promise that I will help you find passage to the Isles, but if you want to see Cathal's murder avenged, we must return to Innislee."

A shadow passed across the elf's face, and she set a hand on her round belly. "I will not go back to that city. There is nothing left for me there except ghosts and nightmares."

"Faylen—"

"No. *Every single day* I have spent in that city has been a living hell. A man I thought I could trust sold me into servitude in a brothel. The woman who bought me forced me to give my body to men who beat me for their own pleasure. Cathal was the only source of happiness I ever found there, and the city stole that from me, too."

Riona's heart broke at the emotion in Faylen's voice. "I understand, and I would not be asking this of you if I did not believe it was necessary. You are the only witness to what happened the morning Cathal was murdered. I need your help if we are to bring his killer to justice. After that, I will see you safely out of Rivosa."

Faylen said nothing for several long moments. Finally, she swept a threadbare cloak around her shoulders and pulled the hood over her head to hide her long, distinctive hair. When she was finished, she turned back to Riona. "I have made the mistake of trusting the wrong people too many times in the past. Do not make me regret trusting you."

They found Aeron at a table in the tavern's main room, his hand hovering over the blade at his waist. He had to feel every bit as exhausted as Riona did, but he was alert, tension corded in every inch of his lithe, muscular body. When he spotted them, he rose and met them at the bottom of the stairs. "I had the owner's son fetch some food from the market for you," he said to Faylen, nodding to a bag slung over his shoulder. "It should be more than enough to last the journey to the Isles."

"Good thinking, Aeron, but she's not sailing just yet." Riona handed him the bag with the documents. "I need you to take her back to Innislee and find yourselves somewhere safe and private to stay. You can use my money to hire a carriage back to the city, and whatever remains will buy you any supplies you need."

Aeron frowned. "...It sounds like you're asking me to leave you here alone, my lady."

"I am. There's something I must take care of, but I'll see you in Innislee soon," she said. "Once you and Faylen are settled, please send word to Amaris that I have been delayed and will return as soon as I can. Tell her to remember what we discussed before I left and assure her that she need not worry about me."

"You're making *me* worry about you. My lady, whatever you're planning, if it's dangerous—"

"It's not. It's simply something I must do on my own," she said, her stomach twisting at the thought of putting Faylen and Aeron in danger. They had never asked to get involved in any of this, and she would do whatever it took to keep them safe. Riona took his hand and added, "Please promise me that you will not follow."

Unease flashed across his face, but he nodded grimly and said, "I swear it."

Riona surprised them both by pulling him into a tight hug. "Thank you, my friend, for everything you have done for me. I am more grateful for it than I can express," she whispered. Then she pulled back and added, "When you get to Innislee, leave a note with Ophelia telling me where I can find you."

He agreed, and Riona turned to Faylen. "I know it will not be easy to return to the city. It cannot possibly make up for what you've endured, but I want you to know that my uncle will pay for Cathal's murder. The Treasurer was a good man, and he did not deserve the end he met."

She nodded. "May the Creator watch over you."

"And you, as well."

With that, they left. Riona climbed the stairs and returned to the room Faylen had occupied, latching the door shut behind her. She watched through the window as Aeron and Faylen started down the street in the direction of a carriage for hire, Aeron leading his horse by its reins. Riona prayed that she was doing the right thing by sending them back to the capital.

Once they'd climbed into their carriage, Riona closed the shutters and lay on the bed, her lids falling shut the second her head hit the pillow. She would need all her strength for what lay ahead. While Faylen slept, Riona had spent all morning studying Cathal's maps, committing every detail to memory.

Tonight, she would go to the Howling Mountains.

Chapter Forty-Four
The Liar

The banquet hall was quiet enough to hear a pin drop. If Auberon hadn't been sitting at the head table, looking out over a sea of more than a hundred people, he might have been able to trick himself into believing he was alone. Tension hung in the air. News that Drystan had rescinded his bid for Riona's hand had spread through the castle like wildfire, and no one—including Auberon—had an inkling of what would happen in the days to come.

He glanced to his right, where Drystan sat with his spine perfectly straight, staring at the double doors at the opposite end of the hall. They had been seated at the end of the table, far from the king's currently empty chair—still a place of honor, but an obvious sign that they had fallen out of favor. Beside King Domhnall's chair sat Prince Eamon, then Duke Valerian. The duke shot Auberon a concerned look. Drystan's drastic decision had thrown everything off balance. Weeks of negotiating, politicking, manipulating...potentially all for nothing.

Drystan set his foot atop Auberon's, pressing gently in warning. "Have faith," he whispered. "The negotiations for the betrothal may be over, but we can still spend tonight advocating for a peace treaty. Convince the council of its necessity, and we are almost guaranteed an end to the fighting."

"We are guaranteed *nothing*," he hissed, his patience wearing thin. "We'll be lucky if we're not thrown onto a ship bound for Torch by the night's end."

"Spare me the theatrics, and focus on doing what you were sent here to do. Find proof that the mines exist. Allow me to attend to politics." Drystan's gaze finally slid to him. "Remember your duty."

Auberon glowered. "As you command, *Your Imperial Highness*. I will do my best to stay out of your way."

The doors of the banquet hall swung open then, revealing the royal family in all their finery: the monarchs and their children, then Lord Lachlan, Amaris, and...

No Riona.

Alarm shot through him as the royals approached the dais. While the others took their seats at the head table, King Domhnall turned to the court and said, "Unfortunately, my dear niece has taken ill and will not be joining us for the feast, but that shall not keep us from celebrating her impending betrothal. Within one week, one of these young men will be promised to Lady Riona. It will be my honor to count him among my family and usher in a new era of prosperity for Rivosa." He looked to Drystan then, ice in his eyes as he lifted his goblet in a toast. "To our future."

A cheer rose from the courtiers. As the king took his seat, servants flooded out of the kitchen bearing platters of food and drink. Auberon studied him. A dozen explanations for Riona's absence swirled in his mind, and not a single one involved illness. She had been in perfect health the night before. He recalled with unease the strange air that had hung over the royals at the negotiations. Something had happened to Riona, and they had known about it then. Had she decided to confront her uncle about the mines? About Cathal's murder? Riona was intelligent, but her righteousness made her stubborn and impulsive. She would charge headfirst into danger if she thought she was doing right by her kingdom and her people.

She could be hurt. She could be—

Auberon gripped the stem of his goblet with white knuckles, imagining it was the king's neck. He still lacked proof that the king had been involved in the murder or that it was connected to the mines, but his gut was rarely wrong. He wouldn't put it past the bastard to hurt his own niece in the name of "protecting" his kingdom's security.

Halfway through the meal, his attention snagged on Amaris. She was sitting between the Crown Prince and Riona's father, halfheartedly stabbing her fork into a slice of wine-poached pear. Every so often, she glanced at the empty seat on Lord Lachlan's other side, a shadow passing across her face. To an untrained eye, nothing would look amiss; the royal family was eating and chatting, laughing as they engaged Eamon and Valerian in conversation, but Auberon could see through the forced cheer. They were tense and uncertain—their shoulders set in stiff lines, their smiles not quite reaching their eyes. And Amaris looked almost...*guilty.*

She knows something about Riona's absence.

After what felt like an eternity, the servants cleared the last of the plates, and the musicians began to play. Auberon immediately stood and started toward Amaris. Before he could reach her, Prince Domhnall took her hand and whisked her down to the dance floor. Frustration flared within him.

Servants filtered through the crowd that was quickly gathering around the dance floor, and Auberon snagged a goblet of wine from one as he wove through the sea of bodies. He needed something to ease the restless, nervous energy rushing through him. Auberon drained the goblet and then swapped it with another from a passing servant's tray. He was about to lift it to his lips when a hand caught his arm and pulled him around. Half of the wine sloshed to the floor, a blood red stain against the white marble.

"If you're planning to sulk and drink yourself into a stupor, go back to the guest house," Drystan hissed, his expression livid. They stood in the middle of the crowd, and Auberon felt the press of the courtiers around them like a too-tight doublet. "You are a prince of Erduria, and I expect you to act like one. Help me convince the advisors to counsel the king toward peace."

"No!" Auberon snapped, louder than he'd intended. A few nobles turned to stare at them. "You want me to creep around in the shadows and stay out of your way? Fine. *You* created this mess of the negotiations, and now you can solve it."

He shoved the goblet into Drystan's hand and stormed off, ignoring the objections of the courtiers as he pushed through the crowd. Drystan could deal with the court himself. Auberon's only concern was the eudorite mines. He left the stifling heat of the banquet hall and stepped out onto the balcony, where he had stood with Treasurer Cathal that very first night in Innislee. The cool winter breeze whipped around him, slicing straight through his doublet. Thankfully, the cold had dissuaded any other courtiers from braving the chill. He was alone.

"You have forgotten your place," Drystan said, his tone laced with a warning. Auberon turned to find him closing the doors to the hall, sealing them off from the rest of the court.

"*I* have forgotten my place? I have done nothing except what was asked of me this entire time. I nearly *died* doing my duty to the Empire!"

"Your duty was to find the eudorite mines, not to fall in love."

The accusation struck him like a spear. A wave of rage flooded him, so thick and suffocating that it passed beyond fury into a strange, eerie calm. When he spoke, his voice came out icier than he'd ever heard it. "Do not speak to me of love, Drystan. All I have is the Empire. All I am, I owe to it. I will never forsake that."

"So you say. Yet your eyes never leave Lady Riona. They betray you."

Auberon did not blink. He did not breathe. He could not,

for he was terrified that the slightest movement would reveal the depth of his feelings for Riona. The feelings that he had begged the Creator every night to strip from him.

He would not give in to the desire burning within him—the need to make every touch linger a heartbeat longer, to savor each laugh or smart-mouthed response, to marvel at the fact that of all the people in her uncle's court, Riona had spent every night in the Royal Theater with *him*. He loved the way she moved with a dancer's grace as she practiced the swordplay drills he'd shown her. He loved that even though she'd had every reason to hate him, she had held his hand as he drowned in his own blood. He loved that she had spent the end of every night in the theater teaching him the song his mother had played for him as a child.

He loved her.

But if she married an Erdurian, it would be Drystan. He was under no illusions to the contrary. Drystan was his Crown Prince, his future Emperor. Everything that Auberon loved about Riona would make her an exceptional Empress, and she deserved nothing less than the throne.

Riona was a means to an end. His pawn. His puppet.

She could never be anything more.

Auberon started toward the doors, desperate to put thoughts of her out of his mind. "You're wasting your time talking to me. Spend tonight swaying the council members to your side."

Drystan set a hand on his shoulder, stilling him. "I know you'll do whatever it takes to complete the task that Father gave you. I only hope you do not destroy yourself in the process. In one week's time, Riona will be promised to another."

Auberon set his jaw and nodded stiffly. "I know."

Drystan released him, and he returned to the banquet hall just as a song ended. He immediately spotted Amaris and Prince Domhnall in the center of the nobles, their heads bent close together. At first, Auberon thought it nothing more than a romantic moment between the couple, but then he noticed the furrow between Amaris's brows as she whispered in the prince's ear, her fingers curled in the fabric of his doublet. They parted and bowed to the court, forced smiles on their faces. Their fingers laced together, they started through the crowd, pausing to speak with noblemen and women in their path.

Auberon stalked along the edge of the room as another song began. Once the court's attention returned to the dancers, Prince Domhnall led Amaris through the nondescript door tucked into the side wall—the same place he had taken Riona during the first banquet. When Auberon reached it, he glanced back to make sure no one was watching and then slipped inside. He found himself in a long, narrow corridor, the gray stone walls streaked with soot from the torches. There were no doors, just an archway on the far wall. Auberon crept toward it on silent feet.

"—all sitting around, pretending everything is fine, while she's out there somewhere," Amaris whispered. "I don't know if she's safe. I don't know if she's hurt."

Auberon stiffened. He shifted just enough to peer through the archway and saw Amaris and Domhnall sitting on a bench in the middle of the courtyard, clasping each other's hands. Moonlight filtered through the opening in the center of the building's roof.

"My father has sent men to find her and bring her home," the Crown Prince said, his voice calm and soothing. "She'll be fine."

"How do you know that? She could be halfway across the Tranquil Sea by now. She could have crossed the border into Beltharos. Percival Comyn would give her refuge if she asked—I know he would. Gather some men and ride to Westwater. Riona will listen to you."

"You said she sent you a note? What exactly did it say?"

"Just that she would return to the city as soon as possible. And she mentioned the conversation we had last night, before she left. That's how I knew it came from her, even though the handwriting was unfamiliar."

If Riona had left last night, that meant she'd been missing for almost a full day. Auberon's chest tightened with fear. It was reassuring to know that she had left Innislee of her own volition, but he still worried about her safety. What had brought on her sudden departure? And who had written that note, if not Riona?

Prince Domhnall frowned. "What did you discuss?"

Amaris hesitated. "Her lover," she finally admitted, and the prince's mouth parted in surprise. "She'd been sneaking out to meet him every night for at least the last week. I fear they've run off together. You *have* to go after her, Domhnall. Bring her home before she makes an even bigger mistake."

A lover? Clever lie, aramati, Auberon thought, impressed despite his concern. *Fears about an arranged marriage. A forbidden romance. It's the stuff of storybooks. Of course Amaris would fall for it.*

Domhnall's expression softened. "If I could, my love, I would ride out this very second to track her down, but I cannot. My father will not allow me to ride off during some of the most important days of his reign. It would raise too many questions, and the suitors cannot learn that anything is amiss. Think of the things they will say about Riona's virtue if they find out that she ran off with a stranger in the dead of night. We might lose any chance at a marriage alliance. If you want to protect her, you must act as if nothing is wrong. Have faith that my father's men will find her."

Amaris's face crumpled. She buried it in Domhnall's chest, her arms slipping around his waist. "I thought she was just sneaking out for the night," she mumbled, her voice muffled. "I should have stopped her."

"You know how headstrong Riona is," he said with a weak smile. "Do you *honestly* think you could have stopped her?"

She let out a soft, hiccuping sound—half laugh, half sob. The prince held her close until she finally leaned back, drying her tears with a sleeve. "Are we doing the right thing?" she asked, her voice so quiet that Auberon had to strain to make it out. "Must Riona lose her home and her family for the sake of some political alliance?"

"Amaris—"

"You could find a way for her to stay," she insisted. "Convince your father to provide Duke Valerian military aid. Guarantee Eamon's father trade and resources as repayment for the loss of the duchy. End the war with Erduria."

"I've tried to speak with him, but he won't listen," the prince growled. "He refuses to take my counsel, or that of any of his advisors. He believes we've all been swayed by their honeyed words and deep coffers."

"You are his son, and you will sit on the throne. The decisions he makes now will shape your rule before you ever wear the crown. Make him see reason."

Domhnall shook his head. "This is right. In time, Riona will understand why this marriage is necessary."

Amaris turned away. "I don't want to discuss this anymore. Go back to the banquet. I'll join you once I've composed myself."

As the prince watched her, clearly debating whether to press the issue further, Auberon returned to the banquet hall and waited until Prince Domhnall emerged. Once he slipped into conversation with one of the nobles at the edge of the dance floor, Auberon stepped back into the corridor.

Amaris was still sitting on the bench, her face buried in her hands, when he stepped into the courtyard. "I know the king wants me to return to the banquet," she murmured when she heard his soft footsteps, "but I just need a minute."

"Unfortunately, I don't think we have much time to spare."

Her head snapped up at the sound of his voice, her cheeks stained with tears. "I'm sorry, I thought—"

"Prince Domhnall isn't going to search for Riona," Auberon said, not bothering to hide the fact that he'd been eavesdropping on their conversation. "I'll find her and bring her back to Innislee, but I need you to tell me everything you can about the night she left. Do you know who sent the note?"

"...I have my suspicions. Riona has a...friend among the castle staff named Aeron. I went to speak with him, but his flat was empty. One of the neighbors told me he hadn't been there in days, and the castle staff said they hadn't seen him lately, either. I don't know where else to look for him."

Auberon offered her a hand up from the bench. "I'm sure we can manage something. Come with me."

Chapter Forty-Five
The Lady

Riona had heard stories about the dangers of the Howling Mountains, but nothing that compared to standing before them. Wind and water had carved the limestone into labyrinthine tunnels and narrow crevasses. Every so often, a freestanding pillar rose from the ground like the trunk of a tree, a silent sentinel guarding the realm of the Rennox. A breeze shot through the tunnels, creating a high-pitched, keening wail that scraped down Riona's spine. Her palm began to sweat around the handle of Auberon's dagger.

Standing before the Howling Mountains, Riona felt very, very *small*.

The entrance of the mine was bracketed with two tall, flat stones, their faces worn smooth by weather and age. As she passed between them, Riona reached up with her free hand and closed her fingers around the eudorite pendant at her throat. She had never given much thought to the necklace, always considering the answer of its origin lost along with her mother when her ship sank, but now it taunted her. Had her mother known about the mines?

A tunnel stretched out before her. Lanterns hung from the ceiling at even intervals, linked with a series of thin tubes that kept the oil at a constant level. Riona removed her cloak and set it by the entrance, along with a lantern she had bought in one of Crafford's markets. The tunnels were well lit, and it would only get in her way if she had to fight her way out. She stalked down the tunnel, a hand running over the uneven stone, and listened for the sounds of men working the mine.

All was quiet save for the shrieking wind.

She kept walking. Other tunnels branched off the main one, each lit with the same series of suspended lanterns, but she stuck to the largest, hoping that it would lead her to the heart of the mine. Every few yards, she marked the wall with a stick of charcoal she'd bought in the market. It would be all too easy to lose her bearings. Everything looked the same; it was all gray stone, occasionally pitted in places where miners had extracted veins of eudorite ore. Some of the depressions in the wall were longer than her arm—long enough for a blade.

This war will not end until the Tranquil Sea runs red with Erdurian blood.

Eventually, the sound of scraping drifted to her from somewhere up ahead, where the tunnel split. She cautiously approached the fork and froze when she saw a lone figure crouching in the tunnel to her right. His hair was lank and scraggly, hanging in limp knots around his narrow, bony shoulders. A threadbare pair of pants hung from his hips. He was facing away from her, muttering to himself as he scratched at the wall with his bare fingers. Blood was crusted on the stone from his torn fingernails.

Unsettled, Riona took a step back, and her boot scuffed against a loose chunk of stone. At once, the man whirled around. He stood slowly, revealing the sharp lines of his ribcage, and studied her through the curtain of hair hanging over his gaunt face.

Then, without a word, he launched himself at her.

Riona's heart leapt into her throat as she spun and raced down the other tunnel. The wind rose to a high-pitched scream, and her pursuer let out an eerie, bloodcurdling wail in answer. It filled the tunnel and burrowed into Riona's bones, the sound neither human nor animal.

Riona pushed herself faster, her grip tightening on the emerald-hilted dagger. *The dagger!* She should have stood her ground and fended the man off, but the thought of plunging the blade into his flesh and watching the light fade from his eyes made her feel sick. If she ran fast enough, she could lose him. She didn't have to kill an unarmed man.

She raced through the tunnels, making a mental note of each turn. Everything looked the same—a blur of pitted gray stone, tinged a pale orange by the light of the lanterns. Pounding footfalls reverberated through the tunnels, echoing and distorting around her. No matter what turns she took, no matter how fast she ran, the man chasing her did not relent. She would have to turn back and face him. She would have to—

There was a crackling sound, and then the ground gave way below her feet.

Suddenly, she was falling, her arms and legs pinwheeling. She twisted and hit hard stone, letting out a cry of pain as the air was knocked from her lungs. Agony shot through her ribs and down her hip, still bruised from her last night of training with Auberon. She had fallen into a sinkhole. Chunks of stone—some as large as her body—lay scattered around her.

Riona rolled onto her side and coughed, pulling her tunic over her nose and mouth so she wouldn't breathe in the dust floating in the air. Gripping her sore ribs, she pushed to her feet and picked up Auberon's dagger, which had fallen a few yards away. She walked over to the edge of the hole and stretched her arm as high as she could. The rim was still several feet above her, well out of reach.

She stumbled back as the strange man materialized through the haze and knelt at the edge of the sinkhole, peering down at her with his head cocked. Riona slowly placed the dagger in its sheath and raised her empty hands. If she had to choose between starving to death in a sinkhole and taking her chances with this stranger, she would gladly take the latter.

"Help me," she whispered, her voice a hoarse rasp. Just speaking those two words sent daggers through her ribcage. "Please."

Something flashed across the man's face—a glimmer of recognition breaking through the madness. Then he stood and walked away.

"No!" Riona cried, not caring if any of the mine workers heard. Anything would be better than dying here, another soul lost in the Howling Mountains. "Come back! Please come back!"

His soft footfalls padded down the tunnel and faded into silence.

Riona whirled, searching for a way out. She scrambled over to one of the chunks of stone and dropped to her knees, trying to push it over to the side of the sinkhole. If she could stack them, build them up enough to climb out, she would be able to escape. She gathered all her strength and shoved, succeeding in flipping the boulder onto its side. She managed it another two times before she fell back, panting and aching. Beads of sweat rolled down her face. She sucked in several deep breaths, setting her bruised ribs on fire, and tried again, her arms quivering with the effort. It was still a good couple of yards to the edge of the hole. At this rate, it would take her an entire day to stack up enough stones to climb out—if she didn't keel over from exhaustion first.

I will not die here. I will make it out.

Just as she thought it, the stranger reappeared in the tunnel above. He lay down at the edge and stretched an arm out, holding a pickaxe in one grimy, bloody hand. He stared at her expectantly.

Guessing at his intention, Riona stepped forward and hesitantly took the metal in her hands. Once she had a firm hold on it, he began to pull her up, his lean muscles straining. She grimaced at the pain that tore through her ribs. As soon as she'd reached the rim of the sinkhole, the stranger's fingers knotted in the back of her tunic and pulled her onto solid ground. They fell back against opposite walls of the tunnel, breathing hard.

Riona set a hand on her heart, trying to calm her racing pulse. "Thank— Thank you," she gasped. "Thank you for saving my life."

Now that he was before her, no haze hanging in the air and masking his features, she could see that he wasn't much older than she was. Under the grime, his skin was smooth, untouched by time. Beyond the curtain of hair over his face, his eyes were a bright, clear blue.

"Why did you chase me?" she asked softly, afraid of scaring him away.

Slowly, he lifted a shaky hand and pointed at her. She followed the line of his finger down to the pendant at her throat.

"You wanted the ore," she breathed. "You worked in these mines, didn't you? Is that why you were scratching at the wall?"

As soon as she said the word *mines*, he clapped his hands to his ears and let out a screech, a strange mimic of the shrieking wind and her own terrified cries. "NO! No, please! Please don't! *Please*—"

"Shhh... Shhhh, it's okay." Riona held up her hands as if calming a wild animal. "I won't make you go back. I only need you to tell me how to get to the heart of the mine."

He shook his head so vigorously his neck popped.

"Please. Whatever has happened to you, I want to help. I know that prisoners have been sent here to mine eudorite ore for the military. Can you lead me to where the others are?"

The stranger studied her for several long moments, then nodded once, a quick bob of his head.

Riona smiled and stood, offering him a hand up. He hesitantly took it, then started down the tunnel the way they had come, his shoulders hunched and steps shuffling.

"What is your name?" Riona asked as he led her through the tunnels.

"Dig! Dig! Dig!" he cried, the words reverberating against the stone. Riona flinched, then forced herself to relax. No one had come to investigate the sinkhole, so she doubted anyone was close enough to hear them. "Dig, filth! Dig!"

"...That's what you want me to call you? Dig?"

He nodded again and scuttled down the tunnel. Riona hurried after him, pity making her heart heavy. Her uncle had condemned this man to a life in the mines. How many others were aimlessly wandering the tunnels, slowly starving? How many were too far gone to save?

Another wail rose, and Dig lifted his head to mimic the wind as he walked. Unease settled deep within Riona's bones, and she wrapped her arms around herself as they descended into the heart of the Howling Mountains.

Chapter Forty-Six
The Liar

Auberon let Amaris return to the banquet first. When he stepped through the doorway several minutes later, he spotted her already making her way toward the double doors at the far end of the room, eager to make her escape. Every so often, a courtier tried to engage her in conversation, but she murmured an excuse and apologized before continuing on her way. One hand rested on her stomach as if she were feeling sick. Auberon glanced at the king. He was once again in his seat at the head table, a look of displeasure on his face as he watched Amaris make her hasty exit. King Domhnall knew the truth behind Riona's absence, which meant that he also knew Amaris was feigning illness to leave the banquet early. Fortunately, she was too far away for him to stop her without making a scene.

Amaris slipped out of the room, and Auberon started after her at a leisurely pace, his hands tucked into his pockets. To his left, he spotted Drystan still speaking with the council members. Lord Farquar was leaning back in his seat, a bored expression on his face, but the rest seemed to hang onto Drystan's every word. The war had cost them lives and trade, and they were eager for the rush of prosperity that would follow the signing of a peace treaty. Auberon didn't bother telling Drystan that he was leaving. He had made it abundantly clear that Auberon was to stay out of his way when it came to matters of the court.

So be it. Drystan could face the court alone while he went off in search of Riona.

Auberon left the castle's main building and started up the cobblestone path toward the guest houses. Amaris was already waiting for him near the front door when he arrived at the house he shared with Drystan, speaking quietly with a castle servant. The future queen stood with her head high and hands clasped, her long braids twisted into a waterfall that spilled down her back. For a moment, as she turned to face him, Auberon was struck by how much the girl resembled Riona. They weren't related by blood, but their mannerisms were nearly identical.

A pang of regret and longing buried itself deep in Auberon's heart. He shouldn't have pushed Riona away. The Creator only knew where she was and what she was doing, but he was willing to bet it had something to do with Cathal's murder. That was the only thing that would have caused her to leave the city with such haste. If he hadn't argued with her, would she have told him whatever she'd discovered? Would she have asked him to join her?

He pushed the thoughts away as he approached Amaris and the servant. When the light from the lantern hanging beside the door struck the girl's face, he realized that it was Ophelia, the servant who had summoned him and Drystan for the negotiations.

"Tell me where Aeron is," Amaris was saying as he met them outside the house. "I've searched everywhere for him, and he's nowhere to be found. He escorted Riona out of the city, didn't he?"

"I don't know anything about it, my lady."

"You must know where they've gone," Amaris insisted. She pointed behind them, to the dark silhouettes of the rolling hills that surrounded Innislee. "They are out there somewhere with bandits and highwaymen roaming the roads. If you care at all about Riona's safety, please, you must tell me where they're going."

"I cannot help you, my lady. I'm sorry."

Ophelia turned to leave, but Auberon stepped into her path. "Ophelia, I don't think you're aware of just how serious this may be. Lady Riona did not run off with a secret lover because no such lover exists. She was meeting with *me* all those nights she snuck out of her father's estate. I was helping her search for Treasurer Cathal's murderer, and I believe she has taken matters into her own hands. She could be in trouble. She could be *dying*. We cannot delay. Where did Riona and Aeron go?"

"I—I couldn't tell you, Your Highness. I don't know," Ophelia responded, her eyes flitting from his to Amaris's and back. It was a tiny but telling movement.

She was lying.

"Are you sure?" he pressed, stepping closer. "Shall I recount for you the horrific death Treasurer Cathal met in that brothel? Or the way that serving girl's throat had been slashed from ear to ear, just to ensure her silence? If their murderer learns that Riona is searching for him, she may meet just as gruesome an end as they did. Is that what you wish for the woman whose token of favor you wear around your neck?"

The servant shrank back. Then a cool mask slid over her features, and she pulled the small obsidian pendant out from under her tunic. "This necklace means that I have sworn my loyalty to Lady Riona. She has ordered me to remain silent, and it is not my place to question her. I can only assume she did not want anyone to follow her, no matter how seemingly pure their intentions." She glanced at Amaris. "I'm sorry I cannot tell you anything, my lady. Goodnight."

Ophelia performed a stiff curtsy and started down the cobblestone path. Auberon started to follow her, his temper reaching the end of its leash, but Amaris caught his arm. "Let her go. She's not going to speak."

His hands curled into fists. "I would marvel at the loyalty Riona inspires in her allies if it weren't so damned frustrating."

"Speaking of allies..." Amaris turned on him. "Riona was meeting *you* all those nights she snuck out? What were you thinking, helping her search for a murderer? What game were you playing? You couldn't have done it out of the goodness of your heart."

"I couldn't have done it because I wanted to see the bastard who poisoned me meet the executioner's blade?"

"You and your brother have been manipulating the court every day since you got here. Of course you had some ulterior motive."

He shook his head and entered the house, Amaris trailing his steps up to his bedroom. She watched as he sheathed a sword and dagger at his hip, then fastened a cloak around his shoulders. "I'm going to find her," he said as he pulled the hood up. "Is there another exit from the castle, one where royal guards aren't stationed? The longer it takes the king to realize I've left, the better."

When Amaris didn't respond, he turned and found her studying him, an unreadable expression on her face. "What?"

"...You care for her, don't you? Perhaps this all began as a game to win her over for your brother's sake, but...that's not how it is anymore. At least, not for you."

He brushed past her and started down the stairs.

"Don't walk away from me, Auberon," she warned, hurrying after him. "If she must leave her home and her family behind, it should be to marry a man who will love her and make her happy. Your devotion to your brother is admirable, but you and I both know that he is not that man. He and Riona are too similar. There's nothing between them, and there never will be. She—"

Auberon whirled so quickly Amaris nearly slammed into him. She gripped the banister as she stopped short, only a few inches between them. "I was sent here to secure a marriage alliance between Riona and my brother, and until we leave this castle for Erduria, I will not stop trying to do that," he said in a cold voice. He was tired of people questioning his heart, his loyalties. He wouldn't give in to his desire. He *couldn't*. "I will find her and bring her safely home, and then I will do everything in my power to ensure that she and Drystan are betrothed."

Without a word, Amaris turned and walked into his bedroom. She returned a moment later with a cloak wrapped around her slender shoulders. "I'm coming with you."

"No—"

"*I am coming with you*," she repeated, her tone leaving no room for argument. She slipped past him and continued down the stairs, leaving him no choice but to follow her out of the house. "If you're right about her hunting down Cathal's murderer, then her life could be in danger. You and I are going to search for her together. Either that, or I can call for the guards and have you dragged before the king. I'm sure he'd be very happy to hear how the ruthless, manipulative Erdurian prince has been sneaking around with his niece at all hours of the night. What will it be, Your Highness?"

Amaris pinned him with her stare. She knew she'd trapped him, but she didn't know just how dangerous her threat truly was. If the king had ordered Cathal's assassination, then his learning that Auberon and Riona had been investigating the murder would only paint targets on their backs. He wouldn't put it past King Domhnall to arrange for some *accident* to befall them once the negotiations were over.

The eudorite mines...

He turned northward and gazed out over the sprawling city, picturing the dark expanse of the Howling Mountains as he'd seen it the day he and Drystan had arrived at Crafford. Riona was brave to the point of folly, and she knew her time in Rivosa was running out. Perhaps, in a desperate attempt to find answers, she had gone to search for the mines. A spark of possibility ignited within him. Few people were brave or foolish enough to venture into the Howling Mountains, which meant the land would be nearly untouched. He might be able to follow the tracks her horse had left.

"I think I know where Riona is," he said as he turned back to Amaris. "I hope you know how to ride."

Chapter Forty-Seven
The Lady

It felt like they walked for an eternity—an eternity with only the dark tunnels, howling wind, and Dig's unsettling, keening cries as company. Riona studied him as they walked, the threadbare pants slung low around his hips and the grime coating his fair skin. How long had he been wandering down here? Did a part of him remember whatever family he'd left behind? She had just opened her mouth to ask when he stopped at the mouth of a tunnel and turned back to her, a grim expression on his face.

They had arrived.

Riona gripped her pendant, suddenly uncertain. The screeching wind had frayed her nerves, leaving her jumpy and unsettled. "Can you tell me anything about the mines? The layout? Where I might find the overseer?"

He said nothing, just pointed down the tunnel.

I'm on my own, then.

She set a hand on Dig's arm, and he stiffened at her touch. "Thank you for your help. Wait for me here, and once this is all over, I'll see you safely to your family, wherever they may be. You don't have to spend another day in these terrible tunnels."

He nodded and stepped aside.

Riona crept down the tunnel, her heart in her throat. Gradually, the sound of snoring drifted to her from up ahead, where she saw several naturally-formed archways in the stone on either side of the makeshift corridor. Each was covered with a curtain of heavy wool. Peering around the nearest curtain, she discovered a large, dark cavern filled with rows upon rows of cots. She could just make out the silhouettes of the slumbering forms atop the mattresses. There had to be more than fifty men in this room alone, each with one ankle chained to his cot.

The prisoners sentenced to work here. How many of them have gone mad after listening to this relentless wind?

She continued on, silently thanking the Creator that they seemed to be keeping track of day and night. The tunnels were quiet and empty, every room she passed dark. Unfortunately, the smooth walls provided no alcoves in which to hide; she would be discovered the second she encountered another person, but there was no helping that. She'd come too far to leave without answers.

Grab any evidence I find and run, she reminded herself. *That's all I have to do.*

Exactly. It'll be easy, Auberon's voice whispered. *Then it's the simple matter of betraying your kingdom's secrets and confronting the king. What could* possibly *go wrong?*

Gradually, the caverns she passed changed from makeshift dormitories to private sleeping quarters. Riona looked into one and was surprised to find it furnished like a lord's manor. A curtained archway in the center of the cavern led to an adjoining room, where a canopied four-poster bed sat, dripping downy cushions and rich furs. Ornate rugs covered the ground, and a wardrobe full of finely-made cloaks and tunics stood open behind the desk. This was how her uncle was paying the men who ran the mine: steeping them in finery, granting them riches he could not afford to bestow. All to keep them quiet and content in the place that would become their tomb.

They thought the king was rewarding them for their loyalty. They didn't realize he was only buying their silence.

Riona walked down the length of the tunnel, peering into each room she passed, then returned to the first sleeping chamber she had found. It was the most lavishly decorated, which meant it likely belonged to the overseer. If she was going to find answers anywhere, it would be there.

A snore rumbled from the adjoining room, and Riona hesitated in the archway. She had to search now—it would be impossible to slip into the overseer's quarters once the workers were awake. She had already been away from Innislee for a full day, and the longer it took her to find the information she needed, the harder it would be for Amaris to explain her absence to the court.

Riona crept to the desk in the center of the main room. It was a massive, pretentious piece of intricately carved wood, more suited to beauty than function. She had stolen a box of matches from the tavern in Crafford, and she waited for another rumbling snore before striking one, hoping that the noise would mask the sound of the flame flaring to life. Under its faint, flickering light, she began to search the drawers.

Several minutes—and several burnt matches—later, she found something: a letter from the king. It was dated just over a month earlier, right around the time Riona had returned from Beltharos. It was unsigned but clearly written by her uncle's hand:

I know the cave-in left the prisoners uneasy, but you must clear it as quickly as possible. Because this is the only mine that hasn't failed, it is imperative that it runs at maximum efficiency. That collapsed tunnel is full of ore waiting to be mined. I am sure the prisoners will be jumpy and discontented, so be sure to remind them of the <u>depth</u> of their gratitude for the mercy I have granted them. Most of them would spend the rest of their days rotting in a cell if not for this opportunity. Their labor will finally win us this war.

The next letter was from the Treasurer.

My friend, I am sorry to hear of the cave-in. Send me the names of the deceased, and I will see to it that their families are alerted of their deaths. I shall make up a story, of course, but the loved ones should still be told. Their service to the crown has earned them this much, despite the severity of their crimes.

I know this is against the king's orders, and I ask for your silence on the matter. Those men gave their lives for their kingdom, and few people will ever know the roles they played in ending this war. Some nights, I question how we can continue like this, sending them to that foul place and deceiving them into believing that they will one day earn their freedom. Yet I suppose there is no use in philosophizing when nothing will change. My Creator and my king have forced me to bear the cost of this terrible operation, and I will repent by remembering each and every man I sent to his death.

I understand that the mine's production will be limited to about half of its previous output while you clear the cave-in and move the bodies. Keep me apprised of the situation. As we have discussed, despite our king's desire to employ every ounce of ore for the military, as Treasurer, I may need to sell a portion of the yield to maintain the kingdom. Your loyalty to Rivosa and your discretion in this matter will be amply rewarded.

For the roles we play in this undertaking, may the Creator forgive us all,

Cathal

Tears stung Riona's eyes as she read the end of the letter, and she dried them with a sleeve before tucking the papers into her waistband. Her instincts had been right the whole time—Cathal had never been the villain. He had been good, honorable, and noble until the moment he died. All he had ever wanted was to save his kingdom from destruction.

"I thought I heard a rat poking around in here," a gruff voice said.

Riona started and dropped the match, which immediately burnt out. A figure stood across the room, holding back the curtain separating the office from the bedchamber. She couldn't make out his features in the faint light bleeding in from the tunnel, but two details were immediately apparent: he was *huge*, and he was holding a sword.

The overseer started toward her. "Who are you, little rat? I don't have any girls in my mine."

She rose and stared straight at him, forcing a bravado she didn't feel. "I am King Domhnall's niece, Lady Riona Nevis," she said, her hand drifting up to make sure that the letters were still hidden under the drape of her tunic. "I am looking into the circumstances surrounding Treasurer Cathal's murder. I know you two were friends. He told you his doubts about the king."

The overseer paused. "He's dead?"

"Yes. He was stabbed in the chest multiple times while attempting to flee the capital with evidence of the mine's existence. I believe the king was behind it, and I came here to find answers."

His head turned toward the archway. "No one's supposed to know about this place."

Thank you for stating the obvious. "I know the king has been running these mines for years. I know he has been sending you prisoners from across the country. But I need proof." As she spoke, Riona silently prayed that he wouldn't notice her slowly inching toward the exit. "I need your help to avenge Cathal's murder."

The overseer glanced about the room, taking in the fine furnishings. He was weighing what she had said against the king's bribes. The silence stretched out between them. Riona stared at the sword in his hand, her heart pounding so hard she was certain he could hear it.

I will not die here.

At last, he lifted his sword, the blade glinting in the sliver of light from the tunnel.

Riona snatched as many papers as she could from the desk's open drawer, then hurtled toward the archway. The dagger was still strapped to her thigh, but she wasn't foolish enough to believe she could fight off the overseer. He was at least twice her size, and she wouldn't be able to get close enough to slip inside his guard. *Use your speed to your advantage,* Auberon's voice whispered, urging her faster. *Run, aramati!*

RUN!

Riona flung the curtain aside just as the overseer reached out and knotted his fingers in her braids. Pain ignited in the back of her skull, and she bit her lip to keep from crying out. The last thing she needed was to wake the miners.

"Not fast enough, girl," the overseer chided as he flung her back into the office.

She hit the ground hard and rolled, letting out a groan when her back struck the side of the desk, another flare of agony shooting through her battered ribs. The chair toppled, hitting the ground with a sharp *crack!* Distantly, Riona heard people stirring in the nearby caverns.

The overseer loomed over her, still holding his sword. There was no doubt in her mind that he could take her head clean off with one swing.

"You can't kill me," Riona wheezed as she pushed to her hands and knees. Out of his line of sight, she slowly reached for the dagger at her thigh. "I'm the king's niece. Kill me, and you will have sentenced yourself to death."

He paused, and that moment of hesitation was all she needed.

Riona shot to her feet and drove the blade upward, hot blood splattering across her face as it tore through fabric and flesh. The overseer dropped his sword and stumbled backward, a hand rising to the slit in his sleep tunic. Riona stalked toward him. She wasn't sure exactly where she had stabbed him, and she needed to make sure that he wouldn't survive to tell her uncle she'd found the mine.

"Bitch," he spat. When she thrust the dagger at his heart—exactly as Auberon had taught her—the overseer caught her wrist in one meaty hand and wrenched it to the side. A cry of pain escaped her as the dagger's blood-slick handle slipped from her grasp. "You don't get away that easily."

He threw her against the wardrobe. Her head snapped back

and struck the wood, causing stars to dance in her vision as she fell to her knees. The overseer picked up his sword and approached her. Riona groaned, struggling to stand. She would not die here.

She would *not* die here.

The overseer laughed. "Oh, you're spirited, that's for sure. There's no doubt you have Nevis blood running through your veins."

"I'm— I'm trying to help. I—"

He lifted the sword and slammed the pommel down on her head. Everything went black.

Chapter Forty-Eight
The Liar

They rode in heavy, worried silence, their horses thundering along the road to Crafford. Every muscle in Auberon's body was taut, charged with an anxious, restless energy that kept him hunched and low in his saddle. He couldn't stop thinking about the fact that they had no idea *where* in the Howling Mountains Riona actually was. The range spanned half of Rivosa's coast, and they would be searching blindly. She could be anywhere.

He studied Amaris out of the corner of his eye. The black cloak she'd borrowed was wrapped tightly around her and pinned to keep it from streaming behind her in the wind. Between sneaking out of the castle and securing two of the Erdurian horses from the stables, they had gone to Lord Lachlan's estate so she could change out of her finery. She now wore fitted black pants—which she must have stolen from Riona's wardrobe—and a pair of leather boots. Her braids were twisted and pinned atop her head.

"We should let the horses rest," she said as they passed along the edge of a lake, already slowing her horse to a trot. "Keep pushing them, and they'll keel over before we get anywhere near Crafford."

"We don't have time to waste." He glanced at the faint rays of sunlight bleeding across the eastern horizon. It wasn't quite dawn yet, but close. Riona had been missing for almost a day and a half. "Besides, we're over halfway there."

"But we will ride for hours yet while we search the Howling Mountains. Dismount, Prince Auberon," Amaris commanded, the words laced with all the authority of the future queen. "*Now.*"

He huffed a breath and dismounted. His poor horse's sides were dark with sweat, its mouth frothing. After offering Amaris a hand down from her own mount—which she accepted with reluctance—he removed his horse's tack and led it to the water's edge. It drank as if it hadn't seen water in days.

"I'm sorry," he murmured, patting the mare's neck. "After we find Riona, I'll treat you to the finest apples money can buy."

While Amaris doted on the horses, Auberon wandered toward the road, stretching his legs. He would never admit it, but she had been right to stop them. His muscles ached from so many hours of riding, and his fingers were stiff from clutching the reins as tightly as he had. He flexed them, wincing, as he gazed in the direction of the Howling Mountains. Riona was somewhere in there, he could feel it. He only hoped they would find her in time. Even if the miners didn't kill her, there were sinkholes, cave-ins, Rennox...

"I'm worried about her, too," Amaris whispered, joining him by the roadside. She followed his gaze north, and they stood in silence for several minutes, consumed by their worries. Finally, she said, "I've been thinking about what you said last night. Riona and I may not be related by blood, but she is more dear to me than a sister. If you do not tell her the truth about your feelings for her, you must allow her to marry Valerian or Eamon. If she does not have a husband who loves her at her side, she will find no happiness in Erduria."

A stab of pain shot through his heart. "She will. Once she and Drystan are married, she will have a wing of the palace and her own staff of servants and guards. She will have every luxury the Empire can provide at her fingertips. Anything she desires will be hers. And Drystan will be a good husband to her."

"You think you can bribe her into being happy? If you believe that, you don't truly know Riona at all."

Auberon opened his mouth, then closed it. The words had felt wrong even before they'd left his lips. The truth was, he couldn't imagine Riona walking the bright, mirrored halls in the palace or wandering through Torch's maze-like markets. He couldn't imagine her enjoying the relentless sun and sparkling beaches. Innislee was in her blood; she was a girl of lashing rain, biting winds, and raging storms. When she let her court mask fall, she was a tempest.

"No," he reluctantly admitted. "In truth, I don't believe she would be happy in Erduria, either."

She turned to him, her brows rising. "Prince Auberon, I believe that is the first time you've ever been honest with me."

He made a face. "My time in Innislee has forced me to adopt some bad habits. I'll endeavor to lose that one as soon as possible."

"Yes, I'm sure you will," Amaris responded, sounding almost disappointed. She studied him for a few long moments. When she eventually spoke, she said, "If you truly mean to hide your feelings from Riona, I want you to swear that after we return to Innislee, you will stay away from her. Soon, she will marry a man she does not love and leave everything she has ever known behind. There is no reason for her to endure any more pain. You and your people have already hurt her enough."

His heart splintered in his chest. She was right. He had been manipulating her and lying to her since the day they met. And even now, he would do whatever it took to secure an alliance between their countries. If he had to use whatever information Riona had uncovered to blackmail the king into accepting the betrothal, he would do it without hesitation.

How could he possibly bear to hurt her more than Erduria already had?

How could he love her, knowing that he would destroy every facet of her beloved kingdom if it meant saving his people?

He was spared having to answer by the sight of someone riding toward them at a gallop, his horse kicking up a cloud of dirt from the road. Due to the early hour, they had passed few traders and travelers on their ride toward Crafford. This stranger, Auberon quickly realized, was neither. He was a lone rider, no cart or wagon, and his urgency immediately aroused Auberon's suspicion.

He turned to Amaris and hissed, "Go to one of the horses. Pretend it's hurt. *Now!*"

She shot him a strange look, but obeyed. As the rider approached, Auberon stepped into the middle of the road and waved his arms over his head, affecting a distraught expression.

"Help, please!" he cried, putting on the rolling accent of Rivosi nobility. The man slowed to a stop before him, and Auberon hastily smoothed the wrinkles in his doublet as he rushed over, grateful he hadn't bothered to change after the banquet. "Oh, thank the Creator you came along when you did, my friend! I'm supposed to be in Crafford in an hour to check on a shipment from the Isles, and I fear my horse has gone lame. Could you take a look? I'm not much of an equestrian myself." He gestured apologetically at his finery, wordlessly explaining his ignorance on the subject.

"Sorry, but I can't help you."

The man started to guide his horse around Auberon, but he reached out and snagged the reins. "I beg of you, it won't take but five minutes of your time. As you can see, we've another horse here. I just need to know whether it's worth tending or if I should simply cut my losses. Just one look—two minutes—and you'll be on your way," he said, nodding encouragingly at the huge beast of a man. This close, he could see that the stranger was not just fair-skinned, but deathly pale, as if he hadn't seen the sun in ages. Calluses covered his hands, and grime was caked around his cuticles and under his nails.

He had come from the mines.

"I'll pay you for your trouble," Auberon continued, ignoring the man's objections. He offered the stranger a sly grin. "You're heading to the capital, are you not? Let me buy you a pitcher of ale and a hot meal. When you're finished, I expect you'll have enough left over to sample the other...*luxuries* the city has to offer. A night in a woman's arms, perhaps?"

He let the words linger, watching temptation chase away the wariness in the man's expression. Finally, he huffed and dismounted. "Fine, I'll take a look."

"Oh, thank you, friend. Thank you kindly."

Auberon led him over to where Amaris was crouching, pretending to examine one of the mare's back legs. "I think it's something to do with her shoe, but I'm not sure," she said.

As the man bent to study it, Auberon pulled out his dagger and buried it in the side of the stranger's thigh. The miner let out a roar and fell to his knees, one hand flying to the wound in an attempt to stanch the bleeding. Amaris recoiled in horror. Auberon paid her no heed as he stepped behind the miner and pressed the bloody blade to his throat.

"Where are the mines?" he snarled. "Where is Lady Riona?"

"You. Fucking. *Stabbed me!*"

"And I will do it many more times if you don't answer my questions. Where is Lady Riona?"

"Who is that?"

Auberon dug the edge of the blade into the man's neck, and he sucked in a sharp breath. "One more chance, and then I start cutting off fingers. Or maybe," he drawled, "I'll take something you treasure more. How much do you think you'd miss your manhood?"

Fear flashed across his face. "Very well. I'm supposed to deliver a message to the king that Lady Riona found the mine. No one is supposed to leave it alive, but she's the king's own blood, so the overseer wants approval from His Majesty before he kills her."

"The king?" Amaris echoed, her voice pinched with panic. "Why would he want Riona dead? And what is this about a mine?"

Auberon ignored her. "Take us to her."

The stranger nodded. "If you promise to let me go after that, I'll lead you to where she's being held. I can't spend one more day in those damned caves."

"How do I know you won't kill us the moment I remove my blade from your throat?"

"My brother works in the mine, too. Promise to help me free him, and you'll have nothing to fear from me. I swear it on the Creator and all the Old Gods."

Auberon looked to Amaris for confirmation. She slowly nodded.

Satisfied, he stepped back and sheathed his dagger. "You have five minutes to tend to your wound and get back on your horse. Then we're heading to the Mountains."

The man muttered curses under his breath, but true to his word, he made no move to attack. Auberon started back to where he'd left his horse's saddle, and Amaris fell into step beside him, scowling. "Don't chastise me for what I did," he said before she could speak. "It worked."

"You could have handled the situation with a bit more diplomacy."

"He was headed to Innislee to see if the king would order her execution. Would you have bothered with *diplomacy?*"

Amaris sighed. "I suppose if it brings Riona back safely, then it was worth it. I'll say nothing more on the matter. You may be an Erdurian savage, but who am I to judge a man for doing what he excels at?"

"I'm not certain whether that was a compliment or an insult."

She let out a quiet, reluctant laugh. "Neither am I, to be honest."

Five minutes later, they mounted their horses and set off for the Howling Mountains. The miner had shucked off his tunic and torn it into strips, which he had then bound around the gash in his thigh. It didn't take long for the fabric to become soaked through with blood—a fact which did not inspire the slightest bit of sympathy within Auberon. The miners had Riona.

We're coming, aramati, he silently vowed, wishing she could hear him. *And I will flay any man who has set a hand on you.*

Chapter Forty-Nine
The Lady

When she awoke, Riona lifted her head slowly, biting back a groan at the throbbing in her temples. Something dry and sticky was crusted to her face. *Blood*. She shifted, trying to wipe it off, and realized with a jolt of panic that her arms were bound behind her back. With a concentrated effort, she dragged her heavy eyelids open and winced at the light filling the cavern.

Riona was bound to a chair in the center of the overseer's quarters. The sheath on her thigh was gone, Auberon's dagger nowhere in sight. Her wrists were tied together with a length of rough rope, and more circled her chest and upper arms. Her ankles were chained to the legs of the chair, looped through the crossbar so she wouldn't be able to tilt back and slip the shackles free. In her periphery, she could see the overseer standing in the tunnel outside, exchanging quiet words with someone beyond her line of vision. Two guards stood watch over her, one on either side of the archway.

"All these precautions for a harmless noblewoman?" she drawled, her lips curling into a smirk that would have made Auberon proud. "I would hate to see how you'd react to someone with real skill."

The overseer stalked over to her. His chest was bare, and thick bandages encircled his torso where she'd struck him with the dagger. "I'm not taking any chances with the niece of the king," he said as he moved to the desk. "With your luck, you'd free yourself only to stumble into a sinkhole and break your neck. I'm not losing my head because some little rat has no sense of self-preservation."

"That's already happened."

"What?"

"The sinkhole. Except I didn't break my neck."

He muttered something under his breath as he shuffled through the papers on the desk. Riona frowned, trying to wade through the haze of pain clouding her mind, as he lifted something to one of the candelabra's flames. It took her a few moments to realize that he was holding the letters she had slipped into her waistband. They must have fallen out after she'd lost consciousness.

"NO!" Riona cried as he lowered the first of the papers to the fire. It ignited immediately, illuminating the harsh lines of the overseer's face as the flames climbed the parchment. When no more than a scrap remained, he released it, letting it drift down to the desk. It crumbled to ash the second it hit the wood. "Stop! *Stop!* Cathal trusted you!"

He said nothing as he burned the rest of the papers. Riona thrashed, fighting her bonds, but they refused to give. When the last paper dwindled to nothing but ash, she slumped back in her chair, defeated. "How could you? Cathal was your friend."

"And His Majesty is my king."

"He has condemned countless people to death for a dream that will only end in more bloodshed. He cannot wield eudorite weapons against the Erdurians. It will be a slaughter."

The overseer's eyes narrowed. "Since when does the Rivosi royal family have any sympathy for Erdurian *dogs?*"

Since I met Auberon.

When she said nothing, he leaned against the edge of the desk and crossed his arms. "I sent a man to Innislee to tell your uncle what has transpired. By tonight, my messenger will return with his orders. I can't promise that you will leave this place alive." The overseer said it nonchalantly, not a hint of remorse or sympathy in his voice. "If I were in your shoes, I would start praying that he has some mercy for you in that heart of his. Creator knows he doesn't have any for the people he sentences to work in this damned place."

"Why did you agree to take this post?" Riona asked sometime later. After his wound stopped bleeding, the overseer had donned a doublet of black and gold brocade and sheathed Auberon's dagger at his hip. He was sitting at the desk, and he glanced over his shoulder at the sound of her voice. His gaze swept over her, cold and dismissive, then turned back to whatever he'd been writing.

"Don't you realize that my uncle will never allow you to leave?" she asked, keeping her voice low and soft, trying to reason with him. "You may have a wardrobe full of finery and a bed fit for a king, but you are as much a slave as the men who work these mines. He will leave you here until you die or go mad, and then he will send another man to fill your place. Why do you give him your loyalty? Why continue to serve him after he murdered your friend?"

Without a word, the overseer rose, walked over to her, and backhanded her across the face.

Her head snapped to the side. Riona gave herself a few seconds to close her eyes, pain ricocheting around her skull, before she turned to meet his stare. "I met one of your miners on my way here. He wasn't much older than I am, and I'm guessing he couldn't have been here for more than a few years. He'd already been driven mad by the wind howling through the tunnels. Does the sound ever get to you? Does it haunt your dreams?"

"*Silence.*"

"How much longer do you have before my uncle sticks another puppet in your place? That's all we are to him. Puppets. Pawns," Riona continued, undaunted. "You said earlier that I should pray that my uncle has mercy for me. If he is willing to order the murder of his own niece, what do you think he will do with you once you've outlasted your usefulness? Do you truly believe that he will allow you to have a life after the mines?"

"*Be quiet!*"

"No. The only way you and the other prisoners here will leave with your lives and your wits is if you let me go. I don't want the eudorite to be mined if *this* is the price we must pay. Let me go, and we—"

The overseer seized her throat in one large hand, sealing off her air. In her periphery, Riona saw the guards at the archway exchange excited looks. "There's no doubt you're the king's blood, little rat. You've got a silver tongue, just like the rest of the court."

Every muscle in her body tensed, screaming at her to fight. Her wrists strained against the rope binding them. Even so, she refused to let him see so much as a flicker of fear cross her face.

"Your uncle may not want you dead," the overseer snarled, his voice muffled through the blood rushing in her ears, "but I bet he'd commend me if I took your tongue. Seems like you're more trouble than you're worth."

Stars flared and died in her vision.

He smirked. "Not so clever now, are you?"

At last, the overseer released her. Riona had just enough time to suck in a breath before he backhanded her again, his ring cutting into her cheek. Warm blood trickled down the side of her face as the overseer stalked back to his desk and sat. He picked up the quill and began writing, then paused when he noticed a fleck of blood on his ring.

"Only a few hours now, little rat," he said as he picked up a handkerchief and wiped the ring clean. "And then we'll see just how brave you really are."

Chapter Fifty
The Lady

A ragged scream tore through the tunnels, too raw—too *human*—to be the wind. The hair on the back of Riona's neck rose as one, two, countless more joined it. The overseer spat a curse and leapt to his feet, his chair skidding across the rug and toppling over.

"Men, stay here and watch the girl," he said to the guards as he strode through the archway, and they murmured their assent.

"Another collapse, ye think?" the stockier of the two asked once the overseer had left, his rural accent so thick Riona could barely make out the words.

"I don't know, but that royal bitch is right—we're all going to die here."

Another wail rose from the tunnels outside. This one was different, though—it was higher, keening, almost an imitation of the howling wind that had given the mountains their name. Riona straightened, recognizing the voice.

Dig!

"Wind madness," the taller guard breathed, pulling his sword from its sheath. Riona was taken aback by the strange weapon. The long blade was made of a rich black metal that shone like obsidian and seemed to swallow the light around it—the same metal that hung at her collarbone.

Eudorite.

"Rennox!" someone shouted, and the word sent a wave of terror down Riona's spine. "All men to the northern tunnels! Grab your blackblades and get to the northern tunnels!"

"Southern! They're coming from the southern, too!"

"—half to the storerooms, half to the tunnels!" another voice cried, overlapping with all the others. In the chaos, Riona could hear the pounding of heavy footfalls, the ringing of blades, and the bloodcurdling screams of the dying. "A dozen Rennox! Remember, men: kill a dozen Rennox and earn your freedom!"

Lies. All to keep them from lying down and letting the Rennox slaughter them. She had never heard of anyone being able to kill a Rennox. No one even knew how they were *alive* in the first place. How could one kill a creature of living stone?

The guards shifted their weight from foot to foot, clearly disturbed by the cries, but they didn't leave their posts. Riona suspected they were more than happy to stand watch and avoid the fight. While they were distracted, she shifted, trying to slip her hands free of the rope. She only succeeded in shredding her skin on the rough fibers.

I will not *die here!*

The sounds of fighting drew nearer. Would the Rennox reach them? She struggled more, tearing her wrists raw. Pain shot through the torn flesh. She was too far from the desk to try and reach something with which to free herself, so she had to hope that the knots would give way before her wrists did.

"Check over there! We have to find her!"

Riona froze, recognizing the voice. *How—?*

Before she could even finish the thought, Auberon burst into the cavern, wild-eyed and breathing hard. He reacted with incredible speed, pivoting and jamming his sword through the gut of the stocky guard before the man could even cry out. The miner staggered and fell, blood pouring from the hole in his stomach.

Auberon pulled his blade out and turned just as the other guard drove his sword toward the prince's chest. The other man was larger, but Auberon had been trained by the finest swordsmen in Erduria. He deflected the guard's blow and then cleaved the man's head from his shoulders.

Riona flinched as it *thumped* to the ground.

Auberon turned to her. Blood was splattered across his face and body, and his knuckles were white around the grip of a eudorite sword.

"*Riona,*" he gasped.

In a heartbeat, he was behind her, slicing through the rope at her wrists. It hit the ground with a soft *whump*, and the rope around her chest and arms followed. Then he swung the sword down on the chains binding her ankles, and the blade sheared through the iron as if it were twine. *Once eudorite blades are forged, they will retain their form until the end of time,* she recalled her mother saying. *The sharpest blade cannot scratch it. The hardest stone cannot blunt it.*

Auberon dropped to his knees before her and gently cupped her face in his hands, running his fingers over the bump by her temple, the gash in her cheek. His touch was so light, she was half-convinced that he was merely a figment of her imagination. She reached up and brushed a strand of hair from his brow, afraid that the movement would break the spell. "Are you truly here?"

A tender, crooked smile tugged at one corner of his lips. "Did you really think I wouldn't come for you, *aramati?*" he whispered, devastation in his beautiful gray-blue eyes. As he took in her raw, bloody wrists and swollen cheek, his features twisted in fury. "Where is the overseer? I'm going to tear him limb from limb for what he's done."

Riona gripped his wrist. "Leave him to the Rennox. I want to go home," she said, her voice breaking on the last word.

Auberon leaned forward and pressed a soft kiss to her forehead. She heard him let out a quiet, shuddering breath as his thumb traced the curve of her cheek, holding her as if he couldn't bear to let go. "I'm going to get you home, *aramati*. I promise."

He took her hand and helped her to her feet. Pain rushed through her ribcage and down her bruised spine, but she forced a brave face as she stood. "The overseer—he has your dagger. I'm so sorry."

"You think I care about that? Daggers—even heirlooms—can be replaced. You, my lady, are not quite so expendable."

"With that, I wholeheartedly agree," the overseer said as he strode into the cavern. He glanced at the bodies of the guards, his gaze lingering on the severed head before meeting Auberon's glare. He raised his sword, which Riona now saw was outfitted with a blade of shining eudorite. "Looks like her knight in shining armor has come to save the day."

"Pleased to make your acquaintance."

Auberon stalked forward, but before he could take more than two steps, the overseer's chest erupted in a spray of blood and gore. Riona lifted a hand to cover her face. When she lowered it, her heart stopped at the sight of the crude eudorite spearhead protruding from the man's sternum.

The overseer staggered, gaping down at the spear in horror. A crimson stain spread across his fine doublet as he slumped to his knees, then fell face-first to the ground beside the bodies of the guards. The shaft of the spear stuck straight out from his back. It quivered once, twice, as he sucked in two wet, shallow breaths, and then fell still.

Riona moved to Auberon's side in a daze, staring at the weapon. She found the prince's free hand and laced her fingers through his. "The Rennox," she whispered.

Just as she said it, a man—no, a *creature*—ducked through the archway. It was stooped to keep from hitting its elongated, humanoid head on the ceiling of the cavern, but Riona could tell that it was easily more than eight feet tall. Its body appeared to be made of the same gray stone as the walls around it, struck through with veins of eudorite ore, yet it moved with as much grace and dexterity as a human. The creature set one foot on the overseer's back and pulled the spear out of the corpse. Its onyx eyes locked on them, and it lifted the spear, the point dripping blood as the Rennox fixed it on Auberon's heart.

The prince swallowed, his throat bobbing, and said the only logical thing one could say in such a situation:

"Fuck."

Part Five
Man and Monster

Chapter Fifty-One
The Lady

Auberon cautiously lifted his sword. "Riona," he whispered, never turning his attention from the Rennox. "I may have made an error in judgment when I decided to trust these creatures."

"Trust them? What do you mean?"

"Let's just say that the Rennox attack wasn't a coincidence. We ran into a friend of yours on our way here."

A friend? Dig?

"Auberon?" a distant voice called. *Amaris!* "Where are you?"

"In here! I found her—she's alive."

He edged to the side of the cavern, keeping Riona close beside him. His thumb brushed across the back of her hand as the Rennox swiveled its head, tracking their movements. The point of its spear was still trained on Auberon's chest. Droplets of blood *plop, plop, plopped* on the ornate rug. It hadn't moved beyond the archway but, for some reason, it hadn't attacked them, either.

Riona studied it warily. The creature was bipedal, with long, narrow limbs that sparkled with flecks of eudorite. Its face—if it could truly be called a *face*—was nothing more than an elongated oval with twin chips of onyx roughly in the place of human eyes.

Movement flashed behind it, and surprise shot through Riona when Dig pushed aside the curtain and shuffled past the Rennox's leg. He grinned at her, then turned and held up a hand to the creature. Its face parted—there was no other way to describe it, as it had no lips that Riona could see—and it muttered a few guttural words in a voice like the scrape of a whetstone against a blade. Dig shook his head and responded in the same strange tongue.

"He's...speaking to it," Riona said, caught between awe and confusion.

"Unsettling, isn't it?" Auberon murmured.

After they exchanged a few more words, the Rennox lowered its spear and stepped aside. Dig's grin widened as he loped toward the archway and moved the curtain aside. Auberon dropped Riona's hand and took a sharp step away as Amaris rushed into the cavern.

"Oh, thank the Creator!" she cried as she threw her arms around Riona's neck. "When we get back to Innislee, I am going to *kill* you for this."

"If we make it back to Innislee, I won't try to stop you," Riona murmured, ignoring the agony that raced through her ribcage as she squeezed Amaris tightly.

Auberon moved to the archway and peered into the tunnel, his grip tightening on his sword. "Come on, ladies. We have to go now, before the fighting gets closer."

"Trust me, we can't leave fast enough," Amaris said, stepping back and slipping her hand into Riona's. "Let's go."

The Rennox ducked out of the cavern, Auberon and Dig close on its heels. Riona and Amaris started after them, and when they reached the overseer's body, Riona knelt and pulled the emerald-hilted dagger from his belt. She didn't have time to search for the sheath to strap it to her thigh, so she slipped it into the leg of her boot and prayed that they would make it out of the mine without having to use it. Then she pulled the ring of keys from the overseer's pocket and removed the shackles from her ankles, tossing them aside with disgust.

Auberon had waited for them just beyond the archway, and he fell into step behind Riona and Amaris when they emerged, consistently checking over his shoulder to make certain that they were not being pursued. Behind them, the tunnel was a mess of blood and broken bodies. Mine workers lay scattered, some missing entire limbs. The sight sent a tremor down Riona's spine. It was all too similar to the aftermath of the battle of Sandori.

She heard a shout and turned back to find two tall, hulking men making their way toward them, picking a careful path through the scattered bodies. From their pale skin and muscular builds, it was obvious that they were miners. Each held a eudorite blade, and one had a makeshift bandage wrapped around his thigh. The wounded one leaned against the other man, wincing with every step.

When Auberon made no move to stop their pursuit, Riona raised a brow. "More friends of yours?"

"Something like that. I may have stabbed one of them."

"Sounds like something you'd do."

"Let's get out of here," one of the miners grunted when they caught up. "I don't want to spend any more time in this damned place than I have to."

"I couldn't agree more," Amaris muttered.

They set off again, the miners trailing behind their small group. Riona shivered as the wind howled in the distance, mingling with the cries of the dying from elsewhere in the mining system, where the fight still raged. Her gaze drifted to the Rennox. Its hulking stature dwarfed the scrawny young man walking beside it.

"How exactly did you come to be allied with Rennox?" she whispered to Amaris. "How did you even discover I was here?"

"It's a long story. I'll tell you once we're in Crafford and you've had some rest. And once that's over, I expect that *you* will answer some questions of mine."

Riona nodded, dreading what was to come. There was no telling what would happen once they returned to Innislee. Her uncle had been keeping the eudorite mines a closely guarded secret for years. Now that Auberon knew they were crafting eudorite weapons, Rivosa might never again have peace. It would only be a matter of time before Emperor Hyperion sent his army to stake his claim on the Mountains, and she knew her uncle would not allow so much as a sliver of ore to fall into Hyperion's hands. He would fight the Erdurians with every resource at his disposal until the bitter end. Neither side could win. Erduria had more men, but Rivosa had eudorite weapons.

They would fight until they destroyed each other.

This is all my fault, Riona thought, miserable. She had never intended for Auberon to learn that his suspicions about the mines were correct. She had only hoped to use him to find Cathal's murderer and root out the corruption in her uncle's court. *Because of me, both our peoples will be slaughtered.*

As they walked, Rennox began to materialize from the adjoining tunnels, standing with their crude spears like silent sentinels. They were waiting, Riona realized, as one after another fell into step behind them. Eventually, a group of more than a dozen trailed them, their spearheads occasionally scraping against the ceilings of the tunnel. It didn't escape Riona's notice that while none of the creatures lay dead among the bodies they passed, some bore deep gashes in their stone flesh. *The eudorite blades—they're strong enough to wound a Rennox,* she realized with a mixture of awe and trepidation. If that was what it could do to stone, it would have no trouble cutting through steel armor.

Finally, a sliver of daylight appeared in the distance. Riona let out a sharp breath, relief washing over her. She glanced back, and Auberon's tight expression softened when their eyes met. She felt the ghost of his fingers skating across her skin, the brush of his lips against her forehead. The broken, helpless way he had said her name echoed in her ears.

Riona. Aramati. Beloved one.

That meant nothing, a voice whispered in her mind. *He only came to verify that the mines exist. To him, you are still a prize to be won, and that is all you will ever be. He only saved you because he could not allow his brother's future bride to be killed.*

For the first time, the voice was not her own. It was the voice of the man who had taught her all her life that Erdurians were ruthless, heartless, remorseless monsters. It was the voice of the king who was willing to sacrifice countless more lives for the chance to destroy his enemies.

And the words it spoke were ones she no longer believed.

When they were only a couple of yards from the exit, a few of the Rennox broke from their group and formed a wall before the mine's entrance. More moved to stand shoulder-to-shoulder behind Riona and the others, trapping them between two impenetrable lines. The creatures lowered the points of their spears as one. Auberon immediately stepped in front of Riona and Amaris and lifted his sword. Behind them, the miners lifted their own weapons.

Only Dig seemed unconcerned. He stepped forward and held his hands out before Auberon. When the prince stared at him in confusion, he nodded to the eudorite sword clenched in Auberon's hand.

Understanding struck Riona. The folk stories claimed that the Rennox were territorial, but perhaps they weren't trying to protect the land. Perhaps they were protecting the ore. "They want it back. They won't let you take it out of the Mountains."

Dig nodded again, an expectant look on his face.

The prince's fingers tightened around the sword's grip as he turned to Riona. "We have to show the court this sword. They must see the proof of what the king is planning to do to my people. With these weapons..." His gaze drifted to the Rennox, lingering on a deep gash in one creature's torso. The blow would have disemboweled a human, even one wearing plate mail. "Riona, he will *destroy us.*"

The Rennox slammed the butts of their spears on the ground, the sound reverberating down the tunnel. Auberon didn't so much as flinch. He fixed Riona with an imploring look. "Help me reason with them."

One of the creatures stepped forward, and her heart stuttered. There was no doubt in her mind that the Rennox would kill him if he attempted to take just one step closer to the exit.

Let him try to take the blade, her uncle's voice urged. *His death would solve all our problems. Prince Drystan no doubt knows the rumors of the mines, but those rumors hold no substance without the things Auberon has witnessed this day. If he dies, the Emperor will be left with only suspicion.*

Riona silenced the thoughts. She could not condemn the prince to death, not after he had risked his life to save hers.

"Auberon," she whispered. "Hand it over."

He set his jaw and reluctantly placed the sword in Dig's waiting hands. When the prince glanced over his shoulder at her, there was no mistaking the anger and defeat on his face. The same emotions rushed through Riona as Dig collected the miners' swords and handed them over to one of the Rennox. More proof of the mining operation slipping through her fingers, just like the letters.

Without a word, the Rennox parted before them. Auberon led them toward the exit, still eyeing the creatures warily. Amaris practically dragged Riona along, a smile spreading across her full lips when they emerged into the bright sunlight. Dig shuffled along behind them. He hissed at the rush of light that spilled over them, throwing up a hand to shield his eyes. The sun was high overhead, the sky a clear, cloudless blue. Riona grinned. She had never seen such a beautiful sight. Even the miners laughed and clapped each other on the back.

Riona directed them to the small clearing where she had left her mare, and Auberon helped her onto the saddle. "Not quite home yet, *aramati*," he murmured, his hand lingering on her thigh for a heartbeat longer than necessary, "but you're safe now."

Until my uncle learns that I know the truth about the mines, she thought, but she held her tongue.

While he, Amaris, and the miners left to fetch their horses, Dig approached her and ran his hands along her mare's flank, gazing at the horse with a mix of fear and amazement. In the sunlight, she could see for the first time the extent of the grime coating his skin. It was a grayish-brown, weeks upon weeks of dust and dirt caked on his flesh. A scraggly beard covered his narrow jaw, the same mousy brown as his hair.

"We'll find a river where you can wash on the way to Crafford," she told him. "And I'll buy you a change of clothes when we reach the town."

Dig looked up at her through his curtain of lank, tangled hair and shook his head. When Riona frowned, he turned back to the entrance of the mine, where the Rennox were standing in the shadow of the overhang, watching them. Each held its spear like a walking stick, the eudorite point gleaming even in the low light of the tunnel.

"Are you afraid of leaving?" Riona asked softly.

He glanced at the sky and back to her. He nodded.

"You have nothing to fear. You must have family who miss you. We can help you find them."

His face crumpled into a look of devastating sorrow. "Nothing left."

"No family left? We can—"

"No. Nothing left," he whispered. "Of *me*."

Riona's lips parted, understanding rushing over her as Dig hung his head in shame. He had spent so long in the tunnels that he had been changed irrevocably, his wits stolen from him by the ceaseless, merciless wind. Whatever remained of the man he'd been did not want his family to see what he had become.

"I'm sorry," she breathed, her heart breaking. "I'm so sorry for what has happened to you. You have my eternal gratitude for your help today."

Dig reached up and clasped her hand. His fingernails were broken and caked with dried blood in the places where they had torn to the quick on the tunnel's walls. He offered her a fleeting smile before starting toward the entrance of the mine. As he approached, the Rennox turned and retreated to the tunnel. He did not look back as he disappeared into the darkness behind them.

Chapter Fifty-Two
The Liar

It was all Auberon could do not to touch her.

He had chosen to ride at the rear of their group so he could keep a watchful eye on the brothers—whose names, he'd learned, were Callan and Halston—but his gaze never strayed long from Riona. She sat tall and proud in her saddle, her shoulders back and chin held high as always. Even after everything she had endured, she held herself like a queen.

Like an empress.

He fought the urge to dig his heels into his mare's sides and ride beside Riona. To feel the brush of her leg against his. To reach over and run his fingers over the cut on her cheek. To remind himself, over and over again, that she was safe.

Auberon dragged his gaze away. In his periphery, he could see the gaping entrances to the Howling Mountain's labyrinthine tunnels, and he tensed as the wind howled through the caverns. Their group rode along the edge of the mountains in anxious and weary silence. They were still in shock from what they had witnessed: Rennox—creatures of living stone—fighting for them.

Fighting at the madman's behest.

Auberon shuddered at the memory. He was grateful for the creatures' aid, but he couldn't shake the terror that had gripped him the moment that Rennox had pointed its spear at his chest. Looking into its onyx eyes had been like staring at death itself. Only once in his life had he felt as helpless and small as he had standing before that creature, and that was a day he did not care to relive.

He reached down to run his fingers over the hilt of his emerald dagger and faltered when he remembered that it was still on the overseer's body. In the chaos of Riona's rescue, he hadn't thought to retrieve it. He held back a sigh. The mine was far behind them now, the dagger lost to whichever miner was lucky enough to loot the overseer's corpse. The loss wounded him more than he would ever admit. He had been carrying that blade for almost as long as he could remember. He had not regretted giving it to Riona, knowing that the blade might one day save her life, but it was different now that he knew he would never see it again. One more piece of his childhood, gone.

Auberon turned his thoughts to the mine. Not only was it real, but he knew exactly where it was located. He'd memorized every turn they had taken as Callan led them into the heart of the Howling Mountains. The fact that the miners were armed with eudorite blades complicated plans for an attack, but he could work around it. The weapons were extraordinary, but the men wielding them were not trained fighters. A complement of soldiers would easily overwhelm them, especially in tight quarters.

See, Drystan? You had no reason to doubt my loyalty, he thought, recalling the argument they'd had the night he left Innislee. He had accomplished half of his assignment, and all that remained was to convince the king to approve the alliance.

His attention snagged on Amaris, riding at Riona's side. *If you truly mean to hide your feelings from Riona, I want you to swear that after we return to Innislee, you will stay away from her,* she had said that morning. *Soon, she will marry a man she does not love and leave everything she has ever known behind. There is no reason for her to endure any more pain. You and your people have already hurt her enough.*

They had been desperate to find Riona, and now their fragile alliance was broken. He understood Amaris's wariness and suspicion. She couldn't possibly know the lengths to which King Domhnall had gone to keep the mine a secret, but she was smart enough not to trust a foreigner with the knowledge that they existed.

Well. Soon enough, the whole world would learn that the king was mining eudorite ore.

Soon enough, the whole world would come for Rivosa.

They arrived in Crafford that afternoon. Auberon rode close behind Riona, ready to lend a hand should she need it. Her back was still straight, her stare fixed on the road before her, yet he knew that her strength had flagged considerably since they left the mine. She was exhausted, hungry, and in pain, but even now, she was too proud to admit it. It had taken them the better part of two hours to reach Crafford, and she had not once asked to stop and rest. None of them had. All they had wanted was to put as much distance between themselves and the Howling Mountains as possible.

Amaris rode at the front of their group with the brothers, who claimed to know the town well. Sure enough, Callan led their group down a few narrow streets and up to a large lodging house just off the harbor. Auberon breathed in the saltwater breeze sweeping off the Tranquil Sea, still marveling at the fact that they had made it out of the mine alive. Right now, he wanted nothing more than a hot bath. He had tried his best to scrub the blood from his face, but he could still feel the ghost of it on his skin. Under his cloak, his clothes were stiff with the dried blood of the men he'd killed.

Callan led them to a nearby stable. Auberon dismounted

alongside the others, noting with a stab of concern the way Riona immediately set a hand on her ribcage once Halston helped her down from her mare. The pain must have finally gotten the better of her. The street was busy and several people paused to stare at their strange group, but Riona didn't acknowledge them at all as Amaris slipped an arm around her waist and guided her toward the lodging house.

Auberon handed his mare's reins to the stablehand, then pulled out a handful of coins and split them between the miners. "Get us some rooms and then tend to your wound," he said to Callan, nodding to the bloody bandage wrapped around his thigh. "Halston, fetch a healer. Send him to Lady Riona's room first."

Callan grumbled something about being stabbed, but he didn't try to argue. Auberon watched the brothers head off in different directions—he didn't entirely trust them not to run off with the money, even though he had promised them a reward upon returning to Innislee. Then he shoved his hands into his pockets and started toward the tavern after Callan. As he reached the front door, he glanced over his shoulder at the Erdurian ship's sails, just visible through the gaps between the houses. Soon, he, Drystan, and Riona would sail to Torch and leave Rivosa's court of vipers far behind.

"Stop fussing over me, I'm fine," Riona objected as Amaris eased her onto the bed in their shared room. Auberon trailed them inside, followed by the healer Halston had procured. "I just need rest, and so do you. We must set out for Innislee tonight."

Auberon leaned against the chest of drawers and crossed his arms. "If you're feeling well enough, we'll set out at dawn tomorrow. For now, we must all rest and regain our strength."

"But—"

"He's right, milady," the healer said as he set his bag on the bedside table and leaned down to examine her. "A four-hour ride is only going to make matters worse. Now, where is the pain most acute?"

"My ribs."

With a grimace, Riona sat up and pulled the hem of her tunic up enough for him to examine her ribcage. Her face tightened in pain, and by the time she sat back against the headboard, a sheen of sweat had broken out across her forehead. Fury rushed over Auberon when he saw what the overseer had done to her. Even with her deep onyx skin, he could see the dark bruises that snaked across her ribcage and around her back.

The healer's expression didn't falter, but Amaris sucked in a sharp breath and lifted a shaky hand to her mouth. It would be a miracle if her ribs weren't broken. Riona had been moving gingerly since they found her, but to walk and ride without allowing even a flicker of pain to show on her face... She was stronger than he had imagined. Auberon dug his nails into his biceps, fighting to maintain his composure as the healer began to gently examine her ribcage. Every small grimace, every sharp intake of breath, tortured him.

He forced himself to remain still, a silent observer to Riona's agony. A cry of pain slipped from her lips when the healer hit a particularly tender spot, and the sound nearly sent Auberon to his knees. Unable to bear it, he stalked over to the window and turned his back on them, his stomach twisting into knots.

"Your ribs are bruised, but they're not broken," the healer finally said. Auberon turned back as he pulled a bottle of shimmering golden oil from his bag and poured in a white powder, turning the mixture a milky beige. He lifted it to Riona's lips. "Ienna Oil and dried Lady's Grace. It will ease your pain and help you sleep."

She pushed the bottle away. "How long until we can return to Innislee?"

"If you plan to ride horseback, I'd allow several days to

recover first. The bruising continues along your spine, and it'll be extremely painful to make the journey. Now please, drink this."

Riona obeyed. Once she'd finished, she leaned back against the headboard and glanced at Auberon, her expression making it clear that she had no intention of following the healer's advice.

"Rest now, and we'll discuss our traveling plans later," Auberon said, shooting her a warning look.

She huffed, but nodded. "Fine."

The healer pulled several jars and bottles from his bag and set to crafting a topical mixture for her minor wounds. Riona winced when he smeared the herbal paste across the lines of bloody, inflamed skin where the rope had scraped her flesh raw. Her delicate, perfect wrists were a mottled mess of shredded skin and scabbing cuts. The sight made Auberon sick—not from the blood, but at the thought of how desperately Riona had been trying to break free. He didn't want to imagine what the overseer would have done to her if he and Amaris hadn't found her in time.

I put her in that position. I put her life at risk. I never should have told her my suspicions about the mines in the first place.

"Finished," the healer finally murmured, long after Riona's lids had drifted shut. He gently dabbed the last of the herbal paste along the cut in her cheek, then returned his supplies to his bag. "See to it that she rests. She can still move about freely if it doesn't cause her too much pain, but no long rides until she has recovered more. If you must return to the capital, take a carriage —it'll be more comfortable for her."

"Thank you," Amaris said, following him to the door. She dropped a handful of coins into his palm. "We're very grateful for your help...and your discretion."

"Of course, milady." He placed the coins in his pocket and handed her a bottle of golden oil and a jar of white powder. "If the pain gets too much for her, mix these and give them to her before bed. Send for me if you need more."

With that, he left to attend to Callan, who was waiting with his brother in the room across the hall. Amaris closed the door behind him, set the medicine on the bedside table, and pulled the blanket up to cover Riona. Auberon watched from where he stood by the window, aching at the tenderness on Amaris's face as she bent down and stroked Riona's hair.

Every trace of kindness vanished when she looked up at him. "Eudorite swords. Mythical blades that could cleave through steel as if it were silk. That could cut a man wearing full plate mail in two without the slightest nick. That is why you came to Innislee."

Auberon crossed his arms. "You saw what those swords can do. If there were even a *whisper* that my people were planning to use eudorite blades against yours, your king would have sent spies into the Empire to verify it, too."

"All you were sent to verify was whether it would be worth it to take the Mountains from us. What do you think will happen once word of the mine's existence spreads? Armies from around the world will come to claim a stake in the Howling Mountains. Rivosa will never know peace again."

He took a step forward, and Amaris moved in front of Riona as if to shield her. "That is why your king must accept a peace treaty between us. Give us a stake in the mines, make us your partner, and we will fight alongside Rivosa. For the first time in thirty years, we can be allies rather than enemies."

Amaris studied him warily. Then she sat on the edge of the bed and took Riona's hand. "I don't trust a word out of your mouth, but I saw the way she was looking at you back in the mine. Riona is the most honorable and moral person I have ever met, and somehow, she has fallen for you. If she can look at you and see someone worth loving, there must be some honor and humanity in your heart. I hope you prove that you are worthy of her."

Every word she said sent one more fracture through Auberon's heart. He wanted to tell Amaris that he would die before he let another person hurt Riona. He wanted to tell her that although he had been sent to secure eudorite ore for the

Empire's military, he could not bear the thought of more Rivosans dying in the war. He wanted to tell her that he deserved every ounce of hatred she felt for him. If King Domhnall refused a peace treaty, Rivosa could be destroyed, and Auberon would be powerless to stop it.

In the end, all he said was, "I don't believe I am."

CHAPTER FIFTY-THREE
THE LADY

The room was dark when Riona awoke. A lantern sat on the table beside her, its flame turned low. She rolled over, wincing at the soreness in her ribs, and found Amaris curled up next to her. The girl's lips were parted, and her chest slowly rose and fell with soft, slumbering breaths. Riona rose and opened the shutters to find a blanket of stars stretching over the city. The street below was quiet, empty with the exception of a few merchants and sailors heading toward the harbor. It was almost morning, then.

Creeping on silent feet, Riona pulled on her boots, slipped Auberon's dagger into her waistband, and left the room. When she descended the stairs to the lodging house's main room, she found a short, round woman kneading dough at a table behind the bar. She glanced up when Riona approached, revealing a smudge of flour across one cheek. Her attention immediately went to the bump protruding from Riona's temple.

"Are ye alright, miss? My niece said some girl came in 'ere yesterday with a ragtag group of strangers, looking like she'd taken a beatin'. I'm assumin' yer her," she said, rounding the table to examine Riona in the light of the lantern hanging over the bar. "Do ye need anythin'? Did— Did the people yer with do this to ye? Should I send for the guards?"

"No, no, they protected me. All I need is something to eat. I know it's early, but I'll take anything you can spare, please."

Riona pulled a few aurums out of her pocket, but the woman waved them away with a warm smile. "Keep yer money, girl. My niece is around yer age, and if she walked into some stranger's lodgin' house lookin' the way ye do, I'd want the owner to take care of her the same way. Sit down. I'll fix ye up somethin' fresh and warm to eat. Ye look like ye need it."

She patted Riona's hand and bustled into the kitchen, her dough forgotten. Warmed by the stranger's kindness, Riona set the coins on the bar beside a decanter of whiskey, then turned to find a place to sit. Her gaze landed on a table near the rear of the room, where a young man sat with his back to her. The light from the lanterns played across his hair, illuminating the auburn strands. She started toward him.

"Shouldn't you be resting?" she asked as she approached Auberon's table. A chipped mug sat before him, and he idly toyed with the handle, his fingers tapping out a rhythm on the ceramic.

"I could ask you the same question." His tone was light, casual, but his stare remained fixed on his drink as he spoke. "Seeing as you're the one who nearly died yesterday."

"I was bound and held captive. There's a difference," she joked. When he still did not look at her, did not smile, did not act like Auberon at all, her mirth faded. She pulled out one of the chairs and sat. "Why aren't you sleeping?"

"For the same reasons as you, I suspect. Too many troubling thoughts. Too many things to consider."

"And not enough time to brood and make vague, cryptic responses. How very mysterious of you." Riona raised a brow. "Is that how you make all the girls in Erduria swoon?"

At last, his eyes met hers. "No. None of those girls matter."

"The rumors from Torch tell a different story."

"I may indulge in a few...distractions...from time to time, but none of them are like you."

She looked away too quickly, heat creeping up her cheeks. "Oh? I'm a distraction now, am I?"

"Eternally. Relentlessly." His fingers tapped that same rhythm again, and after listening for a moment, Riona realized it was the melody of the song his mother loved. He was tapping out the notes she had shown him on the piano. Then his fingers curled around the handle, and he lifted the mug to his lips, downing the contents in a few long gulps. "Which is why it's a good thing that you'll soon be promised to Drystan."

At his words, her blood ran cold. He was going to use the mines to blackmail her uncle into accepting the betrothal. And although Riona wanted a peaceful end to the war—wanted more than anything to spare her people from more needless fighting—she had never wanted it to happen like *this*. With her uncle choosing to fight rather than seek peace. With her betraying her kingdom's most closely guarded secret. With knowing that once word of the mines spread, there would be no end to the armies that would come to stake their claim on Rivosa's land.

"None of this was supposed to happen," Riona said quietly. "I only wanted to find Cathal's killer. I didn't expect... I didn't want you to find out—"

"Riona," Auberon interrupted, his voice deathly soft. "I was always going to find out. Why do you think I suggested our partnership in the first place? Why do you think I steered you toward the possibility of the king's involvement in Cathal's murder? You were always going to lead me to the mine."

The apology in his tone struck her like a blow. She had thought she could manipulate an Erdurian prince, but he had been two steps ahead of her the entire time. *He* had suggested that they search for Cathal's killer. *He* had convinced her that the king was mining eudorite in secret.

Auberon had been planning this from the beginning.

And now, her kingdom would pay the price for her mistakes.

"I wish things could have been different between us," Auberon murmured, still idly tapping out that melody on the handle of his mug. "I wish there were another way to convince your uncle to accept a peace treaty. I wish that ending this war did not require ripping you away from the city you love, but this is how it must be. I have no other choice. I was given my orders, and I must obey them."

She opened her mouth to respond just as the woman from the bar arrived with a platter of bread, fruit, and a steaming-hot meat pie. Riona's mouth immediately began to water at the scent. It was all she could do not to lunge for the spoon the second the woman set the food before her.

"I'll bring ye somethin' to drink, as well." The woman studied Auberon, then glanced at Riona, trying to read the tension hanging between them. "Is...there anythin' else I can do for ye?"

"No, thank you. This is perfect."

"I should try to get some rest," Auberon said as the woman walked off. "And you should, too. Once you're feeling better, we'll see about hiring a carriage to the capital."

He stood and reached for his mug, but Riona caught his hand before he could grab it. A dozen things she wanted to say tangled on her tongue, caught in the stress from the past several weeks and the storm of emotions raging within her.

In the end, she simply reached into her waistband and pulled out the emerald-hilted dagger. Auberon stilled when she set the weapon in his palm. "Thank you for saving my life."

He stared at the blade, a torn expression on his face. Riona wondered whether he was thinking, as she was, of the moment he'd found her in the mine—his hands cupping her cheeks, his breath shaking as he pressed a soft kiss to her forehead, his eyes shining with devastation and devotion.

"You need not thank me, *aramati*. I would save your life a thousand times over," Auberon finally said. He pulled his hand out of her grasp and set the blade on the table before her. "Keep the dagger. It is yours."

"I don't understand. How could King Domhnall be mining eudorite in secret? How could it be possible?" Amaris said late that evening, her brows furrowed. She was sitting on the edge of the bed in the room she and Riona shared, dressed in the same black tunic and pants she'd worn the night before. "Surely word would have spread by now. With so many people involved, something must have slipped through the cracks."

"You saw how the overseer's office was furnished. My uncle must be paying his men extortionate amounts to ensure their silence."

"Money that he cannot possibly afford to pay," Amaris murmured.

Her stomach churning, Riona turned toward the open window, watching the reds and oranges of the sunset reflect off the Tranquil Sea's waves. After finishing her breakfast that morning, she had spent the day resting, recovering from her injuries, and steadfastly avoiding Auberon. When Amaris awoke, Riona had told her everything—from the partnership she and Auberon had forged, to their excursion to the brothel, to the letters she had found in the overseer's desk.

"So if I understand everything," Amaris said slowly, clearly trying to make sense of all she'd heard, "Treasurer Cathal oversaw the operation of the mines and transfer of prisoners on behalf of the king. Eventually, he started to feel guilty about sending so many men to their deaths and decided he'd had enough. He planned to bring proof of the mines' existence to the Selannic king—your grandfather—in an attempt to renegotiate the repayment of the kingdom's debt. But why would King Domhnall have Cathal poisoned at the suitors' welcome banquet? Cathal didn't try to flee with the documents until the morning after."

"Perhaps he discovered plans that Cathal had made to sail to the Isles," Riona responded, every word sending pain through her battered ribs. "Or maybe he was simply paranoid that Cathal would betray his secret to the suitors. We all saw how much wine the Treasurer drank that night. If my uncle is truly so desperate to keep the mines a secret, any excuse would have been enough to justify the assassination."

"Do you believe he's that heartless? If Cathal had managed to renegotiate the terms of the debt, it would have solved all of the king's financial concerns. Why wouldn't King Domhnall have wanted that?"

"I don't know," Riona murmured, unsure which question she was answering.

Amaris leaned back and let out a long breath, absently twisting a thin braid around her finger. "And now Prince Auberon knows the mines exist. What are we going to do?"

"I...don't know." She sat on the bed and wrapped her arms around her knees, overwhelmed by all that she'd learned and all the questions she had yet to answer. Amaris slipped an arm around her waist and held her close, murmuring soft, soothing words in the Selannic tongue.

"We encountered your mad friend outside the heart of the mine," Amaris eventually said. "He looked terrified when he saw us, but he stood his ground and watched us approach. I think he recognized the brothers we were with; I couldn't decipher much of his babbling, but he knew that they'd been forced to mine the ore just like him. It seemed to have inspired a sense of kinship between them, which had endured through the madness that had gripped his mind. Prince Auberon and I tried to speak with him, to ask about you and explain that you were likely in trouble. Without a word, he up and walked away. Just left us behind. We were still standing there, debating how best to find you and sneak out of the mines unnoticed, when he returned with more than a dozen Rennox at his back. I'll never forget that sight. I don't know how you do it, Riona. The loyalty you inspire in those around you is astonishing."

A knock sounded at the door, and Riona straightened as Amaris rose and opened it. She exchanged a few quiet words with someone in the hall, then Auberon walked into the room and leaned against the chest of drawers, crossing his arms over his chest. The sight struck a chord within Riona—last night, he had stood in that very same position while the healer examined her ribs. He had tried to keep his expression blank, but even through the haze of pain and medicine that had clouded her mind, Riona could recall the agony she'd seen in his eyes every time she had let out even the slightest whimper. She remembered his fingers digging into his upper arms, as if he was fighting the urge to go to her, to comfort her.

"We need to discuss our next steps," he said as Amaris closed the door and sat on the bed. "Amaris and I intercepted the messenger the overseer sent, but the miners will have sent word of what happened to your uncle as soon as they recovered from the Rennox attack. By the time we return to Innislee, he'll know that we were in the mines."

"Then we must confront him about Cathal's murder immediately," Amaris said. "There's no use in pretending to go back to the way things were before we left. All the cards are on the table now. We must speak to him and reach some sort of accord."

"I don't trust him not to react violently. He may not hurt you, but he harbors nothing but loathing for Drystan and me. Considering he has already decided to see this war to its bitter end, I doubt he'll pass up the opportunity to murder the Emperor's sons while he has them in his grasp."

"He wouldn't do that," Riona protested, but the words were empty. In truth, she had no idea what her uncle was willing to do in his misguided attempts to protect his kingdom. Despite her feelings about the arranged marriage, she'd loved her uncle. It broke her heart to know that the man she should have been able to trust the most was the villain they'd been hunting all this time.

Auberon raised a brow. "Wouldn't he? He has shown us just how willing he is to eliminate anyone who threatens him. We cannot risk it. Kill the three of us, and his secret is safe once more. I'll send for Drystan, and we can sail to Erduria together. That way, we'll be out of reach of his assassins until we decide what to do next."

Riona shook her head. "We can't leave. If we do, my uncle will twist the story to make it appear as if you and Drystan abducted Amaris and me as punishment for refusing the treaty. We will live every day looking over our shoulders, and we will lose any hope of securing a peaceful end to the war. Our only choice is to confront him in Innislee." She met Auberon's gaze. "And after that, if I must marry Drystan, I will sail to Erduria with you."

Chapter Fifty-Four
The Lady

They left for the capital at dawn the next morning, using the last of what little money Auberon and Amaris had to hire a carriage. Riona sat on the bench opposite Amaris, her head resting against the window frame and her arm draped loosely across her midsection. Her ribs ached with every jolt of the carriage's wheels over the uneven dirt road, but the second dose of the healer's medicine had dulled the pain enough for her to endure the journey. Auberon and the miners had chosen to ride behind their carriage with Riona's and Amaris's horses in tow.

Half an hour into the journey, Riona turned away from the window and found Amaris studying her, a pensive expression on her face. She'd been strangely quiet all morning. "What's wrong?"

"I've been thinking about everything you told me. Thinking about our future. Before we reach Innislee, we should discuss what is to be done about the mines," Amaris said. "What do you hope to gain when we speak with the king? Prince Auberon holds all the cards now, and he won't give up until he gets what he wants—namely, you and the eudorite. You have no right to demand anything of your uncle. You're the one who betrayed his kingdom's secrets to his enemy, and you'll be lucky if you leave the castle with your life."

Riona glanced away, ashamed. "You know I did not intend for any of this to happen. I only wanted to bring Cathal's murderer to justice."

"I understand, but this is different from some courtier assassinating another noble. He is the king, and whether we agree with his decisions or not, he has the right to run labor camps in the mines. He has the right to execute traitors to the crown."

"Cathal was not a *traitor*—"

"He was. He was sworn to secrecy, and he committed treason by conspiring to reveal the existence of the mines to the Selannic king," Amaris said, her voice calm. "I liked him, and I understand that he was trying to help our kingdom, but he was wrong to do so. It was not his place to decide which secrets to keep and which to betray."

"He would *save us from ruin*—"

Amaris leaned forward and grasped her hand. "I know this is hard to hear, but you must listen. His Majesty is not going to stop mining eudorite because you have a moral objection to using prisoners as labor. Neither will Domhnall and I, once we take the thrones. It is our duty to protect our subjects from the armies who will come to take the mines. We will have no choice but to continue forging eudorite weapons."

"And the prisoners?"

A shadow passed across her face. "I do not condone needless death, but they are prisoners, and they sealed their fates when they committed their crimes. If we must sacrifice them to ensure our enemies do not destroy our kingdom, it is the price we shall pay. Better the deaths of prisoners than innocents."

Riona stared down at her hands, Dig's haunting, keening cries echoing in her ears. The thought that more men would be driven mad by the unsettling, screeching wind made her feel sick, but Amaris was right—they could not afford to stop mining. Rivosa was bankrupt, and Erduria now knew that the king had found a way to mine the valuable ore in the Mountains. If they allied, it would spare her people from years of fighting.

"I have always admired your insistence on doing what is right, Riona," Amaris said softly. "But in this, there is no right answer. We are at the mercy of the Empire."

They didn't speak much as the carriage rolled through Innislee's northern gate and began the slow, steady climb up the King's Road. Every minute sent a ripple of dread through her, every revolution of the wheels bringing her closer to whatever awaited them in the castle. Riona looked out the window and was just able to glimpse Auberon riding alone behind the carriage; the two brothers from the mine had broken off from their group earlier and ridden ahead, taking the extra horses with them. They would stay in a tavern until she and Auberon decided to broach the topic of the mines with her uncle.

Finally, they arrived at the castle's forecourt, and the driver announced their arrival to the half-dozen guards at the gate. Amaris glanced at Riona as one of the men rushed into the castle to alert the royal family of their return. "I will say nothing of the mines until you and Prince Auberon decide our next move, but I beg you to be careful. It is more than just our lives on the line."

"I know."

"And Riona—" She faltered when one of the guards opened the carriage door and offered a hand to help her out. She glanced at him, then leaned forward and whispered in Riona's ear, "If you must go to Erduria, be certain it is with the husband who will truly make you happy."

Before she could respond, Amaris pulled back and accepted the guard's hand, gracefully climbing out of the carriage. Riona followed her, being careful not to let so much as a flicker of pain pass across her face as her bruised ribs protested. The healer's medicine had worn off during the journey, but she couldn't risk taking more and dulling her wits.

"I cannot tell you how relieved the king and queen will be to learn of your return, my lady," one of the guards said as he led them toward the open gate. "Your father was beside himself. He and the king sent half the royal guard to search for you."

"Who all knows that I left the city?"

"Save for the royal family, your father, and the guard, no one. Master Kaiden ordered silence on the matter. His Majesty told the court and the suitors that you were ill."

"Good." She didn't doubt that whispers of the truth were already spreading through the court. The guards were sworn to serve the king, but there were more than a few pairs of loose lips in any castle. "Tell me, has anyone of note arrived in the past couple of days, requesting a private audience with the king?"

"Who would you deem someone of note, my lady? We've seen the council members, of course, and there are always men and women coming to the castle with requests for audiences with His Majesty."

"It would have been a man—tall and muscular, with strikingly pale skin. Anyone of that description?"

The guard frowned. "No, not that I can recall, although I wasn't on duty at the gate yesterday. If you'd like, I can ask around and let you know what I learn."

"Yes, please."

"Of course, my lady."

Riona glanced over her shoulder as Auberon handed his horse's reins to one of the guards and started toward them. "What are we waiting for?" he asked as he joined them by the portcullis gate. His lips curled into a wicked grin. "It's time I collect my reward for rescuing the king's beloved niece."

Chapter Fifty-Five
The Liar

The guard led them to the great hall, where the king, Prince Domhnall, and Lord Lachlan were already waiting for them. As soon as he saw his daughter, Lachlan crossed the hall and grasped Riona's upper arms. "Where have you been? Have you gone *mad?*"

Auberon stiffened as King Domhnall stepped forward, but he merely set a hand on his brother's shoulder. "Release her, Lachlan. Let's hear some answers before we begin chastising."

What game was the king playing? More than likely, he'd learned by now that they had been to the mine. Was he only feigning ignorance to keep his brother and son from learning of the secret he'd fought for so long to hide?

"I went to Crafford," Riona responded immediately, swiftly recounting the story they had concocted before leaving the tavern that morning. Her gaze dropped to her feet in feigned shame. "After the performance at the Royal Theater, it all just became too real. The suitors... The arranged marriage. I...panicked, and I fled. I needed some time to clear my head and come to terms with the fact that I am truly leaving Rivosa. It sounds foolish, but until that night, a part of me had always held out hope that there might be a way for me to stay."

A note of raw anguish slipped into her voice, and a pang shot through Auberon. It wasn't entirely a lie, what she was saying. She had survived the Beltharan civil war only to be cast out of her home less than two months later. Auberon longed to move closer and offer what little comfort he could, but he forced himself to stand still, his hands clasped behind his back.

Riona's slender shoulders curved inward. The sight of her misery made her father's ire vanish. Lord Lachlan grasped his daughter's chin and tilted her head up. "I understand, my love. But why did you tell no one that you needed space? That you wanted to leave?"

"You would have stopped me."

"You know it's not safe for a woman of your rank to be traveling alone," the king said. "Although from looking at your face, it seems that you've already learned that lesson."

Riona started to reach up and touch the cut in her cheek, then remembered the raw and broken skin around her wrists. She quickly tucked her hands behind her back. "There was a brawl where I was staying. I was caught in the middle, and that's when Amaris and Prince Auberon found me. It was an accident, that's all."

"I see." King Domhnall turned to Auberon and cocked his head, examining him as a predator might its prey. "How fortunate it is that you were able to find her so quickly, Your Highness. Perhaps you could teach the men in my royal guard a thing or two about tracking."

He offered the king a practiced smile, ignoring the implication in his words. "Fortunate indeed, Your Majesty. And a deed that I hope will prove that my empire is worthy of your trust."

Riona's gaze shot to him, an almost imperceptible flicker of fear flashing across her face. She said nothing, but he could hear her voice in his head, begging him not to bring up the mines. Begging him not to take her from her home again. And even though he could end the stalemate between Domhnall and Drystan with a few words, he held his tongue. If Riona was willing to spend the rest of her life serving Erduria as its Empress, the least he could do was give her one final day in the city she loved. Besides, he needed to speak to Drystan before making any demands. They could not afford to act rashly.

The king's attention slid to Amaris. "And why, precisely, did you trust an Erdurian to aid you in your search for Lady Riona?"

She lifted her chin. "Because no one else would."

Prince Domhnall winced. He took a step forward. "I—"

"When Prince Auberon offered to help me bring her back home, I accepted, and we left without delay. What else was I supposed to do?"

"Let the royal guards do their job," the king responded, "instead of giving the Erdurians yet another opportunity to place us in their debt."

"What of fostering a lasting relationship between our countries? What of parting as allies, rather than enemies?" Amaris demanded. "You've made no secret of your distrust of the princes, and yet you condemn them when they act out of kindness and compassion!"

"He is acting out of a desire to ingratiate himself with our family," King Domhnall snarled. He fixed Auberon with a hateful glare, even as he directed his next words to his niece. "Do not allow his charms to fool you, Riona. He cares nothing for our kingdom, nor for you. He is Erdurian, and he will stop at nothing to further his own goals."

"Considering he and his brother have been advocating for peace since the moment they arrived, he is right to do so," Riona said, the picture of perfect calm. "I am under no illusion that he did this out of anything but loyalty to the Empire, but seeing as a treaty will save our people from more needless death, how can you continue to deny him? Let this war *end*, Uncle."

The king scoffed. "Where Emperor Hyperion is involved, there is no such thing as peace. Prince Auberon, you have my gratitude for bringing her home, but I am afraid that is all you will take with you when you set sail for Erduria tomorrow."

Riona went still. "Tomorrow?"

King Domhnall stared at Auberon. "Since Prince Drystan has rescinded his bid for my niece's hand, I see no point in further negotiation. Tonight, at the banquet, I shall announce Lady Riona's betrothal to Prince Eamon."

Auberon's stomach dropped. This wasn't the end; they still had time. He could go to the guest house and speak with Drystan now, so they could decide how they would force the king's hand into a peace treaty and betrothal without losing their heads in the process. He'd hoped for more time. He *needed* more time.

"Have any of the documents been signed?" Riona asked. "Is Prince Eamon aware that you intend to promise me to him?"

Her father stepped forward and set a hand on her shoulder. His expression made it clear what he thought about his daughter marrying the Kostori bastard. "Not yet. We were just wrapping up a meeting with the council when we received word that you had returned." He turned to his brother. "Domhnall, they've only just arrived. Perhaps we could give them some time to settle in and recover from their journey before making a fuss over the betrothal. Delaying the announcement by a day won't change anything."

Won't it? Auberon thought, watching the king carefully. Domhnall's expression was cool and closed-off, betraying no hint of whatever thoughts were racing behind that stony façade. Finally, he gave a single, shallow nod. "Very well. One day."

Riona let out a relieved breath. She moved gingerly as she dipped into a low curtsy, clearly trying to hide the pain of her injured ribs from her uncle and the others. "Thank you, Your Majesty."

"Of course, my dear. But I expect no further surprises, do you understand? I'll not promise Eamon a wife only to find her missing the very next day."

She smiled. "I understand, Your Majesty."

Riona straightened, and Auberon fell into step beside her as she led him and Amaris out of the castle's main building. The second the doors clanged shut behind them, Auberon reached out and lightly brushed the back of his hand against hers. Some of the tension bled out of Riona's body, and she let the touch linger, her little finger hooking around his.

"One day. That is all the time we have to prepare to confront my uncle about the mines," Riona whispered, dropping his hand as they slowed to a stop near the entrance of one of the castle's gardens, well out of earshot of any guards or servants who might pass by. She glanced at Auberon. "Thank you for not bringing them up back there. Since my uncle said nothing about them, I expect he plans to meet with us in private to learn just how much we've uncovered about the operation, and what we plan to do with that information."

Amaris looked uneasy. "Unless he kills us first."

"As much as he may want to, he cannot afford to kill the future queen, his niece, and the son of the Erdurian Emperor," Riona responded, not a hint of doubt in her voice. "Even if we weren't high-ranking members of the court, too many bodies have piled up since the suitors arrived. His best course of action is to make Erduria an ally."

Auberon nodded. "Let's pray that he sees it that way, too. He's made no secret of just how unwilling he is to put old grievances aside for the sake of his people."

Riona's expression turned icy as she glanced at the main building. "I will not allow him to condemn our people to more needless death. Speak with your brother about how you wish to conduct the negotiations, and we'll meet in the morning to discuss it."

When she turned and started to walk away, Amaris said, "What are you going to do?"

She looked over her shoulder, her eyes locking with Auberon's. "I have just over twenty-four hours until I'm promised to a stranger. I'm not going to waste a single one of them."

Chapter Fifty-Six
The Lady

Riona wrinkled her nose as a rat scurried across her path, the rodent nimbly darting around a puddle of piss before slipping through a crack in the alley's wall. Thin lines laden with drying clothes zigzagged between the buildings that rose high on either side of her, only a sliver of sunlight visible beyond the overhanging roofs. A few yards ahead, Ophelia slowed before a half-rotted door and rapped a couple of times—another peculiar knock, like the one Aeron had used when they'd gone to meet Faylen.

A heartbeat later, the door swung open to a dank-smelling room, a familiar figure filling its doorway. Aeron silently stepped aside so they could enter.

Riona's bruised ribs ached, but she ignored the pain as she ducked under the doorframe and entered the low-ceilinged room. A lantern sat atop the lone table in the center of the room, its flame turned so high that it licked the glass, and a fire crackled in the small hearth in the far wall. Through an archway to her left, Riona glimpsed the footboard and legs of a wooden cot.

As Ophelia turned back to close and latch the door, Riona took in her surroundings. "Did you not feel safe enough in a tavern?"

"I didn't want to risk anyone asking after an elf of my description," a voice called from the other room. The cot creaked, and Faylen appeared in the archway a moment later, grimacing as she kneaded her lower back. Aeron immediately moved to the table and pulled out a chair for her, which she accepted with a grateful smile. "I've certainly endured worse than a place in the slums. I can forsake a fancy feather bed for the promise of safety and anonymity."

"It will only be for a short while," Riona assured her. "I have less than a day until I am promised to one of the suitors, which means we must work fast."

"Certainly. I'm glad to see you in one piece, my lady." Faylen nodded toward Aeron. "It was all I could do to keep our friend here from riding out after you when you didn't immediately return to the city. I had to remind him a half-dozen times that he had no idea where you went after we left you in Crafford."

"I could have found her," Aeron muttered, "if you had allowed me to look at those documents she ordered me to protect."

"And defy the orders your lady gave you?" Faylen responded, her voice teasing. "Perish the thought. I think you'd burst into flames if you ever did something against her will."

He glowered at her but offered no response.

"I'm glad you remained here," Riona said, infinitely grateful that Faylen hadn't allowed him to look at Cathal's maps. The thought of Aeron wandering through the dark, labyrinthine tunnels sent a tremor down her spine. "The overseer of the mine discovered me searching through his office, and the only thing that kept him from killing me was my royal blood. If you had come, you'd have been killed or forced into labor. I never would have been able to forgive myself if I had led you to that fate."

His expression softened, and he asked, "What mine? My lady, where did you go?"

"More importantly, what did you learn?" Faylen pressed, leaning forward. "Tell me Cathal didn't give his life for nothing."

"I found a letter from him in the overseer's desk. He wrote about the king's intention to wield eudorite weapons against Erduria, and his fears that my uncle would sacrifice countless Rivosi lives to gain the upper hand in the war. The king planned to fight until every last Erdurian paid for what we lost at their hands. He would have slaughtered countless innocents. Cathal felt guilty for his involvement in the operation, and he blamed himself for the deaths of all the men who were condemned to work in the Howling Mountains. It would have been damning evidence against the king if the overseer hadn't burned it," Riona said, a note of bitterness slipping into her voice.

She reached across the table and took Faylen's hand. The elf was not crying, but the expression she wore as she stared into the hearth's dancing flames was one of pure grief. Her free hand rested on the curve of her belly. "Cathal was a good man," Riona whispered. "Always remember that. He risked his life to smuggle those documents out of the city so he might save our kingdom from destruction. He sought an end to the war, and now, we may have a path to securing peace with the Empire. When this is all over, you will be free and live in comfort, and Cathal's killer—my uncle—will suffer for what he has done."

"Your uncle? How... How can you promise that?" Faylen asked, the words raw. "How can we stand against a king?"

"Kings are far from invincible," Aeron snarled. "They die just as easily as any other man."

Riona shook her head. "We cannot kill him—not without losing our own heads in the process and severely crippling our kingdom. Brutal as his methods are, my uncle has stood against his enemies in a hopeless war for over thirty years. We will need a leader like that once word of the eudorite mines spreads beyond our borders. My uncle is strong-willed and ruthless in his defense of Rivosa, and he has the loyalty of the soldiers. Their allegiance will not be easily or quickly swayed."

The hope faded from Faylen's face. "I hope you have a plan, my lady."

"We're going to use the people," Riona said, nodding. "I have less than twenty-four hours until I must confront the king, and if we do not do this correctly, we will lose any chance at a peaceful end to the war." She turned to Ophelia, who was standing by the door, silent as ever. "How many helpers can you assemble without drawing suspicion from the crown and guards?"

The girl frowned, considering. "Right now, probably a half-dozen. If you need more, it'll be easier for them to slip out of the castle later tonight, once the banquet is over. I could probably gather about two dozen by midnight."

"They can all read and write?"

"I'll make certain of it, my lady."

"Good. They'll have to make do with the space at hand. Once they arrive, I want them to stay here until tomorrow afternoon, when the Erdurian princes and I go to speak with the king. It's not an ideal situation, I know, but it is necessary. After we leave, you and I will stop by my father's house so I can fetch some money. I want you to purchase food, lantern oil, ink, and as much parchment as you can carry."

"What are you planning, my lady?" Aeron asked.

Riona smiled, concealing the pain in her heart. The time for secrecy was over. Soon, word of the mines would spread beyond Rivosa's borders, and they would have to be ready for the armies that would come to take her land. All Riona could do was try to delay her kingdom's destruction.

With a grim smile on her face, she leaned forward and explained her plan.

Chapter Fifty-Seven
The Liar

Riona didn't attend the banquet that night. Auberon would have worried over her safety—imagining all the terrible things the king might have done to ensure her silence—if not for the subtle nod Amaris had given him when she'd claimed her place at the head table. Riona was safe, likely resting and recovering from her injuries.

Auberon ate the food the servants set before him, every bite tasting like ash. Hatred curdled in his stomach as he stared down the table at King Domhnall. He had detested the Rivosi king long before he'd ever set foot on Rivosa's shores, and that sentiment had only grown since arriving at Innislee. How Riona, a woman so unwavering in her sense of morality and justice, could share blood with a man like Domhnall was inconceivable. Domhnall had lied and killed to keep his kingdom's secrets, yet now he sat at the center of the head table, seemingly without a care in the world, laughing and conversing jovially with his son and Prince Eamon. The rest of the court mirrored his shift in mood. The chatter was louder, the laughter easier, and the wine flowing freely.

At his side, Drystan watched the Kostori prince with a scowl. Auberon hadn't had a chance to speak with him all day; when he'd arrived at their house earlier, he had been informed that Drystan was meeting with Lord Winslow to discuss the terms of a treaty. Judging by his foul mood, the meeting hadn't gone in the direction he'd intended.

Conscious of the guards and servants surrounding them, Auberon leaned in close and whispered, "Eamon should have waited to celebrate his impending betrothal until *after* the papers were signed. By this time tomorrow, you will have won Riona's hand in marriage."

Drystan glanced at him sharply, the harsh line of his mouth softening. "You discovered something when you went after her?"

He grinned, despite the way his chest constricted at the thought of Riona and Drystan marrying. "I discovered *everything*."

A smile broke out across Drystan's face. "Tell me the specifics at the guest house tonight." He clapped a hand on Auberon's shoulder. "If you're right about this, Father is going to heap reward upon reward on your shoulders. You're not going to be able to stand under the weight of all the titles he'll grant you."

He grimaced. "I prefer my rewards in monetary form."

"Why, so you can drink yourself to death before the week is out?"

"Yes, and what a glorious week it will be." Auberon turned his head toward the court so Drystan wouldn't see his smile fade. "But don't worry about me—you'll have a beautiful new wife to comfort you in your grief. I'm sure you'll hardly even notice my absence."

His heart thundered in his chest for the few seconds it took Drystan to respond. When he did, he spoke in a soft, unbearably sympathetic voice. "Since the night you left, I've wanted to apologize for the way I spoke to you. I am truly sorry. It was cruel of me to throw your feelings in your face like that, especially when you've done nothing but try to help me." Drystan paused, then added, "I'm sorry that this will not end the way you wish, but I hope you know that I will do everything in my power to be the husband she deserves."

Auberon reached for the goblet of wine in front of him. "She deserves you, and she deserves the throne. There is no other way I would have the negotiations end."

The words felt hollow before they even left his tongue, but Drystan had the grace not to comment on it. As the servants cleared away the last of the plates, Auberon descended the dais steps and asked the first noblewoman he found to dance, eager to distract himself from thoughts of Riona and mines and murder. He wouldn't be able to leave the banquet for a few hours yet, so he might as well *try* to enjoy the night.

As the night dragged on, he danced with woman after woman, each more beautiful than the last. One with jet-black curls and a silk gown cut low across her cleavage, a ruby large enough to anchor a ship hanging at her throat. Another with golden-brown skin and golden-brown eyes, a dusting of freckles across her cheekbones. Another who hailed from the Selannic Isles, with the same willowy build and long braids that Riona and Amaris shared. One after another after another.

Two hours later, Auberon extricated himself from the grasp of the noblewoman who had latched herself onto him—her painted lips leaving a red smear along the edge of his jaw—and pushed through the throngs of people surrounding the dance floor. He wiped his face with his sleeve and snagged a goblet of wine from a passing servant, quickly draining it. His doublet felt too tight, the air too thick. The ladies with whom he'd danced were beautiful, but they paled in comparison to Riona. He'd been ruined by that first night in Innislee, when he had held Riona close and elicited the first genuine laugh he had ever heard from her. From that moment, he had been hers.

We didn't even get to finish our dance, he realized as he swapped his empty goblet for a full one. It was the last bit of alcohol he would drink—he wouldn't repeat the mistake he'd made the morning Eamon's lackey accosted him. All he needed was something to calm the furious storm of emotions that raged within him at the thought of Riona's impending betrothal.

Yet when he caught a glimpse of a familiar face among the crowd, a long braid trailing down her back and a tray of goblets balanced on one shoulder, he found himself approaching her, reaching out to grasp her upper arm. Ophelia turned to him, a carefully neutral expression on her face as she said, "Your Highness."

"I need you to send a message to Lady Riona," he breathed, keeping his voice so low that only she would hear through the music and chatter. This was stupid, impulsive, but he told himself that they would only discuss the mines. That he would not act on the desire that raced through him every time Riona was near. "Tell her to meet me at the Royal Theater at midnight."

A drunken noble staggered into her, and she deftly maneuvered the silver tray away before he could send it tumbling to the ground. The elf cast an appraising gaze over him, her polite expression turning cold. It made him wonder just how much she knew about his partnership with her lady. Had one of her little birds overheard their argument in the hall after he'd punched Eamon? Did she know just how deep his desire for Riona ran?

Finally, Ophelia dipped into a shallow curtsy. "It shall be done, Your Highness. Good evening."

She walked away, quickly vanishing into the sea of dancers and revelers. He could see why Riona trusted the girl so much: she was quiet and clever, and easily overlooked. She moved like a wraith through the castle; in the weeks he had been here, he had seen her acting as a server, attendant, maid, and messenger. She slipped from one role to another with the ease of an actress donning a costume.

"Thank the Creator you're here," someone said, and Auberon turned to find Valerian approaching him, a troubled expression on the duke's face. He grasped Auberon's elbow and led him over to one of the stone pillars that lined the room, buying them what little privacy he could in the crowded hall.

"Now we can end this disastrous attempt at negotiating and go our separate ways. Please tell me you've found a way to pry Lady Riona out of that Kostori snake's hands."

Auberon didn't bother to ask how Drystan had explained his absence to the court. "Yes," he said softly. "Yes, I believe I have."

"Good." The duke's green eyes lifted to something over his shoulder, and Auberon followed his gaze to where Eamon stood on the dance floor, spinning Amaris under one arm. A shadow passed across Valerian's face. "If there is anything I can do to help you, please tell me. It's not likely I will leave Rivosa with a wife, but I must leave with the promise of military aid—whether it be Rivosi or Erdurian, it matters not. I will not return to life as a slave of a foreign king, Auberon. I will not continue to watch those Kostori bastards bleed my country dry."

Images of Kostori soldiers marching through Kenter's lush valleys, stealing food from the fields and people from their beds, filled his mind. They had devastated the countryside during their invasion, and from what he had heard, they hadn't ceased their destruction in the years since.

Still, he crossed his arms. "You want Drystan to promise you Erdurian support? I came here to end the fighting between my country and Rivosa. Why do you think I'd advocate for sending more of my countrymen to die in a war that doesn't benefit us?"

"Because in exchange, I will give you all of my research into blood magic."

Auberon glanced back to make sure none of the guards or servants had wandered into earshot, then hissed, "Have you lost your *mind?*"

Valerian's expression was grim. "Take my offer to your father once you return to Torch. Pledge me the support I need to free my country, and once Kenter is independent and the power of the crown returned to Glenkeld, I will share with you everything I've learned. I have no doubt that with the Empire's resources and a dedicated team of scholars, you'll be able to uncover more information than I could in a lifetime."

Auberon fought to keep his expression neutral in the face of such an intriguing proposal. Valerian had to be desperate to offer such a valuable prize in exchange for military support, and the research he'd gathered could be invaluable to Erduria. There was no telling what the scholars might discover. The miracles the healers would be able to perform. The military advantages blood magic would provide.

That last thought sent a chill down Auberon's spine. Although he was in awe of its power and eager to aid his empire, he was still too wary of temptation to entrust the public with knowledge of blood magic. The folk stories warned of blood mages for a reason. Once someone got a taste of how powerful he could become, blood magic corrupted him, heart and soul.

He studied the duke. "I'll present it to my father, but I make no promises. Tell me: What would you do if you were not granted the aid you seek?"

Valerian heard the question he didn't dare voice, and his expression darkened. "If you believe that I would murder innocents in order to strengthen my magic, you must think me no better than the Kostori. If I am denied Rivosi or Erdurian aid, I will go to Beltharos."

"And if they refuse you?"

"Then I shall return to Kenter to try and turn the tide from there, as impossible as that feat might seem. I will not accept defeat."

I will not accept defeat. The words buried themselves under Auberon's skin, doing nothing to assuage his fears about Valerian's use of blood magic. "We could kill Eamon," he murmured, so quiet only Valerian would be able to hear. "It doesn't have to be right now if you're concerned about the attention it would attract. There will be plenty of opportunities to slip poison into his food or drink between now and his return to Kostos."

"Don't tempt me. Even if there were no proof of my involvement, King Jericho would wield his wrath over his son's death against my people. I can't risk their lives for the sake of one man, despicable as he may be."

Auberon sighed. "A shame. I was looking forward to hearing the news of his death."

Valerian offered him a dark, fleeting smile, one that promised blood. "Someday. Just not yet."

Chapter Fifty-Eight
The Lady

The lantern hanging from the ceiling of the carriage swayed, casting long, dancing shadows as the wheels clacked over the uneven cobblestones. Riona turned Auberon's emerald-hilted dagger over in her hands, watching the light play across the gemstones. A little voice in her head urged her to turn back. After everything that had happened between her and Auberon, Riona shouldn't be going to meet him. Drystan was the one vying for her hand in marriage, and that would never change.

And yet when Ophelia arrived at her father's estate with Auberon's message, a traitorous little part of her had thrilled at the thought of spending one more night in the theater with him.

The carriage rolled to a stop before the ornate double doors, and Riona sucked in a steadying breath before climbing out. When she stepped into the foyer, the familiar scents of perfume, varnished wood, and dusty velvet rushed over her. She had just reached the archway into the theater proper when she heard the soft strain of a piano, a melody she knew well. The Fall of the Faeries, from the ballet his mother loved. She rolled her eyes. Of course he had found his own way inside the Royal Theater.

She pushed aside the curtain. The theater was pitch black save for the stage, which glowed under the light of countless candles. Auberon was sitting on the piano bench, wholly focused on playing the song she had spent weeks teaching him. Beautiful, light notes danced in the air. They wrapped Riona in their embrace and drew her toward the stage, her feet moving of their own accord.

When she reached the end of the aisle, Auberon turned his head and offered her a crooked smile. "I'm not as skilled as you are," he said as he continued to play, "and I never will be, but I think this would have made my mother proud. I have you to thank for that, *aramati*."

Riona climbed the stairs and sat beside him on the bench, watching his calloused fingers travel over the keys. "You're doing it again—speaking of your mother as if she were dead. Why?"

For a few moments, he played on, considering his words carefully. The song filled the theater, its beauty underscored with notes of longing. "...I told you," he finally said, a haunted kind of sorrow in his blue-gray eyes. "She may as well be dead, for all that she has in common with the woman she used to be. I don't recognize her anymore."

Her chest tightened at the grief in his voice. "Auberon..."

"I've been practicing," he continued, nodding toward the piano. Riona remembered him sitting alone in that tavern in Crafford, his fingers tapping out the melody on the side of his mug. He held her gaze as the last note faded, silence descending over the theater. "I wanted to play for you, just once. I know that you will be promised to Drystan tomorrow, and I know that you believe everything between us was nothing more than an act, but it wasn't. Despite my best efforts, I have fallen in love with you, *aramati*—wholly and eternally."

Her heart stuttered. They sat so close that the length of Riona's leg was pressed against his, so close that she could see the flecks of pure blue in his eyes and the faint little scar that cut into the edge of his lower lip. So close that if she leaned in, they would kiss.

She had spent so much of her life hating the Erdurians, cursing them for the deaths of her mother and Prince Killian. She clung to the scraps of that hatred with desperation, even as the slight smile on Auberon's lips made her stomach flutter. He had become so much more to her than just an ally, and the knowledge terrified her. She could not care for an Erdurian. Even the little time they had spent here, in this place she loved so dearly, felt like a betrayal to her people, to her mother.

"I...don't know how you want me to respond to that," she said carefully.

"Of course you do. What you don't know is that I have begged the Creator every day to stop me from feeling this way about you. You don't know how desperately I want you to walk out that door and never speak to me again." Auberon shot to his feet and crossed the stage, tugging at his hair in agitation. He spun around to face her. "I never planned for this to happen. This isn't how it was supposed to end. I was supposed to use you to gain information about the mines, and you were supposed to fall for Drystan."

He shook his head, his expression one of pure torment. "Loving you is destroying me, Riona. I forget who I am when I'm around you. Even though there can never be anything between us, I want nothing more than for you to tell me that you love me, too."

If you must go to Erduria, be certain it is with the husband who will truly make you happy, Amaris's voice whispered in her mind.

Riona rose. "Why must it end like this? You are second in line for the throne. Marrying you would still secure a peace treaty. It would still end the war."

Auberon shook his head again. "One day, Drystan will be the Emperor, and he will need a woman deserving of the crown to sit at his side. *You* are that woman, Riona. You are strong, and intelligent, and brave, and *just*. You and I could never marry, and you will understand why when you sail with us to Torch." He looked away, his fists clenching and unclenching at his sides. "I should not have asked you to come here. The Creator has always seen fit to punish me, and this—this is the perfect torture. From the moment I saw you, I knew you would be my undoing."

Her heart in her throat, Riona crossed the stage and cupped his cheek, turning him to face her. "If our meeting was your undoing," she whispered, "then it was mine, as well."

His expression shattered at her words. "Riona..."

"I will not marry your brother."

Auberon reached up and grasped her wrist, pulling it away from his face. "You must. You and I can never be."

"Because you believe I would rather have the crown than you? Or because you think that loving me means you're betraying Drystan? Tell me, and we will find some way to make this work. We can have a future."

"We cannot, *aramati*."

When he refused to say more, Riona took a step back, stung and hurt by his rejection. "Then why did you ask me to come here? Why confess your feelings for me? I love my kingdom and my people, but I would give it all up for you. If you asked me, Auberon, I would go to Erduria with you."

Auberon glanced away, a storm of emotions on his face. But he said nothing.

Her heart breaking, Riona turned and walked away, leaving him standing alone in the middle of the stage.

For a moment, there was silence. Then running footsteps pounded behind her, and Auberon caught her hand just as she began descending the steps. She whipped around, her anger and pain flaring, but whatever objection she'd been about to say vanished when his lips met hers.

Shock froze her, only to be swept away by a rush of desire as his hands came up to cup her face, his fingers tangling in her loose braids. His wicked, clever mouth was soft, moving against hers with the same hunger, the same passion she had seen burning in his eyes. She'd wanted this. There was no denying it as his silver tongue slipped between her lips, teasing her own. She threaded her fingers through his hair, pulling him closer, every soft curve of her body pressed against the hard planes of his. He was wicked and cruel and manipulative and deceptive. He was kind and charming and selfless and brave. And she found that she wanted him more than anything she'd ever wanted before.

One of his hands slid down to cup her breast, heat igniting under her skin as his fingers trailed lightly across the curve of sensitive flesh. She prayed he couldn't feel her heart pounding against her ribs. She guided him backward until his legs hit the piano bench, and he sat, an arm wrapping around her waist and pulling her onto his lap. He pulled away only to kiss just below her earlobe, sending shivers down her spine and drawing a soft sigh from her lips.

Auberon leaned back and looked up at her with love and longing in his beautiful blue-gray eyes. "I just had to do that once," he whispered. He reached up and ran a light finger along the edge of her lower lip, something like wonder in his voice as he said, "I've never seen you smile like this."

She hadn't even realized she'd been smiling. She wasn't aware of much of anything, except for the way he was staring at her lips, the way his heart was pounding where her hands rested on his chest. "Marry me," she breathed, "and make me smile like this every day."

"Let's not discuss it now, *aramati*." He gently eased her off his lap, then took her hand and drew her to the center of the stage. "Dance with me."

"We don't have any music."

Auberon smiled, a hand slipping around her waist to rest at the small of her back. "Indulge me."

And then he began to sing.

Riona gaped at him as his rich voice swept over her, filling the silent theater. The song was in one of the northern languages, and although she did not understand the words, there was no mistaking the beauty, the longing, in the words. It was a ballad.

Dehan dhoh-sha mo tuijía, mo chroí

Cuille solis-sa aire mo sudhin
Bhiodha d'iarrain, bhiodha d'ireach
Làhm mo anam tro'na firinne tué
Is, Ceartan, mi dhoja daonan latha tué

Riona wrapped her arms around Auberon's neck and rested her head against his shoulder. He swayed slowly as he sang, holding her in a tight embrace, their bodies fitting together as if they'd been made for this moment. Every touch sent a flare of warmth through her. She didn't believe in soulmates, but every fiber of her being ignited at the utter *rightness* of this moment. Of *him*.

When the song ended, they fell still, neither wanting to break the spell that had fallen over the silent theater.

"We never finished our dance the night that I was poisoned," Auberon eventually said, his breath soft and warm against her ear. "Every night since, I've wanted to know what it would be like to hold you in my arms. To not have to maintain some ridiculous façade for the court or consider what Drystan might think of every little smile, every little touch. Now, I don't have to wonder any longer."

Riona pulled back just enough to meet his gaze. "Marry me, and I will never dance with anyone but you."

Auberon opened his mouth to respond, but then his attention shifted to something behind her. She only had time to register the terror that flashed through his eyes before he shoved her behind him, ripping the sword from the sheath at his hip. She caught her balance on one of the twisting skeletal trees and whirled just in time to see three black-clad figures emerge from the shadows at the edge of the stage, their blades gleaming under the candlelight.

"Stay behind me," Auberon commanded as they swarmed him.

He lifted his sword just in time to parry a blow from the leader, then twisted as one swung toward his side. He spun, forcing the leader back with a savage slash across the man's thigh, and ducked under the whistling blade of his third opponent—a blow that would have taken his head clean off.

The whole thing happened in a matter of heartbeats.

Their swords clashed, rending flesh and sending splatters of blood across the stage, almost faster than Riona could follow. The largest man drove his blade toward Auberon's stomach. The prince knocked the blow aside and lunged, opening a gash in the man's side and earning a shallow cut in his shoulder in the process from another attacker.

Where one man faltered, another struck, keeping Auberon on the defensive. Every time one of the attackers tried to slip past him and get to Riona, Auberon lunged into the man's path, warding him back with a slash of his sword.

Riona unsheathed the emerald-hilted dagger, desperate to come to his aid, but she couldn't see an opening. Auberon fought like a tempest, his blade whistling as it cleaved the air. Blood sprayed, splattering across the skeletal metal trees. She edged closer to the fight, and Auberon's wide eyes met hers. The moment of distraction earned him a deep gash in his upper arm. A hiss of pain slipped through his lips as he tore his gaze away. He had only glanced at her for a second, but the message in his eyes had been unmistakable: *Run! Run now!*

No. She wouldn't leave him to die. Auberon was a skilled swordsman, but even he couldn't take on three men for long. As he moved, she caught glimpses of the gashes in his doublet, blood soaking the fine fabric. He was wounded, and tiring quickly. Riona gripped her dagger tightly, her palm sweating.

She was no warrior, but she'd been trained by an excellent teacher.

As Auberon turned to meet one man's blade, Riona ducked behind him and caught another's sword. She twisted, using her momentum to slip behind him and slide the dagger across his throat. Crimson sprayed, and the man collapsed, gurgling. Riona whirled to help Auberon with the others.

Two left.

They had somehow positioned themselves between her and Auberon, and were slashing at the prince mercilessly, relentlessly. Forcing him away from her. He staggered backward, trying to ward off their attacks. She was going to watch him die. She started toward him, her fingers tightening around the grip of her dagger, just as movement flashed in her periphery.

Riona turned, and a hand closed around her throat. A man—a fourth attacker. She saw his eyes, twin pools of darkness. She saw his face, twisted in cruel, smug victory.

She heard the whistle of his dagger cleaving the air.

And felt white-hot agony when it sank into her chest.

Chapter Fifty-Nine
The Liar

"R*IONA!*"

Auberon let out a roar of fury as she slumped to her knees, blood bubbling on her lips. He lunged toward her, but his two opponents swiped at him in unison, forcing him to yield another step. One carved a shallow cut in his arm, but he barely noticed it. He could do nothing but watch as the bastard who had stabbed Riona ripped the dagger out of her chest and raised it to stab her again.

Over my dead body! The attacker on his left swung his sword low, and Auberon knocked it aside, plunging his own blade into the man's gut. He cried out in pain as Auberon shoved him off the end of his sword and into his other opponent. They went down in a heap of bloody, tangled limbs.

Auberon charged toward Riona. Her attacker's dagger swung toward her chest, but she met it with her own, locking their blades. Auberon's heart leapt at the rage on her face. She would fight the Creator himself to survive. Riona swayed, blood pouring from her wound, but it did not stop her from pushing to her feet and burying her dagger in her attacker's chest.

Again.

And again.

And again.

She didn't stop until he was sprawled flat on his back, his torso a mess of bloody ribbons. Riona stared down at him, breathing hard, the dagger in her hand dripping crimson. For a moment, she swayed, her trembling fingers rising to the wound in her chest. Then all the strength left her body. Auberon caught her just as she collapsed.

"Hold on," he gasped, easing her down to the floor. "Hold on, Riona. Stay with me."

There was movement across the stage. Auberon looked up to see the last attacker shove the other's body off himself and stumble to his feet. Auberon had managed to carve a deep gash in the man's side. The wound wouldn't be fatal if he found medical assistance soon, but Auberon didn't intend for the bastard to live that long. The attacker pressed a hand to his side and ran.

Auberon raced after him, his pulse rushing in his ears. He was near blind in the backstage darkness, just barely able to make out the silhouettes of props and costume racks. Fortunately, the coward who had attacked them was suffering the same problem. Auberon could hear him stumbling somewhere just up ahead. The image of the dagger sinking into Riona's chest burned in his mind. As soon as he caught the man, he would flay the skin from his bones.

"Auberon..."

The word was nothing more than a ragged gasp, but it was enough to stop him in his tracks. He returned to the stage and fell to his knees beside Riona, heedless of the blood that immediately soaked into his pants. Her eyes were shut, but her chest rose and fell weakly. With every shallow breath, more blood poured out of her wound.

"Au—Auberon, I can't..."

"Shhh. It's okay. I'm going to get you out of here." He gathered her into his arms. Her hand flopped limply to one side, the emerald-hilted dagger slipping through her fingers and thudding on the stage as he raced down the steps. "Riona, stay with me. I need you to open your eyes."

"Mm-hmmm..."

"Riona, please. Open your eyes. Listen to my voice." Auberon fought his rising panic as he ran down the aisle, trying not to jostle her too much. *Creator, don't let her die. I'll do anything. Just don't let her die.* "Don't you dare go to sleep, you understand me? Keep listening to me, *aramati*."

She mumbled something incoherent, her fingers curling in the fabric of his doublet.

"Open your eyes, Riona!" he snapped, his voice tight with fear. Auberon burst through the theater's main doors and breathed a sigh of relief when he saw that the carriage Riona had taken to meet him was still waiting by the curb. He needed to find a healer, any healer. It didn't matter if the king's men came to arrest him within the hour, believing that he'd had a hand in this attack. He only needed her to live.

Then an idea struck him, and he called up to the driver as he climbed into the carriage, "The Drunken Monarch—as fast as you can. *Go!*"

The driver cracked his reins, and Auberon fell onto the bench as the carriage lurched into motion. His heart fractured as Riona let out a soft, low moan. He laid her across his lap and pressed his hands to the wound in a desperate attempt to stanch the bleeding. Tears leaked through Riona's lashes, leaving shiny streaks across her dark skin.

"I'm sorry, *aramati*. I'm so sorry. I'm going to get help. I'm going to fix this." The words spilled out of him, barely coherent. "Listen to my voice. Riona, *open your damn eyes!*"

When they arrived outside the tavern, Auberon picked her up and stumbled out of the carriage. He tossed the driver his entire coin purse, then hurried down the alley and into the secret passage up to the castle. Amaris had shown him the hidden exit when they'd left for Crafford; a small door painted to look like stone sat at the bottom of the crag atop which the castle sat, and a narrow, twisting staircase led directly to the royal apartments. Auberon half-ran, half-tripped up the stairs. The entire time, he begged her to hold on, to open her eyes, to listen to his voice.

At last, they reached the top, and he shoved the door open. He raced along the tall stone wall that surrounded the castle buildings, keeping a careful eye out for Rivosi guards. Only when he reached Valerian's house did he emerge from the shadows, startling the guards standing watch at the front door. "Get the duke," he croaked, his voice hoarse.

They rushed into the house. A heartbeat later, Valerian opened the door, the guards at his heels.

"Heal her," Auberon pleaded, unable to keep the desperation from his voice. "Please."

Valerian took one look at Riona and stepped aside. "Put her in the bedroom. Guards, gather the others and wait outside. Wake the ones who are asleep. I want privacy."

Relief flooded him. Auberon followed the duke down the hall and set Riona on the bed. Her head lolled to one side. She'd fallen unconscious, but her chest still rose and fell almost imperceptibly. Valerian pushed him out of the way and bent over Riona to examine the wound, his expression one of practiced calm.

"Give me some light," he commanded over his shoulder. "There are matches on the desk there."

Auberon obeyed. As he moved around the room, lighting the candles and lanterns, Valerian cut away the neckline of Riona's tunic and began murmuring in Kentari Imperial, his fingers following the line of the wound. Auberon leaned over his shoulder, his panic like a noose around his neck. Guilt threatened to swallow him whole. This never would have happened if he hadn't asked her to meet him at the theater, if he hadn't indulged his longing for a future that could never be.

"Will she live?"

"I don't know," Valerian said, the words clipped. Already, Auberon could see his skin paling, dark shadows pooling under his eyes. He remembered with a jolt what the duke had said about blood magic: if he didn't have a surplus of power, healing a fatal wound would kill him.

And yet, Valerian hadn't even hesitated.

"If I brought you one of the men who did this, would it help? You could kill him, take his power." Auberon swallowed. "Save her life."

The duke shook his head. "I've already begun; the connection has been made. One of us would be dead by the time you returned. Plus, there's some sort of ritual required to bind another's life with blood magic, and I don't know how to perform it. We have no choice now but to pray." With that, Valerian switched back to Kentari Imperial, reciting incantation after incantation.

Auberon watched, helpless, as Riona's blood stained the white silk sheets a deep crimson. The sight sent a fresh wave of rage through him, chasing away his terror. One of the bastards who had attacked them was still alive.

He started toward the door, and Valerian paused. "Where are you going?"

"To find the person who did this."

"You can't—you're distraught, injured, and soaked in blood. From what I can see, you have at least a half-dozen wounds, many of which need stitches. Tend to your injuries, change your clothes, and once you've recovered your senses, hunt down the man who attacked you. My guards will help you."

He shrugged off the duke's objection. "I'm going to find him, and I'm going to get answers. Don't try to stop me. And send some men to watch over Lord Lachlan's house. I don't want to risk his or Lady Amaris's safety."

"Auberon—"

"Do it. Please."

At the raw, desperate sound of his voice, Valerian gave a single, reluctant nod. "Very well."

"Thank you," Auberon said, then turned and stalked out of the room.

Chapter Sixty
The Lady

"*Auberon...*"

His name slipped through her lips as she lay on the cold wooden stage, tremors wracking her body. Something warm and sticky coated her skin, pooling around her. Blood. She didn't know how much of it had come from her or how much had come from the man she'd killed. Soon, it wouldn't matter.

Footsteps thudded toward her. She didn't have the strength to pry open her eyelids, but she knew who knelt beside her even before he spoke.

"Au—Auberon, I can't..."

I can't feel my fingers.

"Shhh." His deep, warm voice wrapped around her. "It's okay. I'm going to get you out of here."

The world suddenly tilted, the floor falling out from under her, and pain shot through her chest. Auberon was carrying her, cradling her in his arms. Distantly, she registered the dagger he had given her slipping out of her grasp, but he didn't seem to notice.

"Riona, stay with me. I need you to open your eyes."

"Mm-hmmm..."

"Riona, please. Open your eyes. Listen to my voice. Don't you dare go to sleep, you understand me? Keep listening to me, *aramati*."

You have such a beautiful voice, she tried to say, but the words tangled on her tongue. *I never told you that.*

Darkness lurked at the edge of her consciousness. The pain in her chest had begun to ease, ebbing and eddying with her weakening pulse.

Such a lovely, lovely voice...

"Open your eyes, Riona!" Auberon snapped, and then she heard him yell to someone nearby.

A door slammed. Reins cracked. Hooves clattered against cobblestone. He'd found them a carriage.

Auberon held her close, warming her with the heat of his body. When he pressed down on the wound in her chest, agony momentarily pierced the fog around her mind. Her eyes flew open. Auberon's face was inches from hers, terror scrawled across his features.

"I'm sorry, *aramati*. I'm so sorry. I'm going to get help. I'm going to fix this," he said in a jumble, the words tripping over each other. "Listen to my voice. Riona, *open your damn eyes!*"

She tried. By the Creator, she tried.

But the haze swept over her mind once again, and darkness claimed her.

"*Rijat du'omo, Iei sao. Rijat du'omo, Iei sao. Rijat du'omo, Iei sao.*"

Riona slowly swam through the fog muddling her mind, vaguely aware that the person speaking wasn't the one she had hoped to hear when—*if*—she awoke. She tried to pry open her eyes and found that her lids refused to obey.

"*Rijat du'omo, Iei sao.*"

Heat pulsed within her chest with each repetition of the

strange words. It wasn't anything like the white-hot flames that had ignited within her when the dagger pierced her chest. There was still pain, but a different kind—like the feeling of sitting too close to a hearth. The warmth grew incrementally, easing away the chill that had crept into her limbs.

"Please," the voice whispered. "I'm doing everything I can, but I need you to fight, my lady. Stay with me."

I'm still here, she thought faintly, the words slipping away before she could force her lips to part.

I'm still...

Chapter Sixty-One
The Liar

Auberon rushed into the theater. The stage was illuminated by the countless candles he had left burning, their flames casting dancing light across the still forms slumped on the stage. The corpse closest to the front lay facing the aisle, his sightless eyes fixed on Auberon as he approached. The blood pooling beneath him ran over the edge of the stage and dribbled down into the pit.

Auberon stalked up the stairs, the candles guttering as he passed. The emerald-hilted dagger lay a few feet away, near the body of the man who'd stabbed Riona. He picked it up, wiped the blade clean on the dead man's trousers, and then grabbed a lantern and scanned the floor of the stage. The fleeing coward had been badly wounded, and he wouldn't have been able to run far. It didn't take Auberon long to find the bloody trail he'd left in his wake—droplets here, part of a footprint there, a streak on the edge of a box of costumes... He could imagine the coward staggering through the darkness, tripping over props while trying to hold the gash in his stomach closed.

The wounds he had sustained in the fight throbbed as he made his way through the backstage area. Most of the lesser cuts had clotted already, but the gash in his bicep still leaked blood.

His doublet was soaked—a mixture of his and Riona's blood—and the cold, wet fabric clung to him. When he passed a rack of costumes, Auberon grabbed a wool overcoat and pulled it on over his ruined doublet. It was late, but there would still be people walking the streets, and he couldn't afford to draw attention to himself.

The trail led to a door in the side of the theater, a discreet entrance for the dancers. Part of a bloody handprint was smudged across the doorframe, where the man had stumbled and caught himself before stepping out into the night. Auberon left the theater and followed the droplets of blood along a narrow road and down a tight alleyway.

Soon, he found himself standing before a tavern, music and raucous laughter spilling through its open windows. The trail of blood led around the side and to a door at the rear of the building. Auberon tested the handle and found it locked, but a pass of his dagger's blade through the gap between the frame and the door was enough to unlatch the simple mechanism. The door swung open to a dim, low-ceilinged storeroom, filled with shelves of food and casks of alcohol.

A man was sprawled on the floor, clutching a decanter of whiskey in a white-knuckled grip. His chest was bare, his bloody shirt crumpled on the floor beside him, and a woman was kneeling at his side. Her back was to Auberon, and it appeared that she hadn't heard the door swing open.

"Hold still, you bastard," she muttered as she wove a needle through the skin of the man's stomach. "I can barely see in this light, and your squirming doesn't help."

"Oh, don't worry about making those stitches pretty," Auberon said as he stepped into the room. The woman started, accidentally pulling on the thread, and the man hissed a curse. A cruel grin spread across his Auberon's. "He won't need them for long."

"I-I swear, I can't tell you anything!" the coward blubbered, the words slurred from the whiskey. Auberon tightened his grip on the man's arm and dragged him up the steep stairs that led to the top of the city wall. The coward stumbled, pitching dangerously close to the edge. Auberon yanked him back. He couldn't let the bastard die. Not yet.

"Can't or won't?" Auberon inquired. "One means you can be persuaded. The other means you're disposable."

The man looked up at the wall, his throat bobbing. "P-Please. I only followed orders. Have mercy."

"Mercy," he scoffed, pulling the drunken coward the rest of the way up the stairs. When they reached the top of the wall, the man sucked in a breath as a cold wind swept over them, slicing straight through their clothes. Braziers at each tower glowed brightly against the night. There wasn't a guard in sight, but one was sure to come by on his rounds soon enough.

Waist-high crenelations ran along the outer edge of the wall, and Auberon shoved the man toward one of the gaps. The coward's knees cracked against the stone so hard he whimpered. Auberon gripped his collar and pushed him so he was leaning out over the wall, staring straight down at the dizzying fifty-foot drop below.

"Let's try this again," he snarled. "Who hired you to attack us?"

"Please. *Please*. Just take me back to the tavern. We can talk this out."

Auberon grabbed the man's shoulder and spun him around. With his dagger, he sliced through the bastard's shirt, exposing his pale, narrow torso. The gash in his stomach slashed an angry red crescent from the bottom of his ribcage to his opposite hip.

"You try my patience," Auberon snarled, setting the point of his dagger under the first stitch. The man's breathing hitched, Auberon cut through the first several inches of stitches. Blood immediately poured out of the wound, running in crimson rivulets down the man's stomach. "Tell me: Do you have a family?"

"A wife and a...a daughter."

"How old is your daughter?"

His throat bobbed. "Five."

"If you'd like to see her again, I'd advise you to carefully consider your answer to my next question." Auberon moved the point of his dagger to the next stitch. "Did the king hire you to attack us?"

"It was some lord from the court. I don't know if he was acting on the king's orders or not. His name— His name is Farquar. Lord Farquar."

Surprise jolted through him. "Farquar? Are you sure? Do you have proof?"

He nodded frantically. "Those men I was with... We're sellswords. We go to a man named Vick for work. He'll have a record of the deal."

"It hasn't been destroyed?"

"I don't think so. Vick takes a deposit first and only gets the rest of the money after the job's completed. He wouldn't destroy a contract if it hadn't been paid yet—especially one he could use for blackmail. He owns the Crow and Crown tavern, over on Ravenwood. Go there, and you'll find the contract." The man glanced over his shoulder at the steep drop below him. "That's all I know, I swear. I can't tell you anything else. Please let me go. I need to see a healer."

Auberon's gaze roved over the man—the blood marring his stomach, the tears shining in his eyes, the dark stain growing across the front of his trousers. He could see by the way the coward was trembling that he had spoken true. He was only a hired hand; he had no loyalty to Farquar, no reason to lie. More than anything, he wanted to get home to his family. Auberon smiled and tucked his dagger into his belt beside his sheathed sword. "Do you love your daughter?"

"More than anything," the man gasped, his expression softening with relief.

"And your wife, you love her, as well?"

"She is my life."

Auberon leaned in close, his smile turning cold and wicked. "Then you know how I feel about Riona."

He planted a hand in the center of the man's chest and shoved him, hard. The bastard toppled over the edge of the battlements and screamed as he plummeted, his arms and legs pinwheeling. Auberon watched him fall, not even flinching at the wet *crunch* his body made when it landed in a broken heap at the base of the wall. Elsewhere on the battlements, someone cried out in alarm. Running footsteps thundered against the walkway.

Auberon turned and descended the stairs quickly, being careful to avoid the intermittent patches of moonlight as he started in the direction of the Crow and Crown tavern. He vaguely recalled seeing the tavern's sign on one of his treks through the city. *Tonight, this all ends,* he thought, his fingers curling around the grip of his emerald-hilted dagger.

As he walked, he looked up at the castle, glowing bright and proud from its perch over the city. Riona was there. Bleeding. *Dying.* Auberon yearned to go to her, but he couldn't yet. He had asked her to meet him in the theater. This was his fault, and he needed to make it right.

That, and he couldn't bear the thought of returning to the castle and finding out that Riona had succumbed to her wound. As long as he stayed away, he could let himself believe that Valerian had saved her life.

Distantly, he could hear the watchmen atop the wall shouting orders to one another. Auberon didn't regret killing the coward. He was sorry for taking a girl's father from her, but the man had sealed his fate the moment he set foot in that theater. If Auberon had been the only target of the attack, he might have let the man walk away after revealing Farquar's involvement. He had known how dangerous it would be to enter the Rivosi court as an Erdurian prince. He had accepted the risk.

Riona was different. She was everything he was not: good, honest, thoughtful, selfless... At that first banquet, they had been perfect strangers, branded enemies by the blood running through their veins. She'd had every reason to hate him. And despite that, she had sat with him as the poison took hold of his lungs. While everyone else had panicked, recoiling in horror and fear, she had held his hand and promised that he would survive.

Soon, she would be betrothed to another man. Auberon could live with that. He could live with watching her marry Drystan, with pretending his eyes didn't automatically seek her out every time he entered a room, with trying to forget the taste of her lips against his.

He could endure that torture for the rest of his life, because it would mean she was alive.

Chapter Sixty-Two
The Liar

The Crow and Crown tavern was a simple building of drab gray stone. Its shutters were closed, slivers of light leaking through the narrow gaps in the slats, and the chains suspending its wooden sign squealed as it swayed in the breeze. Auberon pulled his overcoat tighter around himself as he approached the building, and the movement sent another slender river of blood down his arm. He would have to tend to the gash in his bicep soon.

After making certain that the overcoat covered every sign of his wounds, he pulled the tavern's door open. Immediately, the scent of cheap ale washed over him. It was late, but the tavern was full of drunken patrons, and a small band of musicians had set themselves up in the corner of the main room. The bar ran parallel to the wall to his right, and a door just behind it was labeled *Do Not Enter*. He edged around a group of rowdy young men and started toward it.

A woman stood behind the bar, cleaning a pool of spilled wine with an old, stained rag. When she noticed where Auberon was headed, she tossed the sodden fabric aside and stepped into his path. "You can't go in there, sir."

He put on a rough Rivosi accent and said in a low voice, "I

need to speak with Vick. It's about a job he sent some men to complete tonight—a job on behalf of Lord Farquar. Something's gone wrong, and it'll be all our heads if the lord learns of it before Vick does."

She appraised him warily. He didn't know how well she was acquainted with the sell-swords who went to Vick for work, but with his Rivosi accent, muscular build, and the weapons sheathed at his hip, he could easily pass for one of them. Her lips pressed into a thin line, but she nodded and returned to the bar. Auberon murmured his thanks and slipped through the door. It led to a short hallway with two doors, lit with a lantern hanging from the low ceiling. Auberon ducked under it and pressed his ear to the door on his right. Quiet snoring rumbled from within.

Vick.

He pushed the door open, the hinges squealing, and the snoring broke off abruptly. The room was dark, and in the slivers of moonlight bleeding in through the shutters, he could just make out a figure pushing itself upright in the bed.

"Who's 'ere? Who let you in?" a deep, groggy voice called.

Auberon said nothing as he closed and locked the door. A match flared to life, and he turned back just as the man lit the lantern on the bedside table, filling the room with weak, flickering light. He was middle-aged, with a square, stern face and receding black hair. He scowled. "Who're you?"

"I'll give you a hint." Auberon leaned against the door and crossed his arms. "You sent your men to kill Lady Riona and me tonight."

Realization and fear flashed across Vick's face. For a few heartbeats, he didn't seem to breathe.

Then he lunged for the bedside table and yanked open the drawer, fumbling for something within. Auberon crossed the room in a few quick strides and slammed the drawer shut with one foot, crushing the bones in Vick's hand.

"Now, now, let's not be hasty," he drawled as the man bit off a cry of pain. "I only want to discuss a business proposal with you. We can manage that, can't we?"

Vick nodded, looking like he might be sick. Auberon smiled and lowered his foot, then reached into the drawer and snatched the dagger concealed within. He tossed it onto the desk on the far wall, well out of the man's reach. Vick withdrew his hand and cradled it to his chest. A few of his fingers were bent at ghastly angles.

"As you can see, your men's attempt to kill us failed," Auberon began, "which means that Lord Farquar isn't going to be very happy with you. It won't be long before news of the attack spreads, and Farquar is going to make certain that someone else takes the fall for it."

Vick's throat bobbed. "He wouldn't dare. I have the contract he signed. I'll reveal it to the king."

"You think a piece of paper will save you? He just ordered the assassinations of an Erdurian prince and the niece of the king. You'll be lucky to see the dawn. Fortunately," Auberon said, leaning in close, "I can protect you."

"Why would you do that?"

"I want Lord Farquar to suffer for what he's done, and if I go to his house tonight, I'll kill him much too quickly. I would see him rot in a cell for the rest of his days, and you're the key to achieving that. You'll give me the contract he signed and testify against him before the king and court, and I'll keep you alive. Do we have a deal?"

"Yes," he said immediately. "We do."

"Excellent." Auberon took up his position by the door once again. "Fetch the contract and get dressed, and then we're leaving."

Vick cautiously rose, still cradling his injured hand, and picked up the dagger Auberon had tossed onto the desk. Auberon tensed, reaching for the sword at his hip, but the tavern owner only sank to his knees and pried up one of the floorboards near the foot of the bed. He extracted a small box from the hidden compartment.

"Lord Farquar came to me yesterday afternoon and told me to send some men to the Royal Theater," Vick said as he pocketed a few of the trinkets. "When the opportunity presented itself, they were to attack you and Lady Riona and make it look like a murder-suicide. No one would question it, he said. Not with the way you look at her."

Auberon winced. *Is it really* that *obvious?*

Vick handed him a folded piece of parchment, then moved to the wardrobe and began pulling clothes on over his long sleep tunic. Auberon unfolded the paper and skimmed the contents, his gaze lingering on Lord Farquar's elegant signature. He had no proof that Farquar had been working under the king's orders, but it couldn't possibly be a coincidence that they'd been attacked the very night they'd returned from the Howling Mountains. The king had chosen to silence them, after all.

"Alright," Vick said after he'd finished gathering his belongings in a small canvas bag. "Where are we going?"

Auberon folded the contract and slipped it into his pocket. "To the castle."

Dread had formed a heavy weight in the pit of Auberon's stomach by the time they arrived at Valerian's house. He knocked, and after several excruciating seconds, a grim-faced Kentari guard opened the door. Behind him, Valerian was slumped on one of the armchairs in the sitting room. He looked awful—his clothes rumpled, his skin sallow, his eyes glazed with fatigue—but he was alive.

Auberon shouldered past the guard. "Riona, is she—?"

"She's alive," the duke said, grimacing. Auberon's knees nearly gave out at the relief that washed over him. "She's resting in the bedroom. Who's that?"

Vick had followed him inside and was lingering on the threshold to the sitting room, gaping at the duke's sickly appearance. Auberon pushed him into the other armchair none too gently. "This is the man who sent those sell-swords after Riona and me. I promised him my protection if he agreed to testify against Lord Farquar."

Valerian sat up straighter. "*Farquar* ordered the attack? Why?"

"I haven't made very many friends in the time I've been here, if you hadn't noticed."

"Don't be short with me because you're exhausted and in pain. I told you to stay and rest." The duke slumped back. "I assume you're responsible for that man's broken hand, but don't expect me to tend to any more wounds tonight. I'd keel over if I tried to heal so much as a paper cut."

"He can tend to his own wounds," Auberon said, shooting a sharp look at the tavern owner when he opened his mouth to object. "I just need to see Riona."

Valerian waved a hand in the general direction of the bedroom. "Be my guest."

His heart in his throat, Auberon walked down the hall and slowly, quietly opened the bedroom door. Riona lay on the bed, fast asleep, a thick blanket draped over her. Valerian had cut away the rest of her ruined tunic, leaving her in the wide band of fabric that covered her breasts, and bandaged the wound. Her head was turned toward him, the light from the hearth playing across her closed lids, her high cheekbones, her full, parted lips.

She was alive.

She was *alive*.

Moving as silently as he could, Auberon picked up one of the armchairs near the hearth and set it beside the bed. Ever reliable, Valerian had left a pile of bandages, a spool of thread, and a needle on the bedside table. A bowl of water and a rag sat on the floor by one of the legs. Auberon removed his overcoat and ruined doublet and set them aside, then soaked the rag in the water and carefully cleaned the drying blood from his wounds. He shouldn't have left them unattended for so long. A few of the worst cuts were red and inflamed from his trek across the city.

He sterilized the needle in the lantern's flame before setting to work. The gash in his upper arm wasn't very long, but it was deep, and blood leaked out over his fingers as he worked the needle through his flesh. Pain shot through him with every tug of the thread. He clenched his teeth as he moved to a cut along his ribs, then another just above his hip, distracting himself with memories of that night. Riona cupping his face in her perfect, delicate hands. Riona swaying with him, her body pressed against his. Riona kissing him.

Riona asking him to marry her.

As he tied off the last line of stitches, a weak voice whispered, "You're beautiful."

Auberon looked up and found Riona's stunning blue eyes trained on him, trailing over the faint marks that marred his torso. Marks that were not befitting of a prince. "How long have you been watching me?"

"Not long enough," she said, and those three words made his heart race. A faint smile tugged at her lips. "What a pair we make. Now I'll have a scar to match all of yours."

She reached out to trace an old scar along his forearm. It was little more than a pale white line against his tanned skin—a souvenir from his early days of training with Walther. Before her fingers could make contact, his hand shot up and caught hers. "*Don't.*"

Riona frowned. "Why not?"

"Why not? Riona, do you even *realize*—" Auberon stopped and changed tactics before his traitorous heart could betray him yet again. "Last night was a mistake. I should never have said what I did. Done what I did. I'm sorry."

"I'm not. Do you think I don't feel the same way about you, Auberon? You're not the Crown Prince, but you're a son of the Erdurian Emperor. With our betrothal, we can have peace between our countries. We can end the war. Drystan will understand."

The matter-of-fact way she said it sent a spear through his chest. He released her hand. "It's impossible. If you marry an Erdurian, it will be Drystan."

"Why?" Riona demanded, anger flaring. "You expect me to marry your brother—to *produce heirs* with him—while I love you?"

Auberon stood sharply. He wanted to tell her the whole truth, to make her understand why they could never be married, but he couldn't risk it yet. "Forget what happened between us last night. I was a fool for inviting you to the theater."

Riona pushed herself upright, her face twisting in pain. "How can you ask that of me? I have risked my life time and time again for this kingdom. I played the puppet in Beltharos and faced execution. I ventured into the Howling Mountains to find proof of what my uncle had done. I nearly *died* tonight. Have I not earned the right to marry the man I choose?"

"The choice is not up to you!" Auberon shouted, the reins on his temper slipping. He *had* to make her understand. "I was sent here with two orders: to secure eudorite ore for Erduria, and to ensure that you were betrothed to Drystan. I cannot and *will not* marry you."

Riona shrank back, startled by his anger.

Guilt and regret immediately filled him. He pulled on the ruined overcoat, covering most of his wounds, and sat. "Lord Farquar ordered the attack last night. I have written proof and a witness who will stand before the court and testify against him. All we have to decide is whether we will confront the king before the nobles, or in private."

Riona stilled. "Lord Farquar... Are you sure?"

He pulled the contract from his pocket and handed it to her. She read the contents, then read them a second time over, her fingers tightening on the parchment. When she finished, she folded it and gave it back to him.

"Don't worry about it now," Auberon said as he rose and set the emerald dagger on the bedside table. "Try to rest and regain your strength. Duke Valerian and I will ensure that you're safe until we figure out how we want to move forward."

She nodded, and he left. When he emerged from the bedroom, he found Valerian standing at the far end of the hall, leaning against the archway to the sitting room. His expression made it clear that he had heard everything. "I didn't mean to eavesdrop. I heard shouting, and I wanted to make sure you were both alright."

Auberon let out a soft, bitter laugh. *Alright?* How could they *possibly* be alright? "We're alive, which is all that matters."

Just as he was about to pass Valerian, the duke reached out and caught his arm. "Whatever is between you is none of my business, but you should know that when she regained consciousness, the first thing she did was ask for you."

Auberon stiffened, willing a cool mask to slip over his features. "There is nothing between us."

The duke opened his mouth, closed it, then finally said, "If this is about your position, being the second son... I don't presume to know Prince Drystan or Erduria better than you, but I'm sure that if you spoke to your brother and explained how you felt, he would understand. You could be with her."

"If only it were that simple." He started to move past Valerian, then paused. "You still don't remember the last time we met, do you?"

Valerian studied him for several long moments. "Should I? How long has it been?"

"No, I suppose not. It's been a long time since I was last in Kenter." He walked into the sitting room and gestured for Vick to follow him, the duke on his heels. "We'll go speak with Drystan. Thank you for helping her. Make sure your guards watch over the house at all times, and do not let any guests see her. Not even her family. If her condition changes, please let me know."

"Of course. Can I expect an explanation anytime soon?"

Auberon smiled, knowing that even if he refused, Valerian would still protect Riona. Despite his concerns about the duke's use of blood magic, Valerian was a good, honorable man. He was a better man than Auberon. So all he said was, "Perhaps."

Valerian frowned, but didn't object as he led them to the front door and held it open. There was no mistaking the sympathy in his voice as he murmured, "For your sake, Auberon, I hope your brother doesn't win her hand in marriage."

Chapter Sixty-Three
The Lady

Riona stared at the door through which Auberon had left, her hands in tight fists around her blanket. Then she took a sharp breath, and something within her cracked. A ragged sob escaped her as she buried her face in her hands. It was all too much. The suitors, Cathal's murder, her uncle, the mines, the attack, Auberon...

Auberon.

His confession from the night before came surging back, bringing with it a fresh wave of tears. She felt broken and pathetic and pitiful, sitting there crying, but she couldn't stop it.

Despite my best efforts, I have fallen in love with you, aramati —wholly and eternally.

What you don't know is that I have begged the Creator every day to stop me feeling this way about you. You don't know how desperately I want you to walk out that door and never speak to me again. I never planned for this to happen. This isn't how it was supposed to end.

At every turn, he had been there for her. He claimed to be loyal to the Empire above all, but they had both blurred the lines between duty and desire. She hadn't realized just how hard she'd fallen until he had come for her in the mines, until she had seen the agony and desperation in his eyes as he fell to his knees before her and cupped her face in his hands.

She loved him.

A knock came at the door. Riona straightened and dried her tears, wincing as a flare of heat shot through her torso at the movement. It quickly receded, but didn't vanish entirely, pulsing like a second heartbeat just below the bandage covering her wound. That was odd. She must have pulled her stitches. "Yes?"

Valerian opened the door. "Prince Auberon has left, my lady, and I've sent a guard to fetch breakfast from the kitchen. How do you feel?"

"About as well as one would expect. You tended to my injuries, didn't you?" Riona asked, trying to wade through her hazy memories of the past several hours. "I remember hearing your voice, but I couldn't make sense of the words."

He ducked his head. "It was Kentari Imperial."

She studied him—the way his gaze slanted away from hers, his weight shifting from one foot to the other—and frowned. Why had Auberon brought her to the duke, of all people? How had he known that Valerian would help her? "How did you come to know how to heal?"

"Being the politically useless puppet of a tyrant has its advantages—one of those being extensive time for study. I chose healing. After surviving the Kostori siege on Glenkeld, I have a vested interest in learning how to keep my people alive."

"I should be dead right now."

"The wound appeared worse than it was."

She gave him a pointed look. "I felt how deep that dagger went. I shouldn't have survived the night, but Auberon knew that you would save my life. That's why he brought me here, instead of to a healer. How did you bring me back from the brink of death?"

Valerian ran a hand through his golden curls, looking conflicted. Finally, he breathed, "I used blood magic."

Her blood turned to ice. "What?"

He took a step toward her, reaching out as if to reassure her, but faltered when she shrank back in fear. He winced, his hand falling to his side. "I've been studying blood magic for years, trying to find ways for healers to implement it into their practice," he said. "I had never used it on anyone until Prince Auberon was poisoned. That's why he recovered so quickly. He confronted me about it after the ballet, and I told him everything. That's why he brought you here tonight."

Riona gaped at him, dumbfounded. She knew the folk tales about blood mages. She had seen firsthand the destruction the Cirisians had wrought on Sandori during their war with Beltharos. Yet Valerian had never given her reason to feel unsafe around him. In fact, he reminded her of Tamriel and Percival—honest, honorable, and selfless. She didn't fear him.

Riona met his gaze. "Thank you, Valerian. I owe you my life."

"No, you don't. If the wound had been fatal, I would be dead. Your wound was serious, but any healer—if he'd gotten to you quickly—would have been able to sew the wound and stop the bleeding. I only accelerated your own body's healing." He hesitated, then asked, "You're not angry? Or afraid?"

"I am nothing but grateful."

The duke visibly relaxed, the tension in his shoulders easing. "I am glad to hear it. Now, I'll leave you to rest. I'll have your breakfast sent in when it arrives."

"Wait," Riona blurted, just as he turned to leave. She didn't dare admit it aloud, but she found she didn't want him to go. The quiet would leave her too much time alone with her thoughts. "May I ask you a question?"

He nodded and claimed the armchair Auberon had left beside the bed. Riona bit back a gasp as the light from the bedside lantern struck his face. His cheeks were pale and hollow, shadows hanging under his eyes, and his skin was so translucent she could see the web of faint blue veins at his temples—side effects of the blood magic, she assumed with a mixture of horror and curiosity.

"What do you wish to ask me?"

"What does one do when she suddenly finds her court filled with monsters?"

A shadow passed across Valerian's face. "You survive, no matter the cost. You bide your time. And when the opportunity presents itself, you purge the monsters and rebuild from the rubble."

"Is that what you plan to do in Kenter?"

"I pray for as little destruction as possible, but I will do what I must to restore my country's independence. When the Kostori claimed Kenter as a vassal, the nobility who refused foreign rule met the executioner's axe in the city square. Once the first head rolled, it didn't take long for the rest of the nobles to lay down their weapons and pledge fealty. My father was the first man on his knees." Valerian paused, shame darkening his features. "That day, I hated him. Seeing him kneeling in the blood of his friends, knowing that he was the one who let the Kostori troops into the city. He did what was necessary then to save our people, but we have suffered enough under Kostori rule. So yes, I have known my fair share of monsters, and I plan to rid my country of them all."

Riona looked away from the duke's intense stare and tugged at a stray thread sticking out of her blanket. Her uncle was the heart of the kingdom. She hated his methods, but he was the only thing standing in the way of the empire's complete control of the Tranquil Sea. What if Emperor Hyperion did not honor the terms of the alliance they would soon strike? What if he decided that he wanted the eudorite mines for himself? Even if he kept his word, it would not be long before foreign armies arrived to claim the eudorite ore for themselves. Rivosa would need a strong king to stand against them—a king who had been at war since the day he was crowned.

If she revealed her uncle's treachery to the court, she would leave Rivosa with a gaping wound. Most likely, the king would be deposed and his son placed on the throne. Prince Domhnall would make an excellent king in times of peace, but that was not the future they faced. Every battle, every death, would chip away at his resolve. Eventually, he would give in. Their enemies would win, and Rivosa would be ruined.

Riona met the duke's eyes. She felt like a ship left unmoored in a storm, swept into unfamiliar seas. "What do I do, Valerian?"

He set a hand on hers and gave it a comforting squeeze. "That is for you to decide. This is your kingdom. Your people. You must do what you feel is right."

"And if there is no right answer?"

"Then you make the best decision you can."

Riona managed a weak smile. "Thank you for everything you've done for me, Valerian. I am more grateful to you than I could possibly express."

He dipped his head in respect. "I feel honored to count you among my friends, my lady. Whatever happens, wherever you go, you may call on me whenever you need. The Kentari court can be a rather grim place. It'll be nice to see a friendly face from time to time."

Just then, someone knocked on the door, and two guards entered carrying steaming trays of food. The scent made Riona's mouth water. Valerian chuckled at the shift in her expression and rose as one of the guards set a tray before her. It was laden with slices of roasted ham, eggs, fresh fruit, and a warm roll slathered in butter.

"I'll take my breakfast in the sitting room," Valerian said, already starting toward the door. "Stay as long as you like—my guards and I will make sure you're safe. Do you want to send a note to your father or Lady Amaris telling them where you are?"

Amaris. After everything that had happened, she hadn't stopped to consider Amaris's safety. If the attack had been ordered by the king—which seemed likely, considering they'd only returned from the mines a matter of hours ago—he could have sent men to silence her, too. Bile rose in the back of her throat.

Valerian saw her terror and quickly added, "They're fine. I

sent men to watch over your father's estate. Prince Auberon seemed to think one or both of them might also have been targeted, but no such attack has occurred. I've had my men send an update every hour."

Relief shot through her, and she accepted the offer of writing to her father and Amaris. What she would say in the letter, she had no idea. Perhaps she would just buy herself time by claiming she'd woken up early and gone straight to the castle. Perhaps she would tell them everything. If the bodies in the Royal Theater hadn't been discovered yet, they would be once Mistress Rosalie arrived to prepare for the day's practice. Whatever happened, they had hours until she was promised to Eamon, her future sealed.

Hours until Rivosa lost its last chance for a peaceful end to the war.

Chapter Sixty-Four
The Liar

"Lord Farquar will die for what he has done," Drystan snarled as he paced the width of his bedroom. "Trying to kill you and Riona. What was the snake *thinking?* Are you certain he did it on the king's orders?"

"Certain, yes, but lacking proof," Auberon said, rage churning within him. "This has gone too far, Drystan. We must confront the king now, before he and Farquar orchestrate another attempt on Riona's life. And we must get her on a ship to Erduria."

"You said Valerian and his men are watching over her. She should be safe, at least until she's strong enough for the ride to Crafford. Sending her on a week-long voyage right now would do more harm than good."

"Not with the aid of Valerian's blood magic."

Drystan's expression darkened. After they returned from Valerian's house, Auberon had ordered one of the Erdurian guards to tend to Vick's hand and give him a bed in one of the guest rooms, then awakened Drystan and explained everything. Well, everything except the real reason why he'd invited Riona to the theater the night before. *That* little detail he had kept to himself.

"From what you've told me, blood magic still doesn't work miracles. You were confined to a cot for the better part of a week even with the aid of the healing magic. Lady Riona won't be in any shape to travel for at least a few days, maybe more."

Auberon threw his hands up in frustration. He was sitting on the bench seat of the large bay window in Drystan's room, and he turned to stare out at the lightening sky, the castle just beginning to awaken below. "So now what? We simply wait until Riona is strong enough or Lord Farquar sends more men after her? I taught her all I could about self-defense in what little time we had, but she'll be too weak to take on one skilled swordsman, let alone three. Do you truly think it's wise to delay?"

Drystan's expression turned thoughtful, troubled. "Before we decide our next move, we must examine what choices Farquar and the king have before them. They know that you, Riona, and Amaris have been to the mines, and they'll assume that you've told me what you discovered. That leaves them four powerful, influential people to assassinate if they want their secret to remain safe, and that's too many deaths to explain away. They know you survived the attack in the theater, and that we're going to demand retribution for the attempt on your life. And most importantly, *we* know that they are desperate. They wouldn't have attempted to assassinate you and Riona if they weren't panicking. So we let them panic."

"I still think King Domhnall will say to hell with it all and have you and me killed, just to spite us."

"No. Kill us, and Father will send every soldier in his command to Rivosa's shores. Kill us, and they damn themselves," Drystan said, a spark returning to his eyes. He looked almost...*excited*. "This is it. They have played their hand, and they have lost. Today, we secure the peace treaty."

Today, the woman I love will be promised to you, Auberon thought, but he held his tongue. Instead, he looked away, keeping his voice steady and nonchalant as he said, "I told you we would succeed."

"And I beg your forgiveness for ever doubting you." Drystan crossed the room and clapped a hand on his shoulder. "Now, you ought to rest. You look like you've been dragged to the Beyond and back."

"I feel like it, too," he said with a grimace, running a hand through his hair. Every nerve ending in his body felt frayed. "But you're mad if you think I'll be able to sleep after what happened."

"Please. I bet you'll fall asleep in the bath, if you even make it that far. Whatever you do, I want you to stay in this house until you've slept and had something to eat. Right now, you are angry, hurt, and exhausted. The last thing we can afford is you behaving rashly in front of the court."

Auberon nodded again, unable to dredge up the energy to argue. Every instinct urged him to stay with Riona and make sure Farquar's men didn't hurt her again, but Drystan was right: she was safe with Valerian and his guards, and in his state, he would be of no use to her in a fight. Now that the adrenaline from the night before had worn off, he was ready to collapse. "Fine."

"Good. I'll see you later this afternoon. I'm going to get dressed and see what's happening in the rest of the castle. Someone must have discovered the bodies at the Royal Theater by now."

"Be careful."

"I will. Be sensible."

"Aren't I always?"

Auberon left Drystan's room and crossed the hall, shouting down the stairs for someone to send for a servant to fill the bath. While one of the guards rushed off to fulfill the command, Auberon slipped into his room and tossed the ruined overcoat into the corner of the room, then removed his sheathed sword and belt. After a moment's hesitation, he pulled the blade free with the soft scrape of steel against leather. The edge gleamed under the pale dawn light bleeding in through the windows. Auberon smiled, imagining the metal coated in deep crimson blood.

There was one other thing he hadn't told Drystan. Someone had told Farquar that Auberon and Riona would be meeting in the Royal Theater that night. The sell-swords hadn't tailed him from the castle; he knew the feeling of being watched, and he hadn't felt that familiar prickle on the back of his neck until the heartbeat before the attackers charged onto the stage. He and Riona had provided them plenty of opportunities to attack before they had, which meant that the sell-swords had only arrived moments before they'd revealed themselves. They hadn't been lying in wait—they'd been told precisely when to arrive.

Only one man had ever threatened to reveal his secret meetings with Riona to the court. Tonight, Auberon would gladly repay the bastard's treachery.

Chapter Sixty-Five
The Lady

A knock sounded on the front door of Valerian's guest house not half an hour later. Riona was already waiting in the sitting room, her hands clasped in front of her and her legs gracefully crossed at the ankles—still the poised, perfect lady of the court, despite the sickly pallor of her skin and the bandages wrapped around her chest. After demolishing the breakfast the guards had left her, she had forced herself out of bed and taken one of the lightweight linen tunics from Valerian's wardrobe. The fabric was soft against her skin, the loose, airy fit offering some relief from the heat pulsing just above her heart. She was in agony, having been only inches away from death a few hours earlier, but this could not wait.

"Where is my daughter? I will see her *now*."

Riona's father charged through the archway and stopped short when he saw the dozen Kentari guards lining the room, armed and clad in full plate mail. His hazel eyes widened, incredulous, as two stepped forward and began searching him for weapons. "What is the meaning of this?" he demanded.

"It's only a precaution, my lord," Valerian said, leading Amaris into the room. As a guard patted her down, Amaris's gaze dropped to Riona's chest, and the blood drained from her face.

The neckline of the tunic had slipped down, revealing the edge of the bandage over her heart.

Riona pulled her tunic higher and nodded to the settee across from her. "Please sit. There's much we need to discuss."

The guards finished searching her father, and he shot them an annoyed look before taking a seat on the settee next to Amaris. "Riona, what happened? Your message said only—"

"Did you know about the mines?"

He went still. "I beg your pardon?"

"The eudorite mines that King Domhnall has been hiding for years," she said, her voice deathly calm. "Did you know about them?"

He glanced at Valerian and the guards, all of whom looked equally shocked. "We should discuss this in private, Riona."

"Duke Valerian saved my life last night. He has more than earned his right to be here, especially considering it was one of our dear king's most trusted advisors who orchestrated the attempt on my life. I assume that someone has found the bodies in the theater?"

Her father nodded, the blood draining from his face.

Riona leaned forward, her aching wound protesting at the movement. "Tell me you weren't involved in the attack."

"Of course I wasn't," he said, looking appalled that she'd even asked. "I've known about the eudorite mines since my brother conceived the idea, but I refused to have any part of it. They're too dangerous, and the cost—both in lives and in coin—is too high to justify running the damn things." Realization dawned on his face. "The trip to Crafford. That's where you went when you left, isn't it? Riona, you *went* to the mines?"

"The only one that's still operational," Riona said as Valerian looked at her sharply. "Amaris and Auberon rescued me after the overseer discovered me searching through his office. If not for them, I would have likely been murdered on the king's command."

"No, he wouldn't have—"

"He ordered Lord Farquar to have Prince Auberon and me assassinated!" she snarled, wincing when a flare of heat shot through her chest. Valerian shot her a worried look and shifted closer, hovering by the arm of her chair. "He had Treasurer Cathal killed! *He* is the snake at the heart of this court."

Her father blinked, stunned by her fury. He had seen her grieve, seen her mourn, seen her cry, but he had never seen her with pure, unbridled rage coursing through her veins.

"Cathal was going to reveal the existence of the mines to the king of the Selannic Isles," she continued. "Rivosa is in debt, and he was hoping that promising the Selannic king a share of the ore would be enough to repay the money we owe. The king learned of the Treasurer's plans and sent someone to murder him. Cathal was killed for doing his duty."

Her father shook his head, looking like he was going to be sick. "To be honest...I suspected the king may have had a hand in the Treasurer's death. I just..." He faltered, seeming at a loss for words. Amaris silently slid closer and rested a comforting hand on his arm. "I didn't want to believe my brother was capable of such a thing."

"He is. He did it all to keep the mines a secret."

Her father glanced at Valerian, his gaze simmering with distrust. "A secret that is a secret no longer. Now Kenter and Erduria know that we've been mining the Howling Mountains. I may have disagreed with my brother's mining operation, but I held my tongue to prevent precisely this situation. I suppose it was inevitable, but between the Rennox and the natural dangers in the mountains, even the rumors were minimal. I only wish that you had not been the source of the revelation."

"I don't intend to fight over your land, my lord," Valerian said. "All I ask is for Rivosi aid in the war for my country's independence, and as many eudorite weapons as you can spare for my men. I am asking for an alliance."

Her father appraised the duke warily. Then he turned to Riona and said, "And what of the Erdurian princes?"

"I suggest that we grant them the peace treaty and a stake in the mines. And I will agree to become Drystan's bride."

Pain flashed across his face, but he quickly smoothed it away. "That's assuming Emperor Hyperion won't renege on his deal and send an army to claim the Mountains for himself."

"It's a risk we must take. King Domhnall's men know the mines better than anyone, and Hyperion will have to cooperate if he wants to avoid wasting precious money and lives. Plus, with foreign armies certain to march on our land, we'll have our hands full fighting threats from without. We cannot stand against our enemies if we are fighting amongst ourselves."

Her father studied her once again, his expression somewhere between pride and sorrow. "Spoken like a true courtier," he eventually said. "I should have taken you far from Innislee a long time ago. If I'd had my way, you never would have set foot in this wretched city. It has changed you."

Riona smiled, her heart aching. This court, this kingdom, had changed her for the better. It had forged her into the woman she'd needed to become in this world of polished smiles and silver tongues. If she had to, she would go to Erduria and carve out a place for herself in the Emperor's court. She would do what she could to serve her kingdom from afar.

"The blood of kings flows through our veins," she said softly, repeating her uncle's words from so many weeks ago. "That blood comes with a cost."

"One we will never be finished paying," her father breathed, shaking his head. He rose, and Amaris stood, as well. "You seem to have thought everything through. When do you plan to confront the king about all you've learned?"

"Tonight, at the banquet. I need some time to rest and make sure everything is prepared."

Her father rounded the low central table and kissed her temple. "I'll be right at your side when you do, my love. I've kept my silence long enough."

"We owe it to Cathal to see this through," Amaris added, nodding. "What do you need us to do now?"

"Act as if nothing is out of the ordinary. You don't know who was attacked in the theater nor why, and you have no idea who might be behind it. And Amaris—stay safe. Stick close to Prince Domhnall's side, no matter what." Riona wasn't sure why Amaris hadn't been targeted last night, as well—perhaps the king thought her meek enough to be intimidated into silence, or perhaps he simply wanted to wait until a more opportune time to kill her. Whatever the reason, she wouldn't risk Amaris's safety. "My cousin would die before allowing you to be hurt."

"I will. Let's pray that it doesn't come to that."

Riona nodded, the weight on her shoulders lessening at the determined expressions on their faces. For so long, she had felt alone in this city. Her father and Amaris loved her—she had always been certain of that—but their loyalty had always been to the kingdom and court first. Now, she knew that she could trust them completely.

Her father thanked Valerian for his aid and the protection of his guards, and then he and Amaris left. The second they were gone, Riona slumped back in her chair. She was utterly exhausted. It would have been easier to speak with them in the bedroom, but she hadn't wanted them to see how weak the attack had left her. She knew better than anyone the importance of keeping up appearances.

"You did well," Valerian said. He looked as tired as she felt, the shadows under his eyes stark against the vivid green of his irises. Thankfully, her father had been too distracted with talk of the mines to question how the duke had saved her life, and why she'd been brought to him instead of a healer. "But I still think it's unwise to confront the king tonight. *I'm* barely strong enough to stay on my feet, and I'm not the one who nearly died last night."

Riona forced herself to stand, grimacing as the blood magic flared in her chest. Under the bandages, she could feel the heat pulsing, throbbing, as if someone had pressed a red-hot iron to her flesh. She gritted her teeth and started toward the hallway that led to the bedroom. The world tilted beneath her, and she caught her balance on the archway just as Valerian caught her elbow, shooting her an *I-told-you-so* look.

"I have no other choice," she said, carefully making her way down the hall. Her head swam from the blood loss. "If I don't go to the banquet, my uncle will announce my betrothal and have me tossed onto a ship bound for Kostos before the night is over. That's assuming he hasn't arranged another attempt on my life."

"Still, you must give yourself time to rest." He glanced back toward the sitting room, toward the guards, and then added in a low voice, "Blood magic is powerful, but it has limitations. You can't heal through willpower alone."

Riona shot him a look over her shoulder. "Try me."

Valerian followed her into the bedroom and helped her onto the bed. Once she was settled, she nodded to the folded piece of paper on the bedside table. "Can you seal that and have it delivered to an elven servant named Ophelia?"

"Of course." Valerian tucked the note into his pocket. "Thank you for including me in the discussion of the mines back there. Creator willing, with Rivosi aid and eudorite weapons, I may just be able to free my country from Kostori rule."

"You're welcome," she said, smiling. "It's the least I could do after all you've done for me."

The duke dipped his head in respect. "Rest now, my lady. Tonight, all of this ends."

Chapter Sixty-Six
The Liar

He had promised Drystan he would remain in the house until the banquet. He hadn't promised he would behave himself once he left.

Auberon stood in the center of the hall a few corridors away from the banquet. After bathing and resting, he had changed into a fresh doublet the deep crimson of Erduria's royal sigil, a red so dark it was almost black. Golden threads shone along the cuffs of the sleeves and up the line of buttons that spanned from his throat to his navel. His sword hung at his hip, freshly sharpened.

He pulled a piece of parchment no larger than his palm from his pocket. It had been attached to a larger sheaf of papers that had been delivered by one of Riona's helpers earlier that afternoon, lines of elegant, feminine cursive detailing exactly how she planned the night would go. He had read her instructions carefully twice over, then dropped the papers into the hearth and watched the words blacken and crumble to ash. Only the note he had kept. Two words were scrawled across it.

Be ready.

Footsteps sounded behind him, echoing off the stone. A voice laced with victory and arrogance called, "What do you wish to discuss, Valerian? Are you hoping to make one last bid for Lady Riona's hand?"

Auberon turned just as Eamon rounded the corner. The prince stopped, the two Kostori guards at his back nearly slamming into him. The goading, smug smile fell from his lips, replaced with a sneer. "What do *you* want?"

"A word."

"So you feign the duke's signature and get one of his men to deliver a message for you?" Eamon crossed his arms. "I thought such games beneath you."

"Not when I'm discussing my future Empress's safety."

Eamon laughed. "Your Empress? Don't you ever give up? I know losing Lady Riona to me was a blow to the ego for a mighty prince of Erduria, but now it's just getting embarrassing. And here I thought you a fool when you punched me in the face."

When Auberon spoke, his voice came out as cold as the depths of the Tranquil Sea. "Who did you tell about the theater?"

"What?"

"The night I punched you, you threatened to tell the court that Lady Riona and I had been meeting in secret in the Royal Theater. I want to know who you told."

The prince waved a dismissive hand. "What does it matter? So there are some rumors about her virtue. I've won her hand in marriage, so *rumors* are what they shall remain."

Auberon took a step forward, and Eamon's guards edged closer to him, setting their hands on the swords at their hips. He couldn't keep the fury from his voice when he spat, "What does it matter? She nearly *died*, you fool!"

"She—" Eamon froze, his mouth dropping open. "*What?*"

"Last night, she took a dagger to the chest because you couldn't keep your mouth shut," Auberon growled, stalking toward the prince. "Because you wanted to score cheap points with the king and court by calling her virtue and my integrity into question."

"What integrity?" Eamon shot back, but he looked shaken. "The concept is as foreign to you as kindness."

"Funny you should say that."

One of the guards let out a strangled cry, and Eamon whirled as a blade opened the man's throat from ear to ear. The other one followed. Blood sprayed from the wounds, splattering across Eamon's stunned face as the guards gurgled and slumped to their knees, revealing two elven servants standing behind them with bloody daggers in hand. Identical obsidian pendants hung at their throats.

Eamon tore his gaze from the dead guards just as Auberon seized the prince's throat and slammed him into the wall. Eamon winced as his skull cracked against the stone bricks. Auberon unsheathed his sword and leveled it at the Kostori bastard's neck. "Next time you plan to assassinate someone, you'd better make sure to dispose of their loyal supporters, as well," he snarled. "Or you'll find the next throat they cut is yours."

"I don't know anything about an assassination," Eamon sputtered. Auberon dug the edge of the blade into his skin, relishing the fear that flashed through the prince's eyes when a slender red line opened up across his neck. "I swear it."

"Unwitting or not, you gave the king and his men the information they needed to ambush us. I should gut you for it." Auberon cast an icy glance at the bodies of the guards, their blood pooling on the stone, then turned back to Eamon. "But I think this serves as enough of a warning for a coward like you. You haven't won Lady Riona's hand in marriage. In fact, the second I release you, you are going to go to the gatehouse, send for a carriage, and leave this kingdom. The rest of your guards can pack up your belongings and meet you on your ship. Have I made myself clear?"

"You will pay for killing my men. The king—"

"The king will be lucky to still wear his crown once the night is over. And if my future Empress is feeling particularly *unforgiving*, he'll be on his knees in front of the executioner's axe come dawn. Do you really want to pin your hopes on a man who may be dead by morning?" He smiled. "Or perhaps the better question is whether you would care to join him. What do you think Lady Riona will do when she discovers your part in the attempt on her life?"

The prince lifted his chin. "She will see that it was a *coincidence*. I may not have wanted to lose her to your brother or Valerian, but I certainly don't want her dead!"

"Let me put this in simpler terms so you'll be certain to understand," Auberon drawled, watching a droplet of blood well along the edge of the blade and roll down Eamon's neck. "You've lost. Leave the castle now, or end up like those guards. I'll send my condolences to your father later."

Eamon's gaze slid to the guards, then to the servants standing over them. Auberon felt the moment the tension left the prince's body. "No bride is worth this. Enjoy watching your brother marry the woman you love. I hope she kills you both in your sleep, and then your wretched father."

"One can always dream," Auberon said as he stepped back and lowered the sword. Eamon lifted a hand to the cut in his neck, wincing, and then shot him a hateful look as he turned and walked down the hall. He carefully stepped over the bodies of his guards, not even sparing them another glance. Auberon gestured for the servants to follow him.

Shortly after they left, Ophelia rounded the corner, trailed by two servants. The young men at her back rushed forward and took the bodies by the ankles, the blood leaving a dark smear across the tile as they dragged the guards away. "You could have made it easier for us to clean," Ophelia said, watching their slow progress down the hall. "It'll already be difficult enough to move the bodies without anyone spotting us."

"It wouldn't have had the same impact. I needed him terrified."

Ophelia rolled her eyes, and Auberon smiled, surprised by her lack of decorum. "You're just lucky there are so many hidden alcoves and passageways through the castle. Otherwise I'd have left *you* to deal with the bodies."

His grin grew. "I think it more likely you'd have left my corpse beside them."

Despite her clear dislike of him, a mischievous sparkle lit her eyes. "Don't test your luck, Your Highness."

Ophelia walked over to him and pulled a handkerchief from her pocket. After wiping his sword clean, she knelt and began to swipe at the trails of blood left by the bodies. He raised a brow. "You're going to need more than that to clean up the mess."

"The others will come help me once they've finished hiding the bodies. It'll be easier to dispose of them after the banquet." Ophelia jerked her chin toward the hall from which she had come. "Speaking of which, you should be on your way. It was hard enough altering the schedule so that no guards would come by on patrol during your little *meeting*. I don't need any more chances for something to go wrong. If someone finds me cleaning up this blood, it'll be my neck on the line, not yours."

He pressed a hand to his heart and bowed deeply. The elf faltered, her mouth parting in surprise. Judging by the ease with which she flitted throughout the castle, he doubted anyone ever looked twice at her, let alone bowed. "Thank you, Ophelia. I'm grateful for your aid. Truly. Lady Riona is lucky to have someone like you at her back."

A flush rose on her cheeks, and she set to scrubbing a particularly stubborn patch of tile. "You're welcome," she muttered. He could just see a hint of a begrudging smile on her lips.

He carefully stepped over the pool of blood, straightened his doublet, and started toward the banquet hall.

Chapter Sixty-Seven
The Lady

Relief transformed Amaris's face when she opened the front door of Lord Lachlan's estate to find Riona standing before her, a half-dozen Kentari guards at her back. Without warning, Amaris flung her arms around Riona's neck, pulling her into a tight embrace. Riona fought to hold back a gasp as pain ignited throughout her chest, sending a burst of stars through her vision.

"Oh, thank the Creator," Amaris breathed. "All day, I've been terrified that you'd meet some terrible *accident* at the hands of Lord Farquar or the king. I can't tell you how good it is to see you in one piece."

"Same for you. But why aren't you with Prince Domhnall?" Riona asked as she extricated herself from Amaris's grip and stepped into the house. The blood magic flared with every slight movement, an agonizing reminder of just how weak her body was, but she could not afford to wait any longer. She would not give her uncle another chance to hurt anyone else she loved. "And where is my father?"

"He's with Prince Domhnall and the king, going over the details of the betrothal agreement His Majesty and Eamon are meant to sign at the banquet. Your father convinced the king to make a spectacle of signing it in front of all the members of the court. He bought you as much time as he could," Amaris said as she turned back to close and latch the door. The Kentari guards who'd accompanied Riona from the castle set about surrounding the property, joining the men Valerian had sent to protect Amaris in surveilling the estate. She doubted her uncle would make another move so soon, but they could not afford to be careless. "I stayed with the prince as long as I could, but the king dismissed me to return here and change for the banquet, and you said not to give him any reason to suspect anything was amiss..."

Amaris stopped, seeming to realize she'd begun to ramble. She ran a self-conscious hand over the skirt of her burgundy velvet gown, smoothing non-existent wrinkles in the fabric—a nervous habit she'd picked up from Riona. "I'm afraid," she whispered. "Afraid of what he will do when we confront him. Afraid of what tonight will mean for the future of our kingdom. Afraid of what you will face in Erduria."

"As am I," Riona confessed, taking her hand. "But this is what is right for Rivosa and her people. Right now, I need you to help me prepare for the banquet. I'm not strong enough to manage it myself."

Amaris nodded and followed her up the stairs. Riona kept a tight grip on the banister the entire time, the blood magic sending spears of heat through her chest.

"You must have slipped out of the castle unseen, if you managed to evade the king's guards," Amaris said as she trailed Riona into her bedroom. "He would've insisted on keeping you in the castle to protect you from the supposed murderers lurking about the city. Did you take the passage behind the royal apartments?"

Riona nodded, slinging off the heavy wool cloak that Valerian had loaned her. Under it, she still wore her fitted leather pants, borrowed linen tunic, and leather boots. Auberon's dagger hung in a sheath at her hip, on a belt given to her by the duke. She sank onto the foot of the bed, her fingers digging into the bedsheets as pain shot through her chest and down her bruised ribs. Amaris couldn't find out how weak she was, or she'd refuse to let Riona out of the house. Time wasn't a luxury they had. They had to end this *tonight*.

"I'm sorry to tell you that now both Erduria and Kenter know about the secret entrance to the castle."

Amaris dismissed the words with a wave of her hand. "Our lives are more important than a stairwell that can easily be filled in. Domhnall and I will see to it that a new escape is constructed once the suitors leave."

"I hope you never have cause to use it."

"As do I." Amaris moved to the wardrobe, opening the doors and surveying the vast array of colors and fabrics within. She pulled out a gown of sapphire silk, fanned out the full skirt, then returned it to the wardrobe. "Tread very, very carefully tonight, Riona. Your uncle may be a murderer, but he is still your king, and he has the might of the military behind him. Do not make yourself an enemy of our kingdom. You may have Erduria and Kenter as allies now, but you are still only one woman."

A ripple of uncertainty danced down Riona's spine. "I'll do what I must."

"And I'll pray that it doesn't end with your execution."

Riona forced a smile. "My uncle has already tried to kill me at least once. Who says he'll succeed this time?"

"Not funny," Amaris said, but she caught the hint of a smile on the girl's lips as she pulled a cloth-of-gold gown from the wardrobe. "This is the dress."

With her help, Riona undressed and stepped into the gown. The neckline was cut low across her shoulders and chest, the bodice draped to accentuate the curve of her waist before falling in a sheath to the floor. The gold threads in the fabric shimmered every time she moved. Amaris stepped back as Riona turned to the full-length mirror in the corner of the room.

"I didn't consider the bandages," Amaris murmured, a crease

between her brows. The white fabric bandages over her heart shone starkly against her dark skin. "That neckline isn't going to hide your wound."

A slow smile spread across Riona's lips. "I don't want to hide it. Will you help me take the bandages off?"

"Take them off? Are you sure that's wise?"

"The king tried to have me killed. I want the court to see his handiwork."

Amaris frowned, but she didn't argue as she fetched a pair of sewing scissors from the vanity and carefully sliced through the bandages. She slowly peeled them away, and the blood drained from her face when the wound was finally revealed. Even with the duke's magic, it was terrible; swollen and irritated along the line of stitches that held her flesh together.

Amaris's eyes widened, but she didn't say a word as she twisted Riona's braids into a loose updo, which she secured with little gold pins. Once she'd finished, she moved to the vanity table and selected a pair of long chandelier earrings, then slid a pair of heels onto Riona's feet.

Riona turned back to the mirror. The cut and drape of the gown emphasized the curves of her bust and waist, and the low neckline bared her collarbone and long, slender neck. Every inch of her was perfect and polished, save for the garish line of stitches above her heart. Determination swept over Riona as she studied her reflection. This was the woman she'd been meant to become. She would never be as skilled with a blade as Auberon, but she didn't need to be. She was a lady of Innislee's cutthroat court, and if there was anything this wretched place had taught her, it was that a clever mind and silver tongue could be just as exacting as a blade.

Riona felt Amaris's stare as she picked up the belt with Auberon's dagger and secured it around her waist, the emeralds in the dagger's hilt gleaming in the lantern light. Then she took a single, steadying breath and said, "Time's up."

The banquet hall went silent the moment Riona strode into the room, nobles turning one by one to gawk at the strange procession she led. As she walked down the aisle between the two long tables, Valerian and Amaris flanking her, she saw every pair of eyes drop to the wound above her heart. Whispers rose throughout the hall.

She stopped in the center of the room and scanned the sea of faces until she found Auberon, who was standing with his brother near the bottom of the dais steps. The moment his gaze met hers, the rest of the world faded. Her heart lurched. After everything that had happened, she wasn't sure where they stood. He had deceived her, and he had saved her life. He had confessed to loving her and refused her offer of marriage. If his father commanded it, he would destroy her kingdom without a moment's hesitation.

And yet, even now, she could feel that undeniable tether pulling taut between them.

As if sensing her nerves, Auberon offered her a faint, crooked smile and mouthed, *Do not falter, aramati.*

Aramati. Beloved one. The word sent a pang through her chest, memories of their last night in the theater filling her mind. Her body pressed to his, his lips against hers, his hands trailing over her bare skin. Agony and desire in his eyes as he confessed his love for her. Devastation on his face when he swore that there would never be anything more between them.

Riona turned her attention to the dais. King Domhnall, Queen Blair, and the four heirs were already seated at the head table, staring at her with varying degrees of curiosity and confusion. From his place beside the Crown Prince, her father sat with blatant fear in his eyes, his fingers curled tightly around the stem of his goblet. He glanced sidelong at his brother. The king's face might as well have been hewn from marble for all the emotion it betrayed. Even so, Riona did not miss the rigid set to his shoulders, the tension corded through his body.

Riona looked over her shoulder. Behind her stood Valerian and Amaris, then Faylen and Aeron, and then Vick and the brothers from the mine. (She'd been less than thrilled to find out that Auberon had promised his protection to the man who had sent sell-swords to kill them, but had begrudgingly admitted that his testimony would be invaluable.) And behind them, arrayed in two perfect lines, were four dozen Kentari and Erdurian guards in full armor. In her periphery, Riona saw the Rivosi guards lining the perimeter of the banquet hall shift their weight uneasily, their hands drifting to the swords at their hips. Even the Master of the Guard, standing at the rear of the dais, looked uneasy.

A smile laced with venom spread across the king's lips. "Tell us, for I'm certain we are all sitting on the edges of our seats: To what do we owe this unusual display, niece?"

"I know who murdered Treasurer Cathal."

"Who?"

The word came out a command, a warning. A challenge. His dark eyes locked with hers, daring her to tell the court all she knew.

Riona turned to Faylen and asked, loud enough for all to hear, "Can you identify the man who attacked you and Treasurer Cathal?"

The elf scanned the room. It wasn't long before she froze, the blood draining from her face. Riona followed her gaze to Lord Farquar, who was standing at the edge of the crowd with Lord Winslow and another advisor. His grizzled face didn't change, but she could have sworn she saw surprise flit through his eyes at the sight of Faylen. He must have assumed that she'd left the country after fleeing Innislee. Faylen clutched the sheaf of stolen treasury documents close to her chest as she held the lord's stare and said, "It was him. He killed the Treasurer."

All eyes turned to Farquar, who scoffed. "I did no such thing."

"You did. The morning after Prince Auberon's poisoning, Cathal ran into my room in that Creator-forsaken brothel and told me that someone was coming to kill him. He instructed me to take these documents out of the city, to Crafford, and promised he would meet me there once it was safe. That was when Lord Farquar arrived," Faylen said, fury overcoming her fear. Her voice echoed throughout the hall; the nobles had gone so quiet one could have heard a pin drop. "I didn't know who he was at the time; my room was dark, and he was careful to keep the hood of his cloak up so most of his face was in shadow, but I recognize him now. He knocked me to the ground and threw himself on Cathal, shoving him onto the bed. I saw him..." She faltered, swallowing tightly. "I saw him plunge a dagger into Cathal's chest more than a dozen times. I swear it on the Creator and all the Old Gods."

"That is a ridiculous claim. Cathal was a treasured friend and an exceptional advisor, and I mourned his death," Farquar objected. "Is the court now to take the word of some common whore over that of a man who commanded its navy for decades? She said herself that she never saw the attacker's face."

"I didn't say that," Faylen shot back. "When I tried to pull you off Cathal, you turned back and elbowed me in the nose. The light from the hall struck part of your face, and I saw a flash of those remarkable eyes. Deep, emerald green. Between your build and what I saw of your face, there's no mistaking it. You murdered the man I loved," she said, the words as final and damning as a death sentence.

Riona smiled at the outrage on the lord's face. "You poisoned the goblet meant for Treasurer Cathal," she added, raising her voice to keep him from spouting the truth about the king's involvement in the plot. "When you saw that it had gone to the wrong man, you bided your time and answered all the guards' questions, waiting for the king to release everyone from the banquet hall so you could finish the job. But all those hours gave Cathal time to reflect on the events of the night. When he realized that the poison had been meant for him, he fled the castle and went to collect the woman he loved. You followed him, and when the opportunity presented itself, you murdered him and the servant who delivered the wine.

"You are guilty, and you will be held in custody until you can face justice for your crimes." Riona turned to the two nearest Kentari guards. "Disarm and bind him."

Farquar's cheeks reddened with fury, his hand curling about the grip of his sword. "You have no authority to do such a thing. I am a member of the king's council and a respected naval captain." He looked to the king as the guards pulled their swords and advanced on him. "Your Majesty, bring your niece to heel!"

Prince Domhnall shot to his feet, his chair scraping across the floor. "You *dare* command your king?"

King Domhnall stood as well, but his calm, level gaze was focused entirely on Riona. She could see the wheels turning in his head as he carefully appraised the drama unfolding before him, trying to gauge just how much truth she would reveal to the court. Beside him, the queen hurriedly gestured for one of the servants to usher the three younger heirs out of the room.

Finally, the king fixed his attention on Farquar and said, "You always have been envious of Treasurer Cathal's position, Farquar. Always considered the comfortable life he enjoyed worthy repayment for the debt this kingdom owes you. I see you grew tired of waiting for his retirement."

Lord Farquar's mouth dropped open when he realized that his king had just betrayed him. Condemned him. He whirled around and ripped the sword from the sheath at his hip, snarling as the guards lunged for him. Lord Winslow and the others scrambled backward, a few ducking under the banquet tables to avoid the fighting.

The guards did not hesitate. They descended on Farquar, their blades clashing with the ring of steel on steel. The naval captain was a skilled fighter, but the guards were younger and faster, and he was outnumbered. It didn't take long for one of them to disarm the lord and smash the pommel of his sword into Farquar's nose. He reeled backward and fell to his knees, blood bubbling over his lips. The guards wasted no time in subduing him; one bound his wrists behind his back, and the other forced a gag into his mouth.

Riona looked up at the dais and held her uncle's cool stare. *Do you understand now? Do you see that even after everything that has happened, I am still trying to protect our kingdom? Still trying to protect* you? *I could have told them everything.*

"Your Majesty, Lord Farquar is guilty, and for his crimes, he must be sentenced to execution."

Voices filled the hall, some protesting on Farquar's behalf, others attempting to make sense of all they'd heard and witnessed. Many studied Riona with a mixture of fear and respect on their faces. No one had ever looked at her that way, and the sight of the nobles doing so now had her standing a little taller, a little prouder. She was no longer the quiet, submissive girl she'd once been.

King Domhnall knew it, too. She had seen the moment he'd realized that he'd lost—that she held the future of his rule in the palm of her hand. With just a few words, she could take everything from him. He could sentence her to execution for revealing the existence of the eudorite mines to Kenter and Erduria, but in doing so, he would lose the chance to secure two allies in the fight to defend Rivosa's land. Auberon and Drystan would return to Rivosa with an army at their backs, and they wouldn't stop at claiming the mines. They would come for Domhnall's life, family, and crown.

He lifted his goblet to her, his voice cutting through the clamor of the court. "I underestimated you, my niece. I was beginning to fear that Cathal's murderer would never be found, and you have proven me wrong. As such, Lord Farquar is hereby sentenced to die at sunrise tomorrow." Her uncle paused, taking a moment to dredge up the willpower to say, "What reward would you ask of us?"

Out of the corner of her eye, she saw a bright, beaming grin break out across Auberon's face. Today, they would end the slaughter of their peoples.

Riona smiled. "Perhaps we ought to discuss that in private, Your Majesty."

Chapter Sixty-Eight
The Liar

Auberon couldn't take his eyes off Riona. They'd moved to an empty sitting room not far from the banquet hall, where Riona now stood on one side of the cluster of settees and armchairs, regarding the king with open hostility. Even in her fury, she was beautiful; her eyes like twin blue flames, power and unwavering strength rippling off her. The garish wound above her heart was plain to see, a line of stitches tarnishing her perfect ebony skin. Although she had to be in agony, not a hint of weakness showed on her face.

Auberon, Drystan, Valerian, and the others sat on settees and armchairs on one side of the low central table. Opposite them were the queen, the Crown Prince, Amaris, and Lord Lachlan, all of whom were eyeing the Kentari, Erdurian, and Rivosi guards lining the walls with unease. And at the rear of the room, near the closed doors, a bound and gagged Lord Farquar was on his knees between two stone-faced guards.

The lines had been drawn.

Riona gazed across the table at her uncle, a great and terrible beauty in her quiet rage. The sight made Auberon's heart race. Her uncle was finally understanding what a grave mistake he'd made in trying to temper her clever mind and sharp tongue, in raising her to believe her ambition to be a flaw. If he had let her, she would have dedicated her life to Rivosa.

"These foreign royals have changed you, Riona," King Domhnall said, his words clipped. "They have been manipulating you since the moment they arrived, trying to turn you against your family and your kingdom. And now she who claimed to care so deeply for Rivosa stands poised to bring about its downfall."

If the words wounded her, she didn't show it. She didn't even blink. "They only helped me see the truth, Uncle. *You* are the one who has made me your enemy."

"Riona..." Amaris warned softly. "Remember what we discussed earlier."

"Won't you tell us what this is about?" Queen Blair asked, her braids swaying as she looked from her husband to her niece. "We're family, blood of my blood. There are no enemies here."

"Your husband would disagree, Your Majesty," Riona said. "If he'd had his way, Prince Auberon and I would not have lived to see the dawn. The attack in the Royal Theater was an attempted assassination done on his orders, all to keep his precious mines a secret."

Blair's gaze dropped to Riona's wound, and Auberon saw the blood drain from her face. She turned to the king. "Domhnall? What is she talking about? What mines?"

Riona's father set a hand on the queen's wrist. "Eudorite mines in the Howling Mountains. My brother has been running them in secret for over a decade, working to amass enough eudorite weapons to put an end to the war with Erduria."

"Lord Farquar did not act alone," Riona said, her stare still locked with her uncle's. Auberon felt a sliver of fear slide into his heart. The Rivosi guards were shifting, their hands straying to the grips of their sheathed swords, and the Kentari and Erdurian men were tensing in anticipation of a fight. Tension hung in the air. One word from the king would turn this meeting into a bloodbath.

Undaunted, Riona continued, "The king discovered that Treasurer Cathal was planning to reveal the existence of the mines to the Selannic king in order to repay Rivosa's insurmountable debt, but the king couldn't afford to allow proof of his operation to leave Innislee. So he ordered Farquar to kill him, but not before Cathal managed to smuggle documents proving the existence of the mines out of the city."

Faylen set the sheaf of papers on the table and slid them over to the queen, who spread them out with shaky hands as her son leaned in to read. Auberon watched their eyes widen as they moved across the papers. While they read, Faylen detailed the events of the morning Cathal had died, ignoring Lord Farquar's muffled grunts of protest from where he was kneeling across the room.

Then Riona recounted her journey to Crafford and the mines, including the letters she had found in the overseer's office, the wind-mad miner who had aided her, and Auberon and Amaris's rescue. Callan and Halston—the brothers—provided details about the mines, painting a vivid and brutal picture of the cave-ins and Rennox attacks that plagued the men who had been condemned to live and die in those dark, dank tunnels.

Finally, Vick confessed to the parts he and Lord Farquar had played in the attempt on Auberon and Riona's lives, shame scrawled across his face as Auberon wordlessly handed the contract to the queen. By the time they had finished, Queen Blair's face was pale and horrified. She stared at her husband as though he were a stranger.

"How could you?" Prince Domhnall snarled, glaring at his father. "Your obsession with vengeance has blinded you, Father. Has the war not cost us enough? How much more blood must be shed before you see that this is not worth the cost of victory? We could have had peace *weeks* ago."

"Am I to make peace with the men who murdered my eldest son?" the king spat. He shot a hate-filled look at Auberon and Drystan, and Auberon's hand moved to the hilt of the sword sheathed at his hip. "Who murdered my sister-in-law? Would you have me spit on the graves of all who died in the war by joining our family with their killers?

"They would paint me as the villain in this story, when I have done nothing but defend my people since the day I was crowned," he continued, seething. "I swore an oath to protect my subjects and my kingdom, and *every single thing* I have done since those words fell from my lips was to uphold that vow. Do you think that Emperor Hyperion will not send his army to take the Howling Mountains from us once he learns of the mines? Do you think he will hesitate to turn those weapons on our people? I am doing what I must to ensure our kingdom survives against *impossible* odds. We will have victory, or we will die."

"We could have had peace," Riona said.

The look he fixed on her was so full of pity and disappointment that even Auberon felt as if he'd taken a blow to the gut. "If you believe that, truly under the prince's spell. I have heard quite enough of this, Riona. Master Kaiden, have someone find Prince Eamon and escort him to the banquet hall. We will sign the marriage alli—"

"Prince Eamon is gone, Your Majesty," Auberon said, speaking for the first time since they'd set foot in the room. "He has rescinded his bid for the lady's hand and departed for Kostos. He wishes you all to know how deeply sorry he is for wasting your time and calling into question the integrity of your niece, and he hopes you please excuse his blighted existence in this world. He can't help being a bastard, you see. It's in his blood."

The king looked to Master Kaiden, who immediately sent one of the guards to confirm this information. "Why would he leave if he were going to win the marriage alliance?"

Auberon kept his attention focused solely on King Domhnall, but he felt the weight of Riona's stare as he said, "Because I promised to kill him if he did not."

Murmurs rippled throughout the room at Auberon's words. Pure fury swept over the king's face, and he whirled, pulling

Master Kaiden's sword from its sheath at his hip. Erdurian and Rivosi guards alike stepped forward, unsheathing their blades, as the king started toward Auberon.

Drystan shot to his feet at the same time as Riona stepped into the king's path. "Release the sword, and order your men to stand down," she commanded, the words ringing with authority. "I have people waiting all over the city with copies of the documents Treasurer Cathal stole. With proof that you have been sending our people to work themselves to death in the mines, and that you intend to condemn more of our men to the fighting while you prepare for your *decisive victory*. Right now, the nobility believe Lord Farquar operated alone. If any one of us walks out of this room with so much as a scratch, my helpers will spread word of your actions to the entire city. How long do you think they will allow you to rule, once they learn what you've done?"

Auberon looked at her sharply, surprised and impressed. She hadn't mentioned that part of her plan to him at any point. For all that she would condemn him for his manipulative ways, it seemed that the Lady of Innislee had some tricks of her own up her sleeve. From where he stood behind Faylen's chair, Aeron watched Riona with a look of pride and admiration.

The king held up a hand to still the guards. "You're bluffing."

"Am I, Your Majesty?" Riona gestured at Auberon and the others. "There is no going back, Uncle. No more deception. No more *murder*. Once news of the mines spreads, foreign armies will come to stake a claim on the Howling Mountains, and this is your one chance to make allies of those who would happily send troops to join them. Because I love this kingdom, and because I would give anything to ensure my people's survival, I bring you offers of peace."

Heavy silence descended over the room, everyone waiting to see what King Domhnall would say. Riona watched her uncle with a calm, level expression, her thoughts hidden behind a polished mask.

Suddenly, the king began to laugh.

"I hope you see the irony in this, Riona," Domhnall said, his voice bitter. "You say you would do anything for your people, and yet because of your actions, Rivosa's fighting will never cease. *You* led Prince Auberon into the heart of the Mountains. *You* betrayed the secret of the mines. How many men will die to protect our land? To protect their families?"

Riona went rigid, the words hitting their mark. "I—"

"You and I are the same, my niece," the king said, reaching back to hand the sword to Master Kaiden. "Both desperate to save our kingdom. Both weighing the cost of lives lost to the value of lives saved. You fancied yourself worthy of a place on my council, so tell me: what would you have advised? Kill Cathal and that servant and save thousands, or allow proof of the mines to spread and damn all the generations to come?"

She opened her mouth, then faltered. When the king phrased it that way, the choice was simple. Auberon could tell that the answer to the king's question killed Riona to admit, even to herself. He longed to stand up and interject, but this was the moment he'd been waiting for since the night he had punched Eamon—the moment she finally stood up to her uncle and proved herself more than an obedient court lady. The moment she faced what it would be like to rule.

Her perfect veneer cracked, and Auberon saw guilt and raw grief flash across her face. The king seized the opportunity to say in a soft voice, "So you see why I had to ensure your silence on the matter, my dear. Amaris was never in any danger; she and my son will one day rule together, and they will run the mines as I have done, for the security and protection of our kingdom. You and the prince... You would use it to destroy us. It was a sacrifice I had to make for our kingdom. Two deaths so hundreds of thousands could live. And now the blood of all who die defending the Mountains will be on your hands."

The sight of the first tear slipping through Riona's lashes shattered Auberon's resolve. He rose, rage swelling within him.

But before he could say a word, Lord Farquar began to struggle, letting out a series of insistent, muffled grunts. They all turned to look at him. He still wore the gag, and lines of dried blood ran in rivulets from his broken nose, staining the fabric a deep brown-red. He glared at the king, then twisted toward Riona and fixed her with an imploring look. At a nod from her, the Kentari guards dragged the lord forward and unceremoniously dumped him on the floor before the low central table. One pulled the gag down around his neck.

"Do not let him break you, my lady," Farquar said, his words urgent. "You are not like him, or you would have slit Prince Auberon's throat yourself when you went to meet him at the Royal Theater last night."

"Why are you saying this?" Riona asked. Her tears had stopped falling, but the trails they had left down her cheeks shone under the light of the torches. "Why help me?"

"Because I desire to live, and if you allow him to win, he will kill us all." His gaze swiveled to Duke Valerian, who had been watching the entire confrontation unfold in silence. "Take me to Kenter with you when you leave, Your Grace. If you swear to release me, I will tell you all the one thing you have yet to piece together. I will tell you how His Majesty orchestrated the death of Lady Riona's mother."

Chapter Sixty-Nine
The Lady

The silence was deafening.

And then the queen was rising to her feet, storming toward Lord Farquar as if she would torture the information out of the lord herself. King Domhnall caught her arm, and she turned on him. "Unhand me," she snarled, jerking out of his grasp. "Tell me he's lying, Domhnall. Tell me you didn't kill my sister."

Riona watched, her heart twisting, as the king glanced from his wife to his brother, who looked as if he'd just been punched in the stomach. The guards lining the room shifted, whispers rising from the Rivosans. Master Kaiden shot them a glare, swiftly silencing them, but King Domhnall barely seemed to notice.

"Tell me the truth, Domhnall," the queen said. "*Tell me you didn't take Riona's mother from her.*"

Slowly, his eyes returned to her, the confirmation of his guilt etched across every inch of his face. "...I cannot."

She staggered back a step. "You *bastard*."

"Promise me what I have asked, and I will tell you everything," Farquar said, his voice thick through his broken nose. "Duke Valerian?"

Valerian looked to Riona, seeking her answer. Words lodged

in her throat, a dozen answers tangling together—*No. Yes. I don't want to hear it. I have to know.* Her mother, murdered by her uncle. Her ship sent to the bottom of the sea not by Erdurian ships, but by Rivosi ones. Perhaps even by the men and women who had been charged to protect her.

She could feel Auberon's eyes on her. Could feel him standing close enough to touch, to reach out and lace her fingers through his. She wanted to. More than anything, she wanted to collapse, to sob until her tears ran out, to feel his arms wrap around her and to listen to him promise that everything would be alright.

But instead, she merely nodded.

Valerian's voice shook with anger as he said, "Lord Farquar, you have my word that you will be safely transferred to Kenter. You will be considered a subject of the Grand Duke of Kenter, and by extension King Jericho of Kostos, and you will have your freedom and your life."

Farquar turned toward the queen. "Lady Rhea was indeed killed by Erdurians, Your Majesty, but it was your husband who arranged the attack. I was a naval captain at the time and, upon His Majesty's orders, I was to plant rumors in the Erdurian navy that your sister's ship was transporting eudorite ore to the Selannic Isles. He wanted Emperor Hyperion to believe that she was taking a shipment of ore to the shipwrights so they could study the material, find ways to work it into our hulls and weapons, and that he was using the neutral flags to ensure that her ship would reach the Isles unmolested." He looked at Riona then. "And the plan worked. In Emperor Hyperion's eyes, the consequences of breaking the laws of neutrality were little price to pay in order to prevent your uncle from creating a navy armed with eudorite weapons and defenses."

"All those rumors... All those whispers of eudorite mines," Auberon breathed. "They didn't come from Erdurian spies. They came from your *king*."

Although there was no proof, Riona found herself believing

that the lord spoke truthfully. The reason for the attack on her mother's ship had always been a mystery; Erduria had gained nothing by sending her ship to the bottom of the Tranquil Sea. In fact, it was that act that had finally ended the neutrality of the Selannic Isles and pushed them entirely in Rivosa's favor. After that day, no person with so much as a drop of Erdurian blood was allowed in a Selannic port.

Now, it made sense.

Prince Domhnall frowned. At his side, Riona's father sat stiff and pale, looking as if he'd keel over at the slightest breeze. "But after all my father has done to keep the mines a secret..." the prince murmured. "That doesn't make sense. Why would he want the Erdurians to find out about the mines, even as a rumor? He had Cathal killed to keep him silent."

A small part of Riona wanted him to be right. Even after everything her uncle had done, she did not want to face the fact that *he* had been the one to take her mother from her. It was one more betrayal, one more dagger plunging into her broken and battered heart.

"Rumors are not proof, Your Highness," Farquar said. "This was eight years ago. The people were tiring of the war, demanding a peace treaty, and His Majesty needed a reason to keep them fighting. How else could he justify sending more of their sons and daughters to fight a war he had no hope of winning? Allowing a few whispers to find their way into Erduria was a small price to pay to ensure another generation of dedicated soldiers. Lady Rhea was not the queen, but she had royal blood and was married to the king's brother. Perhaps more important than that, she was dear to many influential people in the Rivosi and Selannic courts. King Domhnall found that she was more valuable to him dead than alive."

Riona's father stood and fixed hollow and haunted eyes on his brother. "She was the love of my life. The mother of my child. And you... You stole her from us. I have stood at your side through many things, Domhnall, but no longer."

Across the room, the king stood frozen, his shoulders slumped in shame and regret. Beside him, the Master of the Guard was pale, more blood draining from his face with every charge the king did not attempt to deny. The rest of the guards stood in shocked silence.

Riona grasped the eudorite pendant at her throat, the ghost of her mother's voice echoing in her ears. *Once eudorite blades are forged, they will retain their form until the end of time. The sharpest blade cannot scratch it. The hardest stone cannot blunt it.*

Suddenly, understanding struck her. Riona turned to her father, already knowing what he would say. "She gave this to me before she set sail for the Isles. Where did she get it?"

"From the mines," he responded. "She and I both knew about them—we were the only ones my brother trusted with the truth back at the very beginning, when he started sending men to the Howling Mountains. He wanted us to run the mining operation, and we refused. It isn't right, what happens to men there. The land belongs to the Rennox. She had a piece of the ore made into a pendant and wore it every day as a reminder to him of what it cost us. And he had her killed for it."

"No, that's not—" the king began, and Riona's father turned on him.

"You watched me grieve, and you made me believe you grieved for her, too," he snarled, choking on his fury. "I disagreed with your running of the mines, but I served you because you were my brother and my king. Rhea and I both did, and this is how you repaid our loyalty."

Domhnall opened his mouth to object, but he faltered when Blair walked over to where he stood, her lovely face twisted in grief and hatred. "You robbed your brother of his wife. You robbed our niece of her mother. And now you have robbed yourself of a wife."

She removed her diadem and shoved it into her husband's hands, then turned on her heel and ran out of the room. Prince Domhnall stood and started to follow, but Amaris set a hand on his shoulder and slipped past him, her heels clicking on the stone as she rushed after the queen.

The doors swung shut behind them with a soft click. The guards lining the room shifted uneasily, glancing at one another and then at Master Kaiden, who looked utterly lost for words.

Her uncle let out a choked sound and swayed slightly, staring down at the large central ruby in his wife's diadem. The gemstone shone like blood under the torchlight. "I inherited a debt I cannot pay. A war I cannot afford to lose. What else could I have done? If Emperor Hyperion takes control of the eudorite mines, his army will be unstoppable. His reach will be endless."

"You are the one who planned a slaughter," Auberon snapped, moving to Riona's side. He stood so close that the back of his hand brushed hers. "You cannot accuse him of something you were already intending to do."

Riona turned to Farquar. The sight of the goading lord should have filled her with rage, but when she looked at him, she felt...nothing. She was numb. Exhausted. Heartbroken. "Duke Valerian, please have your guards take Lord Farquar somewhere safe and secure where he can be held until you sail for Kenter. He may have his freedom the second he leaves Rivosan soil, but no sooner."

Valerian nodded and gestured for a couple Kentari guards to escort the lord out. As they dragged Farquar to his feet and hauled him out of the room, Riona tensed, expecting her uncle to fight to reclaim the lord. But he said nothing. His expression—always so carefully composed—was that of a man utterly broken.

So Riona said in a soft voice, "It's over, Uncle. Give Erduria and Kenter a stake in the mines, and they will stand at your side to protect our land and our people. Refuse, and you will fight alone for the rest of your days. It is your choice."

His gaze lifted to hers, and she saw a spark of defiance flash across his face. Even now, his instincts urged him to fight. "How can you claim to love Rivosa when your actions have led to its downfall?"

"I love my kingdom more than anything, which is why I must do this." The smile she gave him was brittle, filled with all of her sorrow, her grief. Her chest felt like it was caving in, shattering under the weight of all that had happened. "You have dug Rivosa's grave. I can do nothing but attempt to delay its demise."

"Father," Prince Domhnall said, and the king stiffened at the sound of his son's voice. The prince approached his father and tugged the queen's diadem out of his hands, then set it on the low central table. "You have done enough damage to this kingdom. It is time we do what we can to heal old wounds."

The king's shoulders tensed, then slumped in defeat. He eyed Drystan and Auberon and said, "A peace treaty, and twenty percent of the mine's output."

Relief rushed through Riona. Finally, *finally*, he was giving in.

"Sixty percent," Drystan responded, the words clipped, "to make up for the attempts on my brother's life. My father will send some of his own men to work the mines alongside yours, overseeing the operation and ensuring that your workers report the numbers faithfully. You'll forgive me if I don't put much stock into your integrity, Your Majesty."

"Thirty."

Drystan scoffed. "Don't insult me. My father will provide you labor and troops. Without us, your kingdom will fall in a year."

"Forty percent. You'll still have the lion's share once Kenter gets its cut. Isn't that right, Duke Valerian? What resources will *you* wrest away from my kingdom and my people?"

The duke rose, unfazed by the king's withering glare. "Twenty percent of the output from the mines, and Rivosa's support in our war for independence—chiefly troops, trade, resources, and naval vessels. I have need of fifteen thousand men or more."

King Domhnall clenched his jaw, but nodded. "I can give you ten thousand at most. I'll not be left without a standing army while you're off campaigning, lest my old enemies decide to turn their sights on my throne," he said with a sidelong glance at the Erdurian princes.

"That will do, Your Majesty. The rest can be arranged when we meet to write the precise terms of the agreement."

"Very well." Finally, the king turned to Riona. "Your future is yours to decide. Go where you choose and marry whom you wish, but from this day forth, you are no longer welcome in this kingdom. You will leave Innislee once you are strong enough to ride, and if you set foot on Rivosan soil again, you will be greeted as a traitor to the crown. Have I made myself clear?"

"You can't do that," Auberon said, stepping forward. "What about the betrothal?"

He waved a hand in dismissal. "Take her to Erduria if you want, but you will receive nothing more from me than I have already agreed to. She committed treason, and I owe her nothing. She is no niece of mine."

Although the words stung—striking deeper than Riona would have expected, given all her uncle had done—Riona was careful not to let it show. She was an exile, a traitor to her kingdom.

Auberon objected again, but the king ignored him. As he walked out of the room, he gestured over his shoulder for Master Kaiden and the rest of the Rivosi guards to follow. Once they had left, Auberon whirled around, fuming, and let out a string of decidedly un-princely oaths.

"Something tells me this isn't going to be an easy peace to maintain," Drystan said with a sigh.

Auberon gaped at him. "You have been insistent upon securing a marriage alliance since the day we set sail from Torch. How could you not press him into promising Lady Riona to you?"

"I will not force a woman to marry me against her will," Drystan said, shooting his brother a look. He turned to Riona. "You have done great things for both our countries today, my lady. If you wish to accompany us to Erduria, my father will grant you a place of honor in our court. And...if you *do* wish to marry, you can still aid your kingdom from Erduria's throne."

Riona saw nothing save for the shadow that passed across Auberon's face as he listened to his brother speak, his gaze steadfastly trained on the wall. Even now, without the need for a marriage alliance, he would still stand aside and allow her to marry his brother if she decided she wanted the throne more than she wanted *him*.

She opened her mouth to tell him what a fool he was to think that remotely possible, but her father stepped forward before she could speak. "If you would, Your Highnesses, Your Grace, I would speak with my daughter in private."

Almost as one, they rose and left the room, Aeron and the others trailing behind them. As she passed, Faylen set a hand on Riona's shoulder and gave it a comforting squeeze.

Only her cousin lingered, waiting until the last guard had left to say, "I had no idea what my father was doing. Cathal... That servant... Your mother..." A pained look swept across Prince Domhnall's face, and he took Riona's hands in his own. "I am sorry you have to leave, cousin, but know that nothing like this will ever happen again. It is the Creator's will that my father wears the crown, but I will see to it that he will be king in name only. Amaris and I will take on the duties of running the kingdom, and I will enlist my mother's aid in negotiating the terms of our debt with our grandfather. We will recover from this."

Riona squeezed his hands and forced a smile. "I trust that you will. Good luck, Domhnall."

"And to you." He pulled her into a tight hug, and Riona ignored the flare of heat that shot through her chest when his doublet brushed against the fresh wound above her heart. In the face of everything else, the blood magic had faded to a dull throb. "Your exile won't last forever, Riona. When Amaris and I ascend the thrones, our first act will be to revoke your banishment and welcome you into Innislee. In the meantime, you will be greatly missed."

Her heart broke as she said, "Try to visit."

He bowed deeply, then left the room. When they were at last alone, her father turned to her, looking as if he'd aged ten years since the night began. Suddenly, the walls Riona had built around herself crumbled. She threw her arms around her father's neck and held him close, breathing in his familiar, earthy scent.

"Oh, my girl," he breathed, his voice thick with emotion. "My darling girl."

"Was I wrong to do this? Have I just doomed us all?"

"No. *No,*" he said fiercely, pulling back to look her in the eye. "My brother set us on this path long ago. You have made mistakes, but in the end, our kingdom will be the better for it. You have ended a war today, my love. Remember that. Your mother would have been proud."

Tears stung Riona's eyes. Her father took her hands and guided her to the nearest settee. "Tomorrow morning, I will resign my position on the council, and we will start anew elsewhere. We can go to Beltharos and petition the king and queen for positions in their court. We can sail to the Selannic Isles and serve your grandfather. We will make the best of this."

Riona allowed herself a moment to picture it—packing up her fine jewelry and gowns and riding to Beltharos, or setting off on a ship bound for the Isles. They could start new lives there. She and her father could serve in one of the courts, and perhaps Riona could even join a dance company and give lessons to the children of the city. They could forget all that had happened here and all that their king had taken from them.

Yet it was a dream, and nothing more. The war with Erduria would finally end, but it would take years for Rivosa to recover from its debts, and the people would need strong leaders to defend their land. Amaris and Domhnall wouldn't be able to manage it on their own.

"Stay here and remain on the council," Riona said, her chest tightening when her father's face fell. "Enlist Lord Winslow's help, and teach Amaris and Domhnall how to rule. Queen Blair won't be able to guide them on her own, and we need someone to keep the king in check. I'll do what I can to help from afar."

"Where will you go?"

Riona smiled then, hope and possibility swelling within her. For the first time in years, her future didn't feel like something to dread. "I'm going to Erduria."

Chapter Seventy
The Lady

"I'll be honest—you never struck me as the religious type," a familiar voice drawled.

Riona turned to find Auberon standing in the doorway of the castle's private chapel, a crooked smile on his lips. Behind him, the sky was a deep, cloudless blue, sparkling with countless stars. The sight of him standing there, starlight playing across his auburn hair, made her heart skip a beat.

He glanced around the room, and a wry smile tugged at his lips. "Did you only invite me here to see if I'd burst into flames upon setting foot on holy ground? If so, I'm afraid I must disappoint you, *aramati*."

As his grin grew, Riona felt all the tension from their previous argument melt away. They had used and manipulated each other, but now they were free. They had won. They could finally leave this court of vipers far behind.

Auberon reached into his pocket and pulled out a folded piece of paper—the summons Riona had sent him just half an hour earlier. She'd wanted to meet with him in private, but she hadn't been able to stomach the thought of returning to the Royal Theater after the attempt on their lives. And with the amount of blood she'd lost, she wasn't strong enough to trek far from the castle. "Ophelia must be growing tired of delivering our messages," he said.

"Then she'll be glad she doesn't have to do it much longer."

They stood at opposite ends of the prayer room's central aisle, and Riona started to walk toward him. Her heartbeat picked up in pace with every step, remembering how it felt to sit on his lap, his lips moving against hers, his fingers trailing up and down her body. Remembering how it felt to dance in his arms, his rich, deep voice wrapping around her.

"I never thanked you for saving my life last night," she said. "Before I was stabbed, I saw the way you jumped in front of our attacker's blades, trying to buy me time to run. You were willing to give your life for me."

His smile softened. "As I am now, and always will be, *aramati*. I would face all manner of man and monster for you."

"Because you love me."

"Because I love you." A flicker of emotion passed across his face, but he turned away before she could identify it. "I told you, last night was a mistake—a moment of weakness. Of recklessness. You shouldn't have sent for me. I shouldn't have come here."

"Then why *did* you come?"

"Because I am woefully short on self-control where you are concerned, *aramati*."

Auberon turned to leave, but Riona quickly closed the distance between them and grasped his hand. "Please don't go."

Before he could protest, before he could tell her that nothing could happen between them, she pulled him into a kiss. He responded at once, his hands trailing along the curve of her waist and holding her flush against him. The blood magic pulsed within her, sending flares of heat through her chest where the stitches tugged, but she hardly noticed. All she could think about was *him*. His fingers tangled in her braids, his hand cupping the curve of her cheek. Her teeth caught his lower lip, coaxing a smile from him that made her heart soar.

She loved this clever, wicked boy.

Riona pulled back and leaned her forehead against his, her eyes closed. "Please tell me there is a future for us."

He was quiet for several long moments, until he finally said in a soft, broken voice, "I can't, my love, but it will be alright. You have everything you wanted. You're free now—free to leave this wretched court behind, free to marry Drystan and rule beside him. Free to become the Empress you were meant to be. I cannot give you that." He leaned back and pressed a soft kiss to her brow, his breath warm against her skin as he whispered, "I only came to say goodbye."

"Goodbye?" Her eyes flew open, and she stepped back. "Why? Because you think I deserve better than the Emperor's second son? I don't want the crown, Auberon. I want *you*."

"Do you think I don't want the same?" He took several steps away from her, love and agony in his beautiful eyes. "I want to spend every day with you. I want to dance with you every night, to hold you in my arms and smell your perfume on my clothes when I go to sleep. I want to meet your eyes from across a room and know exactly what you're thinking. I want to make you smile the way you did after I kissed you the first time. From the very first banquet, I have been yours, *aramati*."

Riona moved to him and took his face in her hands. "Then explain to me why we cannot be together," she said softly.

Auberon faltered, seeming to wage some battle within himself. Riona's heart thundered in her chest as a mixture of regret and despair came over his regal features. He gently grasped her wrists and pulled her hands away from his face. "Riona, I talk about my mother as if she were dead because she *is* dead. I pick up languages and accents easily because I spent most of my life traveling across the northern continent, searching for work and begging for scraps when I could find none. I know about that boy Eamon had whipped because *I* was that boy. *Aramati*," he breathed, "I am not the real Prince Auberon."

Chapter Seventy-One
The Lady

"I *am not the real Prince Auberon.*"

The confession struck her like a knife to the heart. "... I don't understand."

"My real name is Caelan," he said, "and I've been one of Emperor Hyperion's spies since I was fourteen years old. When he received Drystan's invitation to sail to Rivosa and bid for your hand, the Emperor decided to send someone to accompany the prince and confirm the existence of eudorite mines. He knew that posing as Prince Auberon would allow me to get close to your uncle and the rest of the court without drawing too much suspicion." He looked pointedly at the eudorite pendant at her throat. "It allowed me to get close to *you.*"

Riona took a few stumbling steps back, her fingers rising to the pendant. "What?"

The memories of so many nights filled her mind: every smile, every joke, every touch that lingered just a heartbeat too long. How many of those moments had been real? How many had been nothing more than an act designed to lower her guard?

"I was made an orphan when I was five years old," Auberon —*Caelan*—said, pure misery on his face. "I watched my childhood home burn with my parents trapped inside, and I ran with nothing but the clothes on my back and that emerald dagger in my hands. For years, I wandered from town to town, resorting to begging and stealing to put food in my belly." His voice shook with anger, but there was an undercurrent of something else —*shame*, Riona realized as he looked away, his shoulders slumping.

"I didn't intend to fall for you, and I would give anything to take it back," he continued softly. "Whatever we could have been —it is impossible. It is *wrong*. I am no one, and you are a woman with the blood of kings in your veins. You deserve so much more than a spy with little more than a handful of coins to his name. You deserve the Empire's throne. That is why you must marry Drystan."

Riona gaped at him. "Drystan doesn't deserve a wife who is so clearly in love with someone else. Believe me, I know how it feels to love someone who is wholly devoted to another, and I would not wish that pain upon anyone." When he opened his mouth to argue, she added, "Nor could I put you through the agony of watching the woman you love marry and have children with another man."

"I'll take jobs well away from Torch," he responded immediately, his voice full of desperation. "I'll not bother you again, and given time, you and Drystan will find happiness together. He is an honorable man, and he would love you. He would make a good hus—"

"Please, Auberon. Caelan," she said quietly. "Please don't finish that sentence."

He crossed the aisle and took her hands in his. "You could be the ruler of the greatest empire in the history of the world, Riona. You could have everything you've ever wanted at your fingertips. Give Drystan a chance, and you will come to love him. You could be happy with him."

"None of us would be happy if he and I married."

Caelan gripped her hands tighter, his patience reaching its

end. "Do not be a fool, Riona. You ended a decades-long war today, hours after nearly bleeding to death. How much good would you do for both our peoples as Erduria's Empress? You would throw that away for a man who can give you nothing? I won't allow you to do that."

"You won't *allow it?*" Riona repeated, anger sweeping over her. The blood magic pulsing in her chest flared in response, igniting every nerve ending. She fought to stay on her feet as a wave of agony overcame her. "Then why did you ask me to meet you in the theater last night? Why did you confess your feelings for me?"

"Because knowing that I could only ever have that one night with you was better than not having one at all," he said, the words coming out in a rush. "I was selfish, and I was weak, and I was thoughtless. And I am sorry for hurting you, but I am trying to repent for what I've done. Marry Drystan and forget me. Serve your people and mine from Erduria's throne."

Riona shook her head, struggling to keep her thoughts intact as daggers of pain shot through the wound in her chest. The heat had been a steady throb all day, but now, combined with the emotional toll the last several days had taken on her, it was all she could do not to fall to her knees. Valerian had told her she needed to rest, and now she was paying the price for her refusal.

Sorrow and shock and betrayal and anger warred within her, tangling into a knot of emotions that made her heart feel like it was fracturing in her chest. She was exhausted and heartbroken, weak from the attempt on her life and weary from the stress of the past several months. In Beltharos, she had been forced into marriage with a stranger and made the puppet of a bloodthirsty tyrant, and she had faced execution for daring to defy Nicholas Comyn. She had fallen in love and given Percival up so he could marry the woman he loved, and returned to her home only to learn that her uncle was already preparing to cast her out once again. She had been held hostage and threatened with death for entering the eudorite mines. She had been stabbed in the chest for trying to find Cathal's murderer. She had learned that her uncle had orchestrated the attack on her mother's ship.

This was what finally broke her.

She had always known that Auberon would do anything for his country. That he would be ruthless in manipulating the court into accepting the peace treaty. And yet, over the weeks they spent together, something had changed. He could have forced her uncle to accept a betrothal a half-dozen times, but he hadn't. He could have demanded it as repayment for rescuing her from the mines, but he'd held his tongue. He had become her ally, and then the person she had trusted more than anyone in this wretched city.

She had given up the man she loved for his own good, and now, the man to whom she had given her heart was doing the same to her.

"*Aramati*," Caelan begged. "Please. Marry Drystan and sail to Erduria with us."

"No," Riona responded, the word flat and final. "I have been played for a fool too many times—first by Nicholas, then by my uncle, and now by you. I am tired of people using me as a pawn. I am *tired*," she said, her voice breaking on the word, "of people breaking my heart."

"Riona—"

"Once the treaty is signed, you and Drystan will sail for Erduria alone. You will never set foot on Rivosi land again. And the next time I see you, I will bury a dagger in your heart."

He stumbled backward, startled by her fury. Agony flashed across his face before he quickly smoothed it under a mask of perfect calm. It transformed him; his beautiful eyes turned cold and dispassionate, and his lips pressed into a thin, tight line. Just like that, he shifted into the distant prince she'd met so many weeks ago, every trace of softness, of warmth, gone.

Caelan grabbed the emerald-hilted dagger from the sheath at Riona's hip and pressed it into her hand, his fingers lacing through hers as he lifted the blade to the fine brocade of his doublet, directly over his heart. "Remember what I taught you," he whispered, holding her gaze. "Angled like this so it slips through the ribs."

Riona stared at their hands, curled around the handle of the blade. If she wanted to, she could kill him. But when she looked up into his face, she saw the man who had been waiting for her in the theater the night before, playing the song his mother had loved. An orphan who had carved out a place in his court. A spy who claimed to be heartless, but who had been willing to give her life so she would survive.

A man who, even now, she could not kill.

Riona lowered the blade and offered it to Caelan hilt-first. "Take it. It's all you have to remember your parents."

"Keep it, *aramati*." A faint, remorseful smile tugged at his lips. "It saved your life, and that makes it the most valuable gift I can bestow."

With that, he turned and walked out of the chapel.

The second the doors swung shut, all the strength left Riona's body. She collapsed onto the nearest pew and buried her face in her hands, a tempest of emotions swirling within her. Fury and sorrow. Pain and heartbreak. It was all too much.

She sat there for what felt like an eternity, until everything within her went numb. Only the pulsing, relentless heat of the blood magic remained. With shaking hands, she pulled out the emerald-hilted dagger and examined it with new eyes. Suddenly, she recalled something he had said to her after their first meeting in the theater, both of them soaked to the bone after a storm had struck the city:

We are both children of war, my lady. We must help each other when we can.

She had thought he'd been speaking in the abstract, referring to their countries' bloody histories, but the gravity with which he had said it hinted at an old, deep wound. Every so often, he'd let his guise fall. The look on his face the first time she had played his mother's song. The way he had said her name when he discovered her in the mine. The sound of his voice as he sang to her in a dark theater. And it was those moments—those rare glimpses of the man behind the court mask—that had made her fall for him.

For Caelan. Not Auberon.

Riona glanced at the bowl-shaped altar at the front of the prayer room. The moment she had arrived at the chapel, she had been struck with the memory of her uncle kneeling before the altar after Cathal's funeral, the words he'd spoken returning with perfect clarity: *If the world were just, the man who committed this crime would suffer for it a thousand times over. But you and I both know the world is rarely that fair.*

He hadn't been mourning a friend. He had been wrestling with the guilt of ordering that friend's murder.

Her chest tight and her body aching, Riona returned the dagger to its sheath and rose with a grimace. She left the royal chapel and followed the cobblestone path past the royal apartments, to a wide natural overhang that jutted out over the street below. A waist-high wall surrounded the overlook, and Riona set her hands on the cool stone as she gazed out at her city, warm golden light bleeding from the windows of the buildings that sprawled before her.

"I thought I'd find you here."

She turned as her father emerged from the shadows between two castle buildings. "You always come here when you need to think, just like your mother." He slipped an arm around her shoulders and pulled her close. They stood in silence for several moments, staring out at the city, until her father asked, "What did Prince Auberon say to your offer of marriage?"

"Who said I was going to speak with Prince Auberon?"

He fixed her with a knowing look. "I'm not blind, my dear. Everyone can see how much that boy loves you. So what came of it?"

Her chest tightened. It had not been wise to threaten Caelan, but after everything that had happened these past several weeks, rage had been her only refuge. It was all that had kept her from shattering. At that moment, she had wanted to hurt him as deeply as she was hurting.

"Nothing. Whatever had been between us is over now. We will never marry."

He stiffened at her tone. "What did he say? If he hurt you—"

"Nothing like that. It's over, and there is nothing more to it than that."

He pulled her closer, pressing a kiss to her temple. "I'm sorry. But I have some news that may lift your spirits. I spoke with Prince Domhnall and Amaris, and they are going to petition the king to limit your exile to Innislee, rather than the whole of Rivosa. If he agrees, you will be granted Lord Farquar's title and estate. You would oversee the ruling of his sector, and perhaps in a few years, you'd be welcomed back to the capital with a place on the king's council."

"Would the king allow it? I'm not eager to face another attempt on my life."

"Give him some time to cool down, and he will come to see reason. You have ended the war with Erduria and secured us allies who will fight to defend our land. It won't be any time soon, but one day, you will have a place as one of the king's advisors. It's what you've always wanted, no?"

She hesitated. That *was* all she had ever wanted, but now that he had finally said it, the words felt wrong. Riona shrugged off her father's arm and turned back toward Innislee, her fingers digging into the stone wall as she gazed out at her beautiful, ancient city. This was her home; it was all she had ever known until the day she'd left to become Percival's bride.

But now that she had seen the corruption that festered at her kingdom's heart, she knew that she could no longer stay here. She loved her people and her country, but she wanted no part of her uncle's plots. She could never sit on his council knowing that he had orchestrated the attack on her mother's ship, that he had ordered Cathal's murder, that he and Lord Farquar had sent men to kill her. As long as he sat on the throne, Innislee would never be her home. She couldn't look at the city without seeing the ghosts of those she'd lost.

Her uncle was beyond redemption, but he was steadfast in his opposition to his enemies, and he would stand against every foreign army who sought to claim the mines. Queen Blair, Prince Domhnall, her father, and Amaris would rebuild Rivosa in the wake of his destruction. Together, they would save her kingdom from ruin.

They didn't need her help—but she knew someone who did.

Riona turned back to her father, a look of grim determination on her face. "I know what I must do now."

Chapter Seventy-Two
The Liar

Drystan was waiting in the sitting room when Caelan arrived at the house they shared, the rest of the rooms dark and quiet. He'd sent a few of their guards to ready their ship for the journey back to Erduria, while the rest—along with Vick and the brothers from the mine—would accompany them north once the treaty was signed. The prince looked up from the sheaf of parchment before him as Caelan dropped into the nearest armchair and said, "Have the king sign the treaty as soon as possible. We may have peace between our countries, but I have been quite reliably informed that we're no longer welcome in Rivosa."

"'No longer' implies we ever *were* welcome," Drystan responded dryly, toying with the fletching of his quill. "But that can be arranged. I'm working on the wording of the treaty as we speak, and I can have it signed tomorrow, Creator willing. Will Riona be joining us in Erduria?"

Caelan fixed him with a look that conveyed exactly how amenable she had been to that suggestion. "No. I'm sorry I wasn't able to secure you the wife you wanted."

The prince pushed the parchment aside and set his quill

down next to the ink pot. "I wouldn't want her as a wife if it would be torture to you both. I couldn't do that to you."

He shook his head. "It's a wonder you're so kind, having been surrounded by men like this all your life."

"Just because I didn't force Lady Riona into marriage doesn't mean I cannot be ruthless when necessary. We have peace with Rivosa right now, but should the king step one foot out of line—should we hear so much as a whisper of retribution for what has happened today—I will personally see to it that King Domhnall loses his head and his crown," Drystan said. "His son may not be a friend of the Empire, but he doesn't share his father's thirst for Erdurian blood. It wouldn't be difficult to persuade him to maintain our shaky alliance, especially when he's neck-deep in grief."

Caelan scoffed. "Prince Domhnall doesn't love his father that much. He can't, after what he learned today."

"He does," Drystan insisted. "That's why what he learned today cut him so deeply. A love like that rarely severs so quickly."

He shrugged, unconvinced.

Drystan picked up his quill and scrawled another line across the parchment before him. "You're in a remarkably bad mood for a man who just blackmailed a king," he said as he wrote. "If you'd like, you can set out for Crafford first thing in the morning, and I'll meet you there once the treaty is signed and all the details settled. I know you must be eager to leave this awful place."

"I told Riona the truth. I told her who I really am."

The prince jerked upright, knocking over the ink pot in the process. He didn't even seem to notice the dark stain spreading across the table as he gaped at Caelan. "You did *what?*"

"She would have learned the truth the moment we arrived at Torch. I have told her a dozen times that whatever was between us could not continue, but Drystan... She wanted to *marry me.*" His voice broke on the words, a sharp pang of longing striking him so acutely that it took his breath away. "She loves me, and I love her, and I have lied to her from the moment we met. I had to tell her the truth, if only to make her see that there will never be a future for us."

Drystan rounded the low table and set a hand on his shoulder. "If you thought that telling her the truth was right, I will not challenge you," he said, holding Caelan's gaze. "She is free to marry whom she chooses. If she chooses you, my friend, you have my blessing."

Caelan swallowed the lump building in his throat as a rush of affection for the other man swept over him. Drystan was not his brother by blood, but he and Walther were the closest things Caelan had to family in Erduria. "She has made her opinion of me quite clear. The next time she and I meet, it will not end well."

Drystan stiffened. "Will she tell anyone who you are? Are you in danger?"

Caelan shook his head, certain that Riona would keep his secret—for now, at least. "She promised that she would be the one to bury a dagger in my heart. She won't allow the honor to go to one of the king's men."

Drystan didn't look entirely convinced, but he nodded and returned to his place at the table. "Still, I think it best you set out for Crafford at first light. It'd be wise not to remain any longer than necessary. I want our people to hail you as a hero, not a martyr."

"Very well. Have the treaty signed first thing in the morning and convince the king to give me a royal escort to wherever he's storing the ore. If you can spare a few guards, I'll have them accompany me. We're not setting off without our share of the eudorite."

"It'll be guarded by Rivosi soldiers who want nothing more than to see you dead. Better to wait until Father can send men to secure the ore. I don't trust them not to attack you."

A wicked grin spread across Caelan's lips. "Let them try."

Vick was dozing in one of the spare rooms where the guards slept, and he jolted upright when Caelan roughly shook him awake early the next morning. "It wasn't my fault," he blurted in a voice thick with sleep and fear. "I didn't tell— Oh. I thought you were one of Farquar's men, come to kill me."

"Not yet," Caelan responded, perversely amused by the terror that etched itself across the man's face. He may have promised Vick his protection, but that didn't mean he was finished punishing him for the attempt on his and Riona's lives. "Pack whatever belongings you have here and be ready to leave in ten minutes. We're going to Crafford."

"Must we go now? I have to arrange the sale of the tavern and gather the rest of my stuff."

"One of Drystan's men will do that on your behalf. Right now, it's important to keep you safe, and I won't be able to do that if you remain here. Of course, if you no longer want our protection..."

"No, no. I'll get ready," Vick grumbled, picking at the edge of the bandage wrapped around his broken hand. "You'll set me up with a place when we reach Torch?"

"I'll get you a room and see if I can find some work for you. Once the tavern is sold, you're on your own, understood? You can sail right back here for all I care."

The man's expression soured. "This is the thanks I get for speaking out against Lord Farquar? It won't take long for news of his arrest to spread to the public. Don't you think he has powerful friends in the navy who would love to see my head on a spike for revealing what he did?"

Caelan shot him an icy look. "Considering the role you played in Lord Farquar's plot, you should be grateful that a broken hand is the only injury I gave you. I threw one of your men from the top of the city wall."

Vick paled and fell silent.

"I'm glad we could come to an understanding," Caelan said

as he started toward the door. "Tell Callan and Halston to pack their bags, as well. We won't be coming back."

Once the ten minutes were up, Caelan led Vick, the brothers, and a handful of Rivosi guards along the cobblestone path toward the gatehouse. The sky was still dark and dotted with stars, a faint tinge of pale pink light bleeding from the eastern horizon. He wore a fine silk doublet with whorls of gold along the collar, and his sword hung in the sheath at his hip. He tried not to think about the emerald-hilted dagger he was leaving behind, nor of the hatred and betrayal that had burned in Riona's eyes as she held it to her heart.

It is better this way, he told himself. *She deserves better than a commoner with no name and no honor.*

He shoved thoughts of her away as they passed through the gatehouse. Prince Domhnall was already waiting outside with a few dozen royal guards, and he crossed the forecourt to meet Caelan and his small group near the portcullis. "Your brother has already met with my father and Lord Lachlan, Your Highness," he said. "The treaty is signed. I'm to accompany you to the warehouse and ensure that you are given what you are owed."

"A royal escort," Caelan said, surveying the guards already seated on horseback near the start of the King's Road, waiting for their prince.

Prince Domhnall followed his gaze, looking weary. "My father would rather have had you tied to the back of a horse and dragged through the streets, but I insisted we part as friends." He turned back to Caelan and extended a hand. "All we have known, our entire lives, is war. I hope we can build a future where we are partners, not enemies."

He took the prince's hand and shook it, a knot of guilt tangling within him. He hadn't spoken much with Prince Domhnall, but he had struck Caelan as a kind, good-hearted man, with the same clever mind and sharp tongue as his cousin. Perhaps in another life, they could have been friends. "I would like that, too, Your Highness."

Prince Domhnall smiled and gestured for one of the guards to fetch the Erdurian horses, then climbed atop his own mount, a pure white stallion draped in the Rivosi royal colors. He cut a striking figure, his fur-lined cloak tumbling from the clasp at his neck and flowing over the back of his horse. When the guards returned with the Erdurian horses, Caelan mounted up and joined Domhnall at the front of the procession. Out of the corner of his eye, he saw Vick and the brothers edge close to the Erdurian guards, casting wary glances at the Rivosans as if fearing an attack.

"So, what do you think will happen now?" Caelan asked as they started down the King's Road, the narrow buildings rising high around them. The city was quiet, but a few bleary-eyed people opened their shutters to watch the royal procession pass when they heard the clatter of hooves on cobblestone. "Once word of your father's actions spreads."

Domhnall shook his head, looking troubled. "I don't know. I've ordered the guards who were present last night to remain silent under threat of death, but I'm not foolish enough to believe that will stay loose tongues for long. Amaris and my mother are already planning some court events and city-wide celebrations as an attempt to uplift our people and breathe life into the city. If we can present a united front, the people will follow. Terrible though his actions were, my father led us through thirty years of brutal war. The rush of trade we will soon enjoy from the peace treaty will be a welcome change."

He raised a brow. "You truly think that will be enough to make them forget that he organized the murder of the queen's sister? His own brother's wife?"

"No, but we will make them believe that we are as strong as ever. We cannot fight a war on all fronts, and quelling our people's unrest will be our main concern until word of the eudorite mines spreads." Domhnall glanced at him, his expression grave. "But make no mistake, my father's treachery is over. The crown may sit on his head, but the power of the kingdom rests with me."

"Do you think your father will allow it to remain that way for long?"

The Crown Prince shifted in his saddle, confirming that he'd asked himself that very same question. King Domhnall had fought for thirty years to keep his throne, and Caelan doubted he would remain complacent for long. A small part of Caelan feared the Crown Prince would find a dagger in his back within the year.

"For all his faults, my father is excellent at waging war," the prince said, seeming to choose his words carefully. "If that is what he must do to keep his throne, he will not hesitate, be his opponent a foe or family. He has dedicated too much of his life to its service to allow it to be taken from him. He will die with a sword in his hand and a crown on his head."

That could be arranged. But instead, he merely said, "You'll need a strong king on the throne if you are to stand against the armies who will come for the mines."

One of Domhnall's brows rose. "You don't believe I can be that king?"

"He has fought for three decades. You have won one battle, and that was with the aid of King Tamriel's ragtag army. Temper your father's will, but learn from him in equal measure. Allow him to be the king Rivosa needs in times of war, so you can be the king it deserves in times of peace."

A smile broke out across the prince's face. "Now I see why your brother insisted on bringing you with him, Prince Auberon. You hide a clever mind behind those rakish grins and irreverent jokes."

Caelan shrugged. "Clever men make the greatest fools, as I've found."

Prince Domhnall chuckled, and they lapsed into silence as they rode along the King's Road. Caelan let his gaze wander over the city one final time, taking in the tall, proud homes with their ivy-covered façades and wide bay windows. Passersby on the street—workmen off to their jobs and merchants on their way to the market—paused to watch their procession pass, and Prince Domhnall greeted them with a wave and a smile. Caelan followed his lead, forcing a cheer he didn't quite feel onto his face.

When they finally reached the city gate, Caelan twisted back in the saddle and cast one last look at the castle sitting high over the capital. The sky was growing lighter, and the dark gray stone was stark against the vivid pinks and oranges of the dawn.

Riona. The girl who had comforted him while he was dying, when no one else would. The girl who had traded blows and barbed words with him. The girl who had danced with him in a candlelit theater.

The girl who would kill him the next time they met.

Goodbye, aramati.

Caelan turned forward, and followed Prince Domhnall out of Innislee.

Chapter Seventy-Three
The Liar

Caelan had expected the building that held the eudorite ore to be somewhat...grander. More imposing. This was a building that the king had been stocking for the better part of a decade with ore and weapons intended to slaughter the Erdurian forces. The kingdom's greatest-held secret, one that countless people had—knowingly or not—given their lives to keep hidden.

All in all, it was...not what he had expected.

There was an old ruined city a few hours' ride west of Crafford, a place that had been reduced to rubble so long ago no cartographer had bothered to mark it on any of the maps Caelan had ever seen of Rivosa. The remains of an old castle sat crumbling at the foot of a low mountain range, only the bare bones of the building still standing. In most places, the walls rose only waist-high, the ancient stones covered in a thick layer of moss and ivy. A few of the structures bore scars from the cannonballs that had struck them in long-ago battles.

The rest of the city had fared better than the castle, but only marginally so. Most of the buildings were still standing, many without roofs or doors, and the cobblestone streets were thick with mud and overgrown weeds. Upon seeing it, it was immediately clear why the king had chosen to hide his country's greatest secret here: it was a place lost to time, slowly being reclaimed by Rivosa's wild countryside. Most travelers who happened to discover the ruins would not even bother to get close enough to spot the makeshift work camp at its heart.

A modest house in the middle of what had once been the main road served to store the eudorite ore. Caelan stood with Prince Domhnall outside the open doorway, watching a line of Rivosi soldiers load chests of ore into a horse-drawn cart the prince had commandeered for the journey to Crafford. He and the Crown Prince had walked through the building together, marking off the boxes that would go to Erduria, Kenter, and Rivosa, respectively.

He hadn't missed the open hostility with which the Rivosi soldiers regarded him. To them, he was a monster—the ruthless son of the man they had dedicated their lives to fighting. Prince Domhnall's announcement of the peace treaty hadn't changed any of the men's expressions. It didn't matter that the Empire was now one of Rivosa's allies; these soldiers had lost too many fathers and brothers to let go of old grievances. It would take years, perhaps decades, to bridge the rift that the war had cleaved between their people.

"I still find it hard to believe that my father managed to keep this a secret for so long," Prince Domhnall murmured, wandering toward a blacksmith's workshop on the opposite side of the street. The building had been rebuilt and reinforced for the band of Strykers—weapon and armor smiths of unparalleled skill and international renown—who now occupied it. A blast of heat struck Caelan in the face as he followed Domhnall through the doorway. A half-dozen men were hard at work at the forges, lifting pieces of glowing-red metal from the flames or working the bellows to keep the fires burning. "It doesn't seem possible that an operation this large could remain hidden for so many years. How can it be that not a word of this place has reached Innislee?"

Caelan picked up a eudorite dagger from one of the worktables. Its blade was as long as his forearm, the metal such a deep, rich black that it seemed to absorb the light around it. The nearest blacksmith watched him examine the weapon, open hatred on the man's grizzled face. His expression made it clear that he wanted nothing more than to drag the dagger's blade across Caelan's throat.

"They've lived their entire lives being taught that my people are wretched, soulless monsters. They've watched their friends and family sail off to war and never return. And I have no doubt that they've been told all manner of horrific tales about what my people would do to their women and children if we won the war," Caelan said as he twisted the dagger, watching the light of the forges play across the strange blade. "Hatred is a good motivator, but vengeance is a better one."

Domhnall didn't look entirely convinced, but Caelan could see it perfectly in the icy glares the Rivosans shot his way. There were fewer than forty men in the entire ruined city, all thoroughly isolated from the rest of the kingdom. Their days were spent in a scorching forge, crafting weapons to wield against his people, and their nights spent trading stories of the Erdurians' evil. Civilian ships caught in the fighting. Merchant vessels sunk to starve their people. Fathers and sons meeting their deaths in the cold embrace of the Tranquil Sea's waters. Here, their hatred could fester, eating away at them until it was all that remained. Until they themselves were weapons, their hearts as cold and hard as the blades they forged.

Caelan knew that was the case because that was exactly what he would have done, had he been in King Domhnall's place.

A chill crept down his spine at the thought, and he returned the dagger to its place on the worktable. Domhnall led him out of the workshop and onto the main road, the bright sunlight blinding. The Empire had claimed the lion's share of the eudorite, but even after years of mining, the various boxes and crates were barely enough to fill the cart. That was why King Domhnall hadn't ordered his military to wield the blackblades in battle yet.

It was a long, dangerous, laborious process to mine eudorite, and he had wanted to ensure that he had enough to strike a single, decisive victory in the war.

Prince Domhnall's expression was sorrowful as his gaze swept over the boxes and crates, but he smoothed his features into an emotionless mask before striding toward his stallion. Caelan mounted his horse and rode up beside him as the rest of their guards fell into formation around them. Once the last of their men was in position, the Crown Prince turned to address the Rivosi soldiers, who had gathered on either side of the street to see their prince off.

"Let this be an end to the hatred and violence between Rivosa and Erduria," he said, his voice carrying through the ruined city. He looked to each of the men in turn, meeting their cold, grief-filled stares. "The sacrifices of those you have loved and lost were not in vain. This may not have been the victory my father promised you, but because of this treaty, no more children will grow up without their brothers and fathers to guide them. No more widows will go hungry so they can feed their sons and daughters. With this treaty, we usher in a new era of peace and prosperity for both our kingdom and the Empire."

As he spoke, a few of the faces in the crowd softened. Prince Domhnall smiled at them, ever the dashing young prince with his fine clothing and brilliant white stallion, and wheeled his horse around to face the crumbling eastern gate through which they had arrived. Caelan rode alongside him as they set out, the horse-drawn cart clattering over the broken and uneven cobbles, and he couldn't help but admire the prince's confidence. Despite his inexperience, Domhnall held himself like a man born to rule.

"We will heal," the prince murmured as they passed through the broken eastern arch and started toward Crafford. He seemed to be speaking to himself as much as Caelan, willing the future for which he longed into existence.

Caelan had known Kenter was poor, but he hadn't imagined that the grandest of the duchy's ships would be at this level of disrepair. The carrack creaked and groaned as it bobbed over the waves, and Caelan had to fight the bile rising in his throat as it listed to one side. He stumbled, nearly dropping the heavy crate in his arms as he caught his balance on the wall of the narrow hallway in which he stood.

Someone roughly pushed past him, sneering over his shoulder. "Ay, were you born yesterday, you oaf? Find your sea legs or find a new line of work. We haven't even left the harbor yet, and you're walking like a bride after her first bedding."

Caelan spat a Kentari curse at the sailor's back and readjusted his grip on the crate as the man slipped into one of the cabins, ignoring his insult completely. Once the door slammed shut, Caelan let a smug grin spread across his lips. From what he'd observed, the vessel had a crew of eighty or ninety men, and none of them had glanced at him twice as he joined the flurry of ship hands working to load a week's worth of supplies onto the ship. He was just one in a sea of nameless faces. It had only been a matter of finding a threadbare, sun-bleached tunic and trousers among the stores on the Erdurian ship, and then smearing enough dirt and grime onto his skin to hide the fact that his face bore none of the creases that accompanied a life spent at sea under the relentless sun. With a crate in his arms and a rough Kentari accent lilting his words, it was almost comical how easy it had been to slip aboard the vessel.

A faint sheen of sweat had broken out across his brow by the time he arrived at the lowest level, a result of carrying the crate and attempting not to lose the meager lunch he'd eaten. The hall ended with a door guarded by two men in Kentari livery, swords sheathed at their sides. Caelan's mood lifted considerably when he saw them. All that was stored in the hold were the food and other supplies for the week-long voyage to the northern continent; there was no reason for royal guards to be posted at the door.

No reason, unless it held something that Duke Valerian did not want falling into the wrong hands.

The lantern hanging from the low ceiling swayed with the rocking of the ship, causing the shadows on the walls to dance as Caelan approached the door. One of the guards turned to open it for him.

The crate thudded to the ground, splintering into pieces, as Caelan pulled a eudorite dagger from his waistband and slammed its pommel into the guard's temple. The man cried out and whirled, a trickle of blood rolling down the side of his face as he reached for the sword at his hip. Caelan caught his arm and twisted it behind his back until his elbow popped out of place, then shoved him into the other guard, throwing them both off balance. They went down in a heap of limbs and steel as the ship listed, and Caelan swapped his eudorite dagger with a rag he'd doused in a powerful soporific. He didn't want to kill the men—he only needed them unconscious. The blade was meant for someone else.

He stepped over the broken remains of the crate and kicked one of the men in the ribs when he tried to rise. The guard gasped, and Caelan knelt on his chest as he held the rag over the man's nose and mouth. It only took a few heartbeats for the man's body to go limp. The other guard—the one he'd struck in the head—fought to push to his feet. Auberon pressed the rag to his face, and the man fell unconscious in seconds.

Caelan dragged their bodies into another room, and then opened the door to the hold.

A cold smile skated across his lips at the sight of the man standing in the middle of the room, his shackled wrists chained to a lantern hook in the ceiling. Someone had cleaned the blood from Lord Farquar's face, but his nose was still a bruised, broken mess, dark shadows pooling along the bone and around his eyes. Valerian may have given him his life, but it was clear from the pain on the lord's face that the duke wasn't feeling particularly merciful when it came to the newest member of his court.

"Who are— What are you doing?" Farquar asked as Caelan shoved a heavy stack of crates in front of the door, barring the entrance.

"Making sure we have privacy," he responded as he turned back. The confusion and apprehension on the lord's face vanished when Caelan stepped fully into the light, something hateful and wicked unfurling within him.

"Prince Auberon," Farquar breathed.

Caelan smiled, savoring the fear that filled the lord's eyes as he pulled the eudorite dagger from his waistband. This one was smaller than the one he'd been examining at the blacksmith's workshop, the blade only as long as his hand. He had taken it from one of the crates his men had loaded onto the Erdurian ship, deeming it a satisfactory replacement for the emerald-hilted dagger he had given to Riona. How fitting that the first blood it tasted would be that of the man who had tried to end her life.

He stalked forward, all too conscious of how little time he had before another person would arrive with more supplies. Farquar's gaze remained trained on the blade, and he stiffened, his chains jangling. His throat bobbed as he swallowed, but he remained silent. Caelan had to give him credit for his show of bravery, even if it wouldn't last long.

"You tried to have me killed," he said. "If I were the only target of the attack, I might have let you go mostly unharmed. Enough people have tried to kill me that your attempt wasn't particularly noteworthy. Honestly, I had expected worse from the court of my enemies." His voice turned icy, laced with the promise of blood. "But you attempted to murder the woman I love, and you managed to weasel your way out of facing justice for what you've done. Not only that, but you helped instigate the attack that claimed her mother's life. Riona was only a *child*, and you stole her mother from her."

"I was acting under my king's orders. Like them or not, I was a captain of his navy, and I obeyed the commands I was given. Doing so kept us from losing the war. It kept countless innocent people from dying—if Riona's mother had to die to save thousands more, then it was a price the kingdom was right to pay."

Fury flared within Caelan. "That was not *your* decision to make. Not yours, or your king's."

The lord sneered. "Foolish boy. Lady Rhea died to ensure the Selannic Isles would continue supporting us in the war. Riona would have died to keep the eudorite ore from falling into the hands of men like you. Because of her, we are ruined."

"Because of her, your people will know peace for the first time in thirty years," Caelan snapped, then shut his mouth. Farquar was purposely trying to twist his words, to distract him from the terrifying blade in his hand. He shook his head and let his rage rush over him, burning away what little decency and kindness he still had.

Farquar saw the change in his expression, and for the first time, his face contorted in genuine terror. "I was acting on my king's orders," he said again. "Your anger lies with him, not me."

"Perhaps, but the king is instrumental in maintaining the peace treaty. You, however..." Caelan trailed off as he lifted the dagger, the black blade gleaming in the low light. "I think it's time I show you exactly how ruthless Erdurians can be."

CHAPTER SEVENTY-FOUR
THE LADY

Riona stood before the banquet hall's closed doors and sucked in a breath, steeling herself against the rush of heat that pulsed under her skin. After leaving the overlook the night before, she had accompanied her father to his estate and promptly climbed into bed, where she had fallen asleep the moment her head hit the pillow.

The blood magic pulsed incessantly, like a hot brand being pressed to her flesh, but she refused to let any pain show on her face. She would not allow the court to see her weakness.

Footsteps sounded behind her, and she turned to find Duke Valerian approaching from the far end of the hall, a pair of Kentari guards trailing behind him. His skin was still wan from the blood magic, but it did little to detract from the resplendent image he cut as he strode down the corridor. He wore a tunic unlike anything Riona had seen in the southern continent; the green brocade was fitted to his torso, the neckline draping gracefully across his chest to clasp at a line of gold buttons that spanned from his heart to his navel. The gold threads woven into the silk caught the light of the torches as he moved. Under it, he wore fitted trousers and shining leather boots. A ceremonial sword hung at his hip, the pommel shaped like a rearing stag with flecks of raw emerald for its eyes.

The duke stopped beside her and dipped his head in respect, his gaze catching on the line of stitches over her heart. "I won't pretend that I'm not looking forward to leaving Innislee. I'm sorry for all this city and its people have taken from you."

"Thank you. In truth, it will be a relief to leave it all behind. I can't stay here any longer."

As much as the words hurt, they rang with undeniable truth. Even if her father was right about her one day earning a place on the council, she could not endure another hour among the people who had controlled her all her life. Innislee was in her blood—this city of raging storms and poison-laced smiles—but it was no longer her home.

Valerian's expression turned sympathetic. "You brought your people peace, and for that, they will always remember you." He hesitated, then added in a quieter voice, "I know what you gave up to stand here today. And while Auberon and I are about as different as two people can be, I will do everything in my power to be the husband you deserve. It will be an honor to have you as my wife."

Before she could respond, the doors swung open, revealing the vast banquet hall in all its splendor. Torches crackled from their sconces on the walls, illuminating the panels of vibrantly colored fabric strung across the high ceiling. A troupe of musicians sat on the platform at the rear of the room, and their song softened into an elegant, sweeping melody that danced through the air. The shift drew the attention of the gathered nobles, who turned toward the open doors. At the far end of the room, King Domhnall and the others were already seated at the head table, a picture of the perfect royal family. Riona surveyed the table, her gaze catching on the empty seat beside Prince Drystan. By the time she had arrived at the castle that morning to alert the king and queen of her decision, Caelan had left.

Valerian offered her his arm. "Shall we?"

She slipped a hand into the crook of his elbow, and together they made their way down the length of the room. When they reached the steps of the dais, the king rose and spread his arms wide. "My lords and ladies," he called, his voice filling the hall. "It is my great honor to announce the betrothal of my niece, Lady Riona of Innislee, to Duke Valerian of Kenter."

The queen rose and lifted her goblet in a toast. She once again wore her ruby diadem, but there was no mistaking the ice in her eyes when she glanced at her husband. "May the Creator bless your union," she said, focusing on Riona and Valerian. "To your good health and happy future!"

"Hear, hear!" the nobles cried, raising their goblets.

The music swelled as Riona and Valerian made their way to the head table. As they passed his chair, Prince Drystan offered Valerian a nod, no hint of anger or envy on his face. The duke returned it without a word. Two seats of honor had been left for them at the table: one between the queen and Amaris for Riona, and the other between the king and Prince Domhnall for Valerian. Once the duke helped Riona into her chair and claimed his seat, a fleet of servants emerged from the kitchen with platters of food and wine.

Amaris leaned in close and whispered, "I pray that this decision will bring you the happiness you deserve, Riona. But...I must ask why you chose to arrange the betrothal with the duke. You were free—you could have sailed to Kenter and asked the Grand Duke for a position in his court. You don't have to marry a man you don't love."

"Valerian is desperate to free his country from Kostori rule, and I am going to help him win Kenter's independence. I will never be able to repay him for what he has done for our people and for me, but I will not rest until King Jericho has renounced his claim on the land. Petitioning the Grand Duke for a position in his court wouldn't be enough; I would be a minor noble at best, and I'd be powerless to aid his people or ours. Valerian needs someone to stand at his side when he declares war on Kostos, and marrying him is the only surefire way to secure my position in the court. Together, he and I will free the people of Kenter and return stability to the region," Riona responded, keeping her voice low so only Amaris would be able to hear. She glanced at Valerian, who was deep in conversation with her eldest cousin, and a flicker of guilt shot through her. They had never spoken of it in plain terms, but it was clear the duke knew about her feelings for the man she thought she'd loved. "I hope that we fall in love in the process."

"And Prince Auberon? Domhnall told me that he left at dawn this morning, with hardly a word to anyone. Did something happen between the two of you? I was certain that if you chose a husband, it would be him."

A bitter smile tugged at her lips. "It turns out he is not the man I thought he was."

Servants set plates and goblets before them, and they ate in silence, listening to the chatter and music filling the hall. Several times throughout the dinner, Riona caught her uncle watching her from the corner of her eye, a stony expression on his face. He had granted her the betrothal and celebratory banquet in exchange for one promise: that she and Valerian would set sail for Kenter the very next day. *You have meddled enough in the affairs of this court*, he had told her, his voice trembling with barely restrained anger. *Now, you are Kenter's responsibility.*

The last course had no sooner been whisked away by the servants than a hand appeared between Riona and Amaris. She turned, expecting to see Valerian standing before her.

"Lady Riona," Prince Drystan said, "would you honor me with a dance?"

Masking her surprise, she accepted his hand and allowed him to lead her down to the dance floor. They took up a position in the center of the noble couples, their hands clasped, one of Drystan's arms encircling her waist. "Caelan told me that he confessed the truth to you," the prince whispered as they began to move in time with the music, fierce protectiveness on his face. "He also told me that you promised to kill him the next time you see him, but I am afraid I cannot allow that to happen. He may not be my brother, but he is one of my dearest friends, and I will not see him harmed. He has suffered enough in this life already."

Love, hurt, and betrayal warred within her at the mention of the spy, a knot of emotion too complicated to unravel. "He saved my life twice, and because of that, I will not tell anyone the truth of his identity," she said. "That is all the mercy I will grant him."

Drystan scoffed and shook his head. "You two are more similar than you realize. You would do anything for your people and your country, at the cost of your own happiness. He will be heaped with rewards upon our return to Erduria, but even if you forgave him for his deception and begged him on your knees to marry you, he would reject you on account of his common blood. He believes you deserve a throne." The prince's gaze swept over her, a flicker of contempt passing across his face. "You're not even worthy of him."

Riona flinched. She opened her mouth to respond just as the song ended, and Drystan abruptly released her. "Thank you for your efforts in securing the peace treaty," he said, his expression cool. "I wish you happiness in your impending marriage."

The procession that escorted Riona and Valerian to Crafford looked more like a transport of prisoners than a farewell send-off. She and Valerian sat in a carriage marked with the Rivosi royal crest, the curtains pulled back to afford them one final look at the land Riona loved, with its low, rolling hills and wildflower-dotted valleys. It was a remarkably clear day; the sun shone brightly in the cloudless sky, its rays sparkling on the wide river that wended its way along the northern road. Through the window, Riona could see the mounted royal guards her uncle had assigned to their escort, each armed with swords and crossbows and steeped in the Rivosi royal colors. The display was as much a message for her as it was for the Rivosi people, who were already beginning to whisper about the events surrounding Treasurer Cathal's murder and Lord Farquar's arrest: *I am the king of Rivosa, and I will brook no dissent.*

When their carriage rolled to a stop before the harbor, the driver opened the door and offered Riona a hand to climb out. She accepted it, trying not to look at the Erdurian ship sitting tall and proud beside one of the docks as she emerged. A few docks over, the Kentari carrack bobbed on the water. The sight of the smaller ship left no doubt of the state of the country that was to become her home: the sails were patched and worn from the sun, the hull scarred from time and weather.

Valerian followed her gaze and winced. "I asked for our finest ship to sail here, and was promptly informed that that was it."

"We'll make the best of it. Although...perhaps our first priority upon arriving in Kenter should be to strengthen the navy," Riona responded as another carriage rolled to a stop behind the one they had just vacated. The driver opened the door, and her father, Amaris, Lord Winslow, the queen, and Prince Domhnall climbed out.

Amaris ran to her and threw her arms around Riona. "Oh, I'm going to miss you, sister. Write often, and spare no details," she said, her voice muffled by their embrace. She pulled back and looked from Riona to Valerian. "Let Domhnall and me know what aid you need. We don't have much to spare, on account of our debts to the Isles, but we will share what we can."

Valerian pressed a hand to his heart. "Thank you, my lady. You have no idea what this opportunity means to my people. Creator willing, we will soon find ourselves free of the Kostori tyrant."

"Just make sure you keep my cousin safe," Prince Domhnall said as he and the others joined them. He glanced at Riona and winked, his smile not quite masking his sorrow. "Better yet, protect the court from her. That clever tongue can be a fearsome weapon when she chooses to wield it."

"Seeing as it's the only weapon I'm skilled in wielding, it's imperative that I keep it sharp, cousin," she responded.

Domhnall rolled his eyes as he pulled her into a tight hug. When he released her, Riona turned to her father, pretending not to see the tears welling in his eyes. "I'll be fine, Father," she said as he stepped forward and kissed her temple. "You and Mother raised me well."

"I know you will, my love, but it's not easy to see you leave a second time." Pure devastation shone on his face, and she knew he still wished that she had agreed to his offer to leave Innislee and start anew elsewhere. She fought the lump forming in her throat as he gave her a sad smile. "Your new people will love you, Riona."

"And your enemies will fear you," the queen said as she pulled Riona into a hug. Her breath tickled the curve of Riona's ear as she whispered, "Your uncle will pay for what he did to your mother. Not yet—not while we are awaiting the armies that are sure to come for the mines—but one day. I swear it."

When her aunt pulled back, Riona saw nothing but fierce determination on her face. Her aunt was no longer the aloof, distant queen. She would stand beside her son and Amaris and help their kingdom recover from the damage her husband had done. Riona gripped her hands tightly. "When the time comes, do not hesitate."

Queen Blair nodded and pressed a light kiss to each of Riona's eyelids in the traditional Selannic farewell. "Not even for a second," she vowed as she pulled back.

At last, Lord Winslow stepped forward and bowed deeply to her and Valerian. "After all we endured in Beltharos, I am not eager to see you go, my lady. Be safe, and be as fearless as you were while facing Nicholas Comyn. You were the queen Percival needed to find his courage, and now you will be the duchess Kenter needs to gain its freedom."

She smiled, emotion rushing over her. Lord Winslow was not her blood, but he had been the closest thing she'd had to a father during their time in Beltharos. "What will do you now that you don't have me to watch over?"

A proud smile spread across his lips. "I've been appointed Treasurer. You are leaving your kingdom in good hands, my lady." His gaze drifted to the Kentari vessel, and his smile widened. "Do not forget—you may be leaving your family behind, but you still have friends at your side."

Riona followed his gaze to the ship, where a few figures were standing by the railing, waving to them. When told of the betrothal, Aeron, Faylen, and Ophelia had all chosen to sail to Kenter with her. Seeing them now, Riona's heart swelled with affection for her friends.

Valerian smiled and extended an arm toward the Kentari carrack. "I believe our ship is prepared. Are you ready?"

She glanced at the Erdurian ship, the double-headed eagle sigil emblazoned proudly on its sails, and nodded. "Let's go."

Her family followed them to the dock, where they exchanged their final farewells. They all smiled and wished her and Valerian well, but Riona saw tears brimming in several pairs of eyes and had to fight back the urge to cry. She had left Rivosa once before, but this felt different. This felt...final. Riona and Valerian climbed the gangplank, and her heart lurched the second her foot hit the deck. There was no guarantee she would ever see Rivosi land again.

She wasn't just leaving for a marriage. She was leaving for a war.

Riona and Valerian hadn't made it more than halfway across the deck when the captain rushed over to them, Aeron and the others trailing behind him. Riona stopped in her tracks when she saw the alarm on their faces. "What's wrong?" she asked before any of them could speak. Her gaze shot to Faylen's round belly. "Is it the baby?"

"No, it's—"

"There's been a security breach, Your Grace," the captain said to Valerian. "We've been as careful as possible with a ship and crew of this size, but a Rivosan must have snuck onboard while we were loading the supplies. He managed to get down to the hold, where we've been keeping that lord you took prisoner. I'm sorry, Your Grace."

Dread filled Valerian's face. "About what, Captain? Did the intruder set him free?"

The man shook his head. "No, he's still there, but...you should see him for yourself."

The duke shot Riona an uneasy look and ordered the captain to wait to cast off, then led them below decks. Riona blinked against the sudden dimness of the hall, the lanterns hanging from the ceiling swaying languidly with the bobbing of the ship. They passed through several narrow halls and descended rickety, steep steps until they came to a door bracketed by two Kentari guards, each slumped against the wall with their heads in their hands. They snapped upright when they saw their duke approaching, but made no attempt to stand. One blinked at them dazedly.

"What in the Creator's name has happened?" Valerian demanded, looking bewildered.

"It—It was a ship hand, Your Grace," the slightly more alert of the two guards said. He tilted his head, and the light of the lantern hanging above Aeron shone on the large bump protruding from his temple. A small river of blood had dried along one side of his face. "He said he was just going into the hold to stow some supplies. Next thing I knew, he attacked us and forced a rag over our faces, laced with some sort of drug. I just remember falling unconscious and then waking to the sound of screams."

"What did he look like?"

The guard lifted a shoulder in a half-hearted shrug. "Like every man on this ship and half the ones in the harbor. Unwashed. Unkempt. That's all I remember, Your Grace. I'm sorry."

The other guard muttered his assent, still cradling his head with one hand.

The duke opened the door, and Riona followed him into the hold. The scent of blood struck her like a slap to the face. Valerian abruptly stopped just beyond the doorway, halting so quickly that Riona slammed into his back. He whirled around, his face pale, and lifted his hands. "I don't think you want to see this."

But she could already see what he was trying to shield, and her heart stopped. Behind her, still standing in the hallway, Ophelia began whispering a prayer.

Lord Farquar's wrists were shackled, linked with a chain that had been looped around one of the hooks in the ceiling. He looked barely conscious, his entire body weight supported by the shackles and the chain linking them, and his forearms were coated with blood where the metal had cut into his skin. His face was utterly unrecognizable: his skin mottled with dark purple bruises, his eyes swollen to the point that they could not open, and his lips were a ragged, bloody mess of torn flesh. The doublet he wore had been sliced cleanly down the middle, and it hung open over his broad chest. Rivulets of blood trailed down his torso, painting his fair skin a deep, shiny crimson.

It's still wet, Riona realized with a wave of revulsion. The attacker must have left just moments before their carriage arrived at the harbor.

Through the gap in his ruined doublet, she could just make out letters carved into the lord's flesh. Riona started toward him and fought the bile rising in her throat as she pulled the sodden fabric away from the wounds. Lord Farquar stiffened at the contact, a sob escaping his ruined lips.

She peeled the last bit of fabric away and stared down at the three words that had been carefully and ruthlessly cut into Farquar's chest:

Murderous
Treacherous
Snake

Riona lifted a shaky hand to her lips as Farquar began to sob harder, tears mingling with the blood coating his face. She hated

Lord Farquar for his involvement in her uncle's plots and his ability to weasel out of the punishment he deserved, but she had never wanted *this*. Death would have been kinder.

"By the Creator..." Valerian breathed, sounding like he was fighting the urge to be sick. "What manner of monster..."

Riona started to turn away, but a flash of white caught her eye. A folded piece of parchment sat atop one of the boxes just to Farquar's left, the only bright spot among the blood-splattered crates and barrels. She picked it up, a terrible sense of dread filling her as she unfolded it. On one side of the paper were six short lines, written in one of the northern tongues:

Dehan dhoh-sha mo tuijía, mo chroí
Cuille solis-sa aire mo sudhin
Bhiodha d'iarrain, bhiodha d'ireach
Làhm mo anam tro'na firinne tué
Is, Ceartan, mi dhoja daonan latha tué

She didn't speak the language, but she recognized some of the words. It was the song Caelan had sung to her the night they had danced in the Royal Theater. The night he had confessed his love for her. The night Lord Farquar had sent men to kill them. She flipped the note over and found the translation on the back:

Be thou my savior, my heart
Be thou the light that guides me home
In the darkest night, in the fiercest tempest
Let my soul find its equal in you
And, Creator, give me a lifetime to love you

"What is it?" Valerian asked softly, moving to her side. "What does it say?"

Riona instinctively crumpled the paper before he could read it. It felt like a secret, what Caelan had written, and nothing that would do her betrothed any good to know. He loved her, but he had made it clear that there would never be a future in which they could be together. That there was no reason to cling to desperate, foolish hope. He had given her up, and now, she would pledge her life to serving Kenter.

She felt the weight of Valerian's stare as she crossed the hold, pulled the nearest lantern from its hook, and set it atop one of the boxes. She lifted the latch and held one corner of the paper to the flame.

"Nothing," she murmured as she watched the parchment blacken and crumble into ash. "Nothing at all."

Chapter Seventy-Five
The Liar

For the fifth time in as many days, Caelan found himself staring toward Rivosa. A tapestry of stars surrounded him, twinkling across the cloudless sky overhead and reflecting off the churning waves below. It was the dead of winter, and the cold wind off the sea tore straight through his tunic and overcoat. He had given up his court finery in favor of loose tunics and fitted leather pants the moment they cast off. There was no longer a point in pretending he was anything more than a commoner.

The ship dipped over a wave, and his stomach turned. How he hated sailing. He clutched the railing and focused on the horizon, wishing he could see beyond the darkness and distance to Rivosa's shore. It was just over a week since Riona had confronted her king.

Just over a week since he'd lost her.

As soon as the thought occurred to him, he shoved it away. Riona had never been his to lose, and he'd been a fool to ever believe otherwise.

Footsteps sounded on the deck behind him. "Trouble sleeping?"

"Always." He turned as Drystan leaned on the railing beside

him, watching the stars ripple over the waves. The prince's face was calm and composed as usual, as distant and unreadable as the face of the moon shining high above. He was so careful to keep his true thoughts hidden, to wear that mask of quiet confidence, that Caelan often wondered if Drystan ever doubted himself at all. "I was just...thinking."

"About Riona."

"Yes." He hadn't been able to take his mind off her since Drystan had arrived bearing the news of her impending marriage to the Duke of Kenter. "I can't stop thinking about her. And I can't help but think that I never should have come to Rivosa."

Drystan shot him a look of disbelief. "Would you really trade what little time you had with her for never knowing her?"

No. The answer came to him immediately, but he refused to give the prince the satisfaction of admitting that he was right. Instead, he turned back to the water, trying to ignore the churning in his stomach as the ship tilted.

"Don't take this the wrong way," Drystan said, "but I don't think you should continue working as a spy when we return to Torch. Anyone who knows you can see that you're unhappy there. Before Rivosa, you couldn't wait to get your next assignment. To become someone else. To go somewhere new. Until you met Riona, I don't think I ever saw you truly happy. When you were around her, you were like a different person."

"I *was* a different person. That's the point of being a spy."

The prince let out an exasperated breath. "You know what I meant. You've always seemed...content working for my father, but as your friend, I don't think this life is for you. I believe you've been feeling lost for a very long time, and you joined my father's spy network because you needed something to do. The problem is, it's not enough."

Despite himself, Caelan smiled. "Careful. You're beginning to sound like Walther."

Drystan chuckled. "If that's the price I have to pay to make you see reason, so be it."

Caelan sat with his back against the ship's railing, his legs stretched out before him. As the prince settled beside him, he tilted his head back and stared up at the stars, remembering the night he and Walther had sat up on that rooftop in Torch. Only a couple of months had passed since then, but it felt like a lifetime.

Finally, he took a deep breath and said, "I watched my parents burn to death when I was five years old."

"You watched—?" The prince's head whipped toward him, shock on his face. "By the Creator, Caelan..."

He closed his eyes, fighting the onslaught of memories that came flooding back. It was no secret he'd grown up an orphan, but he had never spoken of the deaths of his parents to anyone until the night he'd confessed his identity to Riona. "I can't remember their faces anymore, but even now, I have nights where I wake in a cold sweat, the sound of their screams ringing in my ears. The stench of smoke stinging my nose. They were just two of the countless casualties in the war between Kostos and Kenter, but they were my entire world." He faltered, his heart aching. "After that, nothing will ever be enough."

Drystan was silent for several moments, seeming to struggle for the right words. "I had no idea. Caelan... I want you to know that you will always have a place in Torch, no matter what you choose to do. But I do hope that you will give up this life and find happiness," the prince said. Then he added, "Preferably not with a girl who threatens to bury a dagger in your heart."

Caelan let out a soft laugh. "I'll try."

"Good." The prince rose and offered him a hand up. "Now, I'm going to try and get some rest. Are you going to go back to your cabin as well, or stay out here?"

"I'll stay a little while longer. Brooding agrees with me."

Drystan chuckled as he walked away. Once he'd left, Caelan pushed to his feet and stood at the railing for several long minutes, watching the stars sparkle on the waves. He hated sailing, but he loved the scent of the sea-salt air and the way it rushed over him, tugging on his clothes and hair. Something about it settled the restless, anxious energy that never seemed to leave him. Gradually, the churning in his stomach began to ease, and he returned to his room below decks.

Caelan closed the door behind him and started toward the bunk affixed to the wall. He had left the lantern burning low, and in its dim light, he nearly tripped over the large chest sticking out from under the desk. An expletive slipped from his lips as he righted himself, bracing a hand on the wall just as the ship listed to one side. Bile rose in his throat.

If he never set foot on a ship again, it would be too soon.

Stumbling forward, he sank onto his bunk and dropped his head into his hands, forcing himself to breathe evenly until the nausea passed. As soon as his stomach settled, he pulled the heavy iron key from his pocket, unlocked the chest, and lifted the lid. Inside, countless shards of eudorite gleamed under the lantern light. Some were no larger than his pinky finger. Others were longer than his arm. All the other chests were down in the ship's hold, but he had kept this one in his cabin as a reminder of what he'd accomplished.

Caelan closed the chest, locked it, and extinguished the lantern's flame. He stretched out on his bunk and closed his eyes, letting the gentle lapping of the waves against the hull lull him to sleep. As he did, his thoughts drifted back to what Drystan had said. He appreciated the prince's concern, but the advice was less than helpful. Caelan had nowhere else to go. Six years ago, Emperor Hyperion had saved him from a lifetime of begging and stealing when he recruited Caelan to his spy network and assigned Walther to train him. The Emperor had given him a job, a purpose, and a home. In Rivosa, he had almost lost sight of that, and he would never allow that to happen again.

I am a weapon of Erduria, he thought as the darkness rushed in to drag him into sleep. *Nothing more, and nothing less.*

Part Six
Stolen Moments

Chapter Seventy-Six
The Lady

"This is all very well and good," Emperor Hyperion huffed, staring down at her from his throne, "but I have yet to hear how that led to where we stand today. The complete destruction of Kostos. The ruination of the Kentari countryside. You stand on opposite sides of a war that has ended thousands of lives and ruined tens of thousands more, and yet you sound like no more than two lovesick children!"

Riona shot a glare at the traitor, still standing beside the dais. The sun hung low in the sky, and its rays turned his hair a rich, deep auburn. Caelan smiled at her, but it wasn't the smug, goading grin he had worn that morning, when she had first been escorted into the throne room. In fact, it seemed almost...mournful.

If she didn't know better, she might have thought he was capable of feeling such an emotion.

Riona turned her attention back to Hyperion, and the movement caused the chains around her wrists to jangle. After she began recounting the story of their meeting in Innislee, the Emperor had permitted her to stand on the condition that she allow the guards to bind her wrists and ankles. Part of her had wanted to point out how foolish he was to fear that she would try to escape in front of a room full of witnesses, but her shoulders had been aching so much from the guards' merciless grip that she had opted to hold her tongue. The humiliation of wearing chains was better than the pain of being forced to kneel on marble for hours on end.

"This is only the beginning, Your *Imperial* Majesty," she said, shooting a dark glance at the guard who had corrected her that morning. "If you want to understand why your perfect spy broke from your ranks and *murdered my husband*, you must understand the depth of his obsessive, misguided love for me. There is much yet to share."

"The only person here with an obsessive love for you is yourself," Caelan responded lightly, eliciting laughter from the gathered nobles. "You've been more than happy to talk about yourself for the better part of a day, and still you insist on more."

"*You* were more than happy to interject when it suited you."

An impish grin spread across his lips. "That's because I enjoy the sound of my own voice. I don't pretend to be some righteous, noble figure so I can sleep at night." His gaze swept over her from head to toe, taking in the fine jewelry and layers upon layers of silk skirts. "Unlike some."

"Caelan, that's enough," the Emperor warned. "You are far from blameless in this. Queen Riona, how much time do you require to recount the rest of your history with my former spy?"

She paused, considering. "Three days. Maybe four, if he insists on throwing around more childish insults."

"Better insults than blades," the traitor quipped with a glance at the dagger she'd thrown, still lying on the dais steps.

"I see. Guards, escort her back to her chambers. Lord Percival, you may accompany her, if you wish. If not, one of my men will show you back to your room."

Riona turned toward Percival, who was still standing on the edge of the crowd with the rest of the courtiers. She had purposefully avoided looking at him while she told the story of her exile from Rivosa. She hadn't wanted to see the disgust in his eyes when he learned how hard and how deeply she had fallen for Caelan. But now, she found only sorrow and sympathy on his face, and shame caused a flush to rise to her cheeks. His pity was worse than disgust.

He bowed to the Emperor, picked up Riona's crown from where it lay on the tile, and gently set it on her head. His warm gaze never left hers as he said, "I'll go with Riona, Your Imperial Majesty."

The Emperor waved a hand in dismissal, and the guards gripped her arms to drag her toward the exit. Riona jerked out of their grasp. "I can walk by myself."

They all looked to the Emperor, who nodded. The guards didn't reach for her again, but they hovered close at her side as they made their way out of the throne room, another half-dozen men falling into step behind them. Percival shouldered past the one closest to her and stopped in the middle of the great hall, turning to the man in the lead. "Release her from her chains. She has cooperated with all your Emperor's orders, and she poses no threat to you."

"She smuggled a dagger into the throne room and tried to kill a man with it. She has forsaken what little freedom His Imperial Majesty was kind enough to extend to her."

"Oh, listen to the lord and release her," a voice called from behind them.

They all turned to find Caelan leaning against the doorway to the throne room, his arms crossed loosely over his chest. The gash in his doublet gaped, revealing the slender crimson line where the dagger had nicked him. He pushed off the door frame and stalked toward them, a wicked grin on his lips. Although he addressed the guards, authority dripping from his voice, his attention was solely on Riona. "If she had any more weapons on her, she would have used them on me already."

Percival studied the traitor as one of the guards stepped forward and removed Riona's chains. Questions swam in his eyes, but he had the grace to remain silent as Riona smoothed the wrinkles in her gown and slipped her hand into the crook of his arm, ignoring Caelan completely. "Shall we?"

He nodded, and Riona led him in the direction of her chambers, the guards trailing behind them. She could feel the weight of Caelan's stare on her back, prickling between her shoulder blades, as they left the great hall. Despite everything that had happened since those secret meetings in the Royal Theater, she could still feel the tether pulling taut between them. No matter what they did, how badly they hurt each other, they could never be free of it.

She and Percival walked through the light, airy corridors in silence, their reflections limned in the red-orange light of the sunset streaming through the windows. After what felt like an eternity, Riona said, "You're wondering how I could love a man like him. How even now, I could be so heartless as to love the man who murdered my husband."

Percival shook his head. "You are many things, Riona, but heartless is not one of them. I came to support you, not to judge. You owe me no explanations."

She did. Even if no one else understood their twisted, broken relationship, she had to make Percival understand. "We are the creatures of cautionary tales, he and I," she breathed, her voice soft with sorrow. "We are what happens when one does not forsake the heart for the good of the people and the country. I don't believe I will ever stop loving him, but I will never allow him to win this war. We are enemies by necessity, Percival. Not by desire."

He set a hand atop hers. "You don't have to forsake your heart, Riona. Look at Mercy and Tamriel. Look at Celeste and me. You could rule together."

"No. There is too much spilled blood between us. This will not end until one or both of us is dead."

"Then I shall await news of your victory," Percival said with a small smile, "and pray that it does not destroy you."

Alone in her room hours later, Riona stood before the door to the royal gardens, holding in her mind the image of the carefully pruned hedges and tree-lined walkways that filled the palace grounds. The sky was dark, the moon hidden behind a thick blanket of clouds. What little light managed to escape was weak; she could see only a few yards before everything faded into darkness. Her hand drifted to the door handle.

She paused when her fingers made contact with the cool metal. The quiet, peaceful gardens were no more than an illusion, taunting her with the possibility of freedom. They were crawling with guards, all waiting for her to attempt an escape. She had no intention of entertaining them with a chase. Once, she could have killed them all without ever laying a hand on a weapon, but not now. She would never touch that Creator-forsaken magic again.

The room was silent, but she felt the moment something changed—a prickle on the back of her neck, a charge rising in the air. Her hand fell to her side. "You're late."

"The waiting makes my arrival so much sweeter, *aramati*."

Riona turned. Caelan stood on the opposite side of her bedchamber, framed by the doorway to her sitting room. She had never figured out how he managed to move so silently. Many people would claim it was his training, but none of the other spies she'd met during her time as the Emperor's prisoner had Caelan's preternatural stillness. None of them moved as he did, like a phantom in the night.

The corner of his lips rose as she studied him. He had changed into a fresh doublet of midnight blue silk, whorls of slate gray embroidery curling around the collar. Fitted black trousers clung to his legs and tapered into his shiny leather boots, and he wore no weapon that she could see. He moved to the small sitting area before the hearth and flopped into one of the two armchairs.

"Would it temper your ire to hear that every minute I spent outside your door, waiting to come in, was torture?" He propped his legs on the low table before him and crossed them at the ankles. "You put on a good show in the throne room. It's nice to see that the years haven't dulled your barbed tongue."

Riona didn't move from her place at the door. "What do you want, Caelan?"

"You."

The simple, unapologetic way he said it sent heat flaring deep within her. He made no effort to hide the desire burning in his eyes as they swept over her. She wore a floor-length gown in the loose, flowing style of the Erdurian Empire, so different from the tight, structured dresses common in Rivosa. The drape of the lightweight silk left no curve of her body to the imagination. Its thin straps bared her arms and most of her back, and the slit up the skirt revealed flashes of her long legs with the slightest movement. Caelan's gaze dipped to the sliver of her thigh visible through the slit, then rose to meet hers.

"Did you dress up for me?"

"No."

Yes.

Her heart pounded as he stood and stalked toward her, that infuriating, charming, roguish grin on his lips. With every step, the years and the deaths between them ticked away, until they were once again standing alone atop the stage in a candlelit theater. He reached up and cupped her cheek, his thumb gently tracing the curve of her lower lip. Riona stiffened, pressing back against the cool glass of the door, and his smile grew when he heard her breath catch. He knew exactly how he affected her, and he savored every minute of it.

"I love you, Riona," he murmured. "I have loved you from the moment I met you, and I will love you until my last breath."

Perhaps it was the emotional turmoil from having to stand before the court and relive their doomed love story, recounting all the precious stolen moments and the teasing little quips. Perhaps it was the way he was looking at her now, as if nothing in this world mattered except for her. Perhaps it was something else entirely.

Her resolve shattered.

She closed the distance between them, her fingers threading through his hair as their lips met. His hand slid to the back of her neck, his other arm encircling her waist, and he pulled her flush against him. Desire ignited within her. Damn her, she wanted him—every part of him. Every cruel, kind, manipulative, selfless piece of his broken and battered heart. She would not have him without the shadows that stained his soul. She would not have him without the demons that plagued his dreams.

Caelan's tongue slipped between her lips and teased her own. A shiver trailed down her spine as the hand on her back slid upward, his fingers grazing her bare back before coming around to cup the curve of her breast. Warmth trailed every place he touched. Riona cursed herself for her weakness even as her fingers dropped to the line of buttons along the front of his doublet. When she reached the bottom, he shucked it off without breaking the kiss, leaving him in a thin linen undershirt. Riona slid her hands under the hem, feeling a tremor ripple through him as her fingers traveled along the hard planes of his stomach, honed by years of swordplay.

Caelan broke away with a ragged gasp. "How you delight in torturing me, *aramati*," he breathed, his voice thick with desire.

He dipped his head to kiss just below her ear, tracing the long, graceful curve of her neck. Riona couldn't help the soft moan that escaped her at the caress of his lips against her skin. She wrapped one leg around him and leaned in close, smiling to herself when one of his hands drifted down to her thigh, teasing the slit of her gown higher. His thumb skated lightly across the tender skin at her inner thigh, slowly sliding higher.

At the last moment, Riona twisted, hooking her leg around him and sending him crashing into the door to the gardens. It rattled on his hinges, one of the glass panes shattering when

Caelan's shoulder struck it. Shards rained to the ground as she gripped his throat and leaned in close.

"Enough," she hissed, pretending she didn't see the shock and pain on his face. "You will never have me or my crown. Accept that."

He swallowed, his throat bobbing under her fingers. "We could have everything, Riona, if you would only relent. You asked me to marry you back in Rivosa. Marry me now, and we can rule together. Marry me, and this will all be over."

"I will not disrespect Valerian's memory by marrying the man who could not even look him in the eye as he took my husband's life."

Caelan's expression was imploring. "I have made mistakes, but everything I've done was with the intention of bettering my country. Marry me, *aramati*, and end this war between us before a blade does."

Riona released him and turned away. More than anything, she wanted to agree and end the war, but she could not. She couldn't do that to Valerian. "You should leave."

Glass crunched as he took a step closer. "If I leave, *aramati*, I'm not coming back. We will give our testimony before the court, and the next time we meet, it will be on opposite sides of a battlefield," he said, his voice tormented. "I love you. Tell me you do not love me—tell me you feel nothing but hatred for me—and I will leave."

The words lodged in her throat. Against her better judgment, she turned around and met his gaze. "I can't."

Caelan stilled. He had a hand on his shoulder, cradling the place where it had struck the glass. "Do you want me to stay?"

She nodded.

"Are you sure?"

Creator damn her. "Yes," she breathed.

That was all he needed to hear. Caelan took a few long strides and pulled her into a deep, passionate kiss, his hands cupping her face, tangling in her loose braids. She leaned into him, her heart pounding so hard she was certain he could hear it. She could not disrespect Valerian by marrying Caelan, but this was different. This was love and lust, a release of all the pain and anger and heartbreak they'd endured and inflicted over the years.

She loosened the tie at the collar of his undershirt and pulled it over his head, baring his suntanned skin and the myriad scars across his torso and arms. When she lightly traced the crescent-shaped scar that spanned from his rib cage to his hip—one of the wounds he had sustained that last night in the theater—he stilled and pulled back just enough to meet her eyes. His hand joined hers, his fingers lacing through her own.

"No matter what happens, I will never regret saving your life that night in the theater," he whispered. "You are my perfect torture, *aramati*, and I would have it no other way."

Riona studied the scars, afraid to voice the words threatening to spill from her lips. She wanted to tell him that even though she detested everything he had done, she wanted him. That she hated herself for her weakness more than she could ever hate him. She knew better than to indulge the desire burning within her, but as Caelan had said that last night in Rivosa, they never had much self-control where the other was concerned.

And tonight, she wanted to make a mistake.

"Tonight," she whispered, "I am yours."

Caelan lifted her into his arms, her legs wrapping around his waist, and carried her over to the bed. He laid her down gently and hovered over her, a hand braced on either side of her head as he drank in the sight of her. His eyes roved from her braids, splayed across the silk sheets, to her lips, and then down to the scar just above her heart. Emotion flooded his face as he dipped his head and pressed a soft kiss to the old wound.

"Say it again," he breathed against her skin.

"I am yours, Caelan. Tonight, and every night."

His hand slid up her thigh, pushing the slit of her gown higher, higher, his fingers skating along the inside of her thigh. Before it could go any further, Riona gripped his wrist, stilling him. "The guards in the garden," she whispered, glancing at the wall of floor-to-ceiling windows, the curtains still parted. "They'll see."

Caelan grinned wickedly. "Let them see. Let them tell the world."

Riona awoke to bright sunlight streaming through the windows. She lay naked between the sheets, the silk soft and cool against her skin, flushed from his touch. Despite everything, she did not regret it. She would never regret a night in Caelan's arms. Perhaps in another life, they could have married and ruled together. But in this life, they were limited to forbidden kisses and stolen moments. It should have been enough.

For the good of their countries, it had to be enough.

She rolled over and found the other side of the bed empty. The sheets were in disarray, the pillow still bearing the imprint of his head. Riona pushed herself upright, holding the blanket over her chest, and scanned the room. Empty. She called his name, hoping that he had only gone into the sitting room, but no response came. She was alone.

A note sat on the bedside table, and she picked it up, shifting so she could read it in the light spilling in through the windows. As always, he had left it unsigned, but his hasty, cramped scrawl was as familiar as ever.

I lied yesterday in the throne room. That night on the ship, I went to sleep thinking of Erduria.

But when I dreamt, aramati...

When I dreamt, I dreamt of you.

Dying for More?

I truly hope you enjoyed the first part of Riona's rather blood-soaked journey. Join my Readers' Guild on Patreon for a signed and personalized advance copy of every new release, plus new chapters of upcoming books.

Sign up for my newsletter to stay up-to-date. You'll be the first to know about book releases, giveaways, and great deals. You'll also receive two free novellas from the Born Assassin series.

Join Jacqueline Pawl's newsletter at www.authorjpawl.com

Join the Readers' Guild at www.patreon.com/JacquelinePawl

Acknowledgments

Court of Vipers would not exist without the support of so many incredible people. To my mom and Faux Pas, thank you so much for listening to my venting at all hours of the night and for telling me that one day, I might actually turn this book into something mostly readable. (*Steve.*) Thank you for spending hours editing multiple drafts of this book. And despite rolling your eyes at the romance, for never failing to tell me that I should include a sex scene. That's not happening yet, but maybe someday. We'll see.

To my dad, thank you for always supporting my writing and recommending my books to anyone and everyone you meet. And to Ethan, my brother and best friend for life: Thank you for always asking for updates about my writing, encouraging me when my characters don't do what I want, and putting up with my countless book recommendations. (You really do need to read *Mistborn*, though.)

My eternal gratitude to Judi Soderberg for all your support of my books. Your edits make these characters and this world come to life, and without you, so many more characters would meet untimely deaths. Thank you to Hannah Sternjakob for the gorgeous cover artwork. I can't wait to commission covers for the rest of the series.

Thank you to all my readers for sharing these books with your friends and family, and for embracing all my morally gray protagonists. A special mention to my Patreon supporters: Judi Soderberg, Esther Rosa, Ebony VonRochow, Mary Laing, Tilde Joensen, Cloee, Chelsea, Satvrnn, Emma Vaughan, Utshana Durham, and Kimber Kober.

And lastly, to all the Booktok and Bookstagram readers who took a chance on a new series: I hope you loved Riona's story, and I can't wait to share more of this world with you.

About the Author

Jacqueline Pawl spent her teen years trapped between the pages of books—exploring Hogwarts, journeying across countless fantasy worlds, and pulling heists with Kaz Brekker and his Crows.

But, because no dashing prince or handsome Fae has come to sweep her off to a strange new world (yet), she writes epic fantasy novels full of cutthroat courtiers, ruthless assassins, unforgettable plot twists, and epic battles. She is a Slytherin, and it shows in her books.

She currently resides in Scotland, where she can be found chasing will-o'-the-wisps, riding unicorns, and hunting haggis in the Highlands. *Court of Vipers* is her seventh book.

For news about upcoming books, visit her website at:
www.authorjpawl.com

instagram.com/authorjpawl

tiktok.com/@authorjpawl

patreon.com/JacquelinePawl

amazon.com/author/jacquelinepawl

Also by Jacqueline Pawl

Defying Vesuvius

A BORN ASSASSIN SERIES
Helpless (prequel novella)
Nameless (prequel novella)
Merciless
Heartless
Ruthless
Fearless
Limitless

THE LADY OF INNISLEE SERIES
Court of Vipers

Printed in Great Britain
by Amazon